THE ASSASSIN'S SIN

THE ASSASSIN'S LEGACY SERIES
BOOK 2

LIBBY WEBBER

To request permission contact Libby Webber of Dead or Alive Press at DeadorAlivePress@gmail.com

ISBN 978-1-7377811-5-8 (hardcover)
ISBN 978-1-7377811-4-1 (paperback)
ISBN 978-1-7377811-3-4 (ebook)

Book design by Libby Webber

Dead or Alive Press
Jacksonville, NC

www.libbywebber.com
www.libbywebber.com/deadoralivepress

*For my husband, who will never read this but is deserving all the same.
After too many date nights spent discussing my characters and hours of
fight scene practice—this book is for you.*

PLEASE BE AWARE

This book contains sensitive topics that include the mention of violence against children and the death of children. This book is recommended for mature audiences.

THIRTEEN YEARS AGO

1

MASON

Mason gripped the side of the basin, pushing against the hand shoving his face beneath the water. His arms shook with the effort, his neck screaming in protest. Any longer, and he would drown. His head pounded; eyes bulged in his head. Then the pressure released. Mason stumbled back, taking the sweet oxygen in gulping breaths. He pushed the wet hair from his face and met Maureen Seward's angry hazel eyes, her stern features accented by the two braids along the side of her head, pulling her hair up and out of her face.

"Why are you here?" she demanded.

This was a mistake. Coming to them was a mistake. They were going to kill him. "Please—I—I." He what? He was turning traitor against Mr. Wayward, the deadliest man on the East Coast. No one did that and survived.

A shiver rocked his body as the fall breeze drifted through the tiny shack. He looked at the other two people in the room: Mr. Wayward's own son, John, and Maureen's husband, Andrew. They'd dragged him to a safe house somewhere in the middle of the woods in Connecticut, where no one would hear him scream, and no one would care if they did. Perhaps turning to John had been a mistake. He would die here anyway. "I need protection," Mason said.

"Lies," Maureen hissed. "He sent you here to spy. I'll send you back in pieces." He backed away, bumping into the wall as she advanced. "I'll start with those pretty brown eyes. Let him know we see exactly what he's doing."

Mason's eyes began to water. He'd witnessed Maureen remove eyeballs on numerous occasions in the interrogation rooms beneath the Institute. People usually began talking after that. "No! Please. I'm here for protection! He doesn't have all his screws tightened. He's trying to kill you all!"

"None of our screws are tightened," John said with a cruel laugh. "Besides, we already know he's coming after us," he added, shaking his head. He pushed off the wall, brushing dirt off his light yellow shirt stained with Mason's blood.

"I came to you for help!" Mason yelled, the emotion welling in his chest. After seven years of working under the Senior Assassin of both the Legacy and Legacy Inc, he knew one thing: Mr. Wayward was out for blood, anyone's blood, who stood between him and his profit. He sought out John after receiving an order he would never be able to follow through on. "He's going to kill me if I don't deliver. And I *won't* deliver."

"What's the order?" Andrew asked. Mason licked his lips, the words stalling in his throat as if speaking them into existence would solidify their fate—like it solidified his sister's. His knees went weak, and he dropped to the floor. Andrew kneeled next to him. "We want to help you, Mason." He placed a hand on Mason's shoulder. "What is he planning?"

Mason swallowed the knot in his throat. "One of the kids. He wants me to kill one of the kids."

"For Christ's sake," John spat. "This again? He tried it when Perry was born, and it created the divide. What's he thinking, that if he kills off everyone—"

"Then no one will be able to oppose him," Maureen finished.

She looked pale. "Unfortunately for him, we are too ingrained in the functionality of both Legacies now for him to rip us out by the roots. There will be backlash from the board. From the clients. But the kids. . ."

"Which child?" Andrew asked.

Sweat broke out across Mason's brow, and he met Maureen's eyes across the small space. "An unclaimed one." Maureen's features barely shifted, but he saw the tension grasp her by the neck. "Not Aeron," he added quickly as Andrew's hand tightened on his shoulder. There were plenty of blood families not represented in the room that he could be referring to, but he had a feeling Maureen knew exactly which child he spoke of.

"If you're not willing to give us the name, there's not much we can do," John said.

"We can't not help," Maureen countered, the villainous gaze that dropped him to his knees was gone and replaced with curiosity. "But what do you expect us to do, Mason?"

He didn't want to die—but he would if it saved the kids. "I don't know. But I didn't come into this life to kill the innocent," he said. "I don't care what threat they pose for the future or what leverage they can garner. Senior trusts me. He needs me. But the kids. . ." The raw memory of his sister's murder surfaced as if it happened yesterday. "They need me more. I will give you the name in exchange for a place with you." Silence followed his statement, and he looked up in time to see a silent conversation play out between the three of them. This was why he came here to the next generation of Legacy Blood ready to usurp their tyrant leader. But the longer they conversed the closer to death he felt. He had one more option—a last resort no one would subject themselves to. "Dose me," Mason said. All eyes turned to him.

"Excuse me?" John asked.

"Dose me. You want proof I'm not lying? Dose me with Sin."

Andrew stepped back. "You don't know what you're asking."

Mason opened and closed his mouth a few times before the

words would leave him. "Andrew—I trust you all with my life. I wouldn't have come to you otherwise." His gaze shifted to Maureen. "I've seen you torture dozens of people with Sin. I know what I'm asking. Let me prove it to you."

Maureen and Andrew exchanged a glance, and Andrew whispered something to John. Mason waited with fear clawing into his heart as they decided his fate. No one asked to take Sin. The neurotoxin invaded the mind, made a person face their demons and spill their truths without ever physically needing to touch them. It disabled the nervous system and, if not carefully monitored, left the user in a permanent state of physical and mental torment.

The hushed conversation halted, and Mason held his breath. "Fine," Maureen said. "But know—I won't stop until I'm satisfied with your answers."

"Of course," he said, a whimper leaving him. As soon as he'd received the order, he'd known his days were numbered. "If I'm going to die, it won't be killing the innocent. If I don't eliminate her —I die. If he finds out I came to you—I die. If you don't believe me —I die. I have no reason to lie to you."

"I'll grab Eileen," Andrew said, his voice almost disappointed. He placed a kiss on Maureen's forehead and left, leaving Mason alone with her and John.

Maureen straightened her shirt and rolled her neck. He'd always admired the way she engaged in torture: with precision. Never a word unused or a cut unnecessary. "I could do this a lot of ways." She moved toward him. "The quickest way is to shock your system; dunk you until you're almost dead. Then we'll administer the Sin. I only have the two doses we were able to swipe—but that should be enough to kill you."

"Great," Mason said, his throat tightening at the thought. "But you won't, right?"

A wicked smile graced her face. "Only if I find out you've been lying."

Mason stepped toward her again, heart hammering in his chest.

This was the right move. John pushed him from behind, securing the back of his neck and pushing his head back underwater. The liquid burned as he unintentionally inhaled the water and his body thrashed against the force. His grip slipped from the basin, and Maureen's small hands secured them behind his back. Before he lost consciousness, they pulled him out again, and John held him securely in place. The sweet oxygen didn't feel quite as relieving this time as a plastic bag slipped over his head. He'd barely taken a gasp of air, and the plastic collapsed onto his face, trying to meld with his skin.

His chest constricted, lungs burning. He held his breath instead, but a punch to his gut forced the exhale, and the material attacked again, pulling against his skin. Maureen landed a punch to his jaw. The bag released and slipped sideways as he stumbled, his hands still tied behind him. She attacked with relentless precision and, without a way to defend, every elbow and strike landed and pushed him against the wall.

"Why are you here?" she demanded.

He shook his head. "I want to join you."

"Bullshit."

"There can be no secrets, Mason." Andrew stepped back into the shack—Eileen Gale by his side carrying two syringes filled with the bright blue cocktail, Sin. "Is he ready?"

Maureen nodded. "I'm really sorry about this, Mase," Eileen said and uncapped a syringe. She stepped forward, and Mason looked down, realizing they had not only secured his wrists but had tied a wrap around his arm to easily expose his vein. She slid the metal tip beneath the skin and pressed the drug into his bloodstream. With his heart already beating rapidly, it flooded his system, burning as it raced its way to his heart. Eileen yanked him forward, and Mason leaned back. He knew it was useless, but his body did not want to go back to the water. Fear, as he'd never experienced, choked him, drowning him.

"No! No!" He begged. Maureen gave him a pitying look and

then slammed his head back into the basin. A scream left him, and he sucked in more water. He would drown; fuck the Sin, he was going to drown. He kept his eyes open, afraid if he closed them, they'd never open again—he'd heard of such things happening with Sin. The world would shift in front of their eyes, and what was real and what was a memory was indecipherable. The mental torture far outweighed the physical pain that followed. The body would heal; the mind would never forget what Sin pulled from its crevices.

Eileen yanked him up for air, and Maureen rocked his skull with a few more strikes. They dropped him back under. They repeated the process several more times until, finally, the darkness crept into his vision, and he knew the Sin had taken hold. He hadn't given them the name, so they weren't going to kill him. If he kept repeating that, he would survive.

The lights flickered around Mason's shivering body. He'd woken tied to a chair in the empty shack. Movement in the darkened corner made him jump against his restraints. He gasped. "Who's there?"

The girl peeked out of the shadows. His heart rammed into his ribcage. She wore the exact same clothes the last time he'd seen her —a pink collared dress with mismatched socks, one white, one blue, and dirty white tennis shoes. His heart beat against its cage, his breath stolen like hers.

"Faith." The name trembled from his lips.

She shook slightly in his vision and turned toward the door. *"Mase!"* Her voice vibrated in terror, and she backed away, an invisible force halting her retreat. The bathtub materialized when she hit it. The porcelain tub with clawed feet had just been filled for a bubble bath. Lavender filled his senses, and he gagged. A scream escaped her, and she tumbled backward into the tub, an invisible hand holding her down. His heart doubled in speed, and he fought against the restraints. The ropes cut into his flesh, and he relished the pain; he would skin himself alive to get to his sister.

"No! No! No!" He screamed into the night. "Stop!"

Faith emerged from the water, clambering to her feet, her dress a darker pink, soaking wet. Her brown hair fell in straggly strands against her face, and she pushed them back, sobs interwoven with her catching her breath.

He knew what came next and clenched his teeth in anticipation, but the sound of the shot still rocked his body. Faith spun toward him, her expression blank as her head rocked backward, and she collapsed. Dead eyes stared blankly at him, the blood trickling down her face. Mason's breath stopped—the broken body of his seven-year-old sister lying as he'd last seen her: soaking wet next to the tub, a pool of blood beneath her head like a satin pillow. His stomach turned, vomit chasing up his throat. He heaved out every ounce of liquid he'd swallowed while they tried to drown him. He should have let them drown him.

The door to the shack opened, and the wind distorted the hallucination. Faith's body wavered like a mirage in the air, but he kept his gaze locked on that spot.

Maureen slid into his vision, sidestepping the vomit. "Who is it, Mason?"

He closed his eyes, his body trembling again. The nightmare was nothing new. Being restrained like he was that night was a whole new level of torment. He looked at Maureen through swollen eyes. "Make it stop."

"No."

"You don't understand—"

"Who is she?" Maureen asked.

Who is she? She already knew. "My sister."

"What was Faith doing here?" Maureen moved behind him, leaning over his shoulder. "What did you do to her?"

The words pulled themselves out of Mason. He wanted to

scream he'd done nothing. But the words that tumbled out of his mouth felt more like the truth he hid from. "I killed her." A sob caught in his chest, the raw image still laying feet from her.

"Killed her? Or failed her?"

Mason snapped his head to look at her. "What difference does that make? She's dead." Maureen cracked him across the face, and his head snapped sideways.

"It makes a difference, Mason."

A sob racked his body. "I watched them kill her before the Legacy showed up. The fucking Underworlders."

"Do you blame the Legacy, Mason?"

No. "Yes." The words slipped out, and he slammed his lips together. He didn't. He didn't think he did. It'd been ten years.

"You do," Maureen said. "Is that why you've come here? To take your revenge?"

Mason's head throbbed, and a dull ache started in his hips. He shifted, trying to get the blood flowing to them. "No."

"Why did you join the Legacy if you blamed us?"

Mason bit into his lip, the coppery taste filling his mouth. His body betrayed him, though, the words coming out. He'd been young and idealistic when he joined. "I wanted to change it."

She raised an eyebrow at him. "Change it? The Legacy?"

"Make it better. If the Legacy could be better, it could save more people."

"And how is that going for you?"

Mason's DTS (Death to Save ratio) was in the hundreds, saving hundreds more than he killed. That was a win for him. "I was winning. Until today."

Maureen nodded and moved back in front of him. "Progress. But you have more demons to excavate." She held up the second syringe. "I'll be back when they finish with you." She jabbed the needle into his arm again, his heart pushing the Sin through faster this time as if the first dose had carved a path directly to his soul.

The lights flickered, and bodies appeared around the room.

Mason widened his eyes, looking at each one. They were the men and women he'd killed for both the Legacy and Legacy Inc; his parents leaned against the door with anger in their eyes; his sister blinked in and out of the space between his other ghosts, trying to catch his attention as he took stock of the dead.

He glanced again at Maureen, who smiled. "If there's anything left to you when they finish, I'll get the rest of my answers." She spun on her heel and left, the dead in the room moving in. A bitter cold sunk into his muscles, freezing his bones. The pain seized his back, and he cried out.

"Mason."

He heard his name but refused to open his eyes. If he could have pulled out his eyeballs, he would have. Of all the torture and death he'd administered, the clip of his sister played on repeat until he screamed loud enough to drown out the gunshot. And his entire body seemed to be fighting with itself. His skin burned where he tried to tear through the ropes, and his nerves shot searing lightning throughout his body. But his muscles shook from a cold so intense he was sure hypothermia would set in any moment.

"Mason," Maureen's voice said again, sterner this time. He'd heard that tone used in interrogation, usually followed by a bucket of ice or electrocution. He pulled his swollen and heavy eyelids open, looking up at her.

"Good. You're doing good." His teeth chattered in response to her smile. "We're going to go through some basic information." She waited for him to acknowledge, so he nodded.

"What is your name?"

"Ma-mason St. James."

"What is your sister's name?"

It was a trick question. Depending on the intent of the questioner, he could deny having a sister because she was dead and no longer existed. He licked his lips. He wanted their help. He needed their trust.

"Can you rephrase, more specifically?"

She smiled and nodded. "No need. Whose child did Senior ask you to eliminate?"

Another question with too many variables for accurate answers. She was taking it easy on him. He shook his head again, unable to trust his knowledge. The name, wanting to spill from his lips, could blow up the entire Alliance. He forced out instead, "More specific, please."

"Which child?"

"Katherine Wayward."

Maureen paled. "Are you positive?"

He nodded. "I don't know why," he said, the words pulling themselves out of him as the truth wanted to once Sin dug its claws in. "Please don't ask me why."

She didn't push. Instead, she changed the questioning. "Have you come here to spy for Senior?"

"No."

"Have you come here for revenge for your sister?"

"No. Why would I?"

She paused, tapping her knuckle against her chin. She strode over to the door and opened it. Andrew entered, beads of sweat sitting across his dark brown forehead. How could he be sweating? Mason's body shivered harder in response.

"How much time do we have?" Andrew asked his wife.

"Not long. I'd say about five hours until he's gone completely."

Five hours? How long had he been held captive by his ghosts?

He turned his harsh gaze on Mason. "How are you doing?"

"Terrible," Mason said. "I'm pretty sure I'm dying."

"We're all dying," Andrew said with a smirk. "Now, Mase, there can be no secrets. No lies. This only works with complete trust."

"I have no secrets," he said. "I swear!"

"Tell me about your team."

Mason jammed his tongue backward, trying to stop any words from exiting. He shook his head, knowing it would do little to help. He wanted to keep his team out of it. Safe. Andrew closed the distance, the back of his hand connecting so hard to Mason's face that the chair beneath Mason tipped and slammed him sideways to the ground. White spots appeared in his vision, and Mason whimpered, laying his face on the cold ground. The rubber sole of Andrew's boot pushed into his exposed cheek.

"Your team," Andrew commanded.

Mason sent a silent apology to his team as their names left his mouth. "Shaun Brinks and the hacker known as Storm."

"Legacy or street?" Andrew asked.

"Shaun is street turned Legacy. Storm is a street hacker."

"Tell me about them," Andrew coaxed. "Tell me about Shaun. How do you know him?"

Warmth spread through Mason as thoughts of his best friend crept into his mind, pushing his sister to the dark corners where Mason liked to hide her. "Shaun's dad works for the FBI. They raised me after the incident. They saved me. He's set to be the next Legacy Liaison for the FBI."

"And what about Storm? Who is that? Where did you meet?"

A smile filled Mason's face, the dried cuts on his cheeks and temple cracking open against Andrew's shoe, and the words fell from Mason so easily. "Storm is the best hacker on the streets. We met her through Shaun's contacts at the FBI. I bet she could hack into the Legacy."

"Does Senior know about Storm?"

"No." Cold gripped Mason's pounding heart, realizing he's just compromised two of his most important people.

"Keep it that way." The boot lifted from his face, and he was hauled upright. The shift in his posture set fire to his nervous system, and he screamed out in pain, leaning forward against his bonds until the wave of agony passed.

"They're getting longer and closer together," Maureen said. "We might have less time than I thought."

Andrew pulled a chair up and took a seat, leaning forward to be eye to eye. Mason held his gaze. "I told you there could be no secrets."

"I don't have anymore," Mason answered.

Andrew nodded and looked over at Maureen briefly. "But I have a secret. And it might make you change your mind about joining us." Mason licked his chapped lips, waiting. The older man released a long breath. "I was on the team who eliminated your parents."

The world fractured, forming deep crevices in the reality around him. Faith blinked in and out of them, her dead eyes staring at him as his pulse moved the Sin faster through his body. She was beside Maureen, then directly next to him and he flinched away. She appeared on the other side of him and just as suddenly was by the door. He swirled his head left and right, trying to keep track of her. Then she was right beside Andrew.

The cold burrowed deeper into his bones, and he locked eyes with her. How had he not known? Everything he believed about the Legacy shattered into pieces. His entire reason for existing. "Did he kill you?" Faith regarded Andrew and looked back at Mason. She couldn't answer because he couldn't answer. Mason shifted his focus to the man in front of him. "Did you kill her?" The words were so soft, the pounding in his ears so intense, he wasn't sure he even said them out loud.

Andrew pressed his lips together, and an eternity passed before he shook his head. "No. I did eliminate your parents. It was a Legacy Inc vs. Legacy sting. We were a trial run for Legacy Inc— and your parents. . . Well, the information we received had been falsified. I'm sorry you are finding out this way. It was messy—and obvious Legacy Inc was not ready to come to fruition just yet."

Mason's mouth became chalky. It had been a test. A fucking test. "My family's murder was a goddam test?"

"Yes," Maureen said. Rage like Mason had never known washed

over him, coiling through his frozen muscles. He'd grieved for his family. Joined the Legacy to protect other innocent people—his own personal cause to bring something good out of a tragedy. He'd vowed over Faith's lifeless body he would never let this happen to anyone else. He'd laid to rest the unknowns. The pain. The sheer grief. His entire insides felt as if Andrew just tried to filet him.

"Who killed her?" Mason demanded. "Who killed her?!" He shouted, twisting against his restraints.

"A Legacy Inc asset," Andrew supplied.

"Who?!" Mason sobbed which turned into a scream, the lightning in his nerves finally reaching the base of his neck. He wouldn't survive another shock like that. As soon as the nerve pain reached the top of the spinal cord, detainees died within the hour. He dropped his head back, trying to stem the pain from traveling higher, breaths coming in shorter bursts. Tears streamed down his face. He couldn't die without knowing the truth.

"Shit." Maureen pushed past Andrew and grabbed Mason's chin, turning his head left and right, checking the dilation in his eyes. "Hold on, Mase." She cut through the restraints, the pain increased as the pressure was released and blood flow tried to return to normal. He clutched his stomach and doubled over, holding himself together, his breath labored.

Andrew peered over Maureen's shoulder at his hunched form. "Now that you know this truth, where does your head stand on revenge?"

His heart wanted to murder every one of them. Legacy and Legacy Inc. It beat wildly against his chest, banging for justice. But his mind knew better. His logic outvoted his rage. Orders were orders. And he'd saved so many innocent lives since that day. The Sin answered for him. "I want their name."

"For what end?" Andrew asked.

"To be sure this can never happen again."

"We play the long game, Mason," Maureen said. She grabbed his arm, a yellow syringe poised at his vein. He looked up at her through his swollen eyes. "Our revenge will take decades to achieve. Are you on board with that?"

The longer the game, the more damage he could cause. And the more lives he could save. "I'd wait a hundred years if it meant I could be the one to kill them."

Maureen laughed and released the liquid into his bloodstream. It would take minutes for the antidote to take effect, but he already felt the pressure leave his heart. They would protect him. They would help him save the children. They would let him get his revenge.

"His name is Rufus," she supplied. "Welcome to the Alliance."

PRESENT DAY

2

LUKE

They—they were children. Babies!

Aeron's distraught cry chased Luke through the city traffic as he swerved his motorcycle between cars toward the safe house. He hadn't killed them all, but he'd killed enough—and that was something he would never be rid of. His chest tightened as he got closer. He'd avoided the kids because seeing their faces brought his dead to the forefront. Gabe never really left his side anymore, always just in the shadows, the ice gaze stabbing him should he have a moment of peace or happiness. He didn't deserve peace. He didn't deserve Aeron.

Katherine said they weren't ready for their Granddad to be dead —what if she needed to clean up loose ends? He would move the kids before word got out about the change in command: now his command, that he would not take. Kat would be hunting for him— they'd be locked out of the accounts, the safes, hell, even the buildings. She'd send the Legacy Inc assets after him. That's what he would do. And as soon as word got out that his Granddad was dead, the Underworld would come for them all because Granddad made sure each of them had monumental targets on their backs.

He should have shot his Granddad. The thought circled over

and over in his mind. He should have been the one to end the man who killed his parents and ruined him. He should have. . . no. He shook his head, dislodging the thoughts. Should haves and could haves didn't change what he was. His Granddad may have been the true monster and killer he'd been hunting the last few months, but someone was going to pay. Needed to pay. Not for his parents' deaths, but for the innocent lives he took; for the piece of his parents that died inside him the night he killed Gabe. For turning him into a monster.

That didn't belong to his Granddad. He'd used Aeron to manipulate him, but Rosemary had taught him how to turn off his switch. Showed him how ruthless could be simple, so simple to access. How lives were nothing more than playing pieces on a board he controlled. She gave him a taste for easy instead of right. His Granddad may have been the mastermind, but Rosemary had been the one who'd broken him. His bullet would be for her.

Tell me he's lying. Aeron's final words to him rang in his ears. Even if he could lessen the blow, the look of horror on her face would never go away; it didn't matter how many of the children he'd saved. He'd still done the unspeakable—the unforgivable. What the hell was wrong with him? He revved the engine, recklessly weaving in and out of cars trying to outrun the undeniable truth— he'd become a monster. *Tell me he's lying.*

Fuck Aeron.

The thought ripped through him as he sped off the exit. Fuck her and her brother and their lies. Fuck their looks of horror as the truth poured from him. His Granddad ruined the only good thing left in Luke's life: the respect and love of people whom he'd done unspeakable things to protect.

Ice pierced his spine as he slowed his approach to the safe house —a two-story townhouse situated in Astoria, just over the bridge from the Institute. He'd have to get back there as well, for money and weapons—but first, the children. The shaking in his body had ceased, replaced by the freezing grip of all the innocent lives he took for. . . for what? For *her?* For *love?* Fuck love.

Fuck it all.

He cut the engine and gazed up at the darkened windows, blackout curtains designed to keep the light in at night. He put his helmet on the seat and took the steps to the door two at a time. The door handle was biometrically designed to only open for them, and he wiped his hand on his pants, afraid Katherine may have hit reset on it before he could get here. He grasped the metal handle, and it whirred to life beneath his touch, releasing the lock and swinging in. The hall was dark until the door clicked closed behind him, and then he squinted against the sudden brightness.

"Luke?" Dominic appeared from the doorway on the left. Had Luke not just fucked his whole life up, he probably would have laughed. Dominic stood in black sweatpants and what Luke guessed was a juice-stained white t-shirt. He held a peanut butter container in one hand and a butter knife in the other like he was going to smear the intruder to death with a nighttime snack.

"Dom." Luke raised a questioning eyebrow. "What. . ." He didn't even know what to ask. Two kids bolted around the corner, brushing past Dominic, and Luke stepped back before they ran into him. Eliza, the energetic six-year-old, chased one of the five-year-old Smith twins.

"Quit running inside!" Dom yelled after them, but they had rounded the banister at the bottom of the stairs and raced to the top. Squeals of laughter rang out as they disappeared around the wall.

"I'm sorry," Luke said, unable to grasp what the hell was going on. "What is happening here?"

Dom laughed and waved him to follow with the knife. "Late-night snack?"

"No." As Luke followed Dom into the kitchen, more shrieks and laughter sounded from above. The counters were littered with dirty plates and empty cups, and step stools lined the way. A bag of flour was overturned on the table like mini piles of snow with handprints pressed into them. Dom dropped the knife back into the container and placed the peanut butter on the counter, leaning against it, concern etched into the corners of his eyes.

"Did something happen to Kat?"

Luke pulled his eyes away from the tiny indents in the flour. He counted several sets, each one belonging to a child alive and well upstairs. "No," he said again, looking back at the handprints. He rounded the table, tracing each palm and finger. He was sure he'd find them here, all dead—that he would be too late. "What is going on here? I thought—the caretakers. . ."

"Katherine was afraid they'd be discovered. So when we moved here, Gunnar and I agreed to take over their care." Luke looked around for Gunnar. "He's grocery shopping. Growing kids eat a lot. I thought you were him."

"I could have been anybody—somebody here to kill them!" Anger jumped into Luke's chest, and he took a step forward. "You answered the door with a fucking peanut butter jar—I could have been anybody."

Dom pushed off the counter. "The alarms would have sounded. The biometrics cannot be tricked. Unless you're here to finish the job."

Crack. Luke's fist smashed against the side of Dom's face, and he stumbled into the counter. He went to swing again, and Dominic framed against the inside of his arm and took a circle step back. Luke's momentum carried him past Dom, and he landed hard against the floor, sliding into the step stools. The breath left him, and when he inhaled, his throat tightened. He took several gasping breaths, the cold swarming him. He closed his eyes. Dom grabbed beneath his arms, and Luke allowed him to sit him up, leaning back against the counter, trying to breathe. He couldn't. He shouldn't. He should be dead. He wished he was dead.

"It's okay, man. Deep breaths. In-two-three-four. Out-two-three-four." Luke tried to keep pace with his words because the alternative was to drown in the thoughts circling in his head. Aeron and his Granddad, and the kids he didn't save. But it wasn't working. His breath refused to cooperate. "What can you feel right now?"

Luke shook his head. He didn't want to feel anything.

"Concretely, what are you touching?"

Luke pushed his body down, finding his grounding. "The floor. The counter. My gun."

"What do they feel like?"

"Cold. Sticky. Heavy."

"Good," Dominic said softly. "What can you hear?"

Luke pressed his eyes tighter, listening. He could hear the kids—laughing, running—their footsteps pattering across the hallway. He could hear his heart beating furiously to get out of his chest. He could hear the clock in the kitchen. He opened his eyes, his breathing calmer. Dom sat right in front of him, eyes locked on his. "The kids. The clock. You."

"Better?" Dom asked.

Luke nodded. He hadn't had a panic attack in years; Perry used to talk him down. "How did you know how to ground me?" Luke asked.

"Katherine used to get them after Shay—a lot. What's going on?"

"Have you heard from her? Kat?"

Dom shook his head.

"I fucked up," Luke admitted. "I've been doing that a lot—but this. . ." Luke looked up at the table again. "What were they doing with the flour?"

Dom looked over his shoulder, his face lighting up. "I don't know. Playing. We don't have any tech here for them, T.V.s, or anything. So, they get bored and get creative. They love to bake and do arts and crafts." He looked back at Luke. "You're worried about them."

Luke was terrified for them. Terrified he'd ruined their lives—that he'd saved them just to have them delivered to slaughter. That they'd grow up with nothing but vengeance in their tiny hearts and end up right where he was. "Are they safe?"

Dom let out a sigh. "They are as safe and as happy as we can make them."

"I thought you didn't want anything to do with them."

"*You* didn't want anything to do with them. Gunnar and me? We're not assassins. I miss my cousins and family back home. Gunnar too. These kids need stability; they need love. It's our part of the mission until your Granddad's dead."

Luke swallowed around the knot forming in his throat. "And what happens then? With the kids?"

As if summoned, the herd of children raced down the stairs, bounding into the kitchen. They ran right past him to the table, the oldest boy scooping up a handful of flour and throwing it in the air, so it rained down on everyone in the room. "I got all of you at once! I win!"

"Hey!" Dom said, standing up and turning to the kids. They ignored him, and each grabbed a fistful of flour and tossed it up, their laughter contagious as the flour drifted down and settled on Luke's pants. Specks of white stood out against the dark suit he still wore, and his lips pulled into a smile. They looked—like children. Penelope, with her brown hair and the remarkable birthmark on her cheek they almost couldn't remake, spotted him on the floor, and her eyes doubled.

"Luke!" Before he could register what she said, she threw herself toward him. He caught her instinctively, and she wrapped her arms around his neck. "You came back," she said into his neck.

Luke met Dom's gaze. "I—I."

"Of course he did," Dom said with a smile. The other children raced toward him, giving hugs and smiles he didn't deserve, didn't want, but they warmed the ice out of his system. They dog-piled him, and he slumped sideways, a laugh surfacing while they climbed and jumped on him.

"Enough. Enough!" Dom said, pulling the kids off him and

helping Luke to his feet. "Go wash up for bedtime. Guns will be home in a bit, and if you want to play a board game, you have to have clean teeth!"

The group moved as a unit and scurried back out of the room, except for Owen. He paused in the doorway, holding Luke's gaze. He was only a year from entry into the Institute—he'd already been trained for combat and understood the value the Legacy put on innocent life above all else. Luke didn't detect a trace of malice in his gaze, though.

"I thought you might have died, saving more of us," he said. "I'm glad you're okay." Then he followed the others upstairs, herding the smaller ones as he went.

Luke's chest constricted, and he didn't stop the tears as they forced themselves down his face. They thought he was a hero—just like Katherine had said. Dom's hand rested on his shoulder. "Kat made sure they knew, especially the older ones, that you fought against their Senior Assassin to save them. That you are the hero of their stories, their nightmares."

"And if they discover the truth?" Luke whispered. "That I caused those nightmares?"

"Luke." Dom spun him around to face him. But whatever he was going to say was lost as the hallway darkened and the door clicked open. "Gunnar's back."

Luke wiped his face, turning away from the doorway when Dom went to meet his cousin. He brushed the flour from his suit. They didn't hate him because they didn't know the truth.

"What's going on, Luke?"

He turned back around. Gunnar carried bags of groceries in, a baby in a carrier strapped to his chest. "Is that. . ."

Gunnar nodded. "Scarlett. Do you want to—"

"No," Luke said, backing up, hands raised. He did not want to hold her. He'd murdered her parents. He'd murdered all of their parents. He could have tried recruiting them. He should have done anything else. But that smiling baby pulled his heart. She was alive.

His brain ached from the swell of emotion, gratitude, and self-hate, and he grabbed a cup from the counter, rinsed out the juice, and filled it with water, gulping it down.

Dom returned, more bags in hand. "This is everything."

"Why are you here?" Gunnar asked.

"I just—" Luke hesitated. He'd wanted to get the kids to safety—but they were safe. Hell, they were even happy. An alarm sounded in Dom's back pocket, cutting him off. He pulled out a cell phone and paled.

"What is it?" Luke asked.

"It's a. . . Give me a minute." He pushed past Luke and opened the pantry. Luke followed, confused, until Dom pushed open the back wall of shelves, revealing his tech room, filled with monitors and the whirring of hard drives. The room was easily fifteen degrees cooler than the rest of the house, and Luke shivered as he followed him in. "Close that behind you. The kids don't know about this room." Luke obliged. Dom's fingers danced across the keyboards, and Luke placed his hand on his gun. Was word of his Granddad's death already out? Impossible. It'd only been a few hours—but he had called Katherine. Would she order him killed?

"Fuck me," Dom said under his breath, pulling up a page on the biggest screen. Luke was glad he hadn't eaten—the youngest member of their Legacy team was sprawled out on a rooftop, Lesley's body beaten, a single execution gunshot administered to her forehead.

"What the fuck is this?" Luke demanded. He couldn't pull his eyes from Lesley's lifeless body. Several of her fingers were broken too. He looked to the side of the photo:

CLAIMED/CONFIRMED
Lesley Montgomery.
Known location: Albany, NY; NYC, NY; Montana.
Wanted Dead.
Price: $1.5 mil.

Luke's hands shook, and he grabbed the back of Dom's chair. "Dominic. . ."

"I'm fucking looking, Luke." It took several more minutes until another dossier appeared on the screen, CLAIMED/CON-FIRMED, stamped across the top. "Do you want me to—"

No. Dread settled into his stomach. Luke didn't want to see what was inside that file. "Open it." Luke slammed his eyes shut, but the image was already seared into his mind. Justin's body laid out in an alleyway. He'd put up a fight, his body beaten too, with multiple gunshots to the legs and chest. He opened them again to read the status next to the picture.

CLAIMED/CONFIRMED
Justin Spry.
Known locations: Albany, NY; NYC, NY; Miami, FL
Wanted Dead.
Price: $1.8 mil.

"Where are these coming from?" Luke asked. Dom didn't answer, but his hands moved faster, and pages opened and closed. Luke couldn't keep up. He looked instead to Lesley and Justin. Dead. They were fucking dead. Hunted. He stepped close to the screen, inspecting the pictures now that the initial shock had worn off. Both had been tortured—not beaten. And the only reason for that was they were looking for information. On what?

"Luke." Luke looked over to the screen in front of Dominic. A list of names, Lesley, and Justin's at the top. His eyes moved to the next two names on the list: Aeron and Decius. His world slipped sideways, and he stumbled forward, grabbing the table for support.

"What is this?" Every inch of him hummed. This couldn't be happening. He'd done everything possible to keep them safe. He sold his soul to keep them safe.

"It's an international hit list. It hit the dark web about an hour ago."

"And you just got the alert!" Luke yelled.

"The Sewards' names were just released. I didn't have your other teammates as priority alerts."

"What are those?" Luke pointed to the screen. There were several blank boxes beneath the list.

"I'm guessing names," Dom said. "The algorithm is set to time release information."

"Can you get around it?" More fierce typing answered him. "Dom?"

"Not right now, I can't. Want me to open them up?"

Luke rocked back and forth, staring at Aeron's and Decius' names. "Yes."

Aeron's file opened first.

UNCLAIMED
Aeron Seward.
Known locations: Seward Manor; NYC, NY
Wanted Dead.
Price: $4.5 mil.

"What happens if you click on the locations?" Luke asked. Seward Manor wasn't exactly listed on Google Maps. Dom clicked on the first one. A pin dropped on a map, to the exact location of her home. Dread swallowed him whole. She and Dee were heading straight to their deaths. "What about Decius?" Dom opened the other file; it was the same. His heart hammered in his throat. He needed to get to them—he needed to save them. Fuck everything else. The world could not go on without them—without Aeron. "Give me a phone."

Dom opened a drawer and pulled out a burner handing it to Luke. The screen updated again. They both froze, looking up. Beside Aeron's name, the words CLAIMED flashed onto the screen briefly, and the next few names on the list were revealed. The burner phone fell from his fingers. No. *No.*

"What just happened?" Luke's heart constricted. "You saw that, right?" Luke said. He picked the phone up from the ground and backed out of the room, tearing his eyes away from the screen. Maybe he was too late. Dom stood and reached for him.

"Luke, wait!"

"I have to go. Call them. Call Katherine. Let her know they're in danger. I have to. . ." He rushed out of the room. Gunnar looked up in shock as he ran past him out of the house. The next names on the list had flashed for the briefest of moments: Eileen Gale, Rosemary Wayward, Betty Wayward. Only one of those women deserved to die, and he wanted to be the one to put the bullet in her. He threw his helmet on and started the bike as Dominic raced down the front steps.

"Wait!" But Luke couldn't. He needed to get to the Sewards. He pulled out of the driveway and sped toward the Institute. He'd need weapons, money, and a vehicle. His first mission was to save his best friends. And then he would make sure Rosemary Wayward got exactly what she deserved.

3

AERON

Decius cut the bike's engine inside the Seward Manor garage, and the sudden silence deafened Aeron. She released her stiff fingers from around her brother's waist and bit back the complaint as pain shot through her body. She deserved this pain—every second of it.

Decius yanked off his helmet, the rough movement jostling the stab wound in her shoulder. A moan escaped her then. Her vision blurred, and she slid sideways off the seat. Hands grasped her upper arms, slowing her descent to the ground.

An echo resounded when her helmet met to the floor. "Oh, Aeron." Decius tugged the strap holding the protective gear in place and eased it off. "Why didn't you say something?"

A short laugh escaped her. "You mean while you were doing one-twenty down the highway?" But she hadn't said anything because there was nothing to say. She had ripped their team apart—their family. And Luke—Luke had torn her heart to shreds.

He prodded her shoulder, and her scream echoed through the garage. Blood oozed from the wound, and her fingers twitched as the pain radiated toward them. Decius' nose crinkled, and he moved to check her side where Luke's bullet had struck. His eyes widened.

"How did you not fall off the bike?"

"I don't know," Aeron lied. But the all-consuming thoughts of Luke had kept her distracted from the pain—his look of betrayal as she confessed she knew who killed his parents and his non-denial of killing the Legacy families.

He slid her good arm over his shoulder and supported her weight into the Manor, navigating through the dark house. He turned toward their father's study, and Aeron's heart skipped too many beats. Behind that door sat memories of unwantedness, neglect, and failure.

It also held the start of this entire fuckup—where their father had asked for her help. Where she had felt powerful, needed. Where he had bared his soul to her and convinced her that it was the only way to save Luke. But there was no saving Luke, and maybe there never was a chance for him once his Granddad sunk his teeth in. Was it worth it? The lies. The betrayals. The fleeting moments when the world seemed perfect.

She stilled, not wanting to enter the room. It was behind that door her life changed. "Dee."

"It's where I've been operating from. I need a better look at your side."

"He should have just aimed for my heart." She ground out the words between clenched teeth. "It would have been easier."

He ignored her and eased the door open. Aeron halted. Decius had rearranged the space. The couches sat beside the window instead of the fireplace, and the piles of papers on the desk would have given their father a migraine. They moved slowly toward the couch, and she eased herself down before completely sinking into the cushions, exhaustion begging to take her. Decius tugged up her shirt again to see where Luke's bullet had hit. With the couch steady beneath her, she could see the anger radiating off him. So much had been said in the Wayward garage. So many lies and truths were unveiled. So many secrets never meant for him to hear.

"Dee, what I said about Mom. . ."

"Not now, Aeron." The ice in his voice froze her words, and she sucked in when he probed the area again.

"He just grazed you. I can't believe I'm even saying that: 'Luke just grazed you.'" He shook his head. "I've never seen him look so angry—so devastated." He huffed out a breath and crossed to the desk. Drawers opened and slammed just out of her sight. He appeared again with a medical kit, and she pulled her shirt off. The raw, burned skin turned her stomach, and she bit into her lower lip, welcoming the immediate pain she could control.

Decius knelt by the couch. "I'm going to clean them up the best I can. This is going to hurt."

"It can't hurt worse than how you're looking at me right now." His eyes met hers, and a roller coaster of emotions pulsed through him, the need to understand what happened in the garage, what happened to Luke. He said nothing, though, as he got to work. She gripped the couch as he sterilized and covered both wounds, and she reveled in the burn of her skin while running over the last few hours. How had they ended up here, with Luke hating her, Decius angry at her, and the blood of their Senior Assassin on her hands?

That was easy: because she lied. She lied to all of them. Once he finished covering her wounds, he returned the first aid kit, dropping it on top and leaning heavily on the desk. "We just killed the Senior Assassin," Decius whispered. "We fucking killed the leader of the Legacy." He looked up at her, and past his anger, Aeron saw the panic in his eyes.

"I know," Aeron said, not bothering to correct him. She had killed him. Placed that bullet right between his eyes.

"What do we do now?"

"Nothing," she answered.

"What do you mean nothing? We are going to be executed. Hunted. We should call Mrs. Gale or Mason."

"Why? You heard Mr. Wayward. The Legacy is gone. Dismantled." She leaned back and closed her eyes. The couch was so comfortable she could just sleep. "We should just rest."

"We need to find Luke."

"Need is a strong word. He just shot me."

"Grazed you," Decius corrected. Luke's face swam in Aeron's mind—cold, calculated, furious. She wasn't sure he wouldn't shoot her on sight. "What the hell's been going on?" he asked.

"A lot," Aeron admitted.

"What you said about Dad, about him trying to stop Mr. Wayward. . ."

Aeron released a long sigh and righted herself on the couch. Her head swam, and she braced herself on the coffee table. Decius was by her side in an instant, but she shrugged him off. "I can't do this right now."

"Fine." Decius pulled out his phone but made no move to dial it. Instead, he sat on the table, his knee bobbing up and down, staring at the screen.

"Whatever happened these last few months, tell me you had no choice." His eyes remained focused on the blank screen.

She opened her mouth a few times, closing it almost immediately. At the time—she didn't think she had a choice. But she had. Her father told her as much from the very beginning.

"Aeron." His voice begged for their father to have been the bad guy. Because that would justify her lying to him, justify her driving the blade through their father's chest.

"I made a mistake, Dee."

"Grabbing skim instead of whole milk is a mistake," he shouted before reeling in his temper. "Lying to me? Working with Dad in secret? That's not a mistake." He stood and paced the length of the couch. "How long have you been lying to me?" he whispered.

Too long. She'd been lying to him for too long and knew her answer would tear his heart out. Her answer was just as quiet. "Since Dad dragged me back from Ernie's. After the funeral, the agreement was if I wanted to train with him to earn my spot, I needed to prove I was loyal. And what's more loyal to Dad than lying to you?"

"I thought you didn't want to be in the Legacy."

"I didn't. And then I did, and then I had to lie about wanting to be in. It's complicated, Dee."

"Uncomplicate it, Aeron. Because from where I'm standing, you have a lot of blood on your hands for someone who didn't want to be in this fucking life."

She flinched; the words were a near-physical blow. "What do you want from me, Dee?" Nothing would heal the broken trust right now, but if he would stop looking at her like she single-handedly destroyed their lives.

"What happened to," his words faltered. "What happened to—to M-Mom?" His voice cracked, and with it, a chunk of Aeron's heart cracked too. "What you said about Mr. Wayward. What happened?"

Aeron could barely manage a whisper. "She was murdered."

Decius' dark complex paled. "No. She died in a car accident."

Aeron shook her head, a tear threatening to fall. But if she let that dam break open right now, it would never stop. "'Intentional car wreck,' if I'm to quote Dad. Mr. Wayward had ordered it. It's why he pulled me home from Ernie's. Mr. Wayward placed a price on my head."

Decius shook his head. "Why would he do that?"

"Place a price on my head or kill Mom?" The question mirrored the one she had asked her father a few short months ago.

"Both."

"Because. . ." she ran her hands over her face. "Because Mom wanted out, Dee. And she wanted to take us with her." It was a small lie to spare his feelings. She couldn't remember their mother, but Decius did—in excruciating detail. It would tear him apart to know she would've left him behind. "The point is, she's dead because of him, and so are Mr. Wayward's own sons. As for me?

Mr. Wayward was a bit of a control freak. I was off the grid, and he didn't like it."

"Why leave me out of it?" His voice cracked. "I could have. . . I would have. . ." He ran a hand over his hair.

Could haves and would haves didn't belong in an assassin's language. "Dad knew you would stop us if it became too dangerous for me."

The gears spun behind Decius' eyes. Her confession of being at the Rose Way Hotel, Mr. Wayward beating her nearly to death and not their father, and the realization she killed their father to gain access to the Wayward estate all sank in.

"Why?" He asked again, and Aeron understood what he really wanted to know. Why had she chosen their father over him? But she hadn't. She had chosen Luke over him.

"Because if Mr. Wayward thought Luke wasn't loyal, he'd have killed him."

Decius released a hollow laugh.

"He's been trying to stop Mr. Wayward for years. He's been taking on an army."

Decius' laughter subsided. "What I'm hearing is that Dad gave you an ounce of attention and praise, and you heeled like a trained puppy. We've worked for *years*, Aeron, you and I, to ensure that you could be free from this life. And if what you said *is* true, Mom would have wanted you out, too. Yet, with a few choice words, you surrendered to him." He drew a hand down his face, and anger flared in Aeron's gut.

"He gave me a chance to leave," she said defensively. "I chose to stay and save Luke."

"And Dad used you as a pawn! Dangling Luke's life in front of you to make you dance. Luke hated his grandfather. He would have turned on him any day of the week. If you weren't blinded by. . . If you told me—so many people would be alive right now. Dad would be alive right now."

Aeron swallowed around the lump in her throat, nearly choking on it. "Luke was in danger. I chose to save him."

"No. You chose to lie to both of us—and look how many ended up dead. Aeron, there has only ever been one rule."

No lies.

She couldn't look at him. This was her fault. Every death, every child Luke had killed.

"Before I call Mrs. Gale and drag her into this shitshow, tell me every detail. Every *fucking* one from the time you came home from the garage until now."

A long breath left her lungs. She didn't know the whole story; their father made sure of that. "Mrs. Gale already knows, and I don't know if you will even be able to reach her."

His eyes darkened, the betrayal he was the only one not in the know cutting his features. He remained silent, eyes downcast, waiting for her to continue. Aeron shifted in her seat, wincing in pain as she turned to face him. The past year's events leading up to the murder of their father and Mr. Wayward, their Senior Assassin, seemed disconnected from the rest of her life. How had everything unraveled so fast? She took a shaky breath.

"I can only tell you the parts I know."

His eyes cut to her, and her phone buzzed in her pocket, giving her an excuse to look away. One of Ivan's many numbers lit the screen, relief racing through her body. Speak of the devil. She ignored Decius' glare and answered it.

"What's up, Darth?"

"Where are you?" Ivan asked.

"Home; at the Manor. Listen, I need you here. A lot's happened to—"

"Get out, now." Urgency dripped through his voice.

She sat up straighter. "What?"

"Get the fuck out of that house." Her blood ran cold at his words; Ivan hardly ever swore. "You and your brother's names and known locations have just hit the dark web. I don't know what you did, but your heads are priority number one worldwide."

Aeron's heart nearly stopped, a cold sweat breaking out across her forehead. It'd only been a few hours since she put the bullet in Mr. Wayward's head. Since she assassinated the man who tormented and ruined Legacy families. How had the Senior Assassin protocol already been activated? No one could know she had killed him already. Were there cameras? No. Luke would have told her; he would have—Luke.

He was the next Senior Assassin—the now current reigning Senior Assassin. Was this his first order of business? Put an international price on their heads? No. It couldn't be. He never wanted to be in charge; he'd fought against it. Until she lied to him. Until she confessed she knew the real killer of his parents. Until she learned the lengths he went to protect her. The innocent lives that he took. Her breath caught in her chest. Mr. Wayward was dead, and somehow, her life was none the safer.

"Aeron, what's wrong?" Decius asked. She didn't answer him, trying to figure out who could have done this because Luke wouldn't have. He was mad, but—no. He loved her and Decius. He'd die to protect them, but he. . . he had killed innocent children, whole families they had grown up with. He'd sold his soul to protect her—from a lie. Decius pulled the phone from her grip. "Who the hell is this?"

She could hear Ivan on the other end. She met Decius' gaze.

"Where?" His eyes darkened as he continued to listen. "Fine." He powered off the phone and removed the battery and SIM card before smashing it to pieces.

"Dee?" She stood shakily, and he steadied her by the shoulders. She winced in pain.

"We have probably less than fifteen minutes before this property is breached." A vice gripped her heart, and she looked around the room. The room where her entire life changed just a few short months ago. Where her father let her in on all his secrets—bared his soul, and asked her to help him stop a madman. She hated this place—but loved it too. "That man on the phone, who is he?"

Aeron let a smile cross her face. "Ivan. Dad's apprentice."

"He needs us to grab a set of documents out of the safe, but I don't know where the safe he's talking about is. Something about secret chambers and murdering cars."

Aeron let out a small laugh. She knew exactly where that safe was. "It's in the garage."

He nodded. "Did you want anything from the house before I set protocol?"

She glanced around the room again. Normal people would be worried about pictures, memories, valuables. But they didn't have many of those. She shook her head, a knot lodged in her throat all of a sudden. She would never be able to come back here.

"Alright. I'll grab the go bags and meet you there."

Aeron retraced their steps to the garage, using the wall for balance, her body begging her to sit back down. She passed the bike and the line of cars and walked to the far wall, where her mother's murderer sat hidden. She leaned against the closest car, a black Charger, as the blood loss and shock set into her system. Her body began to tremble, waiting for her brother to arrive.

"Aer?"

She looked over her shoulder as he approached. "There's a key fob in the pocket of my jumpsuit. Over by the sink."

He rushed over, opening up the cabinet and pulling out the dirtiest jumpsuit. He brought it over and pulled out the round button.

"Click it." She watched his face as the wall slid back, the lights slowly coming on. She was not surprised to see the baby blue car was no longer in its place but wsas annoyed the room was empty.

"Great," Decius said, annoyance clear in his tone. "Another secret. It's empty, so. . ." He checked his watch. "We're down to about seven minutes. What are we looking for?"

She didn't know. She could be completely wrong about this being where he meant. She pushed off the car and scanned the room, looking for seams in the drywall. Or any imperfection. "Look for what doesn't belong."

They started on opposite sides, running hands over the walls. This was pointless. They should be running.

"Found it!" Decius called out. Aeron turned, and he was already kicking through the sheetrock. There, set into the wall along the floor, was a dial safe. So small and inconspicuous that if the building were to burn to the ground, it might have been removed by a demolition team without ever being discovered. Decius tried to pull it out, but it wouldn't budge. He stared at the dial as if willing the combo to reveal itself. "Any idea what it might be?"

She licked her lips. "Yeah." This room had been a shrine to their mother. And even though it went against every protocol, she guessed her father didn't apply the rules in this secret room. "Try Mom's birthday."

Decius hesitated.

"December—"

"I know her birthday," he said, cutting her off. They waited as he spun the dials. The door did not budge.

Aeron swallowed around the lump growing in her throat and whispered, "Try her death date."

A heavy silence fell over them, and Decius inhaled slowly before trying the combination. The door clicked open, and relief raced through her.

"What's in there?" What could her father possibly be holding on to in this room that is so important that Ivan knew about it?

Decius pulled out a manila envelope. "We don't have time to look now. Let's get out of here."

Aeron agreed. She rounded the Charger and hopped in the driver's seat. Even in her condition, they both knew she was the better driver. She pushed the start button, and the car purred to life. Decius closed the trunk and slid into the passenger seat, handing her a bottle of water. She shook her head and opened the garage door. They were leaving. She was really leaving forever.

"Did you set the fire?" Aeron asked.

"Started it in the office," he said, and she began backing out but immediately slammed on the brakes. Decius braced on the dashboard and turned around. A black pickup truck raced into the driveway blocking their exit. Aeron watched the two-man team jump out of the car in the rearview mirror, guns drawn.

"Shit!" Decius grabbed Aeron's head and dragged her down, covering her as they fired. She turned the wheel, speeding the car backward out of the garage. The gun fire halted, and Aeron slammed the car into park. Decius pulled two guns from beneath his seat and handed her one. She threw the door open and dropped low, peering toward the enemy. Another truck barreled into the driveway. She took aim and fired, her bullet making a purchase in the driver. The truck swerved off course and slammed into the parked vehicle. The two men dove out of the way, and Aeron and Decius retreated to the rear of the car to take cover.

"Fifteen minutes, my ass," Aeron spat.

"I said *less* than fifteen. There are three of them. If no one else shows up, we can make it out of here just fine."

Aeron nodded, but her head swam. Her entire body rejected the idea of fighting. It begged to just sit. She dropped her head against the trunk, the cool surface shocking. She must be burning up. "I don't know how much fight I have left in me," Aeron confessed.

Decius met her wary gaze. "We only need to make it out of here. I'll handle them. Stay here and don't die."

She nodded again. "The Legacy motto."

He stood, shots firing over the top of the car. She adjusted her grip on the gun and looked around the corner. Two men followed Decius around the side of the Manor. The third headed in her direction. She fired a few shots, dove for the open garage door, and rolled behind the wall. A shot whizzed past, impacting the rear window of the Navigator parked inside. It spider-webbed, and Aeron thought of her side, where Luke's bullet had grazed, the damage spread across her stomach and back.

She pressed her head against the wall. If she could close the door, she would have a chance. She checked the SUV's side mirror. The man was just in sight. Leaning around the corner, she fired another shot, making purchase in his chest. He dropped, and she did, too, sucking in a few deep breaths before pushing herself up.

The car. She just needed to get back to the car. Forcing her feet to move, she stumbled out and came face to face with a bearded man, his brown eyes glinting with victory, his graying beard twitching when he smiled. Her heart slammed into her throat. "Oh, your head catches a pretty price. Drop the gun," he said, aiming at her. She complied, and he pulled out his cell phone to record, motioning her to the ground.

This was it. She was going to die on her knees in her own driveway. She'd lost Shannon. She'd ruined Luke. She'd killed her father and landed her brother on a hit list when she'd killed the Senior Assassin. She dropped to her knees, the pavement digging into her skin, her body wanting to drop to the side with exhaustion. What was there to fight for anyway? The Legacy Families were all dead, with no one else to save. Decius would be fine without her. Ivan could be released from his obligation to help her. And Luke—Luke would probably shoot her on sight.

The gun pressed against her forehead. She took a deep breath, the smoke creeping out from the Manor, burning her lungs. On a different day, she could imagine disarming him, false surrender so she could get the upper hand. But she couldn't muster the strength, the concentration. She couldn't muster the will to fix the mess she'd made, and he'd pull the trigger before she could even move. She'd imagined dying so many times: saving an innocent life or sacrificing herself for a team member. Not on her knees, begging for her life. So she wouldn't beg. She wouldn't bargain. And whoever confirmed her death on the other side of the screen would not see her pleading.

The click of the hammer jolted her nerves, and the barrel pulled back ever so slightly. She squeezed her eyes tighter, and the shot rang out.

4

KAT

Kat glared at the dead body on the floor, the pool of blood blackening at the edges like an evil halo around his head. She squatted next to her Granddad. He had thought himself a goddamn god who couldn't be killed. Someone had closed his eyes, but the slack face and bullet hole in his forehead warmed her soul. She would've preferred to torture him, have him meet death over and over until his brain no longer recognized if it was alive or dead. Stripped his mind of all thoughts except one: Shay. But what was done was done—for now.

She stood and kicked the body. The dead weight barely moved, but the pool around his head wobbled like jello as it congealed. Rage bubbled in her gut. She'd wanted to see the tears slide down his cheeks. The life die in his eyes. She wanted to see his last breath, over and over and over. But even in death, her Granddad had won. She kicked him again and again until a scream ripped through her. Years of planning, killing, and sacrificing were wasted with a single bullet.

"You can't do any more damage—he's already dead."

Kat took a deep breath and looked over to the door. Aunt Betty carried the kitchen meat cleaver and a roll of plastic. Her brown hair cascaded over her shoulders, and the jeans and faded blue t-shirt were a drastic change from the normal business casual required by her Granddad. She looked. . . free. The thought enraged Kat, and she gave one final kick to the body and spat on him. There were so many sins he would never get to pay for.

"Yeah, but what hell is he going to raise from the grave? Because we know he's not done with us yet. Were you able to find Luke?"

"No. Here's his phone." She put down the items and passed Kat a cell phone from her pocket. "Perry is in the shower now but can't promise anything. He looks rough."

Kat nodded. "Does anyone else know he's dead?" She gazed around the room—there were no security cameras on the property—at least before Aeron had come to live there. She needed to keep this under wraps, or there would be chaos at Legacy Inc.

"Perry, us, Luke, Aeron, and Decius, as far as I know. But we're not going to be able to hide this. The protocols for a dead Senior Assassin—"

"For the Legacy? Those have been chucked out a window," Kat answered. "The protocols for Legacy Inc? Once he hasn't checked in for two days, all assets are transferred to Luke, the next in line." The words were sour in her mouth. It should have been her, but Luke had more to lose and was easier to manipulate; therefore, in her Granddad's twisted mind, he was the perfect candidate for the Senior Assassin position.

"And if we can't find him?" Aunt Betty asked, picking up a plastic sheet and shaking it out.

Kat pocketed the cell phone. "We run. The Legacy Inc assets are not to be trifled with. Unless we can find someone to hack into the mainframe." Kat knew exactly who they needed: Aeron Seward's fucking techie. They'd been the only one she knew who could hack into the Legacy system.

The door leading to the house opened. Perry smiled from the doorway, holding two steaming mugs. "Need some fuel?"

"Thanks," Kat said as he approached. Perry handed her a mug.

She took a sip and appreciated the perfect balance of creamer and coffee. He brought the other cup to his mom. Kat kept a steady gaze on him—his features darkening when he approached the body.

"You didn't get your vengeance," Perry said.

Kat moved beside him. "I know." She curled her lip and spat on the body again.

"Are you gonna kill her?" He raised an eyebrow and tilted his head in curiosity.

"Who, Aeron?"

Perry nodded.

"No. We might still need her. Besides, vengeance is getting old these days." The idea of vengeance had kept her alive all these years. The visions of sticking dirty, sharpened objects into his eyeballs. Of sending jolts of electricity through his body, just to see how long his body would convulse after she turned it off. To have him die one hundred deaths before she would end his reign of violence. But vengeance didn't help Luke—she'd watched it destroy him. Her heart constricted in her chest for a moment—that could have been her; that should have been her.

"The vault in his office," Perry began. "How do we access it?"

"If it's not by the Senior Assassin himself, we need three palm scans. Yours, mine, and either Luke's or Rosemary's. But if we had Luke's, then it wouldn't matter."

"What if you all died?" Betty asked.

"Then he would happily have it all burn," Perry answered, deadpanned. He turned to Kat. "So, we need your mother or Luke."

Kat scrunched her nose and handed the cup back to Perry. No. They'd need another plan. Her mother would be impossible to track. "She's been on the run since the yacht incident. I haven't found her."

"Any idea where she would head to?" Aunt Betty asked.

Kat shook her head. She'd spent considerable time blocking out anything her mother had to say—it was usually lies and saturated in ulterior motives. "Do we have to find her?"

"It's her or Luke," Perry said. "And I think Luke might put a bullet in any of us right now."

"And who says my mother won't?" Kat countered. She rubbed the back of her neck. Granddad's death was supposed to be a celebration. His downfall one for the history books. Not a coverup they might not survive. "Let's get this cleaned up and see what we can do without either of them for the moment. Call Dominic and Gunnar, and make sure they get those kids to a new safe house. Have them meet me in D.C. I've got to return before the Division Three assets realize I'm gone."

Perry nodded. "What about Luke?"

"Honestly? Fuck him. He knew we weren't ready and didn't stop her. Let's worry about what we can control." Kat turned toward their Granddad and Aunt Betty, who was waiting with the meat cleaver.

"I'll get him handled and clean this mess up."

"You're legit chopping him up?" Katherine asked.

"How did you think we were going to clean up his body?"

She hadn't thought about that. The cleaners usually took care of the bodies that needed disposing of or the cops. She hadn't cleaned up a crime scene since her training days. A thrill came over her. "Can I do that? I would have preferred to do this while he was alive, but..."

"Of course." Aunt Betty held out the meat cleaver. Kat stared at his limp hand, the one that consistently held a glass of scotch. The one that administered the torture to Shay. With a swift motion and satisfying crunch, his hand disconnected from the body. Aunt Betty picked it up. "Nice work." She held it up to Kat. "High-five?"

Kat doubted that hand had ever administered a high-five in its entire existence. "No." She moved to the other side, the drop of this hand warming her heart. She picked it up, the weight heavier than she anticipated. It would never harm another child. It would never end another life. It would never break another human. She glanced up to Perry, who wrapped the first one in plastic and pushed it deep within the ice chest Betty had brought out earlier.

"Tag. You're it." She tossed the other hand at Perry. His eyes widened, and he fumbled to catch it.

"Kat! That's disgusting!"

She laughed. "Do you want to pluck out his eyeballs, or should I?"

"May I do the honors?" Aunt Betty asked.

Perry pulled the eye scoop from his pocket. "Be my guest. What are we doing about the Legacy?"

Kat stared into the distance. "I'm pretty sure it's dismantled. Luke handled the last family just a week ago. But we *must* keep Legacy Inc moving. He's supplied the world's most dangerous and unfeeling humans with the training and means to turn this society inside out. It will be pure chaos without leadership."

"We need them on a leash," Perry said.

"We need them in a single room so I can eliminate them all in one shot," Kat countered. "Unfortunately, that will never happen."

A muffled vibration sounded, and all three of them stilled. Kat placed a hand on her back pocket, but neither hers nor Luke's phone was ringing.

"That's his," Perry said, jerking his head toward the ground. The sound continued to vibrate. "Should we. . ."

Kat jump-started into action. She reached into his front pocket and pulled out the phone, two words moving across the screen: The Reaper. Her pulse thrummed in her veins, and she shared the screen with Perry.

"Why would he be calling?" Perry wondered.

The Reaper was the deadliest assassin in the force. Sadness slipped in for a cold moment. That could have been her, Katherine Wayward: The Reaper. She had wanted that job as long as she could remember until the night her Granddad sat her down and forced her to watch the torture of the boy she'd loved. The night she watched Shay die over and over until her life mission shifted from wanting to be the Reaper of bad seeds within the company to taking vengeance against the man who ran it all.

She'd thrown herself into training, and when it became clear her Granddad believed she was loyal, she handed the top Reaper position to her best friend, the man who gave her a glimpse of love after Shay's torture. The man who asked her to leave vengeance behind for him.

"Are you going to answer it?" Perry asked, eyebrows raised.

"I can't," Kat replied. "Thumbprint required."

Perry held up the hand and waved it, but the ringing ceased. "Thumbprint or history?" he asked, raising an eyebrow.

"Does it matter?" she countered, not knowing the answer herself. "We missed the call. We need to get into this phone. Any chance you know the passcode?"

"Try 666," Perry mused.

Kat rolled her eyes but was glad to hear his humor had returned. It'd been too long since any of them had enough internal space to just laugh. Her thoughts shifted back to the phone, though, and a tendril of dread laced her veins. The Reaper only answered to the Senior Assassin and protected them at all costs. If Griffin was calling and didn't get an answer...

"How long has it been since you've seen him?" Perry asked.

"Two years."

"How the hell did you pull that off?"

Kat scrunched her nose. The thought of Griffin knocked at the iron case she'd slammed shut around her heart. "A lot of manipulation and excuses." Her phone rang in her pocket. She passed their Granddad's phone to Perry and pulled her own out: Griff. Her heart skipped several beats, followed by pulses of anger surging through her. How dare he call her. He'd made it clear his loyalty was to the dead man on the floor a long time ago. She only had his number, so she knew not to answer.

"What do you want, fucker?"

"Are you with your Granddad?" They'd known each other a lifetime, and he'd smashed her heart into pieces, yet still, her heart quickened at the sound of his voice, the soft rumble stirring a long-buried yearning for easier days, forbidden love, and for honesty.

She peeked over her shoulder at the dead body. "You've barely spoken to me in years, and that's all you care about? I'm not his fucking keeper."

"Katherine, cut the shit. Is he with you?" The underlying panic in his voice paused the sarcastic response on her tongue.

"I'm sure he's around here somewhere."

"He's not answering, and I need to speak with him."

Well, that would be impossible. "He probably left his phone on his desk and went to take a shit. And I've managed to live almost thirty years without that image in my head, so thank you for making me conjure it. Since you don't actually want to talk to me, I'll pass your message al—"

"Where's Luke? Last I knew, you were his keeper."

Her heart thrummed in her throat. If he was asking about Luke —they were out of time. "I honestly have no idea. I have to go."

"Kat." Her name sounded like honey coming from him, but he paused, his measured breathing the only sound until he released a short laugh. "Did you... Is he..."

He couldn't get the words out, but she knew what he wanted to know because he *knew* her—knew her hunt for vengeance, her longing to be free of this man. But he'd chosen her Granddad over her—she couldn't trust him. "No. I did not kill him. Either hims. Now, if you're done accusing me of treason, I have shit to do." She hung up before he could get another word in.

"We're out of time," Perry said from behind her.

She nodded. What were they going to do now? The easiest answer was to get Luke. The next answer was to run. Her phone rang again: Dominic.

"What is it?" she asked.

"An international hit list has just hit the dark web," he said.

Cold clenched her heart. They were too late. "Who's on it?"

"Luke's team. He was here when the alert came through on the Sewards."

"Luke was at the safe house?" Kat asked. Damnit. She should have called Dominic right away and given him a heads-up. He could have stalled Luke—grabbed him. But she'd wanted to see the body for herself and thought Luke had a better sense to disappear.

"Yeah. He went after them—the Sewards. He wanted us to warn them. Should we?"

"You can try and reach them, but the priority is getting Luke to return to us."

"He grabbed a burner."

"Can you find it?" Kat didn't want to get her hopes up, but if they could get Luke back on board—there was a chance they would survive this.

"I'll let you know. Sending you the list." He hung up.

Kat met Perry's eyes, ignoring Aunt Betty's concerned look, and pulled open the attachment he'd sent. A black screen appeared, a list of names at the top, two already crossed off, two names listed, and several locked at the moment. Kat gasped.

Lesley Montgomery - Claimed

Justin Spry - Claimed

Aeron Seward - $4.5 mil

Decius Seward - $4.5 mil

Perry snatched the phone from her, then passed it to his mom, shaking his head. Perry hadn't worked with Lesley, but Kat knew he and Justin had been close. "Fuck. We need Luke."

"Even dead, that man is relentless," Betty said. "Who do you think is confirming the kills?"

"Rufus or some Underworlder," Kat guessed. "Hell, it could literally be anyone; Joe Schmo in Kentucky, for all we know."

"No," Perry said. "He wouldn't outsource. Maybe your mom—or Griffin."

Kat didn't like the sound of that. She took the phone back. There were six more names blacked out. Was her name on that list? Perry's? They needed Luke. They needed Aeron's techie. They needed to keep Legacy Inc running and shut down the hit list. "If we can persuade whoever is confirming the kills, we have a chance. So, let's get into the game."

"So you are going to kill her? And Decius?" Perry asked, and Kat could feel the distress between his words. She and Perry were family, but Aeron and Decius were his family too, more so since they grew up together, lived together, grieved together. If she had to choose between Aeron and Decius or her and Perry—that wasn't even a choice. His heart would heal.

"If they are still alive when we find them? I'm not counting it out just yet."

5

LUKE

The Institute loomed overhead. The last time he'd parked here, Aeron had been on the brink of death, and he'd fought like hell and sold his soul to keep her safe. He tucked his helmet beneath his arm and paused outside the lobby door. The pride he felt calling this place home no longer surfaced. The Institute, the Legacy, was never a home. It was a prison. The lobby was dark. Not pitch black, but the bright light that had always flooded into the street wasn't there. The guards sat in semi-darkness and didn't move when he entered sending a chill down his spine.

"Jerrod?" he called. No response. Wrapping his fingers around the grip of his gun, he pulled it out, set his helmet on the floor, and moved forward. The two guards didn't respond—because they were dead. Shot once in the head while sitting up, as if they knew and trusted their murderer. Ice stabbed into his back, the familiar touch of the ones he killed taunting him. They had trusted him too.

Luke swallowed the bile down his throat and returned to the lobby doors, locking himself in. Pushing Jerrod's chair aside, he leaned over the desk to check the security footage. The wires had been dug out from beneath the desk and cut. The hit list had gone wide—every assassin who had worked with them knew where to find the Sewards. He could search every inch of the building, but what would be the point? Whoever killed the guards was well acquainted with them and knew this building. He needed the go-bag from the residence and the sports car from the garage.

Luke tucked his gun back into the holster, stepped into the elevator, and placed his hand on the door panel, but the car didn't budge. He wiped his palm and tried again, his hand trembling. It whirred to life and began the rise to the living quarters. The door to his apartment clicked open as it always did to his eye scan, and he froze. Boxes were slightly skewed, and the kitchen light was on. Someone had been in the apartment, maybe still was. He closed the door behind him and tapped the screen beside the entrance. He pulled up the security check-in. The last person to enter before him was—no fucking way.

He rewound the video feed, his heart pounding in his throat. Surely the program had glitched. Or someone was fucking with him, rewriting the program to show a dead woman's name. But there on the screen, two figures entered but didn't exit: a hooded figure he couldn't make out and Rosemary—fucking—Wayward.

He drew his gun and spun, deciding which side of the apartment to search first. Movement down the hall toward his parents' rooms beckoned him. He kept his steps soft, moving through the living area, and down the back hallway to the large master bedroom. The door sat wide open, a figure moving around paperwork laid out on the bed. "Who are you?" Luke asked.

With her back still to him, the woman held up a single finger commanding him to wait, a gesture so familiar it hurt. He inhaled to speak again, and cloth slipped across his nose and mouth, a firm hand securing it in place. He grabbed at the hand, his knees buckling. His vision blurred, and he slipped to the ground. Rosemary stepped slowly into view, her hair a knot atop her head.

"Sweet dreams, Luke. We have some unfinished business." She leaned in with a wicked grin as his limbs became impossible to move. And then, nothing.

Luke's body hung limp between the men carrying him, his shoes dragging across the smooth ground. A hood covered his head, and his arms were cuffed behind his back. He kept his breathing shallow, listening over his captors' labored breaths to figure out where they had brought him and who they were. The soft clack of heels on cement echoed around him—a warehouse of some sort. The faint sound of doors opening and closing, a metal chair being moved. The two men shifted sideways—to fit through a door frame.

Luke took his chance. He dropped heavily to his knees, but his legs refused to cooperate when he wanted to kick out, the restraints below his knees registering too late. They dropped him, his face rebounding off the ground. A moan escaped him, and a heavy boot pushed onto his back. The clacking of heels picked up speed as they moved closer. The hood was ripped from his head, the darkness replaced by blinding light he tried to turn away from but couldn't. He cracked an eye open and looked directly into Rosemary's smug face. Fuck. Not only had he not made it to Aeron and Decius, he was caught by the monster he wanted to kill, and she liked to play with her food first. He wouldn't give her the satisfaction.

"You're not convulsing, so that's a good sign." He swallowed back a grunt, her dig at the last time she'd drugged and almost killed him.

He pressed his face to the cool ground, remaining silent and letting the ice-cold floors lower his body temperature. He wasn't going to make it to the Sewards. He wasn't going to be able to warn them. Apologize to them. Explain his sins to them.

She stood, and the men pulled him up, but the chill in his cheek had pulled Gabe and the twins from his memory, and as the two men righted him, their figures appeared against the wall, watching. He willed for the others to come forward, too—Ben and Shannon—

but they did not join him. Luke didn't fight as they dropped him in the metal chair or as it dug into his back, his hands still cuffed behind him and now attached to an anchor on the floor. He didn't flinch at the sharp stab of a needle in his arm or make a peep as the world went hazy again, his head heavy. Maybe his dead would come out and watch him be tortured. They deserved that, at the very least.

"No smart-ass remarks? No banter?" Rosemary asked, moving over, and grasping his chin. "You're taking all the fun out of this." He pulled away, remaining silent. "We can do this the hard way if you want."

"You only do things the hard way," Luke said, breaking his silence. Her face lit up at his words.

"Facts. But I'm not quite ready for you just yet." She ran a hand down the side of his face as his eyelids drooped, the room moving in and out of the darkness. "Wait until you see what I have in store for us." Her wicked grin was the last thing he saw before the darkness took over once more.

6

KAT

Kat paced the short hallway outside the Senior Assassin's office, waiting for Perry's text. She'd flown back to the D.C. Headquarters to make sure it hadn't suddenly burst into flames, and Perry made sure his mom got to the safe house with Dom and Gunnar. They didn't need to be worried about her at the moment.

Getting into the Senior Assassin's office was easy enough. A few rewritten codes and it would be hers. The only person who would get the security alert was dead. The vault and financial records, however, required Luke's biometrics and blood sample to activate. Her phone chimed in her pocket, and she double-checked the message: Perry's thumbs-up.

Find the Sewards, she texted back. Aeron seemed reasonable enough. If they could get her techie in here to shut down the hit list and release the financials, they could all be breathing easier within the day.

She took a deep breath before placing her hand on the scanner. She'd already raided his private study and rooms in the building and found nothing of use—he kept all the good stuff in the vault. A small prick on her middle finger pulled a blood sample, and the lock clicked open. Kat released a long breath and let herself inside. The desk had a single stack of papers and a computer screen. She looked behind the desk to the six-foot-tall vault. It wasn't even concealed. The hard drives and central nervous system of Legacy Inc were just behind that foot of metal.

She leaned forward, hands against the smooth wood of the desk, letting her head droop and enjoying the weight stretching the tense muscles in her neck. With access to the office and boardrooms, she could step into full leadership of Legacy Inc. But without access to the financial accounts, she wouldn't be able to pay them. And money was what kept the beasts in line.

The air in the quiet room shifted, and her shoulders tensed. "Leaving your back open for your enemies, Katherine. Bold move."

She turned around. Carl West, one of three liaisons responsible for the assets of Legacy Inc, leaned against the door frame. The man oozed pretentiousness and greed, and she'd heard not-so-pleasant complaints from assets on his volatile temper. Yet, his blue suit was crisp as always, without a tie—she noted.

"You're out of regs," Kat said, gesturing to his chest. "I believe that is a $2000 fine."

"Only if Mr. Wayward catches me." He quirked an eyebrow, and Kat swallowed the urge to break his nose.

"If any management catches you."

"And where is our Senior?" Carl asked. He moved closer, and Kat pushed off the desk, standing taller, a smirk dancing on her face as he paused.

"He's otherwise occupied. I'll be handling all business for the next few weeks. Is there something you need?"

Carl sized her up and down with a predatory gaze. "What's keeping him occupied?"

"Oh, that's above your pay grade."

"Speaking of pay. My team hasn't been paid for their last assignment."

Kat's gut sank, although she knew this was coming. Deposits were synced with her Granddad's check-ins. No check-in, no payment. "Did they finish the job?" Kat countered.

Carl scoffed.

"I'm just saying," Kat continued and put her hands up in a peaceful gesture. She needed him to believe her, to trust her. "Last time a payment was late, there was paperwork missing. Bring me the file, and I'll double-check it for you."

"I've been doing this a long time, Katherine. I know how to file fucking paperwork." The anger radiated off of him, and she steeled herself for a confrontation. "I want to speak to the man in charge."

"You're looking at her. Now, you can either resubmit the paperwork or wait until our Senior has finished his business elsewhere. Up to you."

His eyes darkened, but he didn't argue. He pulled out his wallet and counted out a thousand dollars in hundreds, holding them out to her. She accepted and raised an eyebrow. "I'll have the rest for you by this evening," he said.

"Bring it to the boardroom at 2100," she commanded.

He dipped his head in understanding, then spun on his heel and left. She closed the door behind him and tossed the money on the desk. Carl would have anyone he could contact notified about her promotion within the hour. He may not know of the other divisions, but he knew enough Reapers to cause some issues. Besides, he hated Kat with something akin to obsession. He had been the third in command until Kat returned from the Caribbean. There had been too many close calls while training with him to be considered anything less than out for her blood. She raked a hand through her hair. They would need to hold board meetings sooner rather than later. Pulling out her phone, she texted Perry:

Send out board meeting invites. Carl already knows.

She moved behind the desk and pulled out the leather chair, hesitating. She'd sat in the seat many times, as a child and as an adult, but this was different. Sitting in his chair, it felt as if the evil he'd done would wind around her, leach into her skin, suffocate her. A chill rocked through her, and she pushed the chair to the corner. There were no other seats in the office. If you were in here, you were reporting in and wouldn't be here long or being reprimanded and didn't deserve to sit. She made a mental note to bring in a new chair at some point. She collected the cash Carl had given and opened the top drawer to the right. The pristine organization of it bothered her. Pens and papers sat in an organizational tray, perfectly in place. Paper clips, a stapler, and tape. Every single item in the drawer sat meticulously aligned and looked out of an office supply advertisement. Rage rippled through her body, and she clenched her fist against the urge to dump it all out. Instead, she tossed the money from Carl on top of it but slid the drawer closed gently, so as not to disturb the contents. She could not make this her own yet.

She inspected the other drawers. The bottom one on the right contained files for each division of Legacy Inc. She pulled one of the black folders out, interested in what information he would keep out of the vault. There were only three pieces of paper inside, which held the hierarchy breakdown of the system that had made him billions and the most feared man on the East Coast. A single division leader, known as a liaison, oversaw three team leaders, each of which had three assets beneath them. He'd compartmentalized the system so well that each liaison believed their division was the only division in Legacy Inc. He'd even trained them on different properties. Headquarters was the only common ground where they might cross paths—where Reapers trained and resided.

There were no names or pictures in the files, nothing to identify who was in each division or team. Each spot, however, held a specialty or two that belonged to each person: Bio-chemical warfare, assassin, coding, a list of languages spoken. Kat pulled out the rest of the files, each containing a single paper. She laid them across the table and laughed. Her Granddad had created the ultimate cheat sheet for any possible assignment he would need done. She shook her head. Should anyone work outside their lane for any mission, it was the last mission they would ever do. Collateral sacrifice, her Granddad had explained when he put her in charge of overseeing Division Three upon her return to D.C. It hadn't been the worst gig—she knew of a handful of assets who would come when she called now. But she needed more information on the Divisions' activities. She shot a text to Perry: *Need case info across the board.* The three dots moved at the bottom of the screen: *Give me ten minutes.*

Kat sat at the head of the boardroom table, waiting for Carl. The table sat up to twenty people, but the largest group to sit in this room consisted of the Waywards, The Reaper, and a select few—never more than ten. Today, the table felt obnoxious for the meeting with each liaison. She eyed Perry, typing away at the computer to her right. He looked better, the bags beneath his eyes had gone, and he'd managed to keep his face clean-shaven.

"Stop staring at me," he said without looking at her, hands flying across the keyboards. He'd managed to bypass the first level of fire-walls and access the files on all active missions. He'd yet been able to access StormLink, the system which monitored all Legacy Inc assets and their direct connection to government assignments and payouts.

Kat's eyes ached from scanning the documents between her arrival and the meeting—but she'd gleaned a few important details in handling the liaisons and Reapers. However, Perry still needed to find Aeron or hack into the financial records and find a way to bypass the hit list and Luke's biometrics to access the money to pay their employees. What if they took a loan out? What if she just killed them all? She rolled her neck back and forth.

This was the first of several meetings with the liaisons and Reapers, and she expected nothing to go to plan. The door to the board room opened. Kat glanced at the clock before looking at the door: 8:50 p.m. He was early. But it was not Carl's cold gaze she met, it was Griffin's warm brown eyes. He kept them locked on hers as he moved to the fourth seat on the left and dropped into it. She hadn't seen him in person in over two years—the intentional rearranging of schedules and faking illness to avoid him took up more of her life than she'd care to admit—and this was exactly why. Heat scorched her body as his gaze scanned her entirety. His dark curls hung past his shoulders now, and his warm terra-cotta skin somehow shimmered even beneath the harsh fluorescent lights; he managed to spin her stomach and send her system into overdrive just by entering the room. She stiffened—not giving him the satisfaction of knowing just how much his presence affected her.

"What are you doing here?" Perry nearly growled.

"I'm in charge of protecting the leader of Legacy Inc."

"Then go protect him," Kat said, regaining control of herself.

"If only I could find him—either hims."

Kat refused to look at Perry. They hadn't been able to stop the series of protocols their Granddad set into motion in case of his demise. Which meant they only had a few more days before the hit list circulating had their names on it. "Perhaps you finally fulfilled your usefulness? Did you consider this is your forty-two hour warning before he sends the dogs out?"

His gaze hardened, and Kat smiled, seeing she had struck a nerve. "If he wanted me dead—I promise we would both know," he ground out.

The door opened again before she could reply. Carl entered with his signature blue suit freshly pressed and a matching tie in place. He dropped a rubber-banded stack of cash on the table. "The rest of the fee, with twenty-five percent interest." She nodded and accepted the money. "I understand there are some housekeeping issues we must discuss?"

"There are," Kat said. "I spent the afternoon reviewing the last missions you've been charged with, and I must say, we've been heavily underutilizing you and your sections." Carl tried to hide the twitch of his lips into a smile but couldn't. Kat had dealt with men like him all her life. Egotistical, narcissistic, misogynistic. She needed him and every other Legacy Inc asset gone, but short of just inviting people into the boardroom and killing them, she needed to know what she didn't know—and at the moment, she didn't know shit.

"Tell me, why haven't you requested a single solo mission in the last six years?"

His eyes stayed tracked on her and folded his hands on the table. He looked at Griffin and then Perry before looking back at her. "My business is with Mr. Wayward, I will be open to discussing housekeeping matters when he is available."

Kat expected as much. A man like Carl on leash meant only two things: he'd overstepped with Granddad and was being punished, or he was being leveraged and protecting someone. Both made him dangerous, but only one was useful to her. "Understood. That's a shame because I have a mission that requires discretion and your particular brand of subterfuge. And the payout. . . well, we could discuss retirement."

Carl remained silent, the internal battle playing out behind his hardened gaze. If he was being chained for stepping out of line, he'd have to refuse—see this as a test. If he was protecting someone, this was an olive branch, his way out. He said nothing.

"I see you are on a tighter leash than I expected," Kat said, disappointment flooding her tone. "What is it he dangles in front of you? Your freedom? Someone else's? Or are you that far up his ass you can't see what's right in front of you."

"You're a vicious fucking bitch." She'd struck a nerve. He stood, taking Kat by surprise, but Griffin was already on his feet, a blade to Carl's throat and a feral look in his eyes. Carl raised his hands in surrender.

Her heart pounded, and she wasn't sure from whose movement. It didn't matter. Carl didn't scare her in the slightest. She intertwined her fingers and leaned forward on her elbows, gaze boring into him. "Say that again—it sounded fucking good." She flicked her eyes to Griffin, nodding for him to step back. He did so reluctantly, the blade leaving a sliver of a cut where he'd almost killed the man. She needed Carl to let the others know she wasn't fucking around.

"I was simply making my departure."

"I haven't dismissed you yet. Sit the fuck down."

Carl lowered himself back into his seat, eyes narrowing. "So, I'm to understand then," Kat continued, "that you are not looking to move up in the company?"

"Not with you."

She let out a soft laugh. "I'm sure he'll be disappointed to hear that." She leaned back in her chair and turned her head to Perry. "Let him know?" Perry nodded and pulled out his phone. When she looked back to Carl, the movement of his Adam's apple was the only indicator he was afraid he'd made a mistake refusing her. "I guess that will be all, Carl." She stood and held out her hand. He followed suit and grasped her hand tightly, and she squeezed back, negating his poor attempt to overpower her. "I'll be sending orders out shortly. Be sure your sections are ready. You're dismissed."

"And the pay we are owed?"

"I took the liberty of digging up the paperwork myself. There were a few errors in them. I suggest you resubmit." He glared for a few seconds longer, then spun on his heel and left. Kat kept her gaze on him until the soundproof door clicked shut.

"If you want to know what your Granddad has over them—you could just ask me," Griffin said from his chair. She flicked her gaze to him. He'd leaned back, hands laced behind his head and feet kicked up on the table. "It will save you a lot of time."

"I don't need you here, Griff. Nor do I want you. I have my own Reaper and she will be here within the hour."

His jaw clenched in response. "Star is not up to the job of protecting you."

"I don't need her for protection; I just need to be rid of you."

Griffin got to his feet, the anger swirling in his eyes she knew only she could provoke. Good. Anger would keep him away from her. "You're playing a dangerous game, Kat. In all the years I've been his Reaper, there has never been a hiatus in communication until now."

"Yeah—*his Reaper.* Don't you have a growing body count to confirm?" Griffin's lip twitched, but he said nothing, and a thrill sparked through her. He didn't deny it. He was confirming the kills on the hit list. What would he do when her name popped up?

"Shit," Perry whispered, and Kat ripped her gaze away from Griffin, but his phone buzzed at the same moment.

"Daddy calling?" Kat spat. It was a deep dig—his family had been killed, Legacy Inc taking him in as a boy—he'd never truly gotten over the loss. But her anger didn't care about his feelings—he hadn't cared about hers. He pulled out his phone and read the message. His shoulders became heavy, and he stuffed it back into his pocket.

"What are you two playing at, Katherine?" He took a step closer, and Kat fought the urge to step back.

"I don't play, Griffin. You want to be more direct in your questioning?"

A knock on the door interrupted them. "Come in!" Kat called. A dark-skinned woman entered. She was shorter than Kat, her frame soft and curvy, and her hair shaved short. She didn't look like an elite assassin, but Star was a top Reaper, and Kat trusted her.

Star nodded to Griffin. "Hello, Reaper."

Griffin bowed his head, his nonchalance and anger melting away as he stepped into his formal role. "I need to go. May I be dismissed, Ms. Wayward?" His jab at her surname tore at old wounds, and she clamped her mouth shut, nodding her answer. He paused beside Star on his way out, whispering in her ear. Star's eyes widened and she nodded.

Kat waited until the door clicked closed. "What did he say to you?"

Star smirked. "He said, 'Don't fuck this up.'"

Kat swallowed around the lump rising in her throat. "Fuck up protecting me or letting me crash and burn?"

"He wasn't specific," Star said, shrugging her shoulders.

"I can take care of myself," Kat said, more to herself than Star.

"Don't I know it." Her smirk widened to a grin, and Kat shook her head. Star had been her Reaper on and off for the past five years. It was how Kat kept tabs on Griffin and knew when to make herself scarce. She was indispensable, but more importantly, she reminded Kat of Shay. Always smiling and full of laughter. She was ruthless in a fight, but her smile. . . "Eyes in the hall?" Star asked.

"Thanks," Kat said. She waited until Star exited before stepping behind Perry to see the latest update:

Aeron and Decius' names had an unconfirmed tag next to them, and a new name graced the screen: Eileen Gale.

Her gut curled, and she let out a long breath. If Aeron was dead, the chances of finding her techie dropped to zero. They were running out of time and options. But Perry's posture shift worried her. She'd just managed to pull him from the bottom of the bottle after Shannon's death, and now Aeron and Decius may both be dead.

"Fuck. That's Shannon's mom, isn't it?" Kat asked. He nodded and she placed a hand on his shoulder. "You good?"

"No." He shrugged hard, forcing Kat's hand off his shoulder. "I'm not fucking good."

She could see his suffering. She knew it like an old best friend. But they didn't have time to work through this. "We need to get these assignments out, and then—"

"When do we call it quits, Kat? We need to shut the whole

fucking operation down. All of it. Everyone. Us included. No one should play god like this."

"I get it. You're in pain. I know that pain, Perry—too well. But we can't just walk away. It's not only our lives at stake."

"You don't get it—it's not just Shannon and her family. That fucking hurts. But while you were babysitting Luke. . . he's not the only one with demons that will haunt him forever."

Kat swallowed hard. "Did he make you—?" She didn't even want to say it.

"No. He knew I wouldn't. I'm not like Luke—I don't have someone worth killing the innocent for. But the shit I saw him do to people—that he had me do to the innocent short of killing them? It was worse. The Legacy was never meant for that—we handled evil people. This is just—we are evil."

She bit her lip and remained silent for a few moments. "I hear you," she said. This was his unhealed heart lashing out, but they didn't have time for it. "For right now, pull the missions he had lined up so we can figure out whom we're sending where."

He scoffed but switched screens, pulling open the StormLink portal where StormTracer, their government handler, requested emergency assignments. There were several assassinations: employees who knew too much, civilians who'd stumbled upon ultra-classified information, and then there were people whom they needed information extracted from.

"Open the interview file." Perry clicked it open, and she scanned the names. If there was one thing her Granddad had been, it was thorough. He hand-picked every mission and who went on those missions. He knew each asset in Legacy Inc—what made them tick and what they would succeed at. She had no idea who would be good for any of this. But idle assassins were the most dangerous kind.

"I feel like I should just put names on a list and throw some darts."

"Maybe we should ask Griffin?" Perry said, reading through the files.

She bristled at the suggestion and turned away. "No. Send Division Three the first nine names. I'll have Star figure it out from there."

"And the rest?"

"Give them to the Reapers. We need to find Aeron and Decius—now. The kills are unconfirmed. Maybe Luke made it to them after all."

7

AERON

The shot rang out.

Aeron's entire body tensed. The barrel slammed against her forehead, knocking her backward, her body sprawling out on the concrete ground. Her eyes flew open, her heart racing, and she scurried back, spying the bearded man lying only feet away, a single shot to his temple. Aeron grabbed his gun and shakily got to her feet, swinging herself around for the next attack. A hit list equaled a single prize, and most hitmen didn't like to share. A dark figure materialized from the tree line, and she fired. They dove sideways, rolled back to their feet, and charged her. Before she could register the distance, they disarmed her, pushed her behind them, and did a full 360 check before turning back to face her. They pulled the hood back, and Aeron's knees gave way from beneath her. Mason caught her and did a quick inventory of injuries, his face darkening at her bloodied state. She looked down at the man who'd almost killed her—who she almost let kill her.

"What the fuck, Aeron!" Mason spat.

His intensity shocked her into talking. She had just knelt there. She hadn't even tried. "I don't know," she admitted. "I just. . . I didn't want to anymore."

"Want to live?" Mason asked.

Was that really what she wanted? To end it? To leave Decius alone to clean up her mess? No. "Want to fight."

His blue eyes held her gaze hard. "Don't ever *fucking* do that again."

She nodded, but that wasn't the whole truth. She didn't want to find Luke—find out what he'd become because of her. What he'd done because of her. "Mason—Luke's been. . ." How could she even put into words what Luke's been doing, what she led him to do? "He's been killing—"

"I know."

Her jaw dropped open. "What do you mean *I know*? You know he's been killing families? Children?" She choked on the last word.

"Yes."

"It's my fault," she whispered. The weight of the lies lifted off her, tears fighting their way out.

"And you think killing yourself would fix it?" He shook his head. "C'mon, Aer. You know better than that. We clean up our messes— not run from them."

She swallowed the lump in her throat and stared at him a few seconds longer, appreciating just how close she had been to death. He was right. She needed to clean up her mess. "What are you doing here?"

"I got the alert and came as fast as I could. Where's Decius?"

"I don't know."

"Get to the car and be ready to go. I will send him your way."

Her heart pounded in her chest. "But what about—"

"You almost just let yourself be executed!" His tone radiated anger, and Aeron swallowed hard. She had. At that moment, the easy answer was to stop fighting.

"Mason. . ."

"We'll talk about that later. I'll send him to you." He didn't wait for her to agree. He handed the gun back to her. She looked from it to him, unable to get the words out. He scooped her into a hug. "In case I don't see you again, I'm proud of you, both of you. Make sure Dee knows that." She nodded, returning the embrace. He took a deep breath before releasing her and sprinting to the side of the house.

Aeron moved cautiously to the car, dropping heavily into the driver's seat. Thankfully, it turned over without an argument. The second truck had made a space for their exit, and she pulled to the bottom of the driveway. The flames danced in the rearview mirror as she looked for Decius. Her hands shook, and she placed the pistol on her lap, gripping the steering wheel. She should be dead. Three times today, she should have been dead.

The passenger door opened, and she whipped the gun up, finding herself looking at Decius, covered in soot but alive.

"Let's get out of here," he said, sliding into the seat and slamming the door closed. She raced toward the main road. The firetrucks could be heard coming down the road, but they would never be able to salvage the property. That was how the protocol was designed. Nothing survived the fire. No one would survive the fire.

"Where's Mason?" Aeron asked.

Decius picked the gun up from her lap, dropped the magazine from the gun, checked the rounds, and then tucked it beneath the seat. "He left out the back entrance."

Aeron nodded. She didn't need to wonder how Mason had found out about them, but she was sure as hell grateful he did. Once they made it to the winding backroads, Aeron slowed, watching their speed as she headed toward the only safe place she could think of.

"Aeron?"

"Yeah?"

"Why is there a hit on us?"

Aeron's mouth went dry. "I killed the Senior Assassin, Dee."

"I know that. I was fucking there. How is there *already* a hit on us?"

She didn't want to answer. There was only one reason she could think of why they would be on a hit list so quickly. "Luke must've—"

"Luke would *never*," Decius countered.

"You don't understand—the things he's done this year—"

"I don't care about the things he's done. He would never put a hit on us."

"I honestly don't know what Luke would do anymore," she said, the image of the nursery crime scene coming to mind. "I've seen what he's capable of. Innocent lives—"

"We all take innocent lives."

"Not like this," Aeron said. She couldn't form the words to explain, Mason's pale face floating in her mind when he'd dropped the sheet over the crib. Had he known when they showed up it was Luke's work? They fell into silence as she sped up. They didn't speak the rest of the drive, and Aeron was a-okay with that. She took the longest route. She released a long sigh only once the gravel driveway sounded underneath the tires. A warm light glowed from the windows of the red barn house, and she noted the 67' Impala parked in Tommy's spot as she parked behind the building.

She cut the engine but didn't move to get out of the car. Her side ached from the drive, and she dropped her head back, taking slow, deliberate breaths. Her last exit from here had not been pretty. Her father had gifted Ernie a broken leg, and Tommy had tried to shoot him. She recalled the mess they'd left behind—and the hurt—the pain that crossed Ernie's face as she left with his attacker.

"Are we just going to sit here, or. . . ."

"I didn't leave here on good terms. I don't know what to expect going in."

"Only one way to find out." He opened his door and stepped out. Aeron followed suit, moving more slowly. She closed the door and managed a few steps before she stumbled, dropping to the ground, knees digging into tiny rocks; a flash of a gun pressed to her forehead sparked in her mind. She swallowed a sob. How the hell had they ended up here?

"Jesus, Aer, you alright?" Decius asked, reaching for her. Aeron did not answer him because the back door creaked open, and she looked up, meeting Ernie's blue eyes. She felt her brother tense beside her. "Is that him?"

Aeron nodded and clambered to her feet. Ernie didn't smile, his face a mask of shock as he rushed forward with a distinct limp he hadn't had six months ago. His face contorted with emotion, sadness, relief, and little anger before he swept her up into a surprisingly gentle hug. Why hadn't she just chosen to stay here?

"I thought you were dead," he whispered.

"I'm harder to kill than you think," she responded, breathing in the comforting scent of motor oil and home cooking.

He stepped back, surveying her injuries and glancing sideways at Decius. "You must be her brother." He extended his hand. "Ernie."

Decius accepted the hand, eying him up and down, no doubt looking for weaknesses, but Ernie was by no means a small man. "Decius."

Ernie half carried Aeron inside, and she reveled in the closeness. This was a man who fought for her and cried for her. A man who loved her like a daughter.

Nothing had changed in the kitchen; the wooden table and mismatched chairs sat waiting for them to enjoy dinner or a cup of tea. As usual, Rita was at the stove, cooking something that smelled heavenly. And Tommy—Tommy looked at her from the doorway to the garage, eyes wide.

"Hey, Princess," he said, all malice from six months ago gone. Was her sudden departure that jarring?

"Hey, Tommy."

He moved to the table to pull out a chair, but Decius stepped around Ernie and grabbed it first, glaring. Tommy backpedaled.

"I've got it," Decius said, tension in his voice. Aeron lowered herself into the chair, smirking at the two men. "Damn it," he swore, looking at her side. Blood had stained through her shirt, and he lifted the hem. "Do you have a medical kit or something?"

Rita reached underneath the sink and pulled out a fully stocked emergency kit akin to the ones they kept at the Institute. "Where'd you get that?" Aeron asked. They hadn't had that the last time she was here, and she recognized the circular cityscape Legacy emblem on the front of the medical bag placed on the table. "Where did you get that?" she repeated.

"He dropped it off after you left," Tommy answered.

"Mason?" Aeron asked. She had forgotten to tell him she wasn't returning after the funeral. Perhaps he brought it as a precaution.

"Your father," Tommy supplied.

Decius paused, the bloody bandage only halfway removed from her side, and shot a look to Tommy before meeting Aeron's confused look.

"When did he come back?" Aeron asked.

"About a month after the incident," Ernie answered. "Him and some scrawny guy. Brought a boatload of cash and some crazy stories and a bunch of computers."

"And you didn't shoot him on sight?" Aeron asked with a small laugh. "Why was he here?"

"A peace offering. Thanks, darling," he said to Rita, who brought over steaming mugs of tea. He took a seat at the table, quiet while Decius worked.

"Don't be up too late," Rita said, pausing to place a hand on Aeron's shoulder. "Welcome home." Rita was not one for talking. She cooked, ran their restaurant, and loved them all. It was nice to be home. Aeron placed her hand on top of hers and smiled up.

Rita disappeared upstairs, and Decius continued the work on Aeron's side. The left flank burned, and not in a hot sense, but the deeper burn of foul healing. He pressed it, blood seeping out more slowly, but Aeron hitched a breath, and her head swam. She braced the table. "Shit, Dee. I think it's infected. It fucking burns."

He nodded. "Alright. I'm going to clean and stitch it. Just relax."

She rested her head on the chair back, aware of Tommy staring at her from the doorway. He hadn't moved. She looked at him through slitted eyes. He wore his blue mechanic's suit, oil and grease-stained. His hair was longer—shaggy blonde framing his sour expression. "What's your problem?" she asked. He didn't answer. He just stared at her for a few more moments before returning to the garage, the door closing behind him. What the actual fuck?

"He's been worried about you." She turned her gaze to Ernie. "Your father told him if we hadn't heard from him in more than a month, he was dead. And if you didn't arrive within a month after that, you were probably dead."

Aeron raised an eyebrow. "I am so confused right now."

"Me too," Decius said. He covered his work with clean gauze and stood up. He stretched his body, joints popping, then washed his hands before sitting down and pulling the cooling cup of tea toward him. He sat straight, ready to pounce at any moment. He kept his gaze on the tea, and Aeron waited for him to speak. So much had been revealed to him the past eight hours—his mother's true killer, his best friend a murderer, his sister a liar.

"Thank you for hosting us," Decius finally said. "But we won't be staying."

"Decius," Aeron said, "it's safe here."

"I don't know any of these people. And if Dad wanted us to be here, we should be running far away. And we need to find Luke."

Luke. Of course. Because Decius couldn't fully comprehend what was going on—because she lied to him. Hurried footsteps sounded down the stairs, the movement too fast to be Rita. Aeron craned her neck and nearly spun out of the chair when Ivan emerged from the dark hall. His eyes roamed over her, and without hesitation, she launched herself from the chair and threw herself into his arms. He stumbled back but returned the embrace, letting go slightly when her muscles tensed. A clattering sounded behind her, and she looked at Decius. His chair was knocked to the ground behind him, and his gun aimed directly at Ivan, his chest heaving.

"He was there the night Dad died," he breathed, not lowering the weapon.

She turned directly in front of Ivan, and Decius adjusted the aim to his head. "You mean the night I killed him," Aeron said because Decius needed to hear it. Accept it, for him to accept everything else he was about to learn. "This is Ivan, Dad's apprentice. You wanted to know what Dad's been up to? You probably shouldn't kill the one person who can tell you." Decius' gaze bounced between her and Ivan. He nodded, righted the chair, and sat back down, his gun now resting on the table beneath his hand. Aeron glanced at Ernie, who hadn't moved, but his eyes had doubled in size.

"Can we all just go to bed?" Aeron asked, fatigue settling in, the ache in her body making it difficult to stand, and she leaned against Ivan, who grabbed her waist to keep her from falling. Ernie's was a haven; guns and Legacy talk—this is where she came to get away from her life. "Seriously. Can we try and kill each other in the morning after a good night's sleep?" Ivan's chest vibrated with laughter behind her, and Decius glared at them.

"So we're not going to talk about why we're on a hit list, or—"

"We're on a hit list because I killed the Senior Assassin," Aeron snapped. Ivan tensed behind her but said nothing. "We're here because I royally fucked up. We're here because Dad's death will not be in vain."

Decius' jaw tightened, and he nodded. "Okay." He looked over to Ernie. "Guest rooms?"

"Up the stairs to the right."

Decius stood, tucking his gun away, and walked past them up the stairs. She kept her eyes on him until the dark stairwell swallowed him up. "I should follow him," Aeron said, stepping away from Ivan. She leaned on the table for support. "Thank you, Ernie."

"We will talk in the morning," he answered. He moved to the sink, rinsing out his mug and turning it upside down on the drying rack. "You have no idea how good it is to see you." He pulled her in for another hug, placing a soft kiss on the top of her head. "Sleep well."

"I always do here." Then it was just her and Ivan.

"So. You killed Mr. Wayward. Does that mean. . ."

"Luke?"

Ivan nodded, searching her face for an answer, but she wouldn't give him the satisfaction of being right. Luke might be too far gone to save.

"He's alive and well at the moment." Aeron could taste the bitterness she wanted to hide and looked away.

"Still worth saving?"

Aeron adjusted her position and felt the burn in her side, reminding her of the fury in Luke's eyes when he shot her. "I need to sleep on that answer."

He grimaced. "Let's go to bed."

She found Decius laid out on her bed. How he knew this was her room, she couldn't be sure, but knew he'd searched every room before settling down.

"What's up?" she asked, clicking the door closed.

"See what I did there?"

"Excuse me?" Aeron said, confused at the sudden hostile tone.

"What I did down there. That's called trust, in case you forgot."

She huffed out a sigh and sat next to him, leaning against the headboard. They sat side by side. "I trust you, Dee."

He ran a hand along his jaw, the stubble scratching his palm. "I want every question I ask tomorrow answered. I don't care if you think it will hurt me. I don't care if you think I will hate you. I won't. I never could."

Her heart constricted. That was why she had lied to him—because he would always forgive her. A lump rose in her throat, and she swallowed around it, nodding against his shoulder. He wrapped an arm around her, and she breathed a bit easier. They were safe. Even if just for the night, she was safe.

8

LUKE

*L*uke woke again, still in the small room, chained to the chair. He didn't recognize the warehouse Rosemary stored him in, the smell completely unfamiliar, but it turned his stomach: the stale coppery scent of death. Running water reached his ears, a river of some kind. Were they still in the city? She'd knocked him out in the apartment, but how long had he been out? He rubbed his chin against his shoulder: at least two day's worth of stubble. His stomach dropped. He could be anywhere—but he wasn't hungry or parched, so someone had been ensuring he received fluids. Moving his arms the best he could, Luke recognized the pull of a PICC line in his right arm leading to a monitor and IV bag. So, she didn't want him dead—yet.

The windowless room pressed in on him. The black walls were designed to conceal the torture done within it and to make cleanup a little easier. The singular lamp overhead cast the corners into such shadows, there could be someone standing there and he wouldn't know. He tried to pull his memory from when he'd been taken. The last thing he could remember was Rosemary tranquilizing him at the apartment and someone... someone helping her.

The door handle turned, and Luke straightened, dread creeping in. She would spend days, weeks, torturing him before killing him. He recoiled at the memory of the torture he allowed Shannon's mom to receive just a few days ago. His heart threatened to choke him as it beat in his throat. He didn't believe in karma, but this seemed like a fitting end. He clenched his fists as the figure entered, but it wasn't Rosemary. A giant entered. He was over six feet tall, and steroid muscles roped beneath his blue button-down. The first few buttons were open, and the sleeves rolled, flecked with blood. Intense brown eyes glinted at Luke from beneath his untamed dark hair, contrary to his close-trimmed beard and mustache.

"You're awake," the man said. Luke kept his mouth shut, eyes not leaving the man's face as he closed the door behind him. Rosemary was a monster he could contend with—the devil he knew. He had no idea who this man was or what he could want. The man stepped closer, and Luke jerked back, but he just raised an eyebrow and moved to the vitals monitor beside Luke. He changed the IV bag and wrote down notes on a clipboard.

"Who are you?" Luke asked, his voice hoarse. The man didn't look to be an errand boy. He looked like a killer—a scary fucking killer.

"The name's Rufus."

Luke dared to ask another. "Why am I here?"

"Because the boss-lady needs you." Rufus finished writing the vitals down, sent a text, and took a seat on a small empty table by the door. Luke wasn't sure it would even be able to hold the weight and waited for the wood to protest. It didn't.

"Rosemary?" Luke couldn't imagine Rosemary needing him for anything.

"Sure," Rufus said. He leaned back against the wall, crossing his feet out in front of him, and smirked. "If it was up to me, I'd have you locked in one of my rooms, seeing how well your body handles the skin being melted off while you're still awake." Luke's stomach turned. "I'm just waiting for her to be done with you." Luke's arms began to tremble, fear coursing through him. He had no doubt Rufus meant exactly what he'd said.

The door opened again, and relief flooded Luke's system at the sight of Rosemary. Her blue jeans and gray sweater looked out of place in a room like this. She glanced at him briefly as if confirming he was awake and alive. Then she held the door wide for Rufus, dismissing him with a simple "Thank you". Rufus' gaze swooped over Luke one more time, and Luke's skin crawled with sudden violation. Like Rufus could already see his skin melting off his body, and he enjoyed the sight.

She closed the door behind him, her shoulders relaxing. Interesting. She didn't like Rufus either.

"Nice friend you got there," Luke said.

"He's the most despicable human on the face of this earth, and the only man keeping him in check is currently presumed dead." She turned to him. "I need some information, Luke."

Presumed dead. So no one knew for sure yet—just that the Senior Assassin hadn't checked in. "I'm not helping you with a goddamned thing." Luke spat at her feet. He would rather die—and probably would.

Rosemary tutted, disgust painting her face. "Do you think I'm happy about our current situation? I really did my best to protect you."

Protect him? Rage exploded from within him, and he lunged toward her, his restraints digging into his wrists, ankles, and chest. His shoulders screamed in protest as he tried to wrench free. "Liar!" The word broke as it left him, and he swallowed back the raw pain begging for him to release the secrets and guilt that ate him up from the inside out. "You are evil," he choked out. "I'll never help you."

She nodded, pacing back and forth like she did when weighing the words she was going to give him, soft and even as they came out. "Where are my daughter's safe houses?" Luke clamped his lips together. Too many innocent lives rested in that secret. "This can be very simple. Tell me where she is, and I will let you go."

"I would rather have Rufus melt my balls off than tell you anything."

Rosemary lunged for him, and he slammed himself back into the chair. Her hands grasped at the armrests on either side of him. "That can be arranged," she whispered. "I would very much enjoy watching you be a plaything at Rufus' hands. But I don't have the time or the patience. Where's my kid?" He remained silent, her breath hot on his face as she remained close, searching his face for weakness. "Fine. How about the money you owe me."

How dare she. "Shannon died," he spat, unable to keep his mouth shut. "I promised you wouldn't see a dime if anything happened to her." Ice seared into his back at the mention of Shannon, and he latched to the feeling of her, of someone there with him.

"You also promised to reign down hellfire on me, but it seems your bark is worse than your bite."

Luke glared, the ice radiating into his heart, seeping into every inch of his body with each pounding heartbeat.

"You can give me the money, or you can give me Katherine. I'll take either."

"And I'll give you neither. I'll take my chances with Rufus."

Rosemary scowled and pushed back away from him. "Which one of you killed him?" she asked. It took a moment for her question to register. She wanted confirmation of his death. She could rot in hell before he talked. "I knew you three wanted him dead. I expected you to be smarter about it. Now, bodies are turning up left and right. Names being crossed off his hit list."

Thoughts drowned each other in his mind. Bodies. Days. "What names?" Luke whispered, but he knew the names—they were seared into his brain. Aeron; Decius.

"Your team—Aeron and Decius and the other ones. As soon as I got the alert, I knew you and Katherine fucked up."

Dead. They were dead? "They've been confirmed?" Rosemary raised an eyebrow. "Have they been confirmed!" he demanded.

"Tell me where Katherine is, and I will tell you if they are."

Breathing was suddenly impossible. If they were dead, there was nothing left for him. No one left for him. Bile rose in his throat, and he leaned to the side, releasing the acidic liquid onto the floor. She sidestepped it and grasped his chin. "Enough. Where are the safe houses?"

A half laugh, half sob escaped Luke. "I would rather die a hundred deaths than save you from your fate." Because if Aeron had been confirmed—Rosemary's name was worth $5.5 million. He knew people who would kill her for free—with a price like that? She wouldn't last a day. "You're next." The terror which filled her eyes was worth a million deaths, and Luke smiled. "There's nowhere on this earth you could hide with a price like that on your fucking head."

"How could you possibly know that?"

"Are you willing to gamble that I'm wrong?"

Her terror melted into a wicked smile that had become so familiar over the past six months. It promised pain, misery, and a never-ending hell-loop of wishing for a death that may never come. She pulled a syringe from her sweater pocket, the bright blue liquid stopping his heart.

"A hundred deaths? I reckon a single dose of Sin will get me what I want." Her cold fingers grasped his arm, fear holding him in place as he watched the blue liquid disappear into the PICC line. Panic seeped into him, his heart pumping, and try as he might, he couldn't slow it. He couldn't pull his panic back. He hadn't had the chance to build a tolerance to Sin or to even learn what could possibly be in store for him. Mason's haunted face floated into his mind. The deadness in his eyes when they'd spoken of it. Would his pain be physical? Would his veins tear his body apart from the inside out? Would he completely lose his sense of reality?

A frigid hand of Death traced up his arm, across his chest, and clamped onto his heart. He gasped, the breath completely freezing inside him. It chased the warmth from his body, triggering violent shivering and teeth chattering.

The door opened again, but his dead had already started to fill the room, obscuring his view—Gabe, Olivia and Sarah in their pink pajamas, Ben, Wilks.

"What are you doing here?" Rosemary asked.

"Me? What are you—what did you do?" A female voice demanded. He looked over at the woman and reeled back. Her brown hair was pulled back into a braid displaying a twisted map of scars along the left side of her face, some of which crossed to the right.

"I'm being useful," Rosemary responded holding up the vial.

The scarred woman closed the short distance between her and Rosemary and grasped the front of her sweater, slamming her into the wall. "You idiot. We only needed his biometrics. A single conversation, and we would have been in tonight. Now the scanners will read the Sin in his system."

Rosemary shoved the woman off, and Luke strained to see around the dead in the room. Rosemary straightened back up, glaring. "And what would you have done with me once he opened that vault? I should have been long out of the game by now."

"You promised to keep my entire family safe. A dead husband is not safe. You can be out when they are."

"How was I supposed to know she would kill him?"

"What about Luke?" His eyes widened at his name. "How did you protect him?"

"My loyalty is to you—not my fucking brother. Luke wasn't part of the deal."

The scared woman's features contorted, and she pulled a gun from her waist, jamming it beneath Rosemary's chin. "And what is stopping me from killing you right now instead?"

"Because if Luke dies, you need me to keep control of this place," Rosemary said, a glint of triumph in her eyes. They remained locked, staring at each other for several moments until the scarred woman removed the gun, glaring daggers. Rosemary swallowed hard. "Besides, how many have you seen through the process? Hundreds? He'll be fine until we need him."

"He better. If they wind up dead because you fucked this up, I will personally see to it you live a long, long life in the clutches of Sin."

A shot rang out, and Luke jumped, his ears ringing and his heart raced, pushing the Sin deeper and faster into his system as the wall beside Rosemary's ear exploded. The cold dug deeper into his body, and his heart pumped faster.

"A warning shot," the scarred woman said. She turned from Rosemary, and her cold gaze landed on Luke but not before Luke caught the clench of Rosemary's fist and the shift of her posture. He smiled. He didn't know this woman—and if she terrified Rosemary, he should be shitting his pants—but anyone who made Rosemary feel like scum on the bottom of a shoe was someone worth knowing. "You'll get out when you finish the job here. And Lucas' life is part of that."

The way his name fell off her tongue rocked at a memory. He did know this woman, or someone very much like her because the woman she reminded him of was dead. He looked around the room filling with the dead—they all looked so solid and real, maybe she was one of his dead. Maybe he'd already lost his grasp of reality under Sin.

She checked the clipboard of his vitals and then leaned close, checking the dilation of his pupils, no doubt. "Who are you?" Luke asked. She didn't answer him.

"What dosage did you give him?" She looked to Rosemary, who hadn't moved from her spot near the wall.

"A full vial," she whispered.

The scarred woman blinked a few times but said nothing else. She pulled out her cell phone, making a call. "Eileen, I need your assistance. . . How bad?. . . . Who?" Her eyes cut to Luke, and he shrank back against the chair. "Can you make it here?. . . See you soon." She pocketed the phone, and Shannon appeared beside her, disappointment etched into every feature. Her red hair moved in the windless room.

"I'm sorry," he said to her. "I never meant to. It should have been me! It should have always been me!"

Shannon glared at him. *"It will never be you, Luke. You will never be willing to die for her."*

"You wanted to know where the kids were," Rosemary said. Luke pulled his eyes away from Shannon. The kids? How could they possibly know about the Legacy kids?

The scarred woman nodded, her hands clasped behind her back as she thought. "You realize he will spill all his secrets. Yours, too."

Rosemary swallowed hard and nodded.

"Right then. Let's leave him to it."

Rosemary nearly ran from the room, but the scarred woman paused, giving one last glance to him before the door clinked shut. It was silent for a moment, a room of ghosts staring at him, his heart racing faster than he ever remember it being able to. Shannon stepped aside, allowing Gabe to take her place directly in front of him. And then the screaming started, the high-pitched wails of the dead.

9

AERON

The sound of yelling jolted Aeron awake. Sunlight filtered into the small bedroom, and the sweet smell of pine trees and motor oil filled her nose. She rolled over to her back, a grunt of pain escaping her as yesterday's events filtered back. The fight with Mr. Wayward; Luke confessing he'd been killing families; hoping for a quick death at the hands of a complete stranger; Decius' anger —Ivan's relief. Her head pounded and swirled, and dehydration was the most likely suspect.

She sat up, pushing against the swirling room around her, and grabbed her side. She hitched her shirt up to find her bandage still white. That was a good sign. A bottle of water and a set of pills waited for her on the desk. She gulped down the water, leaving only enough to wash down the pills. She probably should have stayed in bed, but she cracked the bedroom door, and the yelling intensified.

"She sleeps like the dead! I can yell all I want." A smile crept onto her face. That was Decius. Who had pissed him off? She slowly worked her way down the steps, leaning against the wood paneling for support. She paused in the shadows before the bottom of the stairs.

The kitchen was full. Ivan sat at the table with a laptop, Tommy beside him, looking over his shoulder. Rita stood beside Decius, looking at a burn on his hand, the cast iron pan askew on the electric burner being the obvious culprit, and Ernie leaned in the doorway to the garage, arms crossed and eyes on her. She raised her hand, and he smiled back. She scanned the room again, taking in the atmosphere; even Decius had relaxed. No matter who you were, when you showed up at Ernie's, something inside you shifted. You were instantaneously a part of this family. If they could just stay here forever—but there were ramifications of her actions that needed to be dealt with.

She continued toward the kitchen, not nearly as stealthily as she would have liked. Her foot slipped on the second to last step, and she stumbled into the room.

"Told you you'd wake her up," Tommy said. Decius glared at him for several seconds until Tommy averted his eyes.

"Morning," Aeron said, making her way to the seat beside Ivan.

"Afternoon," Decius corrected. "Actually, it's almost evening." Aeron glanced at the clock above the stove: 3:45 p.m. The sun would set within the hour. Damn.

"We've decided not to kill each other, then?" Aeron joked. "Or were we waiting for me to wake up?"

"We've come to a truce," Ivan supplied. "But we have some pressing matters to attend to." The silence that followed his statement irked her.

"Aeron," Decius started, then cleared his throat and dragged one of the remaining chairs over to her. "Aer, Lesley and Justin are dead."

Blood rushed to her ears, and her stomach knotted. "What?"

"They were the first on the hit list," Ivan said. Aeron's chest tightened. Their team. . . their team was dead. But hope crept in. If Justin and Lesley were first on the hit list, it didn't make sense that Luke ordered the hit.

"Can we have the room, guys?" Decius asked.

"You can have the building," Ernie answered. "We'll go to Rita's Diner. Text us when you finish."

"Thanks." Decius stuck out his hand, and Ernie shook it. Aeron remained silent while Tommy, Rita, and Ernie headed out the back door.

"Can I have some water?" Aeron asked, her head pounding. "And some food. Anything."

"Yeah."

"What happened to them?" Aeron asked.

"I'm not showing you before you eat," Ivan said.

"I didn't ask to see," Aeron responded but was thankful he wasn't going to throw that at her.

"Here." Decius slid a glass of water over along with a veggie wrap from the fridge. "Rita said it's one of your favorites."

Aeron accepted the plate with a nod. When she had found Ernie's, they had taken her in as their own, and she had imagined that this would be what it was like to have a dad who liked having her around and a mom who knew what her favorite foods were. Parents who loved her. Rita had even put a bag of cracked pepper chips on the side. She tore open the bag, dumping the chips out and sticking a few inside the wrap. She took a bite, the crunch satisfying.

"You were really happy here," Decius said.

Aeron took a few more bites before answering. "Yeah. I was." She didn't know if she could say the same now, with Ivan and Decius both here and their names on a hit list, their team dying. "What happened to them?"

"From what I can find," Ivan said, "the hit list went live barely thirty minutes after your kill shot. Lesley and Justin were eliminated within minutes."

"That's so fast," Aeron said, gut-clenching.

"I believe they were already being followed," Decius said.

"And us?"

"You were living with him," Ivan said. "He was watching you."

"But where did the list come from? He was dead."

"I think it was because he was dead," Ivan replied.

So, this was her fault too. Heat flooded her cheeks, and she rested her forehead against her fist, propping her elbow on the table. "The package in the safe was full of tapes." Decius eyed the pile of things next to Ivan, and Aeron silently thanked him for the change of subject. A cassette player, a black book, and several cassette tapes sat on the table.

"I'm going to do a quick sweep of the building; all electronics need to be off. We can shut down the breakers to be even safer." Ivan stood up.

"What is on these tapes, Darth?"

Decius raised an eyebrow at the nickname, and she shook her head.

"I'm not sure." He disappeared up the stairs, leaving Decius and Aeron alone.

Was he going to grill her about what happened yesterday? She took a big bite of the sandwich, hoping to dissuade him from asking anything, but she could see the conversation playing out in his mind.

"Ask me," she said. "Whatever it is you need, ask me."

His gaze met her, and he clenched his jaw, debating the words. "Why did you kill him?"

Aeron placed the food back on the plate and pushed it away, appetite disappearing. She needn't ask which him—he wanted to know why she'd killed their father. "Luke had seriously damaged him during the fight at Shannon's funeral. He was on blood thinners for a recent heart attack and wasn't going to make it. He asked me to kill him—to secure my place in the Wayward Legacy and bring down Mr. Wayward."

"How could you. . ."

"Push the dagger through his heart?" she asked, spelling out exactly what she'd done. She focused on the glass in front of her as their final conversation filled her mind.

'What did you say? How far?'
'I—"
'Aeron. How far?'
'I'd do anything.'
'Then do it.'

She shivered with the memory, his final smile the happiest one she could remember. Aeron could lie and say she pulled on all the painful memories he'd given her, playing out the fantasy she'd had of ending his life repeatedly. The truth was worse. "We hadn't saved Luke yet—we were so close; I couldn't give up." But there was never a chance at saving Luke—she knew that now.

He remained quiet for a few minutes, and Aeron glanced at Ivan standing at the base of the stairs. His eyes were locked on her, and he flushed and looked away when Aeron met his gaze.

"We need to talk about what happened last night," Decius said.

Aeron gave a slight nod, pressure forming behind her eyes. Several deep breaths helped relieve it, but the emotion pressed into her sinuses. She cleared her throat and looked at him. "About what Luke said?"

"Would you, ah, like the room?" Ivan asked.

Aeron chuckled. "You are the eyes and ears of this place right now. You'll hear it anyway." He smirked. And his smile eased the pressure in her face. She turned to Decius. "What part?"

"Luke."

The pressure behind her sinuses returned, and she couldn't stop the tears that pushed their way out. She wiped her face several times and then stood, moving to the sink. She turned on the cold tap and splashed her face. Luke's devastating realization turned her stomach, but she couldn't wash the image away. She dried her face on a paper towel and moved back to the table. Ivan's perplexed look compelled her to speak.

"Luke has been the one eliminating the Legacy families." Her words hung between her and Ivan like a cartoon anvil ready to fall. His expression mirrored hers from last night.

"I'm going to need you to clarify what you mean by that," Decius said.

Aeron dropped her head. There was too much he didn't know. "For the last six months, Dad, Ivan, and I were tracking the deaths of Legacy families. Kids and all. We didn't know who'd been eliminating them—until last night."

Decius' nodded. Her confirmation of Luke's confession was not the explanation he wanted. "We can still save him," Decius said as if reading her earlier thoughts. "I know, you keep telling me we can't —but you didn't see what I saw: he was devastated. Disgusted."

"He traded innocent lives for mine," Aeron said. "Very innocent lives."

"I may have done the same—and so would you." Aeron snapped her gaze to him. "We weren't there, so we can't judge." She wanted to argue, but had their positions been reversed, would she have done the same? Mason dropping the sheet over the crib, his face ghastly, floated back into her mind.

"Not as far as he went," she whispered.

He didn't argue with her. Instead, he picked up the top tape, their father's scrawl across the top: February 13th, 2008. "What about these?" He changed the subject again, and Aeron realized he wasn't going to push for more information just yet. But he would.

"The house is completely clear," Ivan said, going with the topic change. "I've also disconnected the internet for the time being. All cell phones off?" Decius nodded, eyes still on the cassette. "Let's get started." He slid the cassette player to the middle of the table.

"Are you going to let us play it?" Aeron asked, holding out her hand. "Or. . ." she trailed off, not sure what to say. The date, like the code to the safe, was their mother's death date.

He swallowed hard and handed the tape over. She placed it in and hit play. Static blared through the speaker as if the recording device was being hastily moved about, and Aeron turned down the volume as her father's voice started mid-sentence.

". . . hurry up, Mason. Is it on? Good. We're on our way. Say it again."

"Drew, I. . ." Aeron's stomach seized, eyes darting to Decius. His knuckles whitened as he clasped them together at their mother's voice.

"Repeat it, Maureen," their father commanded.

"He's going to kill me. Elijah is going to kill me. I knew it as soon as I left that meeting. I'm not making it home." Her voice broke. "Take them away from this, Drew. Please. Send them far away."

"You know we can't. But I will protect them." The raw emotion in their father's voice brought moisture to her eyes, and she blinked it away.

"Mason, talk some sense into him. Tell him you can get them away from here."

Silence lingered for a few moments, and Aeron leaned in as if they would talk faster.

Finally, Mason answered. "We'll keep them safe, Moe. I swear it."

A sob left their mother. "I don't want this life for her."

"I won't claim her," their father said. "We will put the second phase into action."

"That won't be enough."

"It will have to be, Sweetheart."

"GPS shows us five minutes apart," Mason's low voice interrupted.

"Is it a bomb, Maureen?" their father asked.

"I don't know," she answered. "The look he gave me, it could be anything: sniper or poison. Drew, I—I don't want to die. I don't want to. . ." Silence again. "Should I just pull over?"

"Do not pull over," Mason said. There was a pregnant pause, and then, "He has control over the vehicle. Storm, just confirmed. Maureen, just keep driving normally."

"My love," their mother's voice became softer somehow. "I will love you, forever and ever."

"Don't you dare get sentimental on me," their father said. "We're going to figure this out. I am not losing you; do you understand me?"

"Always so bossy," her voice laughed. There was silence again, and then suddenly, "Shit! The car, Drew!" There was a screech of tires, the crunch of metal, then a soul-searing moment of nothing.

"Maureen? Maureen!" His voice echoed through the still kitchen. "What's the location?" In the space of silence, a car revved —her father's car, racing toward their mother.

Mason responded, "Corner of Pine and Valley."

"I'm almost there. Hang on, Sweetheart!" His voice bellowed. Then more quietly, "Mason, have they answered?"

"They'll meet us there," Mason whispered.

"The kids? Our kids?" His voice broke again.

"I already let Eileen know. Sir—over there."

Another screech of tires. Car doors opening. A bone-chilling wail ripped through the speaker, breaking Aeron's heart in two, each piece trying to climb up her throat, and she swallowed around them; it was the most devastating sound Aeron had ever heard in her life. Shouts in the distance followed, then commotion she couldn't hear clearly, then silence.

They sat in complete stillness, Aeron not even daring to breathe. Ivan hit stop on the player, and chills spread throughout Aeron's body.

"Play it again," Decius' rough voice said, and she met his tear-stained face, which probably matched hers. "Play it again."

She nodded, pulling the device to her and rewinding the tape. The words were not such a shock this time, and Aeron leaned closer, trying to hear the background noise: a car engine, a blinker; was that the sound of texting? She squeezed her eyes against the sound of her father breaking. She turned off the player again, the air around her charged with tension. Why had her father wanted them to hear that? What good came out of listening to the worst day of his life?

"Where the fuck is Mason?" Decius spat. "Aeron?"

Aeron kept her eyes focused on the table in front of her. "I don't know." She swallowed hard. "Play the next one." She didn't want to look at Decius. He'd just found out their mother had been murdered, and then to hear it? She dared a glance, but his face was buried in his hands, his shoulders tense.

"Want me to see if there's anything else on here? Either side?"

"Not right now," she responded, unsure either of them could handle what else happened that day.

Ivan slid the player back toward him and switched out the tapes. "This one is dated a few weeks later." He pressed play. The same static sounded at the beginning before it began playing. Aeron clamped her hands over her ears and pushed away from the table.

The screams pulled her back to 2008, sitting around the kitchen table at the Gale estate the night Seamus Gale was brought home, nearly in pieces. Aeron had heard the screams and ran toward them. But when she skidded around the corner to the garage—the images she'd buried of her best friend's father bleeding and screaming as his team failed to save his life flickered through her mind. Aeron had slammed herself into Shannon, refusing to let her see her father that way. Keara had vaulted past her, though—her screams mingling with the rest.

"What happened?" Eileen Gale's voice cried out.

"It was a setup. It was a fucking setup," her father cried back. She could imagine him raking his hands through his hair, his face distraught. "Can you save him?"

Their silence was filled by the agonizing wails from Seamus.

"I don't know, Drew—there's too much damage."

"Please, Eileen. I can't—I can't be responsible for another death."

"Daddy!" Keara's high-pitched scream cut through Aeron's heart.

"Turn it off," Aeron said. Ivan hit on the stop button. "That was the night—"

"Seamus," Decius said. "The night Keara and Shannon's dad came home. The last night he came home." Decius sniffed and wiped his nose on his sleeve before pulling the collection of tapes toward him, eight in total. He looked at Ivan. "Why did he want us to have these? To relive the deaths of the people we loved?"

Ivan licked his lips, and his brow knitted together. "I don't know."

Aeron picked up her glass and moved to the sink to refill it. She braced a hand against the white ceramic basin and squeezed her eyes shut, shaking her head and trying to dislodge the graphic memory of blood, skin peeled back, and Mason puking in the corner. It wouldn't leave, though. Keara had sprinted into the garage, and Aeron had tackled Shannon to the ground, pinning her so she couldn't get up.

Aeron snapped her eyes open.

"Mason was there too," she said, turning off the tap and spinning around. "Press play. Dad is going to tell him to stop any more of us from coming in."

"I believe you," Ivan said. "I don't need to hear any more if I'm being honest."

Decius looked over the tapes, putting them in date order, and a thought occurred to her. "Why are we not concerned about the hit list at the moment?" Aeron asked, moving behind him. She took a sip of the water and passed the glass to him.

"Your dad and I installed a security perimeter," Ivan said. "We'll have a five-minute head start if they get close."

"How did you manage that?"

"We're surrounded by woods for miles. Do you want me to bore you with the detailed tech side of it, or do you trust me?" Ivan asked, raising an eyebrow.

She trusted him. She trusted her father. "I'm good."

"You said Mason was there?" Decius asked, pointing at the tape player. They obviously already had the security conversation without her. She nodded. "I think it's time we called our Guardian in."

10

KAT

Kat leaned forward against the front of the desk and glared at the vault in her office. Her office—not her Granddad's. He wouldn't be back for it. Her eyes glanced at the phone beside her. She was waiting for word on the Sewards. Their estate had burned to the ground last night. She'd sent a team from Division Two in to do a sweep of the area, but they found only the bodies of a few mercenaries—no sign of the Sewards or Luke.

The air in the room shifted. She'd taken to leaving the office door open. It was now known across Legacy Inc that she had taken the helm. She wanted to be available for any issues that arose with the change of command. This would be the first brave soul to take her up on the offer.

"That is a beautiful view—even with your clothes on." An involuntary smile tugged her lips as Griffin's deep voice pulled on memories of pleasure and violence—most in the same evening. She schooled her features before spinning around. He leaned in the doorway. His jawline was dusted with stubble, and his hair was knotted in a messy bun on the top of his head, a throwing knife stuck through it. The man could kill you with a flip of his hair. "Hello, Kat." He stepped into the office and closed the door. His eyes roamed her body, and a jolt of excitement shot straight to her core when his tongue slipped across his lips. The things that man could do with his tongue.

She mentally shook herself. This was why she couldn't work with him, why she put years between them after his betrayal. "Speak to me that way again, and it will be the last words you say, Reaper."

His half-smile faltered. "What's your game, Kat?" He took a step forward, and she took a step back, surveying him. He could kill her in an instant, and something inside her ached with the thought. They'd once been inseparable, grown up together, trained, and cried together. After Shay was driven insane, he put her back together. She'd spent months learning every scar and blemish on his body. He'd reminded her what a loving and caring touch could feel like. He could undo her with a smile. "Katherine?"

"If you want an audience with me, set a meeting."

"I thought you had a new open-door policy?"

"Not for you."

"I still can't reach him. And he hasn't been seen in days."

"That's a real problem for you. Have you tried the estate?"

His jaw ticked in irritation. "You and I both know he didn't promote you and go off the radar without telling me."

"Do we? Or are you being tested? We know how much he loves his games. The encrypted message came directly from him."

"And the hit list?" He quirked an eyebrow. "He just decided to hit the self-destruct?"

"We don't know what hit list that truly is. He's been finishing off the Legacy for a while now. Just ask Luke." She leaned against the desk again and crossed her arms. "But, since you insist on reporting to me, who are you hunting?" she asked, switching gears, reminding herself she was in charge. Legacy Inc would be hers in just a few days.

"That's a broad question, Kat. Want to stop beating around the bush and ask what you want to know?"

She licked her lips, and he stepped closer, the magnetic pull between them tangible. "Aeron Seward. Is she dead or alive?"

He studied her for several minutes. She would wait all day if needed. "Unconfirmed."

"I saw that myself. I'm asking—"

"I know what you're asking," he said softly. "My answer is the same. Why?"

It was her turn to measure her answer. She could say she was inquiring for Luke's benefit, but Griffin surely already knew that and would bring up the question: where was Luke? She could tell him the truth, but she didn't want to die today. She settled on the question burning in her gut. "What will you do if that is the self-destruct list, and my name comes across it?"

Griffin's eyes glinted, a hungry smile creasing his face that she shouldn't find so sexy. "I would have to hunt you down." He took a step closer. "Spend every moment watching you, studying you, waiting for the perfect moment." He closed the distance between them, holding her gaze. She couldn't look away if she wanted to. Her body vibrated, and he placed his thumb beneath her chin, tipping her head up, his warmth radiating to her core. She gripped the desk, keeping her composure. He would use her the same way she would use him. They weren't good for each other. He would destroy her in a heartbeat again.

She swallowed, mouth dry all of a sudden. "And then you would kill me?" She stared into his eyes, trying to read him. They'd shared something once, but it had been a lifetime ago.

He shook his head, eyes darkening, and he stepped back. The sudden chill sliced into her thoughts. "I honestly would need a pretty good reason not to."

Kat gave a short laugh and nodded, her body still thrumming. "I'll start thinking of some then."

His eyes narrowed, and she could tell he fought the urge to come closer again. "What have you done, Kat?"

The space between them pulled her back to reality. She pushed off the desk, rounding it to put more distance between them. What hadn't she done? Besides, he would be confirming her death if not administering the final blow in just a few days if she didn't find a solution. "That's a broad question," she said without a hint of amusement. She raked her gaze down his body and back up with a smirk. "Do you need something more specific?"

"Kat—"

"In the future, if you require a meeting, you can schedule it through Star. And Reaper?" She raised an eyebrow at him and paused to be sure she had his full attention. "Don't come back here until you have more solid information on Aeron Seward. You're dismissed."

Anger flashed for the briefest second across his face before he spun on his heel and yanked the door open, coming face to face with Carl. Kat sighed. Maybe an open-door policy was the wrong way to go. The two men stared at each other for a moment before Griffin pushed past him.

"Pissed off your pet?" Carl asked, stepping into the office and closing the door.

"He's not my pet. Leave it open." He looked over at her and pulled the door back open. She remained standing behind the desk, hands splayed on top for support, looking down at the coded documents for the government contracts from StormTracer she'd deemed the most important. If it didn't involve national or international crisis prevention, the mission wasn't happening. Three active missions in Central America kept a handful of Division Three assets out of her hair, and she could send another few to handle the European requests sitting on the urgent pile. Carl cleared his throat. Kat looked up beneath her brows and waited for him to speak.

"My leash is tight. What guarantees are on the table for cooperation?"

Kat stood straighter. If her Granddad were alive, she'd be concerned this was a test. They would be pitted against each other before any real loyalty could be tested. But there was no test. He just wanted an out. "When was the last time you were in Europe?"

He licked his lips, shoulders tensing slightly. The last solo mission on file for him had been a European assassination. The after-action report was the least detailed she had ever seen him turn in, and he'd been grounded right after that.

"Six years."

"And how is your son doing?" Kat asked. His eyes widened, the mask slipping for a second before he could school the features back. "Perhaps you should close the door."

He did and moved right to the desk. "How long has Senior known?" Panic seeped into the whispered words, and Kat let him stew for a few moments longer before answering.

"I don't know that he does. I did my own search, but if I can find him, so can he." Dominic had found him because he pulled more than Senior probably ever cared to. The French woman he'd been protecting had kept him on her Granddad's leash, but the child he had been hiding had brought him to Kat.

"Katherine. I—"

Kat smirked. "You what?" Carl had been nothing but a problem for her. He'd sabotaged and slandered her across Division One for the last several years. He probably blamed her for his predicament since he'd been sent to Europe when she returned from the Caribbean. But using a child as leverage was not what she did. He didn't need to know that.

He released a long sigh. "What do you want to keep this quiet?"

She shuffled through the papers on the desk, pulling out a black ops assignment. She'd planned on dealing these to Division Three. But having leverage on Carl? That would be priceless. "How much do you have stacked away?" She looked up.

"Excuse me?"

She raised an eyebrow at him and waited. Every smart assassin had a bug-out account.

"Enough to live on for the next five years."

"All three of you?" He nodded. "Good. You're taking a team with you to Europe for a black ops mission."

His face lit up like Dom's at a comic con. "Are you serious?"

She licked her lips, nodding. "Carl, I don't like you. In fact, it would be in my best interest to shoot you and say you attacked. With our history, no one would doubt me."

"Then why—"

"Because I need the best on this mission, and as much as I hate to admit it—that's you."

She could see the hesitation in him. She just admitted she'd rather kill him. It doesn't exactly garner trust. But she was offering him an out. It would come down to how much he wanted to meet his son—and how afraid for his life he was.

"What's the catch?" he asked.

Kat smirked. "I want you to take a small team to Europe—and I want none of you to come back."

Silence answered her for a full minute. "Are we transferring people to the European compound, or. . ."

"Or. . . ?" She drew the word out. If she gave a direct order to eliminate the other assets, he could call it treason.

He moved to the desk, leaning forward, dropping his voice low. "What is it you are asking me to do?"

She quirked an eyebrow. "The only people who will be privy to this assignment are you, me, and whoever you hand select to accompany you. Once the official missions are complete, should Senior ask questions—accidents happen during missions all the time, and paperwork goes missing."

He nodded, swallowing hard. His eyes shifted to the papers on the desk. "How many missions?"

"Four total."

"I hand-pick the assets?"

"Choose wisely. If these aren't complete—the deals off," Kat said, standing up straight and grasping her hands behind her back.

"Why?" Carl asked, straightening up too.

It was a fair question. "You want out. I want up, and I want an ally on the outside. Do we have a deal?" He remained silent, weighing his decision. "It's either yes or no. I have many other assassins I can offer this to while I put a bullet in you and send your corpse to France to meet your son instead."

His nostrils flared, but he kept his mouth quiet. Good. He should remember who he was dealing with. "I'll have a list for you tomorrow."

"Before you leave this room," Kat clarified. "I need your choices now. You leave tonight."

11

AERON

*A*eron looked around the garage. The Impala she'd been working on had been long since completed and was parked in Tommy's spot. A baby blue 1985 Camaro SS now sat in that location, its engine parts laid out on a drop sheet in front of the car and the interior completely stripped. She ran a hand along the front driver-side fender, tracing a small series of dents as if from a baseball bat. The door in the corner of the garage opened, and Aeron's heart jumped to her throat. The last time she'd seen that door open, her father came to collect her. Luke's parents had been killed. It had set into motion the series of events that landed her with the blood of her father and the Senior Assassin on her hands and their names on a hit list. Tommy smiled from the doorway.

"Hey, Princess. Ivan said we could come back. Mind if I join you?" He waited at the threshold for her permission, like this wasn't his house more than hers.

"Sure."

He closed the door behind him and moved to the front of the car. Idle hands were never an issue here. He started cleaning the parts laid out on the drop sheet. She picked up a rag and sat, too, leaning her back against the bumper. She waited for him to speak. They had never liked each other. But something had changed the night her father had come for her—the night he was willing to kill for her. They worked in silence for several minutes until he cleared his throat.

"I'm sorry about your dad."

Warmth spread through her chest, and she blinked away a few unexpected tears. No one had said that to her and meant it. They'd told her he'd deserved it, apologized he had died that way, or let her know she was better off. No one knew him the way she had in those last few months, except maybe Ivan. And they hadn't really talked about it. "Thanks."

"I didn't know you were such a badass all this time. I probably wouldn't have picked on you, knowing you could kill me a hundred different ways."

"I could kill you thousands of ways," she said with a laugh. "And I thought about it—many times. But I came here to escape that life. This life. I'm sorry I brought it to your doorstep."

"That's okay. Your dad was pretty cool. Even the geek isn't that bad—although, with the scar, I expected him to fight better."

A lump rose in her throat, and she glanced at the car, changing the subject. "What are we working on?" She didn't want to open that dam of her father again just yet. It might not close.

"Passion-build for a man out in town. His wife died, and he wants to take her ashes for a final ride down the coast in the car she bought for him."

So much death surrounded them all the time. Even when you couldn't see it, it lingered just on the outskirts of their vision. "That's both really sweet and really sad," she said. "Pass me that wrench." He held it out, and Aeron took it. She snapped her head around at the sound of tires on the gravel driveway. "Mason's here." She put the wrench down, a sudden dread in her gut. She'd seen him just yesterday—but he'd witnessed her weakest moment. Heat flooded her cheeks. She hoped he would keep that to himself.

"C'mon." She got to her feet and held out a hand. Tommy accepted, and she pulled him up. When they entered the kitchen, Ivan was still in the same spot. "Do you ever move, Darth?"

"No," Tommy answered. "He tried every chair and decided that was his favorite. He'll fight you for it."

"Good. As he should." She smiled at Ivan's raised eyebrow. "Mason's here."

"I know." His brow furrowed, and his leg bounced slightly beneath the table.

She pulled up a chair beside him. "Everything okay?" In the upper left corner of his screen sat the hit list, and next to hers and Decius' names the words: Unconfirmed.

"Shit," he said. But Ivan wasn't looking at the screen—his eyes were glued to the door. It opened, and Ivan stood so quickly she thought the chair would topple over. Mason peered into the room before entering. He sported several cuts on his face and was filthy —still covered in soot from yesterday's fire.

"Hey," was all he gave them as he closed the door behind him.

Ivan pushed past Aeron's legs, bee-lining for Mason. She jumped to her feet but realized Mason had embraced him in a hug as if it had been years since two old friends had seen each other. Jealousy roared in her gut at the familiarity and realization they did know each other, and it dawned on her she had no idea how long Ivan worked with her dad—or who else he knew.

"You two know each other?" she asked.

Mason nodded and moved next to her. "You look like shit." He pulled her up into a hug. "I'm glad you're alive," he whispered in her ear.

"Me too," she responded, and she meant it.

Decius' footsteps on the stairs announced his arrival. He stopped at the bottom, and Aeron reckoned her face mirrored his: puzzlement, disbelief, anger, relief. But he didn't say anything. Just nodded at Mason.

"Good to see you all still alive," Mason said.

"Likewise," Decius responded.

"I'm going to go back to the garage," Tommy cut in. He met Aeron's eyes across the room, a glass of water now in his hand. "Later." He made a hasty exit, and Aeron realized Mason must not have been here with her father. The tension in the room thickened with each passing second. Decius took a seat beside Ivan and pulled out the tape recorder, placing it down in front of him. Mason met his stare and paled.

"You found the tapes," he said, his voice low.

Decius clenched his jaw as if measuring his words before he said them. "We have some questions."

"I actually have a lot of questions," Aeron said, turning to Ivan. This piece of information felt like a betrayal. "I didn't know you knew Mason."

He ran his fingers across his keyboard, biting his lip. "I—uh."

"I practically raised him," Mason supplied, with a smirk, joining them at the table. "At least in the Legacy sense." He sighed deeply. "I know you need answers. But before anything else, we need to make a plan to get you guys out of the country."

"Absolutely not," Decius said, leaning forward. "We need to find Luke first."

"Decius— two of your team are already eliminated; you barely made it out alive. You can't help anyone if you're dead."

"Mase—you've missed some pretty intense stuff," Aeron said, and her side ached with the reminder Luke tried to kill her barely twenty-four hours ago. "Mr. Wayward—"

"Mr. Wayward is presumed dead. The Legacy and the other operation, Legacy Inc, are crumbling. You and every other surviving Legacy member, along with probably the rest of the Wayward family, are on an international hit list that will only get more dangerous with each passing day as more and more assassins flock to claim their prize. I'm not missing anything."

Aeron sat stunned. "How do you—"

"The hit list is his contingency plan. If it's been activated, then he's dead or detained—"

"Oh, he's dead," Aeron said. "I put a bullet in him myself."

"Why am I not surprised?" Mason said with a small laugh. "Remember those very first days when you arrived here? You wanted to bunk and never leave."

Aeron laughed. The freedom Ernie's gave her had trumped everything—almost everything. She'd spent the entire two months eating crap and belonging to no one but herself. And then the reality of her team needing her—or more appropriately, she needing her team—sent her back to New York that first year.

"But with him dead," Mason continued, "we need to run—all of us."

"What about Luke?" Decius asked, bringing the topic back up.

"Fuck Luke," Aeron said, the words coming out harsher than she intended.

Ivan's head whipped over to stare at her. "Fuck Luke?" he said incredulously. "After all we went through. . . after all the sacrific-ing. . . Your dad. . . Fuck Luke?"

"He tried to kill me," she said, but that wasn't the reason she didn't want to see him.

"Eh," Decius started. "I mean. . . he missed on purpose."

"Why are you defending him?" she demanded. He was supposed to be on her side—always.

"Why aren't you?" he countered, his voice rising. "He sold his soul for you."

"I didn't ask him to!" she yelled. "I would rather have been killed. He took innocent lives, Decius." Because of her—but she couldn't voice that last part.

The siblings glared at each other. "Perhaps I am missing some-thing," Mason interjected, pinching the bridge of his nose. "Luke did what? Can we start from the beginning?"

"Which one?" Aeron asked. "The one where I started working with my dad? Or the one where I picked a fight with the Senior

Assassin and nearly died, just for Luke to come in and not finish the job." Ivan sucked in a breath beside her.

"Is that why you didn't fight back yesterday?" Mason asked.

Her back stiffened. It was as if a bucket of ice had been dumped on her. The room went silent, and she ignored the piercing glare from her brother, her eyes focused on the tape recorder in front of him instead. "Can we just. . ." she sighed. She didn't know what they needed to do. She didn't have a plan. She didn't care to have a plan. If they could just stay here, Ivan keeping them hidden, that would be enough. But it wasn't. "Mr. Wayward was using Luke to eliminate families, entire families, because he was pushing the narrative my dad killed his parents. Luke found out I knew the truth for months: his Granddad had murdered his parents. He didn't take the news lightly. Now, you told me yesterday you knew Luke was killing families." Mason nodded. "Little Scarlett?"

"I don't have full confirmation on all," he responded. But that wasn't an answer. Had she misunderstood Mr. Wayward's dying words?

"Did he kill those kids or not?"

Mason sat back, giving her a measured look. "I don't have confirmation on which *ones* he killed."

"But he did?" Aeron insisted. Luke's complete devastation burned into her brain.

"I have confirmed a few. But for all appearances, they were all killed."

Decius' fist came down on the table, and Aeron jumped. "Even more reason to find him. Who knows what he's going through."

"I promise you, I will find him," Mason said. He looked at the tape player. "But perhaps you need some answers first. Have you—uh—listened to them?"

"Just two," Decius said. "The night our mom—that night, and then Seamus' as well."

Mason reached for the tapes, looking at each one. "I thought these had been destroyed."

"Why did he have these?" Ivan asked.

"They were originally going to be used as leverage. However, once we realized how fucked up Senior really was, the tapes didn't matter."

Decius slid the tape player across to him, put in the first tape, and held out a pair of headphones. Mason eyed them warily before pulling them on. Decius hit play. Aeron kept her gaze locked on their Guardian. The world seemed to have dropped onto his shoulders, and he squeezed his eyes shut, tears leaving clean tracks down his soot-stained face. She and Decius exchanged a glance. When Mason hit stop and slid the headphones off, he looked older, as if years had suddenly dropped on him.

"What don't we know, Mason?" Decius asked, taking the lead in the conversation. Aeron let him. Exhaustion set heavy on her suddenly, and she realized she needed more meds. She stood and retrieved the medicine bottles from the counter.

"You don't know anything," Mason answered.

"We know our mother was murdered," Decius said.

"And I know that there's an entire operation dedicated to profit and shutting down the Legacy," Aeron added. "And that there are no loyal Legacy families left standing."

Mason lowered his head to his hands, elbows resting on the table. "I don't even know where to start," Mason admitted. "So much doesn't even matter anymore. The plans we put into motion, the reasons we did—fuck. At the present moment, we need to be focusing on surviving." He peered over at Ivan, forehead still resting in his hands. "First things first—I need you to hack into the mainframe at Legacy Inc."

"Why?" Aeron asked as Ivan shook his head, his blonde hair bouncing around. Aeron's chest constricted, and she had the urge to wrap him in a hug. She returned to her seat between him and Mason.

"Because if we can get into the system, we can shut down the hit list. There are only two ways to do that: Luke's biometrics or Ivan's coding. And we don't have Luke at the present moment."

"Why Ivan specifically?" Aeron asked. She knew he was good, but Mason was oddly specific in his wording.

"I can't," Ivan said, his face paling.

"Of course you can," Mason said with a soft laugh. He stood up and grabbed a glass from the counter, filling it up at the tap. He took a few big gulps before continuing. "It's the whole reason you were recruited."

"Recruited?" Decius asked, but Mason continued as if he hadn't spoken.

"Storm wrote it into the code before she died, Ivan. This has been the plan all along—not all of you getting involved," he said, glancing at Aeron and Decius. "But for Ivan to infiltrate the vault."

"All along?" Decius repeated.

"Decius—this is deeper than anything you could imagine at the moment."

Decius sat back, exchanging a glance with Aeron. She nodded at him. She had royally fucked up last night.

"Last time I tried," Ivan said, a shake in his voice, "we got Wilks killed." The image of Luke shooting Wilks flashed in Aeron's mind. Ivan was still talking, his voice lowered, "I'm positive that's what got Shaun killed too. I can't risk that, Mason. I won't."

There was a pregnant pause. The mention of Shaun ripped at a box in Aeron's mind she'd closed off. Her heart raced, and she looked to Mason, but his back had stiffened, and his eyes brimmed with moisture. He blinked a few times, the tears falling. "That wasn't your fault," he whispered. "That was all me, Ivan."

"What?" Aeron interjected. The box spilled open. Shaun's roaring laughter during a late-night movie. The smell of dinner cooking after a long training day. The sensual touch of his calloused hands up her back. The snap of his neck tingling in her hands. "I thought Mr. Wayward ordered..."

"He did," Mason said, sniffing and running a hand over his face.

"Oh fuck. But I, ah, I told Mr. Wayward that Shaun was passing information to your dad."

"How could you!" Ivan stood up, his body shaking. "He was your best friend—he was a brother to me. How could you do that to us? I've spent this whole time thinking it was my fault!"

"Because Senior was catching wind of the Central American operation, so I needed a distraction. A big one. I didn't know he was going to send Luke in to kill him. I assumed Senior would send me in as a loyalty check."

Sound rushed through Aeron's ears. "Your best friend?" she whispered, heat flooding her face. Memories flittered through her mind of their late-night affairs, unbelievable sex, and long talks of how much she hated the Legacy. Intimate moments, his soft kisses, his genuine shock at her betrayal the night she killed him for Luke.

Mason nodded. "We grew up together. After my family was murdered, Shaun's family took me in. I trained for the Legacy and secured him a spot. He was working with the Alliance when he died."

"The Alliance?" Decius asked.

"That's what we called ourselves, your parents, Luke's, the group of us attempting to reclaim the Legacy roots. But I had to make a split decision." He looked over to Ivan, pleading in his eyes, and then to Aeron. "I didn't consult your father—or anyone. I just. . . I made a judgment call that went wrong. Your father didn't trust me after that."

Decius leaned back in his chair, fingers interlaced behind his head, and a long sigh left him. "You were going to kill your best friend? That's like me deciding to kill Luke. What is in Central America that is so important?"

"A lot. But I was hoping I'd have time to body swap. Killing him would have been the worst-case scenario."

"What was your plan, Mase? Just show up and hope you could find a body that would work?" Aeron asked incredulously. The thought of there being another body that could look like Shaun's, feel as strong and comforting as Shaun's made her skin crawl.

"No. I already had a body double stored."

"Excuse me?" Had he meant to kill him all along?

Mason hesitated. "We all have a body double, Aeron. We change them out every year or so, as needed. It was the first thing we did when I joined the Alliance. I've been switching bodies for years."

"To what ends?"

"Contingency plans for getting out. I've only been able to use them a few times—I've buried more friends than I'd like to think about. But they wouldn't work now—there's not enough time with the confirmation process for the hit list to switch anyone." He paused and looked over to Ivan. "I'm sorry. I should have told you about Shaun. Andrew made it clear I was to keep my distance. But now? We're already on a hit list. Nothing you flag is going to make it worse. Will you do it?"

Silence fell over them. Ivan's eyes were on his screen, and Aeron wished she knew what was going on inside his mind. She'd killed someone important to him; had he known it was her? There was so much about him she didn't know; she'd never asked. Decius pulled the stack of tapes back toward him, reorganizing them for the hundredth time, and Mason—Mason had his eyes on her.

"What?" she asked.

"I'm sorry. I should have told you earlier, too."

"Did you know I was sleeping with him?" The words fell out of her. It didn't matter. He was dead. They were in mortal danger. But Shaun had been a secret she enjoyed—a rebellion against her father. One of the hardest kills she'd ever made.

"What?" Mason and Ivan said simultaneously.

"Never mind," she said, heat flooding her cheeks. She could feel Decius' smirk.

"You were sleeping with him?" Mason repeated. "Holy fuck. It's probably a good thing you did kill him. Your father would've skinned him alive."

"Well, I killed him too, so. . ." Aeron said, but the reality of how much damage she'd done started to weigh her down. She'd killed too many people, people she loved—for what end?

"You were never supposed to be in this deep, Aeron," Mason said, sobering up. "Ever. We were supposed to be getting the two of you out. But we have the chance now. Ivan?"

Ivan wiped at his cheeks and swallowed hard. Aeron made a note to apologize to him later. "I'll do it. Of course, I'll do it."

"You don't have to," Aeron said, although his words sparked a warmth in her chest. "We can find Luke. You should get out while you can."

"And leave you? I'd die first." His gaze stayed locked on hers.

"I've heard that before," Decius said, a warning in his tone. "And he just shot her."

Aeron swiveled her gaze to her brother and raised an eyebrow. "I thought he missed on purpose."

"I'm making a point," Decius said. She smirked. Always the overprotective brother. He couldn't hold his glare, and he cracked a smile instead, a laugh bellowing out of him, and he looked to Ivan. "But hey, good luck with her," he said, still chuckling.

A laugh bubbled out of Aeron as well, the stress clearing from her system. Ivan and Mason joined in, the infectious stress relief spreading through the room. Mason sobered first. "So, we're agreed? Ivan will go to Legacy Inc, and you two are leaving."

"No," Aeron said. If Ivan was risking his life to save hers, she wasn't going into hiding. "We're going with you to find Luke."

Mason nodded, accepting defeat. "Fine. But we're going to need help. Do you guys know where Perry is?"

12

KAT

at tapped her toe inside her shoe as she waited for the bartender to notice her. Mason needed a secure, invisible spot, and she knew Rockstars was completely off Legacy Inc's radar—because it belonged to her, and she made sure of it. Even Perry didn't know about this place.

"Can I get you a drink, Red?" The bartender leaned forward, her smile dazzling even beneath the dim lights. A total of three people were allowed to call her that nickname, and she wasn't one of them. Kat swallowed back the urge to slam the pretty lady's face into the bar top.

"No, thanks. I've reserved The Cove for the evening." Kat held out a thick stack of hundreds and raised an eyebrow. The woman regarded her and the money. No one here knew her—and never would. The Cove was not a room available to anyone unless you showed up with $10k in cash and used the exact phrase Kat just did.

"Of course." She put the money in a locked drop box beneath the register, and Kat glanced at her watch. 2 a.m. Mason would be here shortly. The bartender slid a key across the counter, and Kat took it without a word. She twirled the key between her fingers and made her way through the tables packed with people enjoying lap dances and women serving a variety of drinks. The upscale vibe enticed the patrons to pay more, and Kat made a healthy income from here, all of which was sent to take care of Shay and his family.

There were three bars located inside the club, two on the outside walls and one in the middle across from the main stage. Two women performed on the round stage in the middle of the room, and each lounge chair that surrounded it was filled. The back wall had seven secluded enclaves with bouncers to help the women if needed. Most wouldn't. A requirement for working for her was self-defense lessons. Her men and women were well-trained to handle themselves; bouncers were just there as a deterrent and to be reliable witnesses.

Kat walked past the bouncers and slipped into a nearly invisible doorway leading upstairs, the music dimming to near silence. A single bouncer halted her on the first landing, flexing his impressive muscles.

"This is a private area, ma'am."

"Check with the bartender," Kat said, holding up her key, glad to know her anonymity was protected. She'd made herself invisible to this business to protect Shay and herself. Only the manager knew who she was by sight and nothing more. But Kerry wasn't in tonight, so Kat felt comfortable bringing Mason here. Perry could hold down Legacy Inc for a few hours, and hopefully, by tonight, the hit list would be last week's news.

The bouncer pressed his earpiece, confirming she was, in fact, authorized to be there. "I apologize, ma'am." He stepped aside, and she smiled at him.

"No apologies. You're doing your job and doing it well. I will have a guest arriving shortly. The code word will be Butternut."

"Yes, ma'am. Will you be requesting a dancer or bartender?"

"No. Once he is here, no interruptions."

The bouncer nodded, and Kat moved past him and up the stairs to the next landing. She slipped the key the bartender gave her into her pocket and pulled out a different one to unlock the door. The lights in the room came to life as she entered, and complete silence engulfed her when the door clicked closed. She'd only used this room a hand full of times, a few of those spent hiding from her mother. But today it would be used for its full purpose: an escape room from her Granddad; he might be dead, but he wasn't done with them yet.

She circled the room, making sure everything was in place, and ran her hand across the velvet red couch, pushing away the memories of nights sleeping on it while hiding. She moved to the wall of windows overlooking the club floor. The two-way mirror made her invisible to the world below, just the way she liked it. The room was packed, also the way she liked it—especially at 2 a.m. Money flew at the women performing. Tomorrow night the men would take the stage and make more money than a god. If Luke had found out she had tucked this away, he would be livid. She could have sold Rockstars and would have had enough cash to escape her Granddad before he died—but that was never her plan. She wanted him tortured and dead. Now, she may need to dip into this emergency fund if they didn't get into the vault to keep them all alive.

On the wall opposite the couch was the fully stocked bar. She grabbed herself a glass of water, taking small sips. Being in this room, a place she designed for the end game, brought the panic to the surface that should have set in when she got Luke's phone call. She wasn't afraid to die, but too many assassins would take pleasure in torturing her—doing unspeakable acts before cashing in their prize. *Fuck.* Some wouldn't even care about the money. Her heartbeat quickened, and she moved to the black glass table in the middle of the room.

She took a seat facing the only entrance, bouncing her leg to redirect her racing energy. She didn't know Mason well, but Perry trusted him, which was good enough for her. Perry was overseeing the new safe house for the kids and any problem that popped up at headquarters, which seemed to be in endless supply these days.

The door to the room opened, and music slipped into the room. Kat's entire body tensed, ready to attack. Mason's face poked around the edge of it, and she breathed a bit easier. He'd always been on the fringe of her Granddad's operations—he practically raised Perry. But she didn't know his weaknesses or his reason for living, which made him dangerous. She nodded at him, and he entered, followed by Aeron fucking Seward and her brother. Kat's heart slammed into her throat. She was never so happy to see someone alive. They wouldn't need to do anything drastic. She wouldn't need to sell Rockstars with Aeron's techie available to hack into the vault.

A smile spread across her face until her eyes met Aeron's—who had no idea they were coming to meet her, it would appear. Aeron pushed past Mason and vaulted onto the table, sliding across it. Kat barely managed to scoot back, missing a kick to the face.

"Whoa!" Kat said holding up her hands.

Aeron didn't hesitate. She threw a punch, landing on Kat's cheek and snapping her head to the side. Kat threw one back, making a connection.

"Hey!" Mason yelled, but Kat ignored his attempts to mitigate the confrontation. This was long overdue. She swung again, making contact with Aeron's side. Aeron stumbled and cursed, clutching her side as blood seeped from beneath the white tank top.

"Damn it. I think I ripped the stitches," Aeron said, halting all movement. Kat froze, and Decius pushed past her to get to Aeron's side.

Jealousy traced its way through her system at Decius' tenderness as he checked his sister's wound; it reminded her of Griffin. She stuffed the uncomfortable feeling away and held up her hands in a truce. "You good?" Aeron glared at her, and Mason put a commanding hand on Decius' shoulder. Kat glared at Mason. "If I knew you were bringing a crowd, I would have picked a different meeting place," she said, ice slipping into the words.

"You want their techie, they want Luke, and I need answers," Mason said. "It made sense."

"Fair enough," Kat agreed, only because it was good to see the Sewards alive.

Aeron shot to her feet, shoving Decius out of the way to turn on Mason. "How dare you. I'm not working with her."

"How else did you think we were getting into Legacy Inc?" Mason asked.

Aeron looked back over her shoulder, sizing Kat up. Kat raised an eyebrow in challenge. She needed their techie, but if Aeron wouldn't cooperate, she'd just take the information by force.

"Where's Luke?" Aeron asked.

"I could ask you the same question. He was heading to save you."

Aeron shook her head. "I doubt that." Decius whacked her arm, and they glared at each other, a silent conversation playing out she wished she could understand.

"I haven't met you yet. I'm Kat, Luke's cousin," she interrupted. "Perry and Luke have spoken very highly of you." She held out a hand, and Decius shook it, but he side-eyed Aeron.

"She another one of your secrets?" he asked her.

"Yeah," Aeron answered, sarcasm dripping off her words. "I wasn't sleeping with this one, though." Decius rolled his eyes, and Mason coughed, looking uncomfortable all of a sudden.

"How wired are we in this room?" Mason asked, getting straight to business. His eyes scanned the room, looking for cameras.

"Completely off," Kat said. "No Wi-Fi. No cameras. No way to be tracked in here. You haven't heard from Luke at all?" she asked. A twisting knot started in her stomach as they shook their heads. They needed him—but more importantly, the responsibility of losing him weighed on her. "Take a seat." She gestured to the table, and they sat, Aeron, Decius, and Mason on one side, Kat on the other.

"Let's get all the information on the table," Mason started. Kat raised an eyebrow at him. She'd worked with him a handful of times; he was as loyal as they come and had access to information even she didn't. She was mildly cautious and curious about what he could offer her.

"Yes," Kat said, sitting back. "Let's. There is an international hit list releasing names with very high price tags. Two of your team members have already been eliminated, and you are both unconfirmed at the moment—although I am very glad to see you both alive."

"I bet you are," Aeron said. "Cut the shit. What is it you want from us?"

Kat gave a short laugh, Aeron's anger understandable. The last time they'd spent any amount of time together, she'd made it clear that Aeron's life meant nothing to her—a pawn Kat could clear from the board as soon as she no longer served a purpose.

"There are two ways to shut down the hit list. The easiest way is Luke. With the Senior Assassin dead, the helm has been passed to him. Luke just needs to scan in with the biometrics and take charge," Kat said. "The vault will open, and everything will go back to normal."

"But we don't know where Luke is." Aeron leaned forward, elbows resting on the table. "And I don't care to find him. What's the other option?"

Kat raised an eyebrow at Aeron's sudden distaste for her cousin. "Why are you not interested in finding Luke?"

"We are," Decius said.

"I'm not," Aeron clarified, her cheeks reddened slightly, and she adjusted in her seat, a hand drifting to her side.

"He shot you." It wasn't a question. Luke's state of mind was not clear the last time they talked—this could be why.

"Grazed me," she clarified, and more words seemed to sit at the tip of her tongue, wanting to spill out. Kat remained silent, giving her the space to speak. She had no idea what happened in the garage. What finally led to someone putting a bullet in her Grand-dad? Aeron didn't offer, and Kat would have to wait for the details. The pressing matter was the ticking clock on the hit list.

"Fair enough. Your techie," Kat said. "He's the only person I've ever known to hack into the Legacy system and manipulate it. I want him to hack into it and shut down the hit list. Or, at the very least, get me access to the finances so I can pay the Legacy Inc assets before they realize their leader is dead and money isn't flowing—because that is almost more deadly than the mercenaries coming for you and eventually me."

Aeron didn't miss a beat. "And how do you plan to get him in there safely?"

Kat's lips twitched. "I'm going to walk him in the front door of Legacy Inc and straight to my office."

"That's insane," Aeron said, shaking her head. "No."

"It's a perfect plan, actually," Mason said. "No one knows him. And Katherine is in charge, for all appearances."

"I'm not sending him anywhere with you," Aeron argued.

"I'm not going to kill him," Kat said, annoyed, although the idea did cross her mind as retribution for not getting to torture her Granddad. They could shut this all down and have access to the money by tonight, so her vengeance would have to wait—again. "If we go now, we all can be free and clear by tonight."

"What about Luke?" Decius asked.

Kat met his wary gaze. "We'll find him. I owe him that. But it will be easier without a target on our backs."

Aeron looked over to Mason. Kat removed herself from the table to give them a moment to discuss. She grabbed a tumbler from behind the bar, filled it with ice, picked out her favorite rum —End of Days—and poured a glass. They weren't leaving this room without an agreement. She would kill Decius and Mason to get the information she needed, but honey always worked better for her than brute force. It didn't take long for Mason to approach the bar.

She poured another glass, held it out to him, and raised an eyebrow.

He accepted the drink. "We agree—with one stipulation: I go with you guys."

"Agreed." Kat held out her hand, a smile daring to cross her face. It could be that simple. An agreement. A handshake. A new Legacy Inc. "Drinks anyone?"

Aeron looked over and shook her head, her complexion fading. "Are we done here? I'd like to get home."

"You're not going home," Kat said. "Those mercenaries who hit the manor are the least of your worries. They were desperate. You need to worry about the ones who will slip toxins on the back of your hand, or poison onto your napkin. You made it here in one piece. You're not leaving."

"You can't stop us. We don't work for you," Aeron said and stood up.

"Yes, you do. Everyone works for me. Until Luke's found, I am the Senior Assassin of the Legacy and Legacy Inc. Like it or not, I'm in charge." The truth of the words invigorated Kat. She was in charge—the entire system was hers if she could survive until they unlocked the vault. Aeron scowled and looked at Mason.

"She's not wrong, Aer. She's the current Head Mother Fucker in Charge. But she's also right. This is the safest place for you at the moment."

Mason's phone buzzed before Aeron could answer, and all eyes went to him. He pulled out a burner phone.

"Go." He paced the short room, a female voice sputtering on the other end. "Who?" He stopped walking, dropping his voice low. "I'll fucking kill her. You can tell her that." A scowl darkened his features, and for a moment, Kat saw precisely how dangerous he was. How calculated. "You already know my answer." He glanced around the room at them. "I won't let it happen." He hung up, dismantled the phone, and pocketed the chip. "Change of plans. I know where Luke is."

Decius spun in his chair. "Where?"

"The last place on earth anyone would look for him. It'll take an army to retrieve him, and if we don't go soon, he'll probably be dead by nightfall."

A cold fist wrapped around Kat's chest when his pupils dilated. Only one place she knew invoked that kind of terror. "Don't say it."

Mason's jaw tightened before speaking. "The Playhouse."

Fear crawled up her spine. The name alone called screams from the shadows, hers—along with countless dead. She'd watched associates torn to pieces—friends and foes facing torture no human could possibly withstand, but that was the point. It was an old Legacy training ground that had been converted to a Legacy Inc outpost where Rufus would train assets in New York. But Rufus just enjoyed killing people in as many fucked up ways as possible, and it became a gameland to him. Her Granddad had fed the monster at every turn to keep him in line. Now, there was no one to keep him in line.

"No." She shook her head and sat back. "We can't." They were too close to getting the vault open to risk anything. Luke would have to wait.

"What do you mean 'We can't'?" Decius demanded. "Maybe *you* can't. Just give us the location, and we'll go." He stood up, Aeron following suit more slowly.

"You'll never make it out alive," Mason whispered; his words froze Aeron and Decius.

"I don't care. We can't leave him there," Decius said. "Just give us the location."

"Decius," Mason said. "It's not that simple."

"It's a death trap. The assets took to calling it the Playhouse because the man who runs it, Rufus, doesn't have a soul. He loves to kill and torture people." Kat supplied and looked to Aeron. "And you killed the only person keeping him in line. No one gets out of there unscathed."

She looked back to Mason. Maybe there was another person

who could control the beast. Rumors floated around of Mason being in tight with Rufus. She'd disregarded them because no one worked with that monster voluntarily. Yet, how had he known Luke was there?

"If we have an inside man, perhaps we can. Word around Legacy Inc is you're thick as thieves with Rufus," Kat said. Mason's reaction stayed neutral, giving no indication one way or another. "Are you?"

"It's complicated, Katherine."

She heard the warning in her name. So, he was in tight with Rufus. A chill swept over her, her body immediately guarding itself. There was nothing human inside Rufus. He killed because he liked killing and tortured because he became bored. She'd worked under him for a few months as punishment from her mother when she was in her early twenties. She couldn't recall what the transgression had been for, but the nights he'd forced her to spend in the Playhouse still haunted her.

"Who called you?" Kat countered.

"An old friend. But they can't help us."

"Fine. Do you have an inside man beside Rufus?" Kat asked.

Mason's jaw tightened before he answered. "No."

He was holding back. "Then who gave you Luke's location?" she asked.

"I can't—"

"Then who has him? We shut down the Playhouse months ago."

Mason didn't answer. He grabbed the back of his head, pacing.

Kat pushed. "Surely, if it was just Rufus, you would ask your old pal to hand him over." A slight tick in Mason's jaw let her know she had hit her mark. "If I can't trust you—"

"Your mother has him."

Her eyes sliced across the room, and he met her glare with equal hatred. Her mother was still in New York. Kat had looked for her briefly, but all signs pointed to her retreating overseas.

"Why would she do that?" Aeron asked. "Grab Luke?"

"Because whoever controls Luke has the key to the vault and

power over the deadliest assassin forces on the East coast," Kat answered. Mason wasn't wrong—they'd need an army to get in and out of the Playhouse alive—but she owed Luke and herself. Plus, she didn't have an army; she had three. "Change of plans," Kat agreed, and a fire burned in her veins. She could still have her shot at vengeance. "Let's go storm the Playhouse."

13

LUKE

*L*uke hung his head. The restraints pulled against his wrists, and somehow the chair still felt frozen against his legs despite having been seated there for hours, maybe even days. The soundtrack of the dead became louder when he closed his eyes, but seeing the blood on their clothes and skin, and the bullet wounds in their foreheads was worse. And it wasn't just the innocent he'd killed who haunted him now, but every life he'd helped end. They circled behind him—whispering in his ears while their frozen touch sent white-hot flames of pain down his spine. He clamped his mouth shut, his apology not worthy of the damage he'd caused. He deserved this. He deserved every agonizing second of this torture.

The door opened, and the dead stepped aside, giving Luke a clear view of Rosemary, a smug look befitting of a queen who'd won. "How are you doing, Luke?"

He averted his gaze, catching sight of another figure: Shaun Brinks. Luke's entire being seized. Aeron had killed him—had killed the man she'd been seeing—for him. He hadn't deserved to die. Not like that. And Aeron—he'd never even breached the topic with her. He just. . . What the fuck was wrong with him? Shaun nodded in his direction and leaned against the wall, so similar to the way Mason had outside of Mrs. Gale's torture room, except for the gaping wound at his neck and the blood-drenched clothes he wore. Luke turned back toward Rosemary.

"I see you're a little more coherent. How is the ride treating you?"

"Get out," Luke said between clenched teeth; they chattered together if he released his jaw too long. "I'm not telling you a damned thing."

The door opened again. It was the scarred woman followed by Mrs. Gale. Luke reeled back. She no longer wore the stained and dirty clothes he'd last seen her in when she escaped from Interrogation Room 4, but her left eye was still swollen, barely healed cuts shone on her sunken cheeks, and she had a distinct limp.

What was she doing here? Wait—was she dead too? His breath quickened, eyes widening. "Are you. . . No. . . No!" She must be dead. She would have died before working with Rosemary. Was she killed because of the hit list? Or had her injuries from his interrogation been far worse than he'd imagined? "I'm sorry! I'm sorry," he called out.

"Are you?" Shannon asked, appearing beside her mom. *"Or are you sorry you couldn't outrun your fate?"*

"I didn't mean it," he said, eyes bouncing between mother and daughter. "I swear! I thought—I knew—" But he knew nothing. Shannon's death was entirely his fault. Her ghostly green eyes glared at him. If Mrs. Gale was here, she was dead. His throat seized on itself. "I didn't mean to kill you too."

"Who did you kill, Lucas?" the scarred woman asked.

The way his name rolled off her tongue—god, who was she? He snapped his eyes shut, trying to place her voice. "Say it again," Luke said.

Silence answered. He looked back up, and her eyes roamed around the room. "Leave us," she said, dismissing Rosemary from the room, and didn't speak again until the door clicked closed.

Pulling a chair beside him, she leaned in close. "I'm looking for some people, Luke. I need your help to find them."

"The kids?" he asked, recalling Rosemary's suggestion after dosing him with Sin.

"The kids. Do you know where they are?"

"*Careful,*" whispered a voice in his ear. "*They will know you didn't kill them all—you would have saved those happy little children for no reason.*" He tried to spin to see the person standing behind him. The restraints cut his motion short, twisting his shoulders. He didn't care. The pain brought the room back into focus.

"Who's haunting you, Luke?"

Mr. Seward walked around the woman, and Luke squeezed his eyes shut, shaking his head. When he opened them again, he stood between Mrs. Gale, who hadn't moved, and the woman questioning him. He crossed his arms and put the standard glare in place. He was *so real.* But he was so dead.

"I can see the dead in your eyes. If you tell me about them, if you talk to them—they will let you go," the woman promised. Luke shook his head, but that was a terrible mistake. The world tilted around him, and he swayed, bile rising up again. He choked on it and swallowed it back down. "I've walked many assassins through this process. Trust me."

"*She's not lying, Luke,*" Mrs. Gale said. "*You can trust her. You know that.*"

"I don't even know her," Luke said.

"*Don't you?*"

The scarred woman looked over to Mrs. Gale, too, as if she could see her. Could she? Could she see the dead too? There were so many—how could she not?

"Is she dead, Luke?"

"Can you see her?" he whispered. "Mrs. Gale. Can you see her?"

Mrs. Gale glanced toward the scarred woman and shook her head.

"*No one can see us but you, Luke.*"

"I didn't kill you," he said, panic rising. "I know. I know I killed your daughter—I didn't mean to. It was my fault." He looked at Shannon, her expression softening at his confession. Mr. Seward cleared his throat, Luke's frantic gaze meeting the cool stare of the dead man. "But I did not kill you."

"Who didn't you kill?" The woman asked.

"You did." Mr. Seward said.

"No." He shook his head.

"Didn't you? Didn't you beat me nearly to a pulp? Didn't Aeron give the final pity blow so she could save herself from your Granddad?"

"Where are the kids?" the scarred woman asked again.

Luke's mind fought itself. The truth wanted to pour from him. He wanted to spill the words onto the floor, the Sin begging to bring his secrets out of him. If he told, those kids would die, and Aeron would never forgive him. His heart slammed harder into his chest.

"Where are they hiding?" Mrs. Gale stepped closer.

"A safe house." The words tore themselves from Luke, and he bit into his lip, drawing blood, trying to keep more words from coming out. It was pointless. "In Astoria." The address fell from his lips at the slightest request, and he had to fight the urge to name Dom, Gunnar, and the children. He focused on the dead, tuning out the scarred woman.

"Luke," Mrs. Gale said softly, moving closer to him. *"What happened to Shannon?"*

Shannon squatted down beside Luke, eyes blazing with anticipation like she couldn't wait to hear the truth come out of his mouth. "Rosemary," he said easily. "She set us up. I switched the missions at the last minute with Shannon's help, but Rosemary sabotaged us. She just wanted money to get out."

"The cuts on her body?"

"Rosemary," Luke said, looking back to Mrs. Gale. Tears streamed down his face with the memory of Shannon's final moments. The agony in her screams.

"Did she kill Shannon?" the scarred woman asked, the ice in her voice matching that in his veins.

"No, that was Cage. He's dead. Aeron shot him."

"Jesus. I was about to bring her back in here and slice her to ribbons," the scarred woman said, eyes flicking to Mrs. Gale. Luke looked between the two women again. She *could* see Mrs. Gale. How else would she know he was speaking about Shannon?

Mrs. Gale's hand brushed the tears from his cheeks, and Luke jerked back at the warm touch. "You're not dead." He leaned forward, pressing his face into her hand, warmth filling his face. "You're not dead," he cried.

"No, I'm not," she confirmed.

"Why would you do that? Do you know how many dead are in this fucking room right now? I'm barely holding it together."

"I'm sorry. We needed the information, and the less you fight the Sin, the easier it will be to level you off."

"Please don't go after them," Luke pleaded, the faces of the kids full of laughing while they played with flour in the house. "They're innocent." The scarred woman began speaking, but Luke couldn't understand her as hot white pain radiated up to the middle of his back. His entire body seized, the screams of the dead deafening. When they finally quieted, his muscles relented, his throat burned, and he realized the wail had come from him.

"I'm going to check out the address. You keep him alive," the scarred woman said. She paused at the door, her eyes settling on Luke for a moment. He met her gaze beneath his hooded eyes, the spasm seeming to take all the energy from him. She left without another word.

Mrs. Gale pushed the hair from his sweat-soaked brow. "I'm going to put you under until she returns. It will help stem the nerve pain throughout your back."

He couldn't look her in the eyes. He'd ordered her interrogation on his quest for vengeance—a vengeance manufactured from the start. "I'm sorry about Shannon," he said, his gaze locked on the top of his knees. He didn't want to see Shannon's face either. "I'm sorry about the interrogation. I don't remember ordering it." Bile fought to rise up his throat, but he knew there was nothing left to heave out of his system.

Her hand cupped the side of his face. He leaned into it, the warmth of her touch lowering his heart rate just a smidge. She raised his chin to look directly at him. Shame spread through him at the sight of the bruises and cuts across her face. How could he have demanded Mason do that to her? "You didn't order the interrogation," she whispered. "I did."

He jerked back, pain traveling through his shoulders at the rough movement. "What?"

She had the decency to step away from him and fold her hands behind her back. The words he wanted couldn't even form in his mouth as anger and audacity chased their way through his system. "Mason and I needed to square a few things away."

"You manipulated me."

"Yes." Her answer should have been a fatal blow of betrayal. Mrs. Gale—their healer and mentor—had used him. The shock wore off faster than it should have. He'd been manipulated by everyone he loved, except Decius.

"Are Aeron and Decius alive?"

"We're about to find out." She pulled out a clear vial of liquid and filled a syringe. She stuck it into the PICC line, and his arm gave a tiny tremor. "It's just a sedative. Rest up, Luke."

The room began to sink around him when her words registered. "What do you mean 'find out'?" But the world pulled him into darkness, and for the first time in a long time, dreamless sleep took hold.

14

KAT

Kat stalked the hallway toward her office. If she played the cards right, she could eliminate two of the three divisions in Legacy Inc in a single blow. She needed an inside source at the Playhouse and confirmation beyond Mason that Luke was being held there and that her mother was there. A chill raced down her spine at the thought.

Star leaned against the wall outside the office in reinforced black pants and a black tank, arms hanging down at her sides as if she was tired of moving them. Her head pulled off the wall at Kat's approach. "What happened to you?" she asked.

Kat's tongue licked over the corner of her mouth where Aeron had broken skin. "Has anyone been by?"

"Jerry from Division Three peeked down the hall early this afternoon. He didn't approach, though."

"Griffin?" If anyone could fuck up her plans for tonight, it was him. Star shook her head. Kat placed her palm on the scanner, and the door clicked open. A jolt of excitement raced through her each time it did.

Star followed her in and shut the door. "What's the plan?" she asked. Kat didn't answer. She pulled out the three division folders and two burner phones from the desk. Her safe room was offline—which was great, except you couldn't plan a multifaceted rescue plan without internet. "Kat?"

Kat paused, running her thumb over the phone in her hand. "Do you remember last year—"

"I remember nothing," Star said. Kat smiled and met her gaze across the room. In another lifetime, they would have been best friends. But Kat didn't have friends—couldn't have friends. Every person in her life was a leverage opportunity for her Granddad. But he was dead, and she—no. She wasn't out of the woods yet.

"When was the last time you were in the Playhouse?"

The smile vanished from Star's face. "About two months ago. We went in and shut it down."

"I thought so. Did you do a full sweep?"

"Top to bottom."

"Could you draw me up a blueprint?" Kat asked.

Star gave a measured look that held everything she wanted to say, and Kat could hear it clear as day in her head: 'Why? Are you fucking insane? When do we go?' Star just nodded. "Of course. Um, Kat?" Kat raised an eyebrow at the concern in Star's voice. "Are you going to dismiss me as your Reaper?"

The words sent ice down Kat's spine. She couldn't imagine doing any of this without her. She looked at Star, shocked. "What? No. Why would you think that?"

"With your new position, I thought maybe Griffin—"

"Fuck no." Kat straightened up. She wanted to tell Star what was happening and have the badass with her when she breached the Playhouse. More importantly, when she rebuilt Legacy Inc, she wanted this woman alive and working by her side. "I am conducting a tactical raid on the Playhouse. Senior asked me to test all the outposts for cracks, and I'm doing due diligence is all. I do need a favor, though." Star cocked an eyebrow at her, waiting. "Tell me everything you know about Mason St. James."

"This is a terrible idea," Mason said. He placed the bags of takeout on the table. They'd reconvened at Rockstars since Aeron and Decius' heads were worth too much for them to be wandering around anywhere.

She looked up from the tablet, and her stomach growled at the sweet scent of ramen wafting from the bags, but Mason wasn't looking at her. His eyes were on Aeron. The girl was passed out on her back across the red couch, her arm flung over her face as she snored softly. Decius leaned against the couch with his feet stretched in front of him with ankles crossed arms folded over his chest. His head rested against Aeron's stomach so if she so much as flinched, it would alert him.

"She fell asleep a few hours ago," Kat said. "He dozed off about twenty minutes after her. They look like shit, so I figured I'd let them sleep. I can't go into the Playhouse without an able team."

"It's been a rough couple of days," Mason said and began taking out the food.

"Care to catch me up?" Kat raised an eyebrow at him.

"No."

Kat nodded and pulled a tray of sushi toward her. From what she'd learned about Mason, he was as loyal as they came and somehow had his hands in both Legacies, even though he wasn't a Legacy-blood. Far from it. His family had been murdered in a botched Legacy Inc assignment when he was thirteen—his sister was only seven years old when she was shot point-blank in the head in front of him. The official reports did not identify the killer. He'd pledged his loyalty to her Granddad, who'd brought him into the fold, and Mason never left his side. Or at least it appeared that way. There had been rumors of him being involved with the Alliance—but what his role would be, she couldn't guess.

Kat took a few bites of the food, savoring each one as she refocused on the tablet. The 3D mockup of the Playhouse compound that Star provided was not complete. She slid the tablet over to Mason. "Can you finish out what I have here?"

Mason reluctantly took the tablet, scrolling through what had been created. He sighed and took a seat, putting his feet up on the table and making adjustments to the schematics. It took him only a few minutes to put the tablet back down. "Whoever gave you those prints was pretty accurate. Do you have," he waved his hand in the air over the table while looking for the words that seemed to leave him.

"Holographic display?" Kat asked, laughing. "Here, eat." She pushed a bag of food toward him. "I've got it." She pressed a button under the table, the glass top lit up, and the holographic display of the Playhouse rose up. She moved the food out of the way and whistled. "Damn."

It wasn't just the main building. Mason supplied the entire compound. Three warehouses spread out across the fenced-in lot. The first and largest she knew was an empty shell, designed with a maze and boobytrapped, set up as a distraction. The second was the original Playhouse. It was smaller and quickly ran out of room for Rufus' grand plans. The largest and newest building was the one that gave her nightmares. She touched the glass table in front of her, and the image spun in the air, bringing the back of the compound to her. It wasn't an empty parking lot like she'd remembered. Hundreds of shipping containers covered the area, some of them stacked three or four high.

"What are these?" she asked.

"Holding cells, weapon storage, more torture chambers? I'm not sure about all of them."

"How accurate is this?"

"I was there last month," Mason said, eyes cutting to her. "But Rufus can change the entire layout in hours. He's gotten quite proficient at it."

"Does he still have the wolves?" Kat asked, a chill sweeping her body. At one point, Rufus trained wolves to hunt down people in the building, and at another time, he starved them and set them loose. Most people panicked at seeing the gorgeous animals racing toward them. Kat had been no different.

"No."

A weight lifted from Kat's chest. "It's shut down, so who's he playing with?"

He didn't answer.

"Every time Rufus or the Playhouse are mentioned, your jaw does the slightest of movements, your eyes narrowing for a fraction of a second," Kat said. "Now, I know why I don't like the bastard, but your issue is more personal."

Mason kept his gaze steady, no doubt assessing if she was worthy of his words. "What do you plan to do once your mother is killed and you've eliminated all the assets of Legacy Inc?"

Kat sat back, folding her hands, and resting them across her stomach. Once upon a time, she imagined Luke and Perry by her side as they found the middle ground between the two companies. She'd seen it come to life the day Luke came and confessed he'd put Aeron in the crosshairs. Then it died the night he killed Gabe Woodsworth. The night her mother showed the smallest bit of concern for her. She had no idea why her mother had done it, convinced Granddad Luke was the better candidate for Senior Assassin. She was wrong—Kat had always been the better candidate to take over the company.

"My focus is keeping us alive at the moment," Kat countered. "The future or not future of Legacy Inc is not on my radar."

"Liar."

Kat smirked. "Makes two of us. You didn't answer my question."

Mason licked his lips and looked over again at the two sleeping. "What are you getting out of this, Kat? He's already dead."

"Survival," Kat answered, indulging the line of questioning. "My name is on that list."

"But you have more than enough to keep you safe." Mason's eyes roved around the room. "And if we stuck with the original plan, you could be flying back to the Caribbean by morning, knowing he's safe, too."

It was as if he'd slapped her, the sudden mention of Shay in this room. "How do you know what you know, Mason?"

"You don't get as far into this life as I have without being beyond valuable. I make sure I am."

"And what about now? As you said, he's dead. What's keeping you here?"

"You first," he said.

Kat sized him up. He dealt in secrets and information, but what she wanted wasn't a secret. "I'm not finished yet. My mother has some sins to answer for." Shay's screams were suddenly clear in her mind, an unneeded reminder of how much damage her mother had caused. "When we get into the Playhouse, my mother is mine. Your turn."

"If we're calling dibs," Mason said, not missing a beat, "Rufus is mine."

Kat raised her eyebrows. "What do you have against Granddad's favorite murder man? I thought you were tight?" There was the tick in his jaw again, the struggle to know if he could trust her—should trust her.

"I would have eliminated him a decade ago if I could."

"Why wait? No one would have missed him," Kat said.

His eye slid to Aeron and Decius for a moment before returning to her. "I found something worth more than killing for—something to live for. But those days are numbered too. Rufus is mine."

Kat met his steel gaze and nodded. "What did he do?"

Silence answered her, but it wasn't because Mason refused to talk—she could see the darkness cloud his face, the memory of whatever terrible event pushed him for vengeance. "He executed my little sister."

Her eyes widened. "You've worked with him," she said softly.

And she realized he was as dangerous as her. "Enough for people to believe you're close friends."

Mason nodded. "And you worked with the monsters who tortured Shay, although I know better to believe you let that go." His eyes wandered around the room. "We're very much alike, Kat. We're in this for the long game."

"Who will go with the techie to Headquarters?" Kat asked.

"Perry can handle it," Mason said.

"So, do we have a plan yet?" Decius asked from the floor. Kat shot a glance his way. Aeron was still out cold, but he was wide awake. What she shared had not been private, but the sudden intrusion jarred her all the same.

"We do. Hungry?" Mason held out a container of ramen, and Decius pushed himself up. He glanced at Aeron for a second and joined them at the table. He opened the container, and his shoulders relaxed as he dropped into his seat. He ate for a few moments, eyeing the compound in front of him. Kat didn't know much about him. He wasn't on her radar before—her main concern was always for Aeron—but Perry spoke highly of him. He moved the compound around, zooming in and out, his brow furrowing, probably cataloging questions for later.

"How many people are on the compound?" he asked. "And where is Luke being held?"

Kat looked at Mason. "I don't know," he said. "When it was fully functioning, a staff of fifteen ran and maintained it. Headcount now? We have Rosemary, Rufus, my contact—"

"Who is your contact?" Decius asked. Mason paused, mouth hanging open. Kat sat back and crossed her arms. If he wouldn't answer her, maybe he would answer Decius.

"I can't—"

"Can't or won't?" Aeron asked. Kat's head snapped in her direction. She was sitting up, wiping a hand over her face.

"Aeron—"

"If we're going in to clean house, we need to know who we're up against," Decius added.

Mason looked between the siblings, his armor cracking with each passing second. They may be his reason for living—but they were his Achilles heel.

"Ramen?" Mason asked, holding out a container to Aeron. She glared at him for a moment, then nodded, joining them at the table. Her color had returned.

"Who is your contact?" Aeron asked again.

Mason glanced at Kat for a moment, his walls cracking as he answered. "Eileen." Aeron's chopsticks halted halfway to her mouth.

"Mrs. Gale is holding Luke hostage?" Decius asked.

"That tracks, actually," Kat added. Luke had just spent a week torturing her. She took another bite of sushi. Eileen Gale was a rumored Alliance member—perhaps there were more of them alive than she knew. "So, you're the one who let her out?" Kat's gaze bore into Mason's. "But you can't trust her?"

"I didn't say I couldn't trust her. I can't compromise her," Mason answered.

"Who is she working for?" Kat demanded, leaning forward. "Surely not my mother?"

Mason shrugged. "Your guess is as good as mine at the moment."

"I fucking doubt that," Kat said. She hated working with outsiders but had no choice if she wanted her mother dead.

"Did you say let out?" Aeron asked, interrupting them. "Let out from where?"

"Interrogation room 4," Mason answered.

"But what does that have to do with Luke?" Aeron pushed.

Decius let out a half laugh, shaking his head. "Because Luke was holding her there. Right?" He looked to Mason for confirmation. "Luke called me to let him out of that room—right before we came to you, Aeron."

"And you didn't think to say something?" she asked.

Decius just glared. The fact that breaking his best friend out of one the most hostile interrogation rooms in the Institute had slipped his mind clued Kat into just how rough the last forty-eight hours had been. And the next forty-eight weren't going to get any easier.

"Why was he holding her there anyway?" Aeron asked.

"I don't know," Mason answered, eyes flicking to Kat. It didn't matter why Luke kept Eileen hostage, and she didn't need to give Aeron any more reasons not to find him.

"So, what, Mrs. Gale is torturing Luke for payback?" Aeron asked. Her brow creased, and she shook her head. "I don't buy it."

"She's got a point," Kat agreed. "Eileen doesn't seem the revengey-type to me."

Mason closed his eyes and sighed. "I don't know that she's even on-site. But I trust her with my life, and if she says Luke is there, he's there." The finality in his tone spoke volumes. It would be how she spoke of Perry's words, and Perry said to trust Mason.

"Okay. So maybe Mrs. Gale. That's only three people," Decius said. "This will be a simple smash and grab."

Kat shook her head. "No. My mother wouldn't go in with Rufus on her own. There's a bigger player involved here." But who? Who would her mother trust? Or fear?

"How many people can your mom actually have working for her? You have Legacy Inc accounted for, right?" Aeron asked.

Kat gave a small laugh. "Stateside." Granddad had branched out to several countries, not many assassins, but enough. She choked on her laughter, and her heart slammed in her chest. What if, internationally, they weren't being paid either? She hadn't thought about how his death would impact the overseas divisions. She pulled out her phone and shot a text to Perry. *Check international pay logs.* Maybe she could skim some money from an international branch to pay the DC assets, or maybe she was about to have an international mutiny on her hands.

Decius looked over at her. "What outposts internationally?"

She tucked the phone away. "Spain, Japan, Ireland, several in the Caribbean and South America." She'd reached out to her international contacts when searching for her mother and came up empty. With the Senior position up for grabs, her mother could be in league with any of them. Kat's head throbbed.

"Your Granddad sent me to Costa Rica to finish my father's assignments," Decius said.

"Your dad wasn't working for Legacy Inc, though—quite the opposite," Mason said.

"So, I was doing Legacy Inc shit?"

"I can look into it," Kat said, "but most likely."

"Well, those people are not. . . There's no conscience to some of them. This one lady—her face was completely scarred on one side—"

Mason's container of Ramen dropped from the table. "Shit," Mason said, grabbing napkins and tossing them on the mess. Aeron reached over and helped clean up the spilled broth.

"Who was this scarred woman?" Kat asked, eyeing the mess of broth on the floor, her lip twitching. She figured blood would be the first thing to stain these floors, not ramen.

"The woman in charge of the outpost. She took no shit from anyone, and I watched her torture more people in twenty-four hours and get quality answers than I ever thought possible. It was impressive, actually."

"Her name?" Kat insisted.

"Amara," Decius said. Kat made a mental note to have Perry check the rosters. She knew almost every assassin in Legacy Inc, but she couldn't place the description or name.

Aeron sat back down, and Masson threw away his container and rejoined the table. "Sorry about that. Where were we?"

"Figuring out how many people my mother has working for her," Kat said. "However, I don't know that it will matter. Mason, how much do you know about the division of labor at Legacy Inc?"

"More than I should," he confessed.

Great. Then she wouldn't have to explain too much. She cleared her empty plate out of the way and zoomed out on the compound. "The area is not only set up for close encounter battle, but it's a fucking booby-trapped maze. Mason, give us the tour."

15

LUKE

The door to the room opened. Luke feigned sleep, enjoying the silence before meeting whoever was there to torture him. They moved to his side, and he heard the removal of the clipboard and the scratching of a pen on paper. They didn't disturb him—but he knew the readings on the screen would tell them he was awake. He stayed in the dark a few moments longer, sleep almost retaking him when the door opened and closed a second time. A hand touched his shoulder and gave a light squeeze before disappearing.

"How's he doing?" the scarred woman asked.

"He's managing—but he's still out." Mrs. Gale said. "How are you?"

"Fine."

"That's a load of bull. You're torturing our best friend's kid," Mrs. Gale replied.

"We both know I'm doing no such thing. Rosemary is the one—"

"Just because you aren't slicing him to pieces, it doesn't mean anything. He'll never recover from this. I could have had him leveled off hours ago. Let me level him off."

"Not yet. Mason did a shit job of prepping him for interrogation."

"I doubt Mason ever thought you would be the one interrogating him."

"Well, I'm not done yet."

"Did you find them?" Mrs. Gale asked. Luke's heart thumped. If the kids were dead—

"No," the scarred woman replied. "It was an empty fucking house, with a mess of a kitchen—like a bunch of goddamn children were playing in it."

His shoulders sagged, but he kept his eyes shut and breathing steady. The children were safe. Kat had gotten them out.

"Kids. . ." Mrs. Gale whispered. "Shit. He probably thought you were asking about the Legacy children. Mason said Luke was hiding the ones he was supposed to be eliminating."

"Luke's been the one eliminating families?" Shock colored her words. "Andrew didn't tell me that."

"He probably didn't know. I just found out last week."

"How did we fuck this up so badly?" the scarred woman asked.

"We didn't fuck anything up. We survived." They fell into silence, and Luke fought the urge to open his eyes and see what they were doing. "Are you ready to level him off?"

"Not yet," the scarred woman repeated. "I need to find them."

"Luke doesn't have your answers. You know that."

"You know, I never wanted this life for them. Mason swore he'd keep them safe."

"He has—more than any of us."

"Lucas is killing children. Aeron and Decius are priority number one across the assassin world. I'm sure Katherine and Perry are not far behind them, as they somehow try to float Legacy Inc while cut off from the finances. And Andrew is dead. How has he protected them? If I didn't know better, I would say he played the long game quite well."

A moment of silence followed the accusation and then a loud slap. Luke snapped his eyes open. The scarred woman whipped her head back to face Mrs. Gale, fire in her eyes. She grasped Mrs. Gale's throat and backed her against the wall, fingernails drawing blood where she dug into the skin. Mrs. Gale glared, not an ounce of fear in her body. "You chose to stay away and run the Alliance. He stepped up and has done a damn good job. Jealousy is an ugly color on you, Maureen."

The air in the room vibrated with tension, but his world tipped upside down. Her eyes, the way his formal name fell off her lips, the kindness she showed him under Sin—this was Aeron's mom. She was alive. The breath left his lungs. The catalyst for his killing of all those people and destroying every relationship he'd ever cherished stood alive and well in front of him. Where the fuck had she been?

Maureen's chest heaved a few times before she released her grip. "I knew we couldn't save them all, but Aeron—I thought we would get her out. What if it's too late?" Maureen asked. She moved to the table by the door and sat down, dropping her head into her hands, not even glancing toward Luke.

"You don't give them enough credit. And Aeron? She put a dagger through Andrew's heart to protect them and then a bullet in Elijah's head—consequences unbeknownst to her, I'm sure. But I don't think she needs you to save her, Maureen. Or any of them."

Maureen looked up. The blood drained from his face when her glare met his wide eyes. "Look who's awake. Sleep well, Lucas?"

He nodded, and a sudden wave of nausea swept over him. He looked at the scar more intently and could see her features just below the surface. Her natural beauty had been replaced with anger and trauma. "Hey, Auntie Moe." The words felt foreign coming out of his mouth. They'd buried her. For a brief moment, there was the smallest of hope his parents would be alive too, somehow miraculously raised from the grave. But he'd seen their bodies burn in front of him.

"I hear you've been killing children."

"Maureen." Mrs. Gale's voice held a note of warning.

Maureen rolled her eyes. "I visited the house in Astoria. It was empty. Who was supposed to be in there?"

Luke didn't fight the Sin—there was no need. The kids were safe, and he had no idea where to find them. "The Legacy heirs. I've been saving them," Luke said, surprised by the words leaving his mouth. But Sin never lied. He had been saving them—as many as possible. A weight lifted from his shoulders. He wasn't a villain.

"Mason told me—that was brave to do, defy your Granddad," Mrs. Gale said. "How many did you end up saving?"

"Eight," Luke said. The appreciation in her voice was something he didn't know he needed; confirmation he had made a good decision out of terrible options. "Eight out of twelve."

He avoided looking at Maureen. She'd been dead for over a decade, but for some reason, he wanted her approval—yet he was afraid he'd see Aeron's disgust on her face. So, he focused on the gray floor instead. "Legacy heirs are a different breed," Maureen said. Her shoes appeared in his line of sight, and he looked up. Disgust did not cross her face—admiration did. She looked at him the way Kat did, with the tiniest bit of pity that he'd had to pull the trigger, but something else, almost reverence for making the hard choice. It was the look that had kept him sane on his darkest nights. "You made the right call—the hard one. But it's not going to matter if we don't find my kids. So where are they?"

Luke licked his lips. He'd been focused on the live women, but his ghosts pulled him to scan the room. So many dead he didn't remember killing—but the dead were simply coming to him now. He spotted Mr. Seward to his right, leaning against the wall, a foot propped up and a glass of whiskey in his hand. He met Luke with an unwavering gaze and quirked his eyebrow.

"I don't know," Luke said, his lower back beginning to ache again, the pain surpassing his ability to think and shooting all the way to his shoulder blades. He screamed out in pain. "Aeron has a hideout she retreats to in the summer!" The words launched themselves out of him, and he heaved several breaths, trying to breathe through the searing jolt up his back.

"Where?" Maureen demanded. She moved in front of him and grasped his chin, forcing him to look up. Her green eyes swirled with danger, and there wasn't a doubt in his mind she would kill him if Aeron and Decius weren't found. "I will let her level you off, but I need to know: Where are they?"

He didn't need to wrack his brain too hard; the answer fell out. "I only know of the places on the hit list. That is all."

"What about Katherine? Where would she go so Rosemary wouldn't find her?"

The question caught him off guard. "Her secondary apartment in DC or one of the safe houses in New York City."

"Addresses."

He sent a silent apology to Katherine as the coordinates were out of him before he could stop, and Maureen pulled out her phone and walked away. As if summoned by his guilt, his ghosts came closer again, swarming him. Dave stood at the forefront; the bullet hole in his forehead warmed Luke. Some of these dead deserved it —most of them did. Dave leaned forward, pressing his frozen hands into Luke's thighs. The sensation felt like icepicks were being driven into his quads. He gritted his teeth, but the cold raced to his spine, back tensing with each passing second. The lightning pain wrapped his ribs and shoulders.

"*How dare you give her up,*" Dave said. "*You never deserved her loyalty.*"

"You never deserved her mercy," Luke spat back, his body convulsing.

"Luke?" Mrs. Gale stepped toward him, her body melding with Dave's for a moment, but Dave held tight to his legs, and his body trembled harder.

"Beg me for it," Dave said, a hungry smirk on his face. *"Beg me to stop."*

The ghosts weren't real—but the damage the Sin did was. "Please," Luke begged, self-preservation his only thought. "Please stop."

"Stop what?" Mrs. Gale asked.

Luke looked away from Dave. "Dave. . . he's—my legs, my back. I can't move my legs," he realized. "Please make this stop!"

Mrs. Gale looked over her shoulder to Maureen, who was deep in conversation, unaware his ghosts were roaming so close to her. That he was dying right here in this chair. Mrs. Gale shook her head. "Fuck it." She pulled out a single dose of yellow liquid and put it in the PICC line, but her arm was jerked back before she could push it in.

"No!" Maureen and Luke yelled in unison, Luke for a much different reason than Maureen. The syringe tumbled to the floor, liquid squirting out as it landed on the plunger.

"Not yet!" Maureen said.

She was never going to let him go. Tears ran down his face, blurring his vision. He was going to die here at the hand of his parents' best friends. It was almost poetic since he killed so many of their friends.

"Maureen, enough. We're losing him to his dead. They are causing real, physical damage now—I will not let him die."

"No, we won't," Shannon said.

She came from his left, Shaun right behind her. She wrapped her fingers around Dave's wrists, pinning them in place, the ice burning into his femurs, and he whimpered. What if he never walked again? Shaun winked at him and slipped a knife beneath Dave's throat. Dave's eyes bulged for a second before the hot red blood spilled from his neck and pooled in Luke's lap.

The warmth immediately sedated his tremors, and Dave dropped in front of him, the blood staining his pants. He looked from Dave to Shaun, brows furrowed. "Why?"

"You haven't saved her yet," Shaun said, wiping the blood off his blade and returning it to his hip.

Luke looked to Shannon, his body no longer shaking, and then to her mother. "What happened?" Mrs. Gale asked.

"They killed Dave," he said, flabbergasted. He didn't know his ghosts could be friendly. "Shannon and Shaun killed Dave."

16

KAT

"It reminds me of a huge wholesale warehouse, with rooms built off the end of aisles, and some aisles suddenly turning into mazes and torture chambers," Decius said, zooming in and out of the projected model and tracking possible pathways.

"You're not wrong," Kat said. She glanced at the clock on the wall. It didn't matter how much they prepped Aeron and Decius; they would not be prepared for what they were about to walk into. The door opened—Perry arriving right on time. He looked better than she'd seen him in weeks. Well rested, definitely fed, and clean-shaven. Everyone turned to look at him, but his gaze fell on Kat first, and he nodded. He'd gotten the kids to the new safe house in DC without any issues. She let out a relieved sigh. At least one thing was going right.

Decius rose to his feet, and Perry's face lit up. "You're alive!" Perry said, wrapping him in a hug.

"For now. It's damn good to see you."

Perry took the seat on her right. His presence settled the unease in her stomach she'd been ignoring.

"What's the plan?" he asked.

"I was actually going to ask Aeron that." Kat looked her up and down. Perry and Luke spoke of this girl as if her tactical intelligence rivaled her own. Kat didn't know of many people who could keep up with her, and the idea intrigued her. "I'm curious—how would you play this out?"

Aeron met her gaze with unwavering eyes, a look that would drop any man to their knees. Kat smirked, and Aeron adjusted in her seat. "What's my hand?"

"Your knowns: The people in this room. This compound, which is deadly on its own, think Indiana Jones death-defying boobytraps on steroids. An unknown number of mercenaries guarding and patrolling the property. Could be hundreds, could be none. And we don't know Luke's exact location, nor what state he is in. I'd say the likelihood of him surviving the night is less than five percent. Your unknowns: I have three divisions of assassins at Legacy Inc that are unaware each other exists. The entire Legacy Inc resource department is at my disposal—except for money. I'm short on that at the moment."

She sat up straighter, placing her hands behind her head and stretching her chest. "How many in each division?"

"Thirteen."

"What is the acceptable casualty rate?"

Kat raised an eyebrow and shot a glance at Perry. He smirked and answered. "One hundred percent."

Her eyes doubled. "You want them all—"

"Eliminated," Kat said. "Legacy Inc needs a reset." She could see the wheels turning in Aeron's mind.

"Okay." Aeron licked her lips, knee bouncing beneath the table. Kat remained quiet. Aeron may not have wanted to find Luke, but she had a hunger for the game, the same as Kat. The girl hadn't batted an eye at being requested to drop a rescue plan at a moment's notice—even Perry hated when she put him on the spot. "Chaos. We create controlled chaos, just like the Wilks hit," she said toward Decius. "Except this time, we control both sides." She shrunk the compound down in front of them. "Do you have a pen?" Kat slid a stylus to her.

"You said Dr. Shea's outpost is two blocks south?" Aeron directed at Mason.

"Yeah, through this panel," Mason said, zooming in on the rear corner of the building. "You follow the path between the red trailers; it leads to an exit."

"Will he be in-house?" Aeron asked.

"I'll make sure of it," Kat answered.

"Does Legacy Inc use him the same as the Legacy?"

"Division Two does," Mason answered. "The other divisions have their own medics."

"So, we send Division Two through the back—tell them there's a threat on Dr. Shea from this facility."

"Most of those assets have trained here, though," Perry said. "They know the horrors of the Playhouse."

"Then we tell them Underworlders have hijacked the building and have grabbed Luke. He's the next in line—you all do have a code to protect the line, yes?" Aeron asked.

"Not the same as the Legacy," Kat admitted. "It's technically not a birthright to lead Legacy Inc; that's the appeal—anyone can get there. And if they know Luke is vulnerable, they may take him out."

"Even if they believe Mr. Wayward is still alive?" Decius asked.

"You keep giving them souls," Kat said. "They don't have any. They have no qualms with killing anyone who gets between them and a higher paycheck."

Aeron sighed, staring into the Playhouse. "Then the reward for saving Luke has to be higher than the cost of his life. What can you offer them?"

That was not a terrible idea. And if all went well—she wouldn't owe anyone anything. "I've got some ideas. Keep going."

"We send another division through the front, telling them to kill anything that moves."

Kat nodded. That was pretty close to her plan. "I like it."

"How do we keep us alive?" Decius asked. "Aeron and me. With the prices on our heads—there's no way we will make it out if someone spots us. High paycheck and all."

"You get a tracking chip," Mason said nonchalantly.

"Excuse me?" Aeron raised an eyebrow at him.

"Every Legacy Inc asset is trackable through a biometric tattoo on their ribs of a Rook," Kat said. "The ink is infused with nanotechnology, which gives access to vitals, location, and a host of other things."

"The bird?" Aeron asked.

Kat tilted her head and frowned. "The chess piece."

"Oh, that makes more sense. What do you have, the Queen?" Aeron's eyes flitted to Kat's ribs and back up.

"The bloodline doesn't carry a tattoo. But every Legacy Inc asset gets one. It is the easiest way to track them across the world."

Aeron's eyes lit up. "Are there other ones besides the Rook?" The girl was fascinated, and Kat realized she could talk to her all day.

"None you need to worry about," Perry interrupted, annoyance coloring his words. He turned to Kat, his phone out as he waited for her directions. "Do you want the contacts?"

The mission. Luke. Her mother. For a second, she'd forgotten why they were all there. "Yes. We need every advantage we can get."

"Contacts?" Decius asked.

"They are bionic contacts," Perry clarified. "They will connect with the signal coming from the ink to let you know if you are looking at a friend or foe. Your vision will go green if it is a friendly, red if it's a shoot on command—usually anyone without a tattoo."

"That's freaking cool," Decius said, and Kat caught the jealousy in his tone.

"Legacy Inc's technology far exceeds that of the Legacy," Kat said. It was the biggest perk of Legacy Inc.

"But the intellect of the Legacy far exceeds Legacy Inc," Perry added and then looked to Kat. "I've managed to get limited access to the StormLink program. I'll manipulate the code, so we show up green, and everyone else will be kill-on-sight."

"Luke and Rosemary?" Mason asked, standing up and stretching his legs.

"Luke will be locked away or with one of us. And I'll just have to bank on my mother's skill and notoriety to keep her alive a little longer," Kat said. She turned back to Aeron. "How do we breach it?"

Aeron returned to the Playhouse model, faded light trails running through the building and she traced the glass table in front of her. "We send the divisions in, and then we come in through the rooftops to the catwalk above while the carnage ensues." She zoomed in. The main floor was the maze, but above it, Mason had drawn a catwalk designed to watch over the chaos. Kat always wondered how Rufus moved from one end of the maze to another in what felt like an instant.

"Won't work," Kat said.

"Why not?" Aeron leaned forward, elbows resting on the table.

"The rooftop entrances are only accessible from the inside. We can exit that way, but not enter."

"Damn."

"We will go in with everyone else and then hit the ceiling access panels. What about eyes and ears?" Kat asked. "The contacts are useful, but not enough."

Aeron ran her tongue over her teeth, her internal debate clear on her face. How much was she willing to ask of her techie? "He can get us into the controls, but Mason, you secure the control room so no one can interfere with the feed." She looked back to Kat. "We'll need someone to be home base if he's going to touch the vault tonight with Perry."

Asking Dom or Gunnar to come back here after getting them settled in DC was a risk—and a lot to ask. Perry raised his eyebrows. "Your Reaper?"

"I was thinking Dom or Gun," Kat admitted. But bringing Star in would solidify her place in the rebuilding of the institution and would keep her safe. "But that's a better option. Aeron, get your techie to this address." She scribbled coordinates to a safe house in Brooklyn. "Perry will meet him there. What's his name?"

Aeron hesitated. She loved this man, loved him enough that she had to think twice before risking his life to save the other man she'd loved. "Ivan."

Ivan. The name was a disappointment, and she didn't know why. She'd spent six months chasing this man down, and Ivan didn't live up to the hype in her mind. "Let's get to it. We need to be ready to move within two hours."

"So, we're going to war?" Decius asked.

Kat smiled. "We're going to war. Grab your armor vests and cargo pants for this one, kids. It's going to be a doozy." A thrill shot through her. She forgot what it was like to work with people on her level. Dom and Gunnar were amazing, but they had limited knowledge and skill set. And she couldn't live with herself if something happened to them. But working with Aeron and Decius and Mason —it was like working with Griffin again. Her heart skipped a beat, and she shut the thought down, turning to Mason.

She searched his face. He was keeping something from her; she could feel it. "We could use some type of inside man. You have no one?"

"I didn't say that. I have plenty, but not for what you two have planned."

"Could you go in first and negotiate his release?" Kat asked.

"I might not make it back out."

"I thought you and Rufus were tight."

"He's not who I'm worried about."

"My mother?"

His jaw tightened before answering. "In a manner of speaking." He sighed. "I'll go in first, but if I don't make it out alive—"

"We don't do that," Aeron interrupted. "You are making it out. We all are."

"Always the optimistic one," he said, smiling at Aeron. But in that look, Kat knew what he was going to say: make sure the Sewards are safe.

"I'll do my best," Kat said. "And I'm trusting you." The words were like sand in her mouth. The people who were supposed to protect her failed miserably, and she'd learned trust wasn't something she could afford—but sometimes it's worth the cost. "I don't have time to deep dive on this Ivan, but if he fucks this up, your life is mine. Not your fucking death—your goddamn life."

He smirked at her, and although it should have felt threatening, it eased her mind to know he knew exactly what was at stake.

17

AERON

eron sat on the blue sofa inside the safe house apartment in Brooklyn, her knee bouncing. Katherine had gone to activate the two divisions, and according to Perry, this scale mission never happened with Legacy Inc. She would need to relay the gravity of the situation for them to be on board because they could say no. But Katherine had sweetened the pot: All who succeeded in this rescue mission would be promoted immediately to the E.A.S.—the Elite Assassin Squad. Pay would be tripled, and they'd have first pick for a position in any overseas location. She seemed confident they would all join. Decius had stayed behind to clear his head—or get some sleep was more likely. He could sleep like the dead when stressed. And Mason was going to retrieve Ivan. She wanted to see him before going on this suicide mission.

"Will you stop that?" the woman on the couch beside her snapped. Star, Aeron reminded herself. Katherine's Reaper—a short woman who looked less like an assassin and more like an aunt who did roller derby. Aeron stood, straightening out her black cargo pants, and took to pacing instead, getting used to the bulkier clothing. This wasn't a pre-planned quick assassination. This was a raid with the real possibility for casualties and no one to help them. So they needed to bring more supplies.

"What do you need, Aer?" Perry asked from the computer in the corner. "I've never seen you like this before a mission."

She wrung her hands behind her back. She'd never been on a mission like this. "I don't know. I just don't feel good about this."

"Good. We shouldn't. There is a good chance none of you make it out."

"What happens then?" Aeron asked. They hadn't talked about the worst-case scenario because, in a normal mission, it was never considered. If you died, the Legacy just kept going. But she'd made a promise to her dad she didn't intend to break. "What would happen with Ivan?"

Perry shrugged and leaned back, crossing his arms. "First, I'll make sure you have extravagant funerals. Then I'll split the payload with him and Star and shut the entire thing down. I'm not running that place."

Aeron gave a short laugh. But that brought up something Aeron had never understood. "Why did Luke get picked over you?"

He scrunched his face. "Granddad didn't have enough leverage to keep me in line."

Aeron's stomach turned. Luke had been nothing but a pawn since his parents died. No. Even before his parents died—when he had to kill Shaun. The door to the apartment opened, and her heart skipped a few beats when she met Ivan's blue gaze. The worried look he wore disappeared, and he broke into a grin.

"Aeron!" He shouldered past Mason and scooped her into a hug, lifting her feet off the ground. She hugged him back, the motor oil and pine scent of Ernie's instantly calming her. He stepped back. "Shouldn't you be strapped up and getting ready to storm the castle?" She raised an eyebrow. "Mason filled me in."

An unfamiliar well of emotion clawed at her chest. Maybe she just wanted to protect him—keep that promise. She'd come to see him off and tell him good luck. But she should tell him that they were going to save Luke and he didn't have to do this. Or tell him she would see him on the other side—one way or the other. But instead, the words that came out were, "Don't fuck this up, Darth."

He laughed. "I'll do my best." He handed her a set of earpieces. "One for each of you. I can get you tapped in with Star having access, but Mase will need to keep the signal clear from the inside and get the camera feed up and running."

"No promises," Mason added. "I might not even make it past the front door."

Aeron caught the flinch on Ivan's face. "Can we just pretend you will make it out?" he asked. "That all of you will?"

"Who's pretending?" Aeron joked and bumped his shoulder. He visibly relaxed. "Perry, this is Ivan."

Perry extended a hand, and Ivan accepted. "You're my own personal bodyguard for the night?" Ivan asked.

"Let's hope I'm just an escort."

"C'mon, Aeron. We've got to go." Mason held the door open for her.

"Be careful," Ivan warned. "You're still not at one hundred percent."

The concern sent a swirl in her stomach. "I'll be above the battle most of the time. You be careful, and don't—"

"—die?" He chuckled. "Yeah. I know. C'mere." He hugged her, his worry pressing into every inch of her being. She squeezed him back, holding on for a moment longer than he did. "Go finish the mission." He pushed her toward the door before she could argue, and she followed Mason without a word.

18

LUKE

"*D*id you say your dead are killing each other?" Maureen asked.

Luke's pulse slowed dramatically. Warmth worked its way up from the pool of blood in his lap to his back. His muscles relaxed. The room was beginning to clear out of the dead. Shaun and Shannon leaned near the door. "Yes," he answered. "What does that mean?"

"Either your mind is starting to fracture and destroy itself, or you're finally fighting off the Sin," Mrs. Gale answered as if one of those wasn't a complete death sentence.

"Either?" Luke asked, his voice rising several octaves. "How do you know which?"

"That's the fun part—we don't," Maureen said, a grin twisting her face. Mrs. Gale picked up the syringe—the liquid half gone. "Go grab another. We'll level him off." Mrs. Gale nodded and disappeared through the door, leaving him alone with Maureen.

She pressed her hands together in front of her, scrutinizing his very existence. How had she survived the car crash? They saw the body—a body. It was so long ago he couldn't even remember what it looked like.

"Where have you been this whole time?" Luke asked.

She quirked an eyebrow at him. "You're asking why I didn't come back," she clarified. He nodded.

She gave a soft laugh, a half-smile somehow darkening her features. "The first year, I was in a coma and hooked up to a ventilator. You can imagine my surprise when I finally woke up. I was in a foreign county, alone, with tubes making sure I stayed alive. The only shock bigger than that was when I finally got a glimpse of this." She waved a hand in front of her face. "I'm not vain—far from it, but I was no longer the woman I was."

Luke licked his lips, taken off guard by her candidness, a complete one-eighty from the woman who pinned her best friend against the wall and drew blood just moments ago. "That accounts for a year. It's been thirteen."

She swallowed and looked away. "It took four more years of surgeries and physical therapy before I could even care for myself. I was like an overgrown child—and just as pathetic." She looked back at him. "By the time I was of any use, Aeron had completed her first kill—and it was too late."

"To come back? Your kids needed you. Your friends—"

"Agreed that staying away was the best option. The Alliance had been disbanded, and those associated paid for their disloyalty with dead family members and a lifetime of fear Elijah would stop having mercy one day, and they would all burn. As far as he knew, the Alliance died with me."

"But it didn't," Luke said. He'd heard whispers of the Alliance—a group of rogue assassins who tried to take down the Legacy Blood. Nothing that ever implicated his parents or any of the original families had anything to do with it. "Mrs. Gale said you run the Alliance." She didn't deny it, but she did look away from him. "Why?"

"If I came back, I would have put our entire operation at risk—I would have put all of you at risk. Your Granddad was nothing if not ruthless." She looked back and smiled at him. "Although I would say you all gave him a run for his money, and boy, did he love his money."

Luke couldn't share in whatever she found amusing. They were broken—all of them. Damaged beyond repair. "If you could do it again, would you do it again?"

She moved to check his vitals, not answering. "You are certainly full of questions." She tipped his chin up, tilting it side to side. "Looks like you broke through it."

He did feel better. His urge to spill his every thought no longer strangled him, his bones didn't ache, and his dead didn't call to him. "How long will it last?"

"Hard to tell. Rosemary was trying to kill you with that dose. But if you can keep your heart rate down, we can have it cleared out of your system in a day once the serum is administered."

"And if I can't keep my heart rate down?"

"Do you feel that pressure in your spine? Not the chair. The pressure." He swallowed and closed his eyes, feeling out his body, something he hadn't done in ages. They used to meditate for hours —he couldn't even think of the last time he slept that long, forget about meditating. He traced the muscles down his spine with his mind until he found a growing pressure that touched between his shoulder blades. He opened his eyes and nodded. "That is the neurotoxin infecting your spinal cord. Once it reaches your brainstem, you're dead. Even if you can't feel the effects right now, it's still climbing. But as your blood pressure rises or your emotional state becomes compromised, the pain will return—doubled. It will race to your brain. Without the serum, you'll be dead in hours."

Luke took several long breaths, tapping his toes in his shoes to track his heartbeat, but it began to climb again. And as his heart raced, the dead appeared. He needed a distraction.

"Why didn't you kill Rosemary?" Luke asked. "I mean, if you knew I would cooperate, why not kill her?"

"I owe her."

"It must have been a huge favor."

"You can't even imagine," Maureen said, not elaborating.

The room fell dark, and the hair on Luke's neck stood on end. Emergency lights clicked on from above the door, and an alarm sounded outside as if the compound had been breached.

"What the hell?" Maureen moved to the wall, pressing on it. A dark panel lit up, revealing a screen. It took only a few moments for her to pull up the security cameras. Luke scanned the nine mini screens that popped up, all of them changing between several cameras every few seconds. He saw a large warehouse in the center of the compound, where most of the figures on the screen were headed. A group approached a smaller building in the front, and several ran along. . . were those shipping containers in the back? The door pushed open. Luke eagerly looked for Mrs. Gale with the first dose of serum. She entered with Rufus—no serum in sight.

"We have a situation," he said.

"Obviously," Maureen responded. Luke chuckled, and Maureen turned on him, eyes flaring and all traces of the woman he'd just spoken to disappearing. She radiated power and violence. "Shut it. Your parents are already dead; adding you to the grave won't weigh on my conscious at all. Will you shut him up?" She directed to Mrs. Gale.

Mrs. Gale nodded, picked up an oxygen mask from the side of him, and pressed it to his face. "Wait," Luke said, moving his head as far away from the oxygen as possible. "Where is the serum?"

"I can't," she said. "The recovery protocol is specific. If we miss a dose, we can't save you. And we need to handle whatever this is first."

"What is the problem?" Maureen asked, looking up at Rufus. He seemed to shrink under her gaze.

"Legacy Inc has breached the perimeter." Luke's chest swelled with hope. Kat was coming for him. He didn't kid himself for a second that she would have come to save him if he wasn't the Senior Assassin and the only one with access to the vault and the money. But a win was a win, and he would gladly take it at this moment.

"How the hell did they find him?" Maureen asked.

Mrs. Gale took a step closer to Luke and pressed the oxygen mask firmly on his face. "Just breathe easy."

"I'm not sure, ma'am," Rufus said.

"Where's Rosemary?" Maureen asked.

"She's organizing the assets we have here—but we're grossly outnumbered."

"What defenses does the Playhouse have?" Mrs. Gale asked. Luke took deep breaths from the mask, his mind quieting, the dead retreating.

Rufus' face fell. "None. This was never meant as a stronghold." They fell silent, watching the security footage. "What are they doing?" Rufus asked.

Maureen studied the screens. "Zoom in there." Rufus pulled up the screen. Katherine smiled at the camera and flipped the bird before covering the lens. "Huh," Maureen said with a smirk. "Like mother, like daughter, it would appear." She looked over to Mrs. Gale.

Mrs. Gale smiled. "I remember when we crashed the compound in Costa Rica. We were just as brash."

"And deadly," Maureen said. "We'll need to keep him safe until we can get our hands on her."

"Would you like me to handle her?" Rufus asked, a cruel smile on his lips.

"No. She makes it out alive. You keep Luke safe—no one gets into this room, understand me?" Rufus eyed Luke, and it made his skin crawl.

"Understood."

"Let's go, Eileen. We'll level him off after."

Eileen dropped the mask, and Luke called out before they could leave. "Wait!" The temperature in the room began to fall again, the warmth leaving and the dead coming back. "Don't leave me here!

Don't leave me here with them!"

Maureen frowned. "In your condition, this is the safest place for you." There was a knock on the door before she could leave. Rufus opened it.

"Hey," he said, surprised at who was there.

Mason patted Rufus on the back, the way Luke would Decius, as he stepped past Rufus into the room. Relief washed over Luke. For all the fucked up shit he'd done, Mason would never abandon him. He would make it out alive.

Maureen's voice lowered. "What are you doing here?"

Mason looked from Maureen to Mrs. Gale to Luke. His face twisted in disgust, and Luke's stomach turned. He deserved that look. It was the one he gave himself every time he looked in the mirror. He may have been saving people, but he was still a monster.

Mason pushed past Maureen, but she grabbed his arm and spun him back toward her. "What are you doing here, Mase?"

"Pleasure to see you too, Maureen." He dipped his head. "I'm here for Luke." Luke's eyes doubled. Mason had known all along that Maureen was alive?

"I don't think so."

"I wasn't asking."

"No," Maureen said.

Mason gave a short laugh. "I was sent in to negotiate for Luke. However, there are about thirty Legacy Inc assets breaching the perimeter as we speak with a kill-all order. Give us the Senior Assassin, and I will let you live."

Maureen glared at Mrs. Gale. "Not in for the long game, huh?"

"Mase," Mr. Gale said. "Are you serious?"

He glared at Maureen but spoke to Rufus. "Can you give us the room?"

Rufus scanned the room once and nodded. "I'll be just outside."

"Luke, are you doing okay?" Mason asked, looking past Maureen. A knot lodged in Luke's throat, and he nodded, words refusing to form for him. The room began to dim again. No—that was his consciousness. He looked over to Mrs. Gale, his head drooping. It hadn't been oxygen in the mask—it had been a sedative, and he fought to stay awake.

Mason waited until the door clicked shut before he spoke, but when he did, his voice was filled with venom. "You want to talk long game? I have spent the last thirteen years doing nothing but waiting. I've catered to the establishment that killed my family. I've befriended the man who executed my little sister. I traded my vengeance, every day to raise your children and protect them while you hid away—terrified they would hate you when they find out what you did to their sister. And I would do it again."

"How fucking dare you," Maureen said, seething.

"I traded her life for yours once before. Don't think I won't do it again."

The color drained from Maureen's face, and Mrs. Gale gasped beside him. "What did you say?" Maureen's voice was barely a whisper, and Luke leaned forward to hear.

"How do you think I managed to keep her alive?" Mason asked. "To win that favor with Senior we so desperately needed?"

Realization graced Maureen's face. "You never expected me to walk away from that car crash."

Mason smirked. "If we weren't at the wrong place at the right time, you wouldn't be here. But right now, all that matters is we need Luke out of here alive. So tell me, what's more important: Your kids or your Legacy?" Maureen lunged for Mason. They collided in the middle of the room, and Luke fought against the darkness. Mrs. Gale joined the fray, but he couldn't tell who was helping who. His eyes refused to stay open, the noise of the fight the only thing he could hear until a sudden shot went off, and the darkness took him.

19

AERON

"How's your side?"

Aeron looked at Katherine sitting next to her on the wall surrounding the Playhouse. Their legs dangled off the side, and their breath rose in puffs of smoke in front of them in the cold night while they waited for Mason's signal. "It's fine," Aeron said. The physical pain had become like emotional pain—if she could stay distracted and get her adrenaline pumping, it wouldn't bother her right now. And right now was all that mattered.

"Still infected?"

Aeron shook her head. "The antibiotics are working. It just doesn't want to close. Once we have Luke back, it'll heal properly. I don't think chick fights and deadly rescue missions are recommended after being shot." She could feel Katherine's smirk beside her.

"I really hope we all make it out alive. I like you, Aeron."

Aeron smiled. It was the nicest thing Katherine had ever said to her. "Thanks."

"I've never trained with another woman who was on my level before. I've always been the lone wolf in my family, but this is refreshing. Don't get me wrong, my mother is smart, but we're different creatures. She is short-sighted at times—and selfish. It makes her predictable and easy to manipulate."

"But not you," Aeron said.

"No. I've been planning this vengeance for years against my granddad and mother. You unknowingly stole one—I forgive you, by the way. But I will die getting the other."

"Thanks. And that sounds a little short-sighted yourself," Aeron countered.

"We can agree to disagree," Katherine said.

"I don't want to pretend I could imagine the pain they caused you, the damage she's inflicted on you. But, Katherine, he's dead. And she's running. You could be leading Legacy Inc. You should take the fucking crown."

She didn't say anything, and Aeron let the silence descend on them. She couldn't imagine anyone having as much hate in their body as Katherine did for her mother. If she had another moment with her own—but her mother wasn't a murderous assassin who manipulated her entire life.

Static came through the earpieces, and Katherine straightened beside her. "Last room to the left," Mason said, followed by a high-pitched screech in her ear. Aeron ripped the earpiece out, Katherine doing the same beside her.

Katherine tentatively put hers back in, and her face scrunched in anticipation. "Repeat?" Aeron waited, not putting hers back in— her ear still ringing. But she didn't want to know what she'd just heard. If Mason was dead, then how the hell would they survive? Her heart pounded, and she sucked in a few steadying breaths. Dead or not, they couldn't turn back now.

"Repeat?" Katherine said again beside her. "Shit." She pocketed her earpiece, and Aeron followed suit. "Looks like we're going in deaf and blind." She stood up, reaching a hand down to Aeron. "Ready to go?"

Sweat rolled down Aeron's neck, the lights of the Playhouse blinking on and off around her. Bodies littered the floor. Most were from headshots, some from precise blade work, and some from the archaic boobytraps set throughout the maze. They all rested in a haze of red in her left eye. It'd taken some time, but she learned to look through the flashing colored alerts.

The layout of the Playhouse had been altered. Without Mason in the security room, a way to communicate, or a workable map—they were fucked. She needed to get to the catwalk, but finding the ceiling panels had proved difficult. Ivan hopefully had better luck than them.

She scrunched her nose and stepped past a smoldering body. The wall above it was singed, the flamethrower still lit within it. According to Mason, most of the boobytraps were single-use. Rufus loved the idea of resetting the traps each time. Thankfully, most had been set off by the Legacy Inc assets before they entered.

The door to her left creaked open, and she spun, gun raised, coming face to face with Decius. A green haze surrounded him. He had a cut across his cheek, and his face was flushed with adrenaline. They nodded and lowered their weapons, and a wave of relief rushed through her.

"This isn't the same layout," he said with a humorless laugh. "Where's Katherine?"

Aeron shook her head. They'd lost track of each other as soon as they'd entered the darkened building. "Any luck finding the access panels?"

Decius shook his head and then looked up. He quirked an eyebrow and fired several shots to create a hole. "There's one." He smirked, and Aeron gave a short laugh. She should have thought of that.

"That's one way," she said. He cupped his hands, and she paused with one foot in them, her grip on his shoulders shaking just a bit. "Ready?"

He nodded, and boosted her toward the ceiling, but the hole

needed to be bigger for them to fit through. She grabbed the edges of the drywall and started pulling. Running steps sounded down the hall. "Get on my shoulders."

Aeron climbed, balancing on his shoulders as someone rounded the corner. She kept ripping at chunks of drywall to make a sizable hole. Dust fell in her eyes, and she swiped it away to see again. Pain seared in her left eye. "Fuck." She squeezed her eye shut and kept digging. Decius took aim and fired. He missed, and the slide locked out.

The man sprinted toward them. Decius reached up, and without a thought, Aeron dropped her arm down, releasing a throwing knife. It slid from Aeron to Decius' palm and then sailed directly to the throat of the man. He jerked to a halt, hands clutching his neck, then dropped to his knees. Aeron returned to the ceiling. She'd opened a spot large enough for her to climb through and could see the edge of the catwalk above.

"I see it," Aeron said, grabbing onto the metal walkway, her shoulders and vest catching on the drywall as she pulled herself up. Once on top, she laid on her stomach and reached down for Decius, who had already field-stripped the bodies for weapons and ammo. He passed a Glock and magazines up to her and then backed away, giving her a smile.

"What are you doing?"

"I'm going to double back. Go save Luke." He disappeared before she could argue. She was getting really tired of that assignment. She rolled to her back, taking several breaths. Her eye burned, and she licked her fingers clean and pulled out the contact.

"Shit." The small lens sat on her fingertip with a rip right through it. She let it fall to the metal flooring and pulled herself up slowly. Her side ached, and she didn't need to look—she'd reopened the wound. If they all made it out of this alive, she was going to shoot Luke on principle.

The grated catwalks covered the entire space in a perfect grid, crisscrossing the building—except for a large square space further down the walkway: an observation deck to the bullpen. The inter-rogation room holding Luke was on the back wall. Aeron picked up the Glock and magazines, slid the extras into her cargo pockets, and ensured she had a round in the chamber.

The catwalk creaked beneath her steps, and she slowed near the observation deck and looked over the edge at the glass ceiling. There were two entrances to the bullpen across from each other, each with tables on either side of them. From this angle, she counted ten bodies sprawled in pools of blood, with Rosemary and an unrecognizable woman in the center of the wreckage. The tension was visible between the two, and Aeron wished she could hear what they were saying. The woman shook her head, and Rose-mary looked like a woman pleading her case.

A chill raced through Aeron, and she resumed her hunt for Luke. She spied ladders hanging off the side of the catwalk at the back wall. Last room to the left, Mason had said. She moved to the corner ladder and saw the access panel directly below. Her palms slipped on the metal handles as she lowered herself, and her stomach flipped. Balancing on the bottom rung, she squatted, gripped the handle, and froze. What if he wasn't there and instead she met a room full of hostiles? What if he was in there and refused to go anywhere with her?

She swallowed the fear in her throat. No matter what was below, she needed to find Luke and get him home. She yanked hard. The door swung open more easily than she anticipated, and she leaned back, hanging off the ladder—but no shots came her way. Moving with care, she peered into the room. It was dark, painted black, and she could see emergency lights glowing faintly. The access panel sat against the edge of the wall, and she had to lean in further to see the entire space.

The back of his head was the first thing her eyes landed on, followed by his wrists tied behind a metal chair with an IV kit and vitals monitor working beside him. And he was alone. She lowered herself into the room, dropping to a crouch for several seconds in case someone moved out of the shadowed corners. No one came. "Luke?" she whispered. He didn't respond.

She looked closer. His head was tilted forward, and his fingers limp behind his back. He was out cold—or dead. The thought jumpstarted her adrenaline, and she rounded to the front and dropped to her knees, catching sight of the monitor tracking his heart rate beside him. His face was lax, a sleeping form amongst the chaos. She'd loved watching him sleep, the stress of life unable to touch him in those moments. Emotion welled in her throat, and she sniffed, blinking away tears that couldn't be shed right now. How had he ended up here, lying to her, selling his soul?

Muffled gunshots sounded in the hallway. She needed to wake him up. "Luke." She shook his shoulders. His head lolled to the side, but he didn't wake. "C'mon." She tapped his cheek. "Luke. Get up." Nothing. "Fine." Aeron reeled her hand back and slapped him as hard as possible across the face. The sound echoed in the room, Luke's cheek instantly reddening. Instead of guilt, she felt good. She laughed, her anger and frustration wanting another hit. She pulled her hand back again when a small groan left his lips. She paused.

Luke's eyes fluttered open, and he looked up at her with hooded eyes. "Oh no," he said, the words coming out half-slurred. "No. You can't be dead. Shaun is going to be pissed. He'll never let me have a moment's peace."

He wanted to talk about Shaun and peace now? She slapped him again; every ounce of emotion she couldn't let fall down her cheeks funneled into her hand. His eyes popped open, and his head snapped up. "Fuck, that hurt."

"Good. Hold still. I'm going to get you out of here." She undid the restraint on his wrist, and his shoulders slumped forward, a moan leaving him. How long had he been stuck like that? She passed him a lock pick, and they each worked on an ankle in silence. Then with quicker fingers than she expected, she disconnected the IV running to the PICC line and capped it closed. She needed to secure the tubes from snagging on anything. A glance around the room showed nothing useful, and then she slapped her hand to her forehead—the medical tape inside the fucking cargo pants. It took only a minute to dig it out and secure the two hazards hanging off his arm.

"Let's go."

He pushed himself up but immediately dropped back into the chair. "Damn it. My legs. Aeron. . ."

She looked over her shoulder at the door and back at him. The emergency door would be straight down the hall, past the bullpen —a straight shot. Only the hallways lining the bullpen and the bullpen itself were what they needed to worry about. "We don't have far to go. C'mon." She helped him up, throwing his arm across her shoulder. She gritted her teeth against the pain in her side and hated how comfortable it felt to have him leaning on her at the same time. He took a few tentative steps, the strength returning as he utilized the muscles. As soon as he could hold his own weight, she stepped away—she didn't want to be with him or around him— yet he was everything she knew and loved.

"Follow me." She checked the Glock one more time, the weight heavy in her hand. She grasped Luke's hand with her free one and cracked the door, peering down the hallway. She could hear agonizing screams from the bullpen, but the main hallway looked clear. He stepped into the hall behind her, his body movement erratic, like he was trying to avoid touching the air as they headed toward the exit, slowing them down. "C'mon." She tugged on his hand. "We have to move."

They made it two doors down when the wall beside her exploded. Aeron turned and threw herself on top of Luke, landing chest to chest. She raised the gun and fired once toward the first hallway, unable to see where the threat was. She kept her head low, straining to see down the darkened corridor. Their breath mingled, and she held back a gag. He smelled awful. His bloodshot eyes widened with their sudden contact, and he tried to press himself away from her into the ground. Whatever Rosemary had been doing had him by the balls. "Fuck."

A muzzle flash from the hall caught her eyes, and then a searing pain raked down her arm, the bullet grazing her tricep. Aeron screamed in frustration. She was really tired of being shot. Without looking, she fired three rounds. She reached up and grabbed the handle of the closest interrogation room and gave silent thanks as it turned beneath her hand. Gripping Luke by the collar, she hauled him into the room and shut the door. She leaned against it and closed her eyes.

Logistically, all Legacy Inc assets should have eliminated themselves. Which meant Rosemary had a small army of her own. It didn't matter. The exit was so close; she just needed a new plan. She looked at Luke. He stood frozen, eyes bulging, and his breathing labored. Aeron looked around the room, but it was completely empty. Not even a chair, so the catwalk was not an option. Plus, she didn't know how well he could run the rooftops out of here. But taking him through the labyrinth of hell didn't sound too promising, either. He'd have to stay here, in the empty room, where at least he couldn't hurt himself.

"Luke." She waited for him to acknowledge her. It took a good fifteen seconds before he could pull his eyes away from the corner to her. "I'm going to leave you here, where it's safer—"

"No!" He stumbled toward her, dropping to his knees. "Please don't leave me like they did."

"Rosemary is being handled by Katherine."

"No, your mother and Mrs. Gale," he said, a sob catching in his chest. "They just left me there in the dark, chained to the chair. I don't want to be alone with them. They're trying to kill me."

Your mother. The words ripped at the fresh, raw wound inside, and she swallowed around the lump rising in her throat, the urge to slap him again tingling in her palm. He was high as fuck, she reminded herself.

She grasped him by the shoulders, guiding him to his feet and then toward the darkened corner behind the door. It would give him a second to respond if anyone came in. She pushed down on his shoulders, and he sat. She squatted in front of him. He looked terrified, sweat dripping down his face, but he shivered as if stuck out in an ice storm. Her hand hovered next to his cheek, and she realized it wasn't all sweat—he was crying.

The swirl of anger and pity fought inside her, for him, for her, for the innocent lives they'd destroyed. None of it would matter if he died here tonight. She ran her thumb across his cheekbone, wiped the tears away, and then kissed his forehead softly. "Just wait here," she said, closing her eyes and stuffing the swirling pains away to deal with another time. "Don't move. I'll be back when I clear the hallway."

He nodded, eyes on a spot just over her shoulder.

"Luke!" She grabbed his chin, forcing his eyes on her. "Did you hear me, Lulu?" His eyes were dilated. He wasn't seeing her at all. He twitched again, scurrying away from an invisible threat to the right. "Let me hear it," she said. "Stay here."

"Stay here," he repeated, the glossiness in his eyes completely in control. Aeron released his chin and hoped whatever terrified him kept him pinned to that spot as she raced toward the hall.

20

KAT

Kat smiled as she looked down another hallway, spying two more dead bodies hazed in red. The carnage in the Playhouse was unbelievable. Their plan had worked flawlessly. She'd stopped checking for Legacy Inc identities after the first twenty bodies and easily passed at least twenty more. Now she just looked for the haze of red around the body marking it as assets or an unknown to make sure she didn't stumble across Aeron or Decius dead in the bunch.

She was close to the bullpen now, some deeply buried feeling of familiarity tugging her along the way. The lights dimmed as she turned down the next hall, no longer sneaking around. Her eyes adjusted, her gaze running over the bodies: red, red, red, red, green. No. Heart slamming into her chest, she hurried forward. The green haze surrounded a body propped against the wall.

The head turned in her direction, and Decius nodded, a slight upturn of his lips. "These contacts are the coolest fucking thing ever. I didn't even think about shooting you."

"All good until you lose your fucking chip and become a target," she replied. "Are you alright?" She slowed her pace and looked down at him. Three bullets punctured the front of his vest.

"Yeah. Just the wind knocked out of me." He patted his chest.

Kat nodded and extended her hand, pulling him to his feet. "Where's Aeron?"

He pointed up. "She should be to Luke by now. I was clearing out as many stragglers as I could on my way there."

"You're in the right direction, at least. C'mon." They moved forward in silence. Kat felt the shift in the hall behind them. "Move!" She slammed Decius into the wall, and a blade whizzed past her ear. She looked back, but before she could aim her weapon, the assailant dropped to the ground.

Decius pushed off the wall, forcing her to step back. He held his Sig up between them and flashed his teeth with a smile. "You're welcome."

She rolled her eyes but smiled anyway. "You're welcome." They backtracked, taking a look at the woman on the ground.

"This isn't one of your guys."

"Was it the flying knife that gave it away?" Kat knelt beside the woman. Decius' bullet entered through her neck, and blood trickled around her head and shoulders. Kat grabbed the collar with her fingertips and gingerly pulled it down but saw no markings. She checked her wrists—clear.

"Any idea who she belongs to?" Decius asked.

"No." Kat pulled up the side of the dead woman's shirt, and Decius helped her undo the armored vest. They rolled the woman to her side, exposing her ribs where Legacy Inc assets were marked. "Well, that's interesting." On her side was not just a rook, but the Legacy Inc rook embellished upon the handle of a dagger. It stretched down her ribs, the blade outlined in black with scrawling blue script inside. She leaned closer, trying to make out the inscription on the blade. "Flectere Si Nequeo Superos, Acheronta Movebo."

"Wait." Decius grabbed her wrist before she could drop the shirt. "She doesn't belong to you?" Kat didn't dignify him with an answer and stared. He bit his lip before continuing. "'If I cannot move heaven, I will raise hell'. There was a handful of, well at the time, I thought they were Legacy, but Legacy Inc assets with that same tattoo in Costa Rica. Including Amara. I thought it was strange—we're not allowed to have markings. But I was also deep in my father's shit at the time and didn't ask any questions. Plus, until a few days ago—I didn't know Legacy Inc existed. So tell me, who are we actually at war with?"

"That is a fantastic question." She dropped the shirt and stood. So, Amara rocked the same tattoo. Dom had come up blank in his quick search for her, and she hadn't had the chance to track down Griffin to ask. "When we get out of here, I need you to brief me on that mission. I can't find a record of it anywhere, and we don't have an active compound in Costa Rica."

Decius' eyes widened for a moment, and then he nodded. "Of course. Which way are we going?"

"Bullpen is straight ahead. I'm checking the security room, maybe get an idea of what happened to Mason, and find my mother. Luke will be in the next hallway." They moved as a unit, scanning for threats and stepping over bodies. Too many to be just Legacy Inc, and now she knew why. A hand gripped her ankle, and she nearly tripped. Decius's arm shot out to steady her, and he administered a kill shot to the head without even looking down, his eyes on her.

"You good?" he asked.

She nodded, pulling herself free from him. He'd moved without hesitation, the clear loyalty to her and their mission not missed. And he was kind. At that moment, she understood why Luke and Perry would do anything to save the Sewards—they were worth saving.

The entrance to the bullpen was on the left, and they paused just outside the door frame. "That next hallway is interrogation," Kat whispered. "To the right is our exit." Decius peered past her, then nodded.

"The red door," he confirmed.

"Yes. To get Luke, go left down the hall, pass the bullpen, and then all the way to the end. You'll find Luke and Aeron—I hope."

She peered into the main room. It was empty, except for the dead. Where the hell was everyone? "See you on the other side," Kat said and stepped inside. She'd almost been killed the last time she'd been near this room. She turned and looked back at the entrance, realizing it was the exact spot Rufus had stood waiting for her to die. The haunting memory of the wolf chasing her toward the bullpen wound around her, and she swallowed hard, unable to push it away.

Her feet slid out from underneath her, the blood pooling and slowing her race to the bullpen. If she could get to the bullpen, outrun the feral wolf and get to Rufus, he would call them off. Sharp teeth grazed her calf. Kat cried out, running faster, not looking back. She could hear the nails on the floor behind her and feel the blood running down her leg.

The bullpen was mere feet away. The wolf's teeth struck again, and Kat fell to her side just outside the entrance. She met Rufus' hungry gaze as he stood inside the doorway. The wolf pounced, and she screamed in terror. "Call it off!" she begged.

Rufus rotated the metal chain around his fist and shrugged. She hadn't made it into the bullpen, so he wasn't going to help her. Kat framed against the wolf's neck to keep its jaws from closing around her throat. Her arms were shaking, her torso screaming in pain where the nails dug into her flesh. "Rufus!" she cried. "This isn't funny anymore!" She'd glanced over at him, but his eyes were focused on the wolf, running his hand down that stupid chain like a security blanket. He couldn't hear a word she said.

The hot breath filled her every sense. Saliva sprayed from the starving wolf's mouth, soaking her arms and face. She was going to die as a fucking wolf's dinner. "Please!"

The wolf yipped and retreated from her. She bolted upright, thankful he'd changed his mind, when Perry raced toward her, gun in hand. The wolf dropped to its side, whining. It looked at her as if she'd betrayed it— when all it wanted was a meal. Perry dropped to his knees at her side.

"Fuck, Kat, are you okay?" He checked her legs for bites, but they were minimal grazes. She pulled up her ripped shirt, the punctures to her abdomen were painful but superficial—she was fine. Yet she couldn't take her eyes off the wolf. This majestic animal had been starved and tortured. It was like her—a prisoner in someone else's game.

"What are you doing here?"

The wolf vanished from sight, and Kat spun around, her heart lurching into her throat. She'd buried that night because she never thought she'd return here. The wolf had led her back to the bullpen.

"Hello, mother." Kat shook the memory, burying it one more time.

"Is this your doing?" She waved her hands in the air. "Attacking the Playhouse for Luke?"

"No." Kat shook her head and moved closer. "I'm not here for Luke."

Her mother scoffed. "Katherine, we need to go. Whatever scheme you've come up with, it won't work. You have no idea what you're up against."

"Tell me," Kat indulged. She pulled a knife from her waistband, slipped her finger in the circle grip, and spun it around. "What am I up against?"

Her mother eyed the blade. "There is an entire sect of assassins you know nothing about."

"The ones in Costa Rica?" Kat guessed. She should have known her mother was double-dipping—or was it triple-dipping at this point? "What did they promise you to take Luke? Money? Power?"

"Your life," her mother answered.

The blade halted in Kat's hand, and she cocked her head to the side. "I find that hard to believe. You have to actually care about something for it to be of value."

"Believe what you will. But we need to leave."

"Who are they? The ones with the daggers down their side?" Kat asked. She'd climbed too high to run now. And Aeron was right.

She wanted her mother dead, but Kat really wanted the fucking crown.

"Those belong to the Alliance."

Cold traced its way through Kat. "The Alliance? I thought they were dead."

"Oh, they're harder to kill than you think. If you're not coming with me, fine. But I'm leaving." Her mother brushed past her, and Kat caught her arm.

"Like fuck you are. As I said, I didn't come here for Luke."

The realization crossed her mother's face. Kat swung, her elbow connecting with her mother's nose. It crunched beneath the force, and Kat smiled at the blood, fueled to keep going. She swung again and again, her mother blocking. A kick to Kat's torso pushed her back, and the breath left her. "Ugh." Her mother pounced, and it was like being in the training room when she was a teen. No mercy. Each blow landed with full power, each kick nearly bringing Kat to her knees—except she wasn't afraid of her mother anymore.

Kat rotated the blade in her fist and slashed, the metal slicing into her mother's forearm. It was her turn to suck in a breath, and Kat struck again. Each slice was barely a portion of the pain Shay had suffered. Kat was going to drag her into one of the Interrogation rooms and see how long her mother would last.

She kicked again, backing her mother into the wall. "You are going to feel every ounce of pain you've ever dished out."

Her mother smirked, eyes sliding over Kat's shoulder. Before she could turn, a hand grasped her hair and yanked. Kat fell, her body dragged backward, the sound of metal on the cement floor close to her. Her heart rammed into her throat. She secured her free hand to the assailant's wrist and sliced with her knife across the arm that held her. Hot blood poured down her face, but the pressure released. She scrambled to her feet and came face to face with Rufus.

"Welcome back, Red."

"Don't call me that," she spat, eyeing the chain he looped casually in a circle.

"I'm told you are to make it out of here alive. No one specified in what condition," he said, malice dripping around the words as he advanced. Kat held her ground. Rufus was many things: dangerous, violent, and ugly. But he was predictable. He swung the chain, and Kat stepped toward him, framing the swinging arm, and then latching on. She took a circular step back, planted her foot, and dropped her shoulder forward. Rufus flew over her and slammed onto the ground. The floor vibrated beneath them, his arm still securely in hers.

But her confidence was overshot. A drop like that would have knocked the wind out of anyone—but it didn't faze him. With pure strength, Rufus yanked her forward. She tripped over him and rolled, landing on her back. He rose to his feet, the chain still in hand. Kat swallowed the fear that wanted to surface and bared her teeth instead. "I have no issue with you, Rufus. This is between me and my mother."

"I'm not going anywhere," he said.

Her mother held a hand out to her. "You know a losing fight when you see one, darling."

Kat glared and refused the hand, pushing herself up. "What do you want? He said you didn't want me dead. I promise I don't extend the same courtesy to you."

"So much anger," her mother said, and Kat saw a small ounce of sadness cross her features. "I've done the best I could for you."

"You destroyed me," Kat snapped.

"I made you stronger." She had the audacity to look proud as if abandoning and trading her daughter's freedom for her own would win her mother of the year.

Kat scoffed. "Fuck you." She felt the shift in Rufus behind her and turned in time to see his foot connect with her chest. The air ran from her body, her ribs crying as the force propelled her backward, and she landed on her ass. She tried to suck in a breath, but her lungs weren't ready yet. She tried to relax her ribcage to get air before he pounced. He didn't move; he just stood above her, glaring down.

"What, are you fucking my mother or something?" Kat asked, catching her breath.

"Or something," her mother answered. "Get up. I have something to show you."

"If I'm going anywhere with you, one of us will be in a body bag."

"Enough," her mother scolded, brow furrowed. And for a moment, Kat felt ten years old again, being told to sit down and be quiet, to stop making things a big deal, to just go along with it.

Kat bolted to her feet, anger drowning out the grief that wanted to surface. Her mother may have taught her to fight, manipulate, and use people, but she also taught her to be quiet and obedient. It wasn't until Kat met Shay that she understood how powerful she was and how much her voice mattered. It wasn't until those secluded months in the Caribbean that she learned that love wasn't supposed to hurt—and that her mother never held an ounce of it for her.

"Yeah, Mom. Enough." Kat retreated a few steps, keeping both of them in view, and pulled her blade back out. "You know both of us aren't making it out of this building alive." Her eyes shifted to Rufus, and with a flick of her wrist, she sent the blade flying. It found purchase in his shoulder. She had been aiming for his heart, but it would do.

He stumbled, and she charged. Using his body as a running ramp, she stepped on his bent knee, then his quad. His body leaned back, and she stepped on his sternum, riding him down to the floor like a fallen tree. Kat dropped one knee to his chest and pinned his head to the ground with the other to keep his face away from the knife. She wrapped her fingers wrapped around the handle and twisted. She could feel the muscles and tendons tearing beneath the blade, but it seemed to do nothing to him as he reached up and grabbed her by the waist, tossing her to the ground.

"You little bitch," he growled. Maybe it had done something. She rose to her feet again, breathing harder. The punch landed before Kat even saw his hand rise. Her head rocked backward, and she stumbled into a table. He reached out, his hand encasing her throat. "I may not be able to kill you, but I will bring you to the brink of death."

The hand tightened around her neck. She dug her chin down and shoved back into him, her eyes daring him to try harder. He squeezed again and pushed back. It was what she'd been waiting for. She slid her ass onto the table and gripped Rufus' wrist with both hands. He leaned in, and Kat dropped her body to the side and rotated her leg over his head. The force of her hips through his straight elbow rewarded her with a satisfying pop. Two kicks to the face, and Rufus backed away from her.

Kat glanced at her mother and saw a Glock aimed at her chest. "Go ahead," Kat challenged. But Kat already knew she wouldn't. As much damage as her mother had done, she had never physically harmed Kat herself, even in training. She just allowed others to do it. Kat whipped another throwing knife from her waist and threw it. The blade sailed in slow motion, end over end, toward her throat, and for a millisecond, Kat wanted to take it back. It found a home in the left shoulder instead, and relief washed over her. She wasn't ready for her to die—yet.

The gun lowered with the impact. Before Kat could pounce, Rufus grabbed her by the hair again and slammed her to the ground. On a good day, Kat couldn't manage Rufus solo—she thought he would be busy jerking off to the carnage happening in his house. She never imagined him in league with her mother. She tried grabbing onto his hands, but he slammed a knee into her chest, and the air left her. His sheer size allowed him to kneel on her chest and pin her hand above her head. She tried to buck her hips, squirm, or move anything, but it all required oxygen, which had suddenly become scarce. Her ribs bent under his weight, and she stopped moving, conserving what air she could get.

Her mother frowned and came to kneel next to her. She held Kat's dagger in her hand and traced the flat edge down her daughter's sweaty face. Regret danced in the corners of her downturned mouth, and her eyes softened. "You can never understand this, but you were supposed to be my sacrifice, Katherine. Instead, you became my penance. I'm not ready to lose you yet. Please, I need you to calm the fuck down and come with me."

"Lose me?" Kat ground out. "You lost me the day you tortured Shay."

The regret stayed on her mother's face, but Kat saw the switch behind the eyes—not for what she'd done, but for what she was about to do. The gaze moved to Rufus. "She's all yours."

Kat looked up at the vicious smile. "Coward!" Kat yelled as fear buzzed through her body. She would rather fall on her own blade than be Rufus' plaything. "You don't even have the balls to do it yourself."

Her mother held up a hand. "I am no such thing."

Rufus leaned with more of his weight, the pressure doubling, and her ribs bowed beneath him. She looked up and glared, not giving him the satisfaction of hearing a sound from her. A smirk met her, and she resisted the urge to spit in his face.

"I've fantasized about this since the day you left here." He smirked and licked his lips. A chill ran through her. "This will live in my head for a very long time."

"Oh, I wouldn't bet on it," Kat ground out.

"Always a smart-ass remark from you."

Kat cut her glare to her mother and faltered. She had seen that look in her eyes on missions, but never directed at her, and suddenly Kat couldn't take her eyes off the knife. The tip pierced the inside of her elbow, and she sucked in a breath, clenching her teeth together as the blade made slow and agonizing trail toward her shoulder. "It's okay to scream, darling. They all do."

Kat pressed her lips closed. She was supposed to kill her mother. She was going to save Luke and run Legacy Inc. Her mother smiled as if reading her thoughts. "I'm going to take you apart inch by inch—just like I did to that boy. We'll see if you last as long as he did."

The blade dug deeper, and she repeated the movement, hardly a centimeter from the last cut. Fear seized Kat as she realized she might die here. Rufus slammed a hand over her mouth and nose. She widened her eyes and struggled against him. She couldn't breathe; she couldn't think. The blade cut again and again, the pain near unbearable. Her entire left arm shook, and Rufus squeezed her wrists tighter.

"No one is coming for you," her mother whispered. "No one in this world cared for you the way I did." Kat shook her head against Rufus' palm. It was a lie. Perry cared for her. Dom and Gun cared for her. None of them came here with her, though. None of them would be able to save her. She stopped struggling, tears stinging her eyes, and she blinked, letting them fall, the blackness of unconsciousness seeping in. She was alone. She'd come to the Playhouse alone. She would die alone. Rufus released her mouth before the sweet darkness rescued her, and she sucked in a breath. And when the blade cut again, even deeper, Kat cried out in agony.

21

AERON

The hall was clear, except for a single body. Aeron moved toward it, unable to tell if this had been their shooter. The older man was dead—throat slashed—so there was still a threat somewhere. She scanned the area, her gun ready to fire. A commotion echoed from the closest hallway to the bullpen, and she moved closer to figure out their direction.

She ran her thumb over the grip of her gun and dropped her head against the cool wall. The chances of them making it out dwindled by the second. She should have convinced Ivan to run for it. Her heart gave a painful thump at the thought of never seeing him again. What if she died before she got to see Decius one more time?

The sound moved closer—running footsteps headed her way. Before she could retreat, a man rounded the corner running full force. He gripped the edge of the wall for stability and ran smack into her. The Glock flew from her hands, and he fell on top of her. "Fuck," Aeron breathed, clenching her teeth against the pain radiating around her ribs. If the stitches weren't popped before, they sure as hell were now.

He didn't even have the chance to secure her to the ground,

though, as a woman as dark as her father with a curly black mohawk vaulted around the corner. She threw a flying knee at the man's head and dragged him off of Aeron.

They scrambled for a top position, neither paying her any mind. She crawled to her gun, but another woman with dark-cropped hair and her face splattered with blood arrived before she could reach it. Aeron froze, taking notes from the dead man inches away, and lolled her head to the side. The woman glanced at her and then at the two entangled on the ground. Aeron kept her eyes half-cracked open to keep the door securing Luke in sight.

"Quit playing with him, Izz. They've sent more in, and we're running out of time."

A shot went off. Izz stood up, kicking the motionless man once. "I'll grab him." She ran a hand along the purple and green braids on the side of her head and headed for the end of the hall, where Luke had been held.

Dread crept into her veins. They were looking for Luke. Aeron shot a glance at the other woman. She had to be older than Mason —maybe late thirties. She had the confidence and power of an assassin who had been in the business long before she should have been. What would they do with Luke once they had him?

"He's not there," Izz said, coming out of the room. "You're sure she said this one?"

The older woman glared and placed her finger on her ear, and Aeron spotted the earpiece secured for communications. Apparently, not all of them were flying deaf and blind tonight. "He's not there." She fell quiet for a moment, and then, "Yes, ma'am."

More footfalls raced down the hall, and the woman looked behind her. "Check the other rooms; I'll hold them off."

Izz moved into the next room as four more people emerged from the hallway, shots firing. Aeron inched closer to her gun, keeping an eye out for Izz. If she opened the next door, the game was up. The other woman disarmed the four assailants, keeping them occupied with hand-to-hand combat. Izz returned to the hall and glanced at the woman before she moved to the next room where Luke was hiding.

Aeron's fingers brushed the grip of her gun. She couldn't let her open that door. With a lurch forward, she grabbed the gun and fired toward Izz, clipping the doorframe near the handle, then dropped her body back to the ground.

"Motherfucker!" Izz yelled and turned to join the fray with the older woman, not even glancing her way.

The hairs on Aeron's neck stood. With as much stealth as she could muster, Aeron tilted her head toward the other end of the hall. Someone moved in the shadows, crouched low near the wall, and coming right for her. She rolled to her belly and raised the gun again. They froze, hands up in front of them.

'Are you okay?' They signed in American Sign Language.

Aeron gave the slightest of nods. Without her contact, she had no idea who this could be.

'Good. I was going to kill you if you were dead,' they signed, moving closer.

She smiled at her brother and then flipped him off. He was such a dick. He crept to her side, still unnoticed by the group engaged in unnecessary combat. These women were elite assassins. Their outward grace and relaxation in the complete chaos was Aeron's first sign. The shit-talking from Izz was the second.

"You good?" he asked, eyes roving her for any major injuries.

"Yeah. I just needed a nap," Aeron replied, and he smirked. "Luke's in the third room. He's fucked up, badly."

"Bodily?" Decius asked.

"Mentally. He's on something. I told him to stay until I cleared the hall."

"You're certainly kicking ass at that," he said, the returned humor giving her a burst of energy.

"Want to get sushi tonight?" Izz called out to the other woman. Aeron looked over at them. The man Izz had been entangled with spun away from her, blood spurting from his neck. His body fell, and her gaze landed right on Aeron and Decius. The blade left Izz's fingers before Aeron could blink, barreling toward them. Decius parried it with his forearm, and it clattered into the wall, dropping on Aeron. She tensed, and Decius put a hand on her shoulder. "Stay dead a moment," he whispered before addressing the women. "Are you asking me out, Izz?" Decius called, standing up and moving toward them. "I thought knife-play happened after dinner but before the movie."

"Well fuck me raw, Jude. Look who's in the Playhouse," Izz said, a smile spreading across her face.

"Great. Care to lend a hand, or are you just here to look pretty again?" the older woman called. She'd dropped another one of the assailants.

Decius kept his pace slow. "Since when do you need help with some Underworlders, Jude?"

Another man dropped. The last backpedaled down the hall they'd come from. "I don't. You still could have been a gentleman and offered."

"I like my balls where they are, thanks. What are you doing down here?"

"She sent us to retrieve an asset. What are you doing here?"

"Same," Decius said. "Maybe she thought you weren't up for the job."

"Listen, pretty boy," Jude said. "She just has a soft spot for you because—"

Aeron didn't get to hear why someone had a soft spot for Decius. The wall beside him exploded, and Izz dove on top of him, his Sig skidding across the floor. Aeron sat up, ready to pounce, but Izz pushed Decius behind her and fired back down the hall. Seven more attackers rounded the corner. This was insane. Legacy Inc people were surely gone by now, so who the hell were Rosemary's people fighting?

Aeron clambered to her feet, swaying with the sudden movement, and she realized the top of her cargo pants was drenched in blood. She took a few steadying breaths and joined the fray, holstering her gun in favor of blades. Decius nodded to her as he and Izz battled three combatants. Aeron attacked another, who had been heading for Luke's door. She hit him with a series of elbows to the face, his nose and cheekbones cracking under her strikes, then ran her blade across his throat. His eyes widened, and he gripped his neck, blood pouring through his fingers. He let out a choking sound and lowered to the ground. Aeron stepped back, eyes on him until his life had left, and then looked to Decius, quirking an eyebrow.

He lowered his brows and dipped his head down. Great. He wanted her to attack him.

"There are too many!" Decius called out. "What's the plan, Izz?"

"I swear, if this is a fucking test, I'll kill Amara myself," Izz responded.

"Izz, we can't risk him," Jude said. "Decius, can you hold this down?"

"Yeah, no problem." Decius raised his hand—her signal. She pushed into the crowd, past Jude fighting three of them and into the middle of Decius and Izz playing punch-face with the others. She swung on Decius, her fist cracking him across the face. He stumbled back and then returned the strike. She ducked under his arm, moved to his backside, and pushed him forward. A scripted fight that put Aeron safely behind him.

Izz moved in for her, and Decius grabbed one of the Underworlders and hip-tossed him right into her path. She stumbled back and glared. Another man slipped past Decius, his fist nearly connecting with Aeron's face. She fended off the blows, her arms becoming sluggish. He landed a kick to her stomach. Pain encircled her entire midsection, and she tasted the vomit in her mouth. He kicked again, and Aeron grabbed his leg, spinning him around and tossing him into the wall. He smacked his head and fell unconscious. She swallowed back the vomit as he crumpled to the ground in front of Interrogation Room 1.

"Let's go!" Jude moved toward the bullpen, her two remaining opponents on her heels.

"I'm fucking coming," Izz yelled, grabbing her attacker and following Jude, pausing only to give Decius one last look. "Find me after this shitshow, and you'll be saying that tonight." She winked at him and disappeared from view.

Aeron's mouth dropped open, an astonished laugh leaving her. Decius shook his head, giving a slight cough of embarrassment. The man he'd thrown looked up at them. With the lack of commotion in the hall, Aeron took a better look.

"Who do you work for?" Decius asked.

"Joel. Joel Dowers," the man practically cried.

"The trafficker?" Aeron asked. Joel Dowers was a low-level scum to the human trafficking ring in New York. She'd worked with him to get entry the last time she'd done a rescue mission. He wasn't high enough up to be involved in any Legacy or Legacy Inc affairs. It didn't make sense. "Let's just kill him and get Luke out of here." Decius nodded, and Aeron passed her Glock to him.

"No!" the man cried out. "I—" Decius pulled the trigger, the sound echoing in the now empty corridor.

"Don't move!"

Aeron looked up. Luke stood in the darkened hall, Decius' fallen Sig in his hands. Her heart seized until their eyes met: clear, focused. His aim shifted over her shoulder, and she stilled.

"No!" Decius called. Aeron's eyes shifted from Luke to her brother as Decius dove in front of her, and Luke pulled the trigger.

"Decius, no!"

It was too late. The bullet moved in slow motion. Aeron's heart stopped in her chest as it barreled into Decius. His body jerked back, crashing into her, and she tumbled backward. Luke's next shot made purchase in the threat he'd seen behind her, and the three of them landed in a heap on the ground.

"No!" She scrambled to turn him over and check his vest. Decius grunted, and relief flooded through her. He wasn't dead. He grunted again and tried to sit up. "I'm okay."

Aeron slipped behind him, her hands under his armpits to help him sit up, and froze. Thick, warm liquid coated her right palm, and she nearly dropped him. She closed her eyes and took a deep breath. "No, you're not," she managed, her voice calm against the dread building inside her.

Luke stood where he was, his mouth open in a silent scream. "Dee?"

"Luke, I need you," Aeron said. She leaned Decius against her chest and reached around, unstrapping the vest.

"I got it." Luke appeared beside her and tugged the Velcro apart, his fingers turning red as he gripped the panel and pulled. He removed the armor and tossed it aside. Aeron saw three bullets in the front of the vest and looked down, pulling up his blood-soaked shirt. Dark bruising already colored his chest, and she leaned her forehead against his head but said nothing. There would be no telling how much damage was already done before this.

"Fuck me," Decius said as he moved his hand under his armpit where Luke's bullet had struck.

She leaned him forward slightly, and he grunted, blood gushing onto her hand again. She steeled herself and checked his back and other side. "There's no exit." She scooted out from behind him and laid him down on his side. "Sorry about this," she said, and jammed her knee onto the hole to stem the bleeding.

"Goddamn it, Aeron!" he screamed, and she smirked. That was a good sign. She reached into her cargo pocket and dug around for a pair of gloves and a chest seal. She tossed the latter for Luke to open, and she pulled the gloves on. But Luke's hands were slick with blood, and they shook too hard for him to open it. "Gimme that." Decius snatched the package and used his teeth to rip it open, then held the plastic circle out to her.

Aeron moved her knee, and blood poured from the wound. She took the gauze from Decius and wiped at it, trying to clear the area.

"Okay, give it to me." She pressed the first part of the clear plastic bandage to his side and waited, holding her breath while Decius exhaled, then pressed the seal down, smoothing it out the best she could.

"I think that's good," he said, his brow wet. She sighed with relief and stripped the gloves off, tossing them aside. They needed to get out of this hellhole, but now she had two of them to worry about.

Luke sat back on his heels, running a hand over his face. "Dee, I'm—I'm—" but he couldn't get any more words out. What do you say to the best friend you just shot?

"I thought you were one of the assets," Decius said, voice soft. "I looked over, and the contact lens—it was red. Aeron had said you were safe in a room."

"He was supposed to be," she said, glaring at him.

"I know. I'm sorry! Fuck!" Tears streamed down Luke's face again, and Aeron stood, moving back toward the hall, putting space between herself and him. There was only one way out—straight down this hall and past the bullpen. "You should have left me to die here."

"Never," Decius said, grabbing Luke's trembling hand. "We're family. We don't give up like that." Decius's next cough came with a dash of blood, and Aeron and Luke exchanged glances.

"Dr. Shea is two blocks away," Aeron said, moving back to her brother but looking at Luke. "If we can get out the back entrance, follow the red shipping containers, and it's just two blocks down. Can you make it?" The haze had crept back into his eyes, his gaze shifting around the hall, but he nodded. "Good. Let's go."

They hauled Decius to his feet and put his armored vest back on. Luke slipped his arms beneath Decius', supporting him as he walked. Maybe the assassin gods would be on their side tonight. She took the lead, Luke and Decius following. She peered down the first hallway, and not a soul was in sight. "Move," she said, covering the opening as they passed it. Luke covered her back as she bolted across the opening, and then froze. Luke, doing the same as a scream left the bullpen area.

"What is it?" Decius asked.

"Kat," Luke answered for her. Katherine screamed again.

If anything happened to her—how could they guarantee Ivan's safety? Their safety? "I have to help her," she said.

"Aeron," Decius started. She thought he was going to talk her out of it, tell her she couldn't go. Instead, he gave a half smile. "Be careful."

She looked at Luke. "The exit is down the hall. Decius knows the way."

Luke nodded, but she needed to see it—the clarity in his eyes.

"Look at me!" His red eyes stared back at her. The fog was gone, replaced with pain and regret, but he was in control again. "Okay. Tell him Katherine sends her regards." She looked to Decius, his complexion ghostly already. She stroked the side of his face, wanting to memorize every detail. "I love you, Dee. Best big brother ever."

"I'm not going to die, you idiot. It's hardly a hit."

"Decius. . ."

"This isn't goodbye." He reached for her, the sharp inhale the only sound of pain he'd give her, and grasped the back of her head, pulling her forehead to his. Tears burned in her eyes, and she let them fall. There was too much to say and nothing to say all at once. Memories flashed through her head: running around the manor as children; getting underfoot of their parents at the galas hosted by their mom; her mother's laughter, a musical sound she'd forgotten all about until now; the first day at the Institute when Decius made sure no one bothered her—that she didn't get lost; toasting to drinks at Club Sapphire; their father's disheveled appearance after Decius challenged him for head of house; the way his face lit up when he laughed. She wanted to secure every memory in her mind.

He pulled back too soon and kissed her forehead. A sob racked her body, and she nodded. No words were needed. If he died, they would be the last she ever spoke to him; if he lived, they were wasting time they desperately needed.

"Go," she said and sprinted toward the bullpen. Katherine's screams push the pain at her side out of her mind. She skidded to a halt just outside the entranceway. In the middle of the room, a giant man pinned Katherine to the ground, her hands secured above her head, his knee driving into her stomach. Blood covered her face, and a look of pleasure curled his lips as she screamed again. Aeron's gaze moved past him to Rosemary squatting on the other side, pulling a bloody blade down the length of Katherine's arm.

"You're an ungrateful child," Rosemary said once Katherine's scream subsided.

"I'm not a child, and you were a shitty mother," Katherine snarled, sweat dripping down her brow. "If you're going to kill me, fucking do it."

"Oh no," Rosemary said. She wiped the blood from the blade on Katherine's cheek, and Kat turned her head, eyes landing on Aeron. Aeron put a finger to her lips and circled behind the pair while Rosemary continued. "I'm going to leave you in pieces, and no one will be able to put you back together."

Aeron could hear the shudder in Kathrine's breath as she inched into the room, circling behind the man and Rosemary. She didn't have a plan. Her hands shook too hard to trust her long-range accuracy, so giving Katherine an opportunity to run would have to be enough. The man's head snapped around and landed on her, hunger in his eyes. Aeron was only feet from him—it was too late to stop now. She dove for his neck, wrapping one arm around it and swinging her legs toward Rosemary. Aeron connected and yanked the man down to the floor, and the three of them tumbled off Katherine.

Aeron got to her feet and backed toward the other entrance. The man stepped toward her, and Rosemary placed a hand on his arm, a feral smile crossing her face. "Perfect. Two for one. She will regret ever cutting me out," Rosemary said. "Take as long as you can with that one, Rufus."

Aeron swallowed hard. This was the Rufus she'd heard so much about. She was going to die. She was going to be tortured and killed protecting the fucking Waywards. She shook her head and squared her shoulders, dropping into a deeper stance. He might kill her, but she was taking parts of him with her. "Let's go, you ugly fucker."

He took a step and then stumbled forward, his head dropping. She met Katherine's eyes over his back and nodded. She soccer-kicked Rufus' face, and he stumbled to the side, dropping to his hands and knees. Katherine turned to Rosemary, and Aeron jumped on Rufus' back, locking her arms around his throat. He stood and threw his body backward to the ground. She would have screamed in agony, but her lungs had no breath. Her arms loosened from him, and he peeled away her grip and she rolled to her side as he stood up. The world swam in front of her as she tamped down the urge to puke. His heavy boot pressed on her shoulder, pinning her down. Her chest heaved with unsteady breaths, and she stared up at a gun barrel, Rufus grinning down at her.

"Aeron! Get the fuck up!" Katherine screamed from a few feet away. "None of us are dying tonight!"

No, they weren't. Aeron's fingers slid from her side to her waist in a single motion. She grasped the curved blade from her belt and sliced it through the jeans Rufus wore, making purchase in his shin. Blood sprayed her face, and she squeezed her eyes closed. The pressure released enough for her to drive his leg away. She bounded to her feet and wiped at her face, but he was already advancing again. "The things I will do to you will make your mother cry."

"My mother's dead," Aeron spat back while retreating. Panic sunk into her core. They could manage if it was just getting to the exit, but commotion echoed down the hallway outside the bullpen —the other assassins on their way back. From the corner of her vision, Aeron spied a scarred woman entering the bullpen, running directly for them.

"Drop!" the woman screamed, looking right at her. Aeron didn't know of a friendly person in the building, but this seemed like the woman Decius had met in Costa Rica—the woman in charge of the assassins who had just saved him. Aeron took a chance and dropped. The scarred woman dove over her, tackling Rufus to the ground, and then bounded back up, knives in hand. She sliced him across his forearms and thighs, forcing him back toward the wall.

"Stand down!" a male voice shouted, echoing through the room. All movement halted for a single second, then Rufus shoved the scarred woman and bolted for the hall. She gave Aeron a furrowed, stern look and then raced after him. Aeron looked around for whomever it was that could command the entire room. A man stepped away from the back wall, a gun in each hand, and her pulse thrummed through her body. He had one poised at her and the other at Katherine and Rosemary as he moved forward. His gait oozed power, looking sharp in the tailored black combat clothes. His brown eyes raked over her, but it was the long curly hair knotted atop his head with a chopstick that made him memorable. This was no Underworlder. This was a high-ranking Legacy Inc asset with enough clout to scare off Rufus.

"Griffin, no!" Katherine yelled, taking a step closer to Aeron.

He paused, looking between Aeron and Katherine. Aeron dared a look, too. They were only feet apart, Katherine in between her and Rosemary, who the other weapon was aimed at. He shook his head. "Sorry, Kat. They're on the list." Aeron whipped her head to look at Rosemary. Her face paled, bringing Aeron a spark of joy to see the fear there. She could die happy knowing Rosemary would be joining her.

22

KAT

"And I will be, too," Kat said, and her heart slammed into her chest. What the fuck was Griffin doing here? "The list isn't what you think it is. Stand down." He didn't move, his face a complete mask.

"I have to." And though his words were filled with regret, Kat had only a second to choose. Griffin's shots went off. Kat saw the shock of betrayal cross her mother's face as she threw herself on top of Aeron. They landed in a heap on the ground, Aeron moaning. Kat's palm pressed against a warm slickness on Aeron's hip, and panic surged through her. Luke and Ivan would never help her if Aeron died. Mason would just kill her. But more importantly, she didn't want Aeron to die.

"Aeron?" Kat looked at the blood seeping from beneath her vest.

"I'm not hit," she gasped, and relief flooded Kat's system. "My side."

Kat stood and wiped the blood on her pants. She held out her hand, helped Aeron up, and shoved her toward the door. "Get out of here!"

Aeron didn't need to be told twice. She sprinted for the opening, another shot following her as she rounded the corner.

Kat spun around, eyes landing on her mother's still form. Her breath froze in her chest. She would skin Griffin alive if he'd killed her. That right belonged to her and her alone.

"What the fuck, Katherine!" he spat, eyes blazing.

"What the fuck?" Kat said incredulously. "What the fuck! I said stand down."

"And I don't answer to you."

She scowled and moved to her mother, watching for signs of life. Her chest rose ever so slightly, and the bullet wound in her leg warmed Kat's entire being. She flicked her gaze to Griffin. He'd re-holstered his weapons, his ears alert as his head rotated from side to side, but he didn't come any closer and didn't chase after Aeron.

She took a knee next to her mother. She'd imagined this day so many times. Much like with her Granddad, the circumstances were far from what she'd expected, and a pang in her chest offered a small child's hope that her mother would look to her with love and affection. But when her eyes opened, they contained no such emotion. Anger and betrayal swirled within them. Kat had the slightest urge to ask her why—why she didn't love her? Protect her? What had she done to warrant such disdain? She spoke before Kat could get any words out.

"You are an ungrateful bitch. And a terrible fucking daughter. After everything I did for you—"

Heat flooded Kat's vision. "Everything you did for me? I was a child when you threw me to the wolves. You're just mad I came back leading the pack. You reap what you sow, Rosemary." With lightning speed, Kat smashed her elbow into her mother's face. The snap of the woman's head hitting the floor rendered her uncon-scious. Kat braced her left hand on her mother's sternum and took a breath, her arm shaking beneath her weight. Although she couldn't see the damage, the feeling in her fingers had drastically decreased, and a small worry crossed her mind, wondering if she would ever have full use of her arm again.

"Fucking hell, Kat." Griffin moved close and wrapped his rough fingers around her wrist. He lifted her arm, eyes scanning her tricep. "Who did this?" Warmth spread through her, and she cursed internally. His touch sent electricity to her core, and her mind flashed to nights filled with violence, just like this one, that ended with them wrapped in bedsheets.

"Remove your hands from her, Reaper." The words pulled Kat back to reality, and she tugged her hand away, leaning to look around Griffin. He lowered his head, shaking it. Star's gun was trained on Griffin, and she met Kat's gaze. "Well, answer him," Star said, raising an eyebrow at her. "Who the hell did that?"

She'd never been so happy to see her Reaper—even if she was supposed to be in a safe house across the city. Kat waved her hand over her mother's body. "Who else?"

"What are you doing here, Star?" Griffin asked, voice low and dangerous. He stood, creating space between them, his body posture ready to attack.

Kat ignored the sudden chill accompanied by his distance and stood, too. "Yeah, Star, answer him," Kat repeated back to her.

A smile danced across Star's face. She never took anything seriously—except murder. "Everything went dark. Both sides. I wasn't waiting to find your body in the rubble tomorrow."

Kat turned back to Griffin. "And why are you here?"

"It's your mother's last known location."

Of course, he was here to handle the fucking hit list. Anger swelled in her chest. She thought for a moment he was there to help her—but how could he? She refused to tell him the truth about her Granddad. "You can mark her as claimed," Kat said. "She will not be leaving this building alive. Star, give me a hand."

Star holstered her gun and walked past Griffin, her eyes shooting daggers. "Move it, Reaper."

Anger flashed across his face and he stepped closer. "Katherine, please think this through."

"I have. Every night since I left that island." Almost every night, she reminded herself. There were nights when Griffin had brought her complete silence, and it had been bliss. "Either shoot us right now or go find another body to claim."

Without a word, he turned on his heel and walked out of the bullpen. Kat didn't know what she expected, but leaving her again was not it. She sighed and reached under her mother's armpit, the body lighter than she'd anticipated. She looked up and met Star's gaze. Kat smiled. Her mother was wrong. She did have people who cared about her.

"Where to?" Star asked.

"Let's take her to Interrogation."

Star waggled her eyebrows, and they dragged her limp body to the hall, careful as they slipped in blood and tripped over bodies. The cleanup of this place would be impossible. They'd be better off setting fire to it. Her eyes widened, a smile stretching her face.

"I know that look," Star said. "What are you thinking?"

"Maybe we could just set her on fire while she's alive and then let the whole fucking place burn."

"That would be too easy," Star said. "And you don't like easy." Kat couldn't argue with that.

Star turned the handle to the interrogation room nearest the exit, and the door slid opened. The emergency lights in the room illuminated a metal chair with chains in the center of it. Kat saw a sink to her left, with an open medical kit on the counter beside it. But on the right, was a table with recently used blades, the blood still crusted along them—it was perfect.

"Let's strap her in," Star said. They tossed her into the seat and secured her wrists to the chair's arms for easy access to her fingers. When Kat bent to lock her mother's ankles, her head swam slightly, and her fingers tingled. She steadied herself with a hand on the floor before standing back up.

"Let me see that," Star said, looking at her arm.

"No. It's fine," Kat argued, although it was far from fine. Her fingers had lost all feeling, and she wasn't sure they were even responding to her anymore. But blood had soaked into her mother's pants from the gunshot, and she didn't want to risk her bleeding out.

"Kat, please. Let me."

She shook her head. "I need to do this alone," Kat said, her heart becoming heavier with each passing second. She needed to do this.

"I'll keep guard right outside," Star assured.

"Thanks. When I'm done, we'll leave through the ceiling."

"See you in a few hours."

The room went silent as the door clicked closed—a soundproof room for hours and days of torture. Star was right; the cuts along her tricep needed to be handled. She moved to the med kit. It had been rummaged through, but there was a bottle of hydrogen peroxide and gauze. She splashed some water on her arm to wash as much blood off as she could. Her shirt was too filthy to use as a towel, so she patted her arm dry with the clean part of her mother's shirt. The cold peroxide burned and sizzled when it touched the wound, and Kat hissed, letting it clear what it could before she dried it again.

Once she'd stemmed some of the bleeding, she turned her attention to the woman who wrecked her life. Her mother's head had dropped back, her neck completely exposed. Kat envisioned waking her up by the slow, agonizing sawing of her neck, deep enough to cause unbearable pain but not deep enough to kill her. But Kat needed answers. She placed her hands on her mother's wrists and leaned in to inspect her closer. Her hair had grayed, and wrinkles pulled at her once gorgeous features. And her nose looked better smashed into her face. This close, Kat could see past the blood to the scars of battles and beatings.

She moved a hand to her mother's thigh, the wet material guiding her to the bullet hole. She pushed her thumb in as deep as it could go. Her mother's eyes shot open, her head coming forward as a scream left her until her eyes hit Kat's, and she slammed her mouth shut.

Kat snatched her mother's chin, forcing her to look right at her, and pushed harder into her thigh. "It's okay to scream, Mother. They all do."

Her mother kept her lips clamped shut, her entire body shaking with pain, eyes glaring at Kat. If that wouldn't break her, Kat had plenty of other ideas. She picked up her hand, satisfied with the slump of her mother's body as a response. It wouldn't be fun if her mother just gave in.

"Going to kill me?" her mother asked, breath ragged, body shaking and covered in sweat.

"Eventually." Kat let all her anger and despair drip into the words. She took the time to reorganize the blades and knives along the table in size order. She picked up the middle scalpel, and dried blood flaked from the handle. "But first—I think I'll start with your fingers."

23

LUKE

"C'mon, Dee," Luke said, hoisting him beneath the arms. He'd looped Decius' left arm over his shoulder, supporting him across the back as they escaped the last of the compound hell. The color is Decius' face faded, his eyes and weight drooping. Luke stumbled, nearly dropping him to the ground. He leaned them against the closest building. Dr. Shea's was still a block away. "Decius?"

Decius' head lolled sideways. Fuck. "C'mon, man. You can't fucking die on me. Aeron needs you," his voice hitched. "I need you." Luke gave several hard taps to the side of his face, rousing him. "That's it. C'mon. Wake up."

Decius lifted his head, blinking slowly. "Quit hitting me."

Luke laughed, hysterics creeping in. "Quit trying to die."

"Then you shouldn't have shot me," Decius said with a half-smile. Luke returned it, but his insides turned to lead.

"We're almost there." They stumbled the last block. The doctor's office was an end unit beside an alley. No lights were shining from the front windows, so Luke led them down the alley, looking for the side door. It was nearly at the back of the building, a green metal door with a tree of life magnet indicating the doctor was indeed in. Luke pounded on the door until it swung open, and he looked directly down the barrel of a shotgun.

"Katherine sends her regards," Luke said. The barrel dropped. The older black man moved his gaze from Luke to Decius.

"Fuck me. Get him in here." Dr. Shea looped Decius' other arm over his shoulder, and together they brought him into an operating room. Luke gingerly laid Decius down. A younger Hispanic man raced around the tiny room, hooking up IVs and setting out medical equipment. Dr. Shea took no time removing the bullet-proof vest, exposing the wound. Luke grasped onto Decius' hand and averted his eyes, but not before seeing there was too much damage. In the bright room, the skin was burned and peeled back, blood bubbling against the chest seal as Decius took shallow breaths.

"I'm sorry," Luke said, looking at his best friend. His brother. He wiped the sweat off Decius' brow. "I'm sorry." He didn't know what else to say. He was sorry he shot him, sorry he lied to him, sorry he hadn't let Rosemary put a bullet in him that night in the Woodsworth estate.

"I need to put him under," Dr. Shea relayed quietly.

"Okay," Luke said. "Did you hear that, Dee?"

The slightest movement of his head confirmed. A jolt of electricity shot up Luke's spine, and he tensed, gripping the table with his free hand for support. He'd managed to block out the ghosts to save Aeron, but Mrs. Gale had told him he'd be down to hours if his heart rate spiked. The pain had nearly reached his skull—another shock like that, his brain would fry, he could already feel it. The pain subsided, and with it, his dead blinked into existence around the room. He shivered and kept his eyes locked on Decius, but he could feel his grip on reality slipping.

"Call Mason," Decius said, although it sounded more like a moan.

"What?" Luke asked, caught off guard.

"Call Mason," Decius repeated. "Aeron needs backup." Always the big brother.

"Can I use a phone?" Luke asked. Dr. Shea pointed to a bin filled with burner phones on the counter. Luke stretched out, fingers barely reaching, but he wasn't letting go of Decius' hand. He tipped the bin, grabbing the first phone he touched. He spun a few times—he didn't know how to reach Mason. All Legacy communications had been terminated, and he never bothered to learn the Legacy Inc protocol.

"The Legacy line still works," Decius said with a slight cough, blood spraying from his lips. Luke nodded, dialing the number with shaking fingers. The last time he saw Mason—he wasn't sure he was even alive. Would Maureen have let him walk out of that room? Maureen. He needed to tell Decius about his mom.

Mason answered on the second ring, and the tension in his chest eased slightly. "Go."

"Mase—"

"Luke?"

"Decius has been shot. I shot Decius." A knot exploded in his chest. He'd shot his best friend. A sob rocked his body.

"Is he. . ."

"We're at the doctor's. But Aeron—she's still inside."

"How bad is it, Luke?"

Luke looked back at Decius; his eyes had drifted closed, his hand now slack in Luke's. His frantic gaze landed on the older man.

"I put him under. I need you out so I can work."

"Luke!" Mason's urgent voice yelled into his ear.

The nurse pushed Luke from the room, the door swinging shut. Through the square window in the door, Dr. Shea and the nurse moved in a blur. No, he was crying again. He swallowed hard. "It's bad."

Luke waited directly outside the operating room, peering through the window. Dr. Shea and his assistant worked diligently, and Luke leaned against the wall, bouncing his head on the hard surface and fiddling with the cell in his hand. The constant knock to his skull seemed to keep any pain from shooting through his nerves and up his spine. Where was Aeron? Mason? Should he go back to them?

A chill brushed his arm, and he refused to see which ghost wanted his attention. *"I can't believe you shot him,"* Shannon said. He didn't respond. Maybe she would put him out of his misery.

Pounding reached his ears, and it took him several seconds to realize it was the door he'd entered. He pushed off the wall, side-stepping Shannon, and yanked the door open. Mason rushed past him toward the operating room.

"Wait!" Luke followed, but as he picked up the pace, his heart pumped faster, and electricity jolted up his spine. He crashed to the floor, eyes watering, muscles refusing to listen to him. A sound between a scream and a cry left him.

This was it. His sins finally caught up to him.

Mason grasped his shoulder and turned him over, searching his face. "What did they give you?" he demanded.

"Sin." Luke's parched mouth scratched the word out like sandpaper. And for some reason, shame filled him, and heat flooding his face.

"Fucking Maureen. Where's the pain?"

Luke placed his hand on the base of his skull. Mason ran a hand over his face, eyes darting toward Decius. Luke dropped his head back to the ground, blinking the tears to clear his vision. Mrs. Gale told him he would have barely an hour—he just wanted to live long enough to say sorry to Aeron one last time.

"Stay here." Luke nodded into the ground. He didn't think he could stand, let alone go anywhere. The muscles in his back twitched, and he gritted his teeth. He turned his head to look into the propped open door, Mason and Dr. Shea arguing over Decius' limp form. That should be him on the table, not Dee.

The nurse moved to put his hands inside Decius, and Dr. Shea exited the room. "What are you doing?" Luke cried out. "I'm not worth it. Save him!" He struggled to stand as the doctor approached, but his arms refused to hold his weight, and his head hit the ground again.

"I'm not having two dead Legacy Assassins on my floor; I don't care what price your heads fetch." He held a syringe filled with yellow serum. "A temporary antidote." Luke couldn't pull away—and he didn't want to. He wanted to live. Dr. Shea nodded at the PICC line. "Makes this easier." Luke didn't fight, eyes locked on the yellow liquid that could save his life as it disappeared into his system. "It will take some time—but that will stop it from killing you, for now."

Luke couldn't think of anything to say, thanks didn't seem to cover it. So he just nodded, and Dr. Shea and Mason disappeared back into the room. He didn't deserve it, especially if Decius died. Banging sounded at the door again. Aeron. He stumbled to the door, face-planting several times before he reached it and yanked it open. Aeron's bright eyes met his, and her concern for him for a moment trumped everything. She was alive and as beautiful as ever, especially drenched in blood and grime. She'd made it back to him.

"You're okay," she said and threw her arms around him. The void in his soul filled a little. He hugged her tight; she fit right against him his head resting on top of hers. They stood, wrapped together, taking deep breaths.

"Where is he?" she asked against his chest. Luke pointed to the room, and they moved arm in arm to see the fate of her brother and his best friend.

24

AERON

*A*eron stood at the small square window, looking in at the operating room. She'd removed her tracking chip, crushed it, and shed her vest. The constricting garment made breathing impossible when she finally saw Decius in the operating room light. Luke stood behind her, his arms wrapped around her in comfort. If she was going to watch her brother die, she didn't want to do it alone. This was no place for him—for anyone. This was a place of death. How many people had she seen lay on a table just like that and never get back up? Decius' eyes were closed, his body unmoving. Dr. Shea, a nurse, and Mason worked on Decius' wounds. The damage was beyond repair; even she could see that from here. But they kept working, and she refused to look away. Her heart banged against her ribcage, begging him to open his eyes again, just one more time.

"Did he say anything?" she finally asked.

He shook his head and pulled his hand from her waist. "You're bleeding."

She glanced down at his hand covered in blood. Her adrenaline had been so high she hadn't felt it after running from Katherine. Aeron turned and looked up at him, anger flaring in her chest.

"Yeah. You shot me." His face paled. She could trace the panic rushing through every inch of his body, and she let him suffer for a few moments longer. "In the garage."

His eyes dropped, and he shook his head, stepping back. "Oh. I—"

"If you tell me you forgot, I will punch you in the goddamn face." She clenched her fists at her side.

"No. I—I don't even know how long I've been gone. It's only been a few days?" He turned his back to her, searching inside a medical bag on top of the chair beside him.

She looked back into the room; Decius hadn't moved at all. A slight breeze brushed her side, and she snapped her head back to Luke. He held a bandage between his teeth, a needle, and a thread in one hand. He held her gaze, waiting for permission before moving. She gave a tiny nod, heart pounding. In one moment, she wanted to kill him—hate him for what he's done to them. In the next, she craved this, the trust and gentle touches. He pulled up her shirt, sucking in a breath; she followed suit when he prodded the wound.

"Ah, fuck, Aeron. I'm—" But like shooting Decius, nothing he could say would undo the kind of damage he'd inflicted. She watched as he cleaned and re-stitched the wound, clenching her teeth to keep from crying out and waiting for him to look up, for him to explain, apologize, or ask the questions he needed answers to. But he didn't. He covered the work and turned away from her. She readjusted her shirt and continued to watch them work on her brother, disappointment flooding her.

He returned to his spot behind her, an awkward space between them now. She reached back, returning his hands to her waist. She couldn't do this alone.

"Are you okay?" he whispered.

"No." The last seventy-two hours had been hell, and they weren't even close to the finish line yet. They managed to save Luke, but did Ivan open the vault? Did they even need Luke? Her emotions were an indecipherable swirl of anger and relief—relief that she'd made it out alive and that Luke had gotten Decius here. But he would have been fine if Luke had just stayed in the goddamn room where she'd put him.

Decius' limp arm fell off the table, a velvet pool of blood forming beneath his fingertips. His body began to tremble—no—maybe that was her. Was this how he felt watching her die on the table just a few months ago? How could she ever walk away from this? She would die here, too.

A cold hand touched her shoulder, and she didn't need to look to see who it was. She squeezed Luke's hand as the raw pain of death ripped through her. The machines in the room blinked wildly, but nothing they did would help him now. She dropped to her knees, gasping for breath. She would never breathe freely again. Luke wrapped his arms around her again, but she shoved him off.

"Get away from me!" she screamed, the words making way for the pain.

"Aeron. Please. . ."

"No. No. No." She shook her head and backed away from him. It may have been an accident, she may have been grateful to see him just moments ago, but he'd killed her brother. He'd taken away the last family member she had. She backed into the wall, hugging her knees to her chest.

He was gone. Decius was gone.

The door opened, and Mason stopped short. "Aeron—"

The sobs rocked through her body, her breath refusing to catch. He dropped beside her, and she leaned into him, crying freely into his chest. "It'll be okay," he whispered, wrapping her tight to him. But he had to say that. It would never be okay again. Her brother was gone—her best friend, her protector. And she wasted so much time lying to him. Rage bubbled in her core and burned as it left her in a visceral scream. She choked on the sobs. This was her fault. She'd damned them all.

"I hate to do this," Dr. Shea said, and she looked up, his frame blurry. "You have to go. We've got a security alert."

"But Decius," Aeron gasped. No way in hell was she leaving him here.

"I'll handle it," Mason assured. He pulled her to her feet, wrapping her in a bone-crushing embrace—she never wanted to let go. She took several deep breaths. Controlled. Calm. Their mission wasn't over yet. He raised an eyebrow, and she nodded, wiping her face. Decius didn't die for her to get caught here. "You and Luke go back to the safe house."

She clenched her fists and glared at Luke. She didn't want to be near him, or see him, or forgive him. "I'm not taking him."

Mason touched her cheek lightly. "We need him. Decius would want—"

"Decius is fucking dead." Another sob threatened to choke her and she swallowed hard. "I can't—"

"You must."

She took a few more breaths, eyes moving to Decius' limp body. He hadn't died for them to fuck this up now. "Let me see him," she said.

Dr. Shea stepped in her line of sight. "You need to go. Here." He placed five vials filled with yellow liquid in her hand. "He's going to need a dose every two hours, the next one in ninety minutes, and a full IV treatment."

Aeron tore her eyes away from Dr. Shea, glancing down at the vials and then at Luke. He sat on the floor, head buried in his knees, and hands clasped behind his neck, rocking back and forth. Was that how she'd looked after Shannon died? She could almost feel the two of them, Shannon and Decius, staring at her and waiting for her to get her shit together and save Luke like he'd saved them so many times. He looked up, bloody tears tracked down his face, and she took a step back, bumping into Mason.

"What the hell is wrong with him?"

A dark shadow passed across Mason's face before he answered.

"They dosed him with Sin." A shiver raced down her spine. "I know you're angry, Aeron. But we need him alive. You need him alive."

"I'm not going to kill him," Aeron said, the words ringing true as they passed her lips.

"Just checking," Mason said. She glanced over her shoulder at him, and he gave a small smirk. "You have killed a lot of unexpected people this year."

She smiled, the absurdity hitting her hard. "Where am I supposed to get an IV kit?"

"Under your bed," Mason said. "There's an entire setup there."

"I feel like I should feel violated that you were in my room, but thanks."

He chuckled. "He's going to have fits of pain up his spine. If it reaches the base of his skull, administer another dose and knock him out with this." He put another vial in her hand filled with clear liquid.

She was a terrible medic—always had been. How the hell had she become the one in charge of something like this? She looked back to Decius—could she have done something different to keep him alive? Shannon would have saved them both. Pain ripped through her heart at the thought, Shannon's laughter echoing in her mind at her predicament. She pocketed the vials and pulled Luke up to his feet, the anger in her heart settling into concern. She hated him on so many levels at the moment, but she loved him, too. Decius had loved him. Grief swept through her body, and she squeezed her eyes together, Ivan's words creeping into her mind, pausing her before they entered the alley.

'Still worth saving?'

25

KAT

The door to the bathroom creaked open, and Kat let out an aggravated sigh. What else could possibly go wrong? She needed to shower and get on the road back to Headquarters. No one had shown up at the rendezvous point, and she couldn't reach Perry or Mason. The only thing that had gone right had been the agonizing screams of her mother.

"Star, I'm showering. Whatever emergency is happening, it can wait ten more minutes. It's been a fucking night."

"I'll make sure I tell her," Griffin's rough voice answered. Her heart skipped several beats, and she pressed against the wall for support until the anger crawled up her throat. She grit her teeth against the memories his voice stirred inside her again, the ones she'd pushed away. She'd spent the last four hours reliving all the wreckage her mother had done to her—Shay's torture clear in her mind as she repeated each blow, each slice, each death on her mother. Now, the memories hit her like a ton of bricks, and she couldn't stop how Griffin's voice so easily pulled her to a better time and place as the water cascaded over her.

He smiled at her across the table, the Caribbean air warm against her skin. How he could wear jeans and a white button-down at the beach would never make sense to her. At least he had his hair tied into a knot on his head, a slim dart tucked inside of it.

Laughter danced up the beach toward them, and Kat laughed too, the sound contagious. She squinted, glancing toward the crystal clear water at Shay and his two cousins, Dominic and Gunnar, as they tossed a ball back and forth. Carefree. She raised an eyebrow at Griffin as he stared daggers at them.

"You need to leave him," Griffin said, fiddling with his cup of water.

Kat laughed. "Are you jealous, Griff?"

"I'll always be jealous of anyone who steals your attention from me. I'm an attention whore." He turned his eyes to her, mirth shining in them. He placed the empty cup down, pushed his chair away from the table, and leaned his elbows on his knees.

"Whatever it is, spit it out." She'd never seen him so tongue-tied.

He huffed a laugh before meeting her eyes again, their intensity pinning her in place. "Come back with me, Katherine."

She shook her head. She would never leave. "I'm happy here, Griff. Like happy-happy."

"And that's what I'm concerned about." He stood up, pulling out the slim dart from his bun, letting his hair drop around his shoulders. He raked a hand through it, twirling the weapon between his fingers absent-mindedly—a sign he had much on his mind he wasn't going to share. "We don't get to be happy. He'll make sure of that."

Kat shook her head. "I tried coming home. Granddad refused me for years. And now? I'm so far off the grid here—if he's going to make me go back eventually, I'd rather enjoy my freedom while I can."

"That's how he'll break you. This—" he nodded to Shay. "He is a bad idea. Break it off now and come home with me."

Kat turned her gaze back to Shay and the boys, tossing a football. Their laugh was infectious, and she smiled. She couldn't give this up. "I can't."

"Then do it for them. They have no idea how dangerous you are —who you really are. Don't let them be the next casualties in your Granddad's chess game."

"I'm staying here," Kat answered, but a small hint of dread crept beneath her skin. He was half right—their days may be numbered, but she intended to make the most of them.

"Then you're a fucking idiot." He stood and waved at the group playing football when they turned his way. "They don't deserve what will happen to them."

"Neither do we," she said. "We deserve to be happy too."

"No, we don't. We do bad things, Katherine. We are the bad things. And I think you've forgotten how ruthless he can be."

Kat shook the memory free and took a deep breath. There was too much unsaid between them—too many years, too much distance, too much pain. She cracked open the shower door enough to stick her head out and glared at him. He sat on the countertop, fiddling with a throwing knife. He still wore his bloody and grimy clothes, except for his feet—which were bare. "Why are you here?"

"I need answers."

She closed the shower door again and braced her hand against the wall. Her heart pounded in her chest, her body rallying against her logic, wanting to run to him like all those years before. But he'd broken her heart—ripped it out and then ran to lick the heels of her Granddad. He didn't deserve any reaction from her at all.

"She's dead. You can confirm her," she said, stepping back under the water. "Now I've answered your question. There's not much else to say."

"Why did you choose to save the Seward woman over your mother?"

Kat swallowed hard. The betrayal on her mother's face when Kat dove to save Aeron was etched in her brain. She shouldn't care. It shouldn't hurt. That woman—that monster—tossed her to her Granddad like disposable gloves. "Aeron is more useful to me alive than dead. My mother was an obstacle. A thorn in my side who would betray me to save her own hide."

He remained quiet, and she hoped he would just leave. She grabbed the shampoo and began washing the grime out of her hair. She scrubbed her scalp harder as more memories she had long buried surfaced: long nights beneath the covers, ignoring their duties, indulging in only each other; stake-outs in the van, where she insisted Star Wars was better than James Bond, and he'd almost choked on the sandwich he'd been eating; the thrill of fighting alongside him, the adrenaline rush of his knives sliding past into an enemy, knowing he'd keep her safe. Tears stung her eyes, and she rinsed out the shampoo, letting the shower wash them away. She missed the last memory the most.

"You need to leave," she said, regaining her composure. "Please, just fucking go. It's been a long night."

"I'm sorry, Kat."

"Don't be. She deserved to die. You know that."

"No. I'm sorry. For that night."

The words crashed into her. She'd waited for this apology for years, for an explanation of his sudden abandonment of her for her Granddad. She should have been used to it by then—her mother had done the same. She didn't answer him; it was too late to apologize. She picked up the bottle of conditioner and continued washing her hair.

"You woke up next to me every night for four years crying out Shay's name," he said, barely audible over the water. "Was I jealous? Never. But I was heartbroken and angry for you." She froze, listening hard. "I had been drinking the night we fought, so I wasn't thinking clearly. That's not an excuse, but it played a role in what came next. It had been a particularly rough night for you—you never remembered in the morning, but your screams, Kat, the pure anguish? I needed to know what he'd done to you."

He shifted off the counter and moved to stand next to the shower. She barely dared to breathe, their fight fresh in her memory like the day it happened. She'd woken up to an empty bed, heart racing when Griffin barged into the room, sweat-covered as if he'd gone for a run.

"What's going on?" Kat asked, wiping the sleep from her face.

"What have you and Perry been up to?"

"Huh?"

"Have you been actively building against him?" Griffin asked.

Oh. Was she still planning a mutiny against the entire Legacy Inc establishment? "You don't want the answer to that."

"Kat, you have to let this go!" He moved over to the bed, climbing onto it and kneeling in front of her. "Shay was a casualty. Let him go."

Anger flared in her chest, and she pushed him away. He dropped back to his butt, eyes wild with fear. "Never," she hissed. "He will continue to ruin people—innocent people. I will not let it go."

"It's your own fault!" He prodded her in the chest. "I told you to leave. I told you to leave him!"

An iron hand gripped her heart. "And if that was you he did that to? Would you want me to just sit back and let it go? I would die on the spot, Griff. He will pay."

Griffin clambered off the bed, the alcohol wafting off him when he moved. "I can't do this; watch you commit suicide and drag us all down with you. You will meet the same end as Shay, and I will not let that happen."

"Griff!"

"No." He shook his head. "I can't—I won't." He left without a backward glance. It was the last time she'd voluntarily spoken to him.

"I asked him how he'd done it." Griffin's voice broke with the words, pulling her back to the present. She pushed her wet hair back and leaned closer to the door. "I asked him how he broke you."

"He didn't break me," Kat responded automatically.

"Yes, he did. He took all your sunshine and drowned it in vengeance. Have you slept soundly since that night in his office?"

No. Sleep was not a luxury she indulged in, because he was right—she was broken. Her throat tightened, and she squeezed her eyes together, regaining her control. She was broken like Luke, hell-bent on vengeance—heart irreparable. "He's never broken you, though," she replied, letting out a long breath. "Is that because you have a cold heart, or you're better at hiding it?"

"He broke me before I ever landed in the Caribbean," Griffin admitted. "He asked me to retrieve you. If I failed, I would suffer a fate worse than death—I would be tossed out of the Legacy." A slight sob left him. "To me—an orphan kid who never had a real family—I wasn't risking that. I'd lose my found family; I'd lose you—my best friend." He placed his forehead on the door, and she leaned in, too, letting her tears mingle with the water. "You were so fucking happy, Kat. You glowed when you talked about Shay. You loved each other. What kind of friend was I if I took that from you? I was fucking happy for you."

Kat swallowed back the knot in her throat. Her Granddad was always three moves ahead of everyone.

"I was stupid," he admitted.

"We were young," Kat countered.

"I was the reason he tortured Shay. He never intended on setting me loose. My punishment was to watch you suffer. To love you, knowing I was responsible for what broke you."

The iron grip that held her heart closed for the past four years lessened its grip. The master manipulator had killed three birds with one stone: her, Shay, and Griffin. "You left me." The words tore themselves out of her chest.

"I did."

"Why?"

"Because he promised that as long as I did what he said, he would leave you alone. I saw what he did to Shay. What your mother did to Shay. I'm so fucking glad you killed her. He made me watch the footage the night I left you, and suddenly your nighttime screams were more terrifying." The iron fist opened a little more, and Kat's cracked heart beat painfully. "I don't know if he was showing me my fate or yours if I refused him. I wasn't willing to find out."

She wiped the tears from her face and turned off the shower. She opened the door a crack, held out her hand, accepting the towel he offered, and dried off before wrapping it around herself. She should hate him. His confession should have solidified her anger. But there were too many dead. Too many broken people because of the secrets they kept. She opened the shower door and met his gaze, his eyes puffy too.

"Why are you here?" she asked again.

"I can't find our Senior Assassin. Or our next in line. I have a growing body count, just witnessed the biggest massacre in any Legacy history, and I'm only killing people to keep Shay's fate from happening to one of us. I know you hate me. I did that intentionally. But I've never stopped loving you. I've never stopped protecting you. So please, tell me. Did you kill that bastard?"

Her heart hammered, knowing he spoke the truth.

"No," she said. "But he is dead."

Relief flooded Griffin's body, and he dropped his head back, a laugh escaping him. He put both hands on his head and paced the small sitting area in the bathroom. "Did he suffer? Please tell me he suffered."

Kat crossed her arms and leaned against the wall, shaking her head. "I'm sure the shot Luke administered caused some drawn-out pain. But a single shot to the forehead put him down quickly."

"Luke killed him?"

"Aeron Seward." She pushed off the wall, heading to the bedroom to find some clothes. Her body ached, and sleep suddenly called her name. No. She needed to find out who survived the night —if anyone, and what happened to Perry and Ivan.

"Really?" He followed her to her room, repositioning himself against the wall again.

"Yeah. She's quite the firecracker." Kat really hoped she made it out. She would never admit it out loud, but before Aeron walked into that bullpen, Kat had given up, her mother's words settling deep in old wounds. 'No one is coming for you.' And then her eyes landed on Aeron. She and her brother were a rare breed—what she imagined the prestigious and honorable Legacy would produce.

"What's your plan now that you've got your vengeance?" Griffin asked.

Kat averted her eyes. She hadn't allowed herself to think past washing the blood off herself after no one showed up to the meeting point. She needed to make a plan: either take charge or liquidate the strip club and run. But she couldn't leave now. There were the kids with Dom and Gun. And Luke—she'd used him and then let her mother sink her claws into him instead of her. Then there were the Sewards.

Something about them felt familiar—right? "I take the fucking crown," she said. "Legacy Inc will be mine. But I need to find them —all of them. Perry, Aeron, Decius, Mason, Luke." She looked back at him. "And I need information. Everything you know."

He smiled, eyes crinkling. "I've waited years for you to ask me that. Your arm looks horrendous," Griffin said. "Will you let me look at it first? Please?"

Kat looked over her tricep. She had only let Star do a quick clean, enough for her to get Tegaderm patches on it so she could get in the shower. She didn't want to see or know what her mother had done. What final scar she'd been left with.

He stepped behind her, placing his hands lightly on her shoulders. A chill ran through her body. For years, she'd denied herself any connection. And when she did indulge, it was always just sex. She let him spin her around, his face inches from hers. A hand slid under her chin, and she looked into his eyes. The pain, regret, and love blazing in them for her.

She licked her aching lips, wanting to taste him again. "Are you going to just stare at me?"

His lips quirked into a smile before he crushed his lips to hers. The breath left her, heat pooling in her center. A hand secured itself in her hair, pulling her closer as if they could meld into a single being. The other roamed her back, her side, her ass. A moan left her, and she threaded her fingers through his hair, pulling him even closer.

They broke apart after several minutes, foreheads pressed together, her heart racing, and her entire body buzzing. She fucking missed him so much. He cupped her cheek and kissed her forehead. "I'm going to shower, clean that mess on the back of your arm, and then you and me are not leaving that bed until the world is on fire," he said.

She laughed. "So, in like twenty-five minutes?"

"We can let the world burn for a little bit before you save it."

"We save it," she corrected. "Go clean up, Reaper." She pushed him on the chest. "I won't wait forever."

26

AERON

*A*eron whipped the car into the gravel parking lot behind Ernie's. Tiny rocks pinged against the bottom of the vehicle, and her knuckles were white as she gripped the steering wheel. The ride from Dr. Shea's had been silent. Her mind replayed Decius' hand dropping off the table the entire time. An emotional ball had slammed into her throat, and she couldn't talk around it— she could barely breathe.

Luke had pressed his feverish head against the cold window and didn't look at her. It wasn't until about an hour into the drive she realized he'd fallen asleep. The ball finally dislodged as she pushed the brakes, screaming his name. He didn't rouse a bit, and she couldn't stop any longer to see if he was even still breathing. They needed to put as much space between them and the Playhouse as possible.

She skidded behind the barn and put the car into park. The back door to the house was already open, a tall silhouette in the frame waiting. For a moment, she thought it was Ivan—the GPS alerting him she was safely back. But as she bounded out of the car, Tommy's rougher exterior came into view.

"I need to get him inside!" Aeron said, rounding the front fender to the passenger side. To be sure they weren't followed, the forty-five-minute drive took nearly twice as long. He needed a dose of yellow serum—now. Tommy pulled the door open before she could reach it, and Luke fell forward, Tommy barely catching him.

"Who the fuck is this?" Tommy asked.

"Not the person I wanted to save," Aeron said, the words raw as they came out.

"Where's your brother?"

She met his raised eyebrows with the signature Seward glare because anger was keeping her going right now. Anger would save Luke's life and, hopefully, all of theirs. If she started thinking about Decius, Luke might end up dead.

Between the two of them, they managed to get Luke into the house and laid out on the living room couch. "Get the medical bag," Aeron said, pulling out the vials and placing them on the stained coffee table. She hadn't really looked at him since the warehouse—the stubble on his face was days old, and blood-stained tear tracks were smeared on his face turned her stomach—and he reeked. Tommy dropped the bag next to her. "I need a syringe." She checked the PICC line was still intact. They'd planned to torture him for weeks. She glanced back up at his slack face. What had he gotten himself into?

The syringe shook in her hand. How the hell was she going to get this attached? Tommy placed a steady hand on hers. "Let me. How much does he need?"

She passed the syringe and handed him one of the containers. "The whole vial. One every ninety minutes." She dropped to her butt and leaned against the couch while he filled the syringe and administered the antidote. Luke's chest began to rise and fall more rapidly, and his eyes fluttered open. She couldn't tell if he was here or not. His body tensed and shivered, his eyes widening when they landed on her.

Tommy capped the syringe and stood. "I'll be in the kitchen."

"Wait." He paused in the doorway and looked back at her.

"There are IV bags and a setup in my room, under the bed. Can you get it?" He nodded and left her alone with Luke. She turned back to him; his body remained frozen as if held down by invisible forces while his eyes roved the room in terror. "Luke?" Her voice was barely a whisper, but he whipped his head as if she'd screamed at him.

"Aeron. Is that really you? Are you—are you dead too?"

She turned to kneel beside him. "Why would you think I'm dead?" She didn't know much about Sin, its effects, or the pain. Just that it terrified every adult assassin she knew growing up. They all got the same dark expression as Mason when it was mentioned.

"They're all dead. Maybe I'm dead. Am I dead?" He tried to sit up, his face contorting in pain and fear. "Is this hell?" She put her hands on his shoulders, encouraging him to lie back down.

"Shhh. You need to rest."

His hand shot to hers, the sweaty palm securing her fingers in a vice grip. Her knuckles ground together and, she ripped it away. "You're warm," he said. She opened and closed her hand a few times, the sudden lack of heat from his sending a chill through her body. She moved her hand to his forehead. He was burning up. He put his hand on top of hers again, and she left it. "You're warm," he repeated.

"You're feverish," she countered, unsure what to say to him. How had they gotten to this point? Her best friend, her lover? She couldn't even talk to him. She didn't want to look at him.

His glossy eyes bore into her. "You're warm, so you're not dead. When they touch me—they're freezing."

Aeron had no idea what he was talking about, so she changed the subject. "Do you have any pain in your back?"

He dropped his hand from his head, and it flopped on the couch in exhaustion. "No." She pulled back her arm, and he raised his fingers slightly. "Don't leave me." Aeron swallowed back the emotion trying to surface. She adjusted herself, pulling the coffee table closer, careful not to knock any vials off. She took a seat on it and picked up his hand in hers. His grip tightened for a second, and she rubbed her thumb across the back of his hand, avoiding his gaze. "He's dead?" His question took a shot at her composure, and her sob almost broke free, her throat and eyes burning with unshed tears. Aeron just nodded in response.

"Aeron, I'm—"

"No." She shut him down. Whatever he had to say, whatever apology or explanation, she didn't want it while he was high and dying. A final confession was a way out, and she wasn't giving that to him. "You're on your fucking deathbed, and we don't do that shit."

His lips quirked slightly, but she couldn't share the sentiment. Where the fuck was Tommy? She looked up to see him standing in the doorway; how long had he been there? Tommy gave a slight start when Aeron met his eyes, and he flushed. He'd been there long enough. He brought a black bag and placed it on the floor. It only took minutes to set up the IV stand and hook up the bag. Luke's eyes fell closed again, the IV drip entering his system. Aeron scanned the room for potential dangers and came up empty, then checked to make sure the windows were locked.

"You worried about him escaping?" Tommy asked.

"No. Accidentally dying." She picked up the vials off the table and headed back to the kitchen. She placed them in the coffee cup cabinet and scrubbed her hands in the sink, the bright light allowing her to see just how filthy they were.

"Holy fuck," Tommy said from behind her. "How much of that blood is yours?"

Aeron's lips quirked in a smile and looked down at her blood-soaked clothes. "Quite a lot, I'd bet." She turned and leaned back against the counter, pulling up her shirt. The bandage Luke had put on was mostly clean, but the shift of the material pulled on dried wounds on her torso and back. Tommy's eyes widened. "Don't get weird on me, but will you check my wounds?"

He nodded, brows furrowed and eyes unblinking. She pulled

her shirt over her head, the crusted blood ripping free. Every muscle ached now that her adrenaline was gone. She dropped the filthy fabric into the trash and looked down. Several superficial blade marks crossed her sides and arms on top of the other scars already there. Her shoulder wound from Mr. Wayward had healed, the scab looking worse than the injury. She spun around and looked over her shoulder. "Anything super deep?"

He stared with his mouth open. "I. . ."

"Gaping—any big gaping wounds?" There were definitely a few open; the trickles of blood tickled like small spiders crawling down her back.

"Can't you feel them?"

She swallowed hard. "I feel a lot right now. The state of my body is the least of the pain."

His forehead creased, and he moved closer. His fingers lightly roved over her back and traced her tricep. "This is the widest and deepest." He brought his hand up from behind, holding his thumb and pointer finger about two inches apart, his face etched with concern.

She tried not to laugh at his absurd reaction but couldn't help it. Her laughter bubbled up. "Is it. . ." she tried taming the laughter. "Is it bleeding?" She laughed again, and he just stared at her, hand still raised with his finger and thumb apart.

"Not really."

"Then I'm not worried." The words came out with more laughter. She turned back to the sink, plucked a cup up from the dish rack, and filled it with water. She gulped the first glass and then filled another, sipping it. She didn't want to throw up.

"Want me to cover it?"

"No. I need to shower."

"What happened tonight?" Tommy asked. He'd moved to the table, sitting in Ivan's seat in front of his laptop.

"Nothing good. Any word from Ivan? Or Mason?" she asked, side-stepping his questioning. She didn't want to talk about it or even acknowledge it. She moved to the table, too, easing into the chair beside him, peeking over his shoulder at the screen. Darth Vader images dropped from the top of the screen like raindrops. Tommy slid a finger onto a fingerprint scanner, and the screen saver evaporated, showing several windows open on a carousel—the front one a snapshot of the security cameras.

"That's how I knew you were almost here," Tommy said. "Are you hungry?"

She was, and she appreciated his attempt to keep her distracted. "I am. But I'm going to shower first. Can you keep an eye on him?"

Tommy's gaze flicked to the living room. "What if he wakes up?"

"Leave him. Unless he's screaming. Then come get me." She pushed herself up, her muscles protesting. "We have frozen pizza?"

Tommy scoffed. "In Rita's house? No. They'll be home soon. I'll have her bring food."

"Thanks." She walked around the table, pausing to peer in on Luke. He still dozed fitfully on the couch. Hopefully, he wouldn't die while she bathed.

She pulled a towel from the hallway closet and flipped on the bathroom light. The room was small, nothing compared to the luxury of her bathroom in New York. She normally didn't care, but access to a large tub and the ice machine sounded nice right now. She hung her towel on the rack, turned on the shower, and caught a glimpse of herself in the mirror. Dark circles sank beneath swollen eyes, cuts grazed her cheeks, and Rufus' blood smeared her face. Her chest tightened—Tommy's reaction wasn't dramatic. She looked like she'd survived a war.

The cold water battered her body, taming the inflammation and burning all the open cuts. The water pooled at her feet, forming a line of red along the basin of the white tub. She bent to wipe it off, and a sob choked out of her, the vivid image of a velvet pool of blood beneath Decius' hand creeping in—the steady drip off his fingers tips. She turned the water off, uncaring that she was only half clean. She grabbed her towel, the blue cloth darkening as she dried off with shaking hands. Shit. She'd forgotten clothes.

She peeked her head out of the bathroom. Ernie and Rita had returned already, their hushed voices carrying up the stairs, but the smell of food sickened her. Going back downstairs wasn't an option. With the dirty towel wrapped around her, she moved silently to her room, clicking the door closed and taking several deep breaths. Just get dressed and go down to check on Luke.

Aeron flipped her light on and froze. Decius' clothes were on her bed, his jeans and hoodie carelessly tossed like he would pick them up when he got back—because he was supposed to. She dropped to her knees, her stomach turning, and she curled into the fetal position, clutching the filthy towel around her. The emotional knot in her throat prevented her from breathing, and as her stomach lurched, the dam broke. Sobs rocked her body, her entire being shaking. Each time she inhaled, it somehow made the pain worse. How could breathing make it worse? With each exhale, she thought she would never catch her breath again. The sobs wouldn't stop. She cried. Full, snotty, heartbreaking wails: for her brother, for herself, for her father, for Shannon, and for Luke. Because she had done this—ruined them all with a single lie.

She cried, her body shivering, her throat swollen, her soul broken. It could have been minutes, hours, or days she stayed curled on her floor before her door creaked open. She'd fallen to her side, her head too heavy to pick up off the ground. She didn't even look up to see who the feet approaching her belonged to. The mercenaries could just come and get her—it didn't matter anymore. But the feet that padded toward her were bare. Rita's soft face entered her vision as the woman squatted beside her and pushed her hair from her face. She placed a glass of water next to her and pulled a pillow from the bed to slip underneath Aeron's head. The warmth of the quilt settled over her like a long-needed hug, and she let her eyes drift closed.

27

LUKE

uke forced his eyes open, the heavy feeling of a medically induced sleep and the tug of an IV uncomfortably familiar. He gripped the back of the couch, his body protesting as he sat up in the unfamiliar wood-paneled room. A blanket was tangled around his legs, and he ripped it off. He was too warm with it on. He smiled. He was warm.

The room was dated—an older home with brown carpeting. The couch was sunken in, the scratchy plaid material probably older than he was. The sun came in through two frost-kissed windows, framing a wooded landscape. The only other piece of furniture in the room was a stained coffee table in front of him that held several mugs, an open Legacy med kit, and empty vials. Dr. Shea. His heart pounded, the world around him spinning—the Sin, Rosemary, Aeron's mother. The torture he'd endured flooded back to him; each moment, each person had pulled on a deep well of self-disgust. Then, Aeron had shown up, and—oh shit, he'd shot Decius.

He pressed his hands against his face, the image of Decius dead on the operating table blinking into his mind. He needed to find Aeron. He unclipped the IV from his PICC line and hung it up.

"Oh, good. You're awake."

Luke snapped his head toward Mason, who stood in the doorway, a mug in his hands.

"Where am I?" Luke asked.

"A safe house in Connecticut," Mason said, entering the room and sitting on the coffee table. He put his mug down next to the other five. He looked exhausted—deep bags beneath his eyes and a barely healed cut across his forehead. Luke noted he didn't meet his eyes. Instead, he grabbed Luke's wrist, checking his pulse. "How are you feeling?"

"Like I should be dead," Luke whispered. It wasn't meant as a metaphor. He only had a few clear memories, but what he did recall in stark clarity was shooting his best friend and then watching him die.

"Let's be thankful you're not."

"Are you?" Luke asked. Mason released Luke's wrist and grabbed the back of his head, looking to the ceiling. "You can't even look at me."

Mason dropped his hands and met Luke's eyes. They were hard to read, but there was none of the joyful light that usually shone in them. "Luke, I'm trying here. Okay? I just walked through the Playhouse, the complete massacre we orchestrated to save you. And I—I need to focus on this. Are you alone, or do we have unseen company?" Mason grabbed Luke's chin, turning his head from side to side.

Luke looked away as soon as Mason let go, expecting to catch a glimpse of Decius, but the room was completely void of his dead. "We're alone."

"Well, that's a good start."

"How is she?" Luke asked, a slight ping in his chest. After Shannon died, Aeron was inconsolable. He needed to see her and explain what happened. He glanced around the room, expecting Shannon to appear at the thought, but it remained empty.

Mason dropped his head in his hands, taking several deep breaths. When he looked back up, he wiped away the moisture from his cheeks. "Her brother is dead, Luke. She's terrible." He wiped his hands on his pants. "I'm going to remove the PICC line. Stay still."

Luke nodded. Mason turned Luke's hand over, resting it on his thigh. It took three alcohol wipes to clean the area, and Luke was mesmerized by the clean patch of skin. Only then did he realize he was still in the clothes Rosemary had grabbed him in, covered in vomit, blood, and piss. He must smell disgusting.

"How long has it been since Rosemary grabbed me?"

Mason placed gauze on the insertion site and applied pressure before pulling the long tube out. "Four days. Five?" He furrowed his brow. "I know for you, it feels like weeks. I remember that feeling. How is your head?" He placed the PICC line in a plastic bag on the table and put a Band-Aid on Luke's arm.

"It's quiet," Luke said. His mind was clear—no pain—but without his dead, it was like he was missing a piece of himself. They had pulled on things deep inside of him, reminding him what it meant to be human. And now he felt—fine.

Mason's gaze bore into him, and Luke looked away. He didn't need Mason worried about him. They needed to be concerned about Aeron. "Listen, what you just went through—the way you did. . ." Mason sighed, looking away. "I'm sorry."

"Why? You didn't pump me full of Sin."

"No." Mason stood up and began to pace. When they were younger, Mason would pace when trying to put together a lecture on the spot. Luke couldn't handle one of those lectures right now. "I should have protected you better."

Luke stiffened, the memory of Mason in the Playhouse returning. "You were there—in the room."

Mason nodded. "What do you remember?" Luke looked at the floor, furrowing his brow. "I won't judge you, Luke. But you have no idea how dangerous the woman who did this to you is. And the extent she will go to get you back and gain access to Legacy Inc, and worse. If you can remember anything—"

"You mean Aeron's mom?" Luke said. "The scarred woman."

Mason kept his features schooled. "Yes."

"She just wants to see her kids, Aeron and De—" Luke could feel the blood drain from his face. Mason pressed his lips together and nodded.

"Imagine how angry she will be to learn you killed her son."

"It was an accident." But Luke remembered the cold switch he'd seen in Maureen, from kind to deadly in a moment.

"I don't think she will care." Mason picked back up his mug. "I need you to shower and eat something. We're far from being out of the woods, and we need to discuss our next move and figure out who is still alive."

Luke nodded but didn't have an appetite. He leaned back, closing his eyes. Decius was gone. It didn't seem real.

"Luke," Mason called. "Now."

The kitchen was full of people Luke didn't know: a large man with tattoos washing dishes, a scrawny woman with wispy hair reading a book at the round table, and a man with blonde hair and blue eyes in a mechanics jumpsuit eating pancakes next to a laptop. The tattooed man spotted Luke first, a smile lighting up his face, and Luke took a step back.

"Good to see you up. You had us worried." He dried his hands on a dish rag and extended one to Luke. "I'm Ernie."

Luke eyed the hand but didn't shake it. Mason glared at him from the stairwell. "C'mon. The bathroom is up here."

Luke followed slowly. His back was stiff and in pain, as if he'd been hit by a car. They reached the landing and turned right, and Luke paused outside the first closed door, soft sobs reaching his ears. He put his hand on the door frame and leaned closer. Aeron.

Mason grabbed his arm and tugged, shaking his head. "Not yet."

"I need to see her," Luke said. The memory of her arms wrapped around him tugged at his chest. He wanted to hold her. "Please."

Mason looked him up and down, his face twisting in disgust. "You're still covered in her brother's blood."

Luke looked down at his clothes again. "Yeah." He shook his head. "You're right."

Mason tossed Luke a towel and handed him a stack of clothes. "Take your time. Are you sure you're feeling okay?"

"I'm fine," Luke answered, but he wasn't. Maybe once he showered, the dam would break, and his tears would drop. Or when he saw Aeron, it would hit him. That would do it.

It took three full-body scrubs to feel clean, and then he washed his hair and body one more time for good measure. The water was nearly freezing by the time he got out. He dried off and caught a glimpse of himself in the mirror; the reflection looking back at him was exactly the same. He had a few cuts and bruises, but he looked refreshed—alive.

The jeans and hoodie Mason had given him fit fine, and he wrapped his filthy clothes in his towel to throw out. When he opened the door, he stopped short. Mason sat on the floor. He closed the book he'd been reading and looked up.

"Feel better?" Mason asked.

"I feel the same, just clean."

"And what is 'the same'?" Mason asked, standing up.

Luke licked his lips, sizing up his Guardian. He had always been there for Luke—even when he was doing the unthinkable. His shoulders tensed, waiting for the ball of ice to form in his chest at the thought of Gabe—but nothing happened. He looked over his shoulder, but the boy was nowhere to be seen.

"Luke, we need to talk about what happened in the Playhouse."

Luke shook his head and walked past him, pausing again outside Aeron's door. It was quiet now. He closed his eyes, putting his hand against the wood. He could almost feel her. "I don't want to talk about it." He pulled away, headed to the kitchen, and then out the back door. The frozen cement bit into his bare feet, his ears tingling with the cold as his wet hair seemed to freeze the second he stepped outside. He looked around for a trash can but didn't see one. Instead, he dropped the bundle of clothes near the side of the house and went back inside. Everyone had cleared out except for Mason.

Mason put a steaming mug on the table and motioned for him to sit. Luke did, pulling the coffee toward him. It smelled delicious, and his stomach gave a small rumble. He took a sip; it was perfectly brewed.

"I'm worried about you," Mason said.

"I'm fine," Luke answered. It seemed to be the only thing he could say. But it couldn't be the truth. Maybe if he could see Aeron, explain to her. . .

"Luke, you just killed your best friend."

"I know." He took another sip of his coffee.

"You wanted to comfort his sister while covered in his blood. What the hell is wrong with you?" Mason demanded.

"I don't know!" Luke yelled back. And then softer, "I don't know." Was this denial? No. He killed his best friend. He watched him die. Felt that pain along with Aeron. "I wasn't think—"

"You're not feeling anything, are you?"

"I'm feeling plenty," Luke answered. "My back is killing me. And I'm feeling pretty annoyed with this conversation."

"You killed Decius."

"Accidentally."

"Luke." Mason pressed the heels of his palms to his forehead, taking a few slow breaths before looking back at him. "You. Killed. Your. Best. Friend. Accident or not, you should be feeling something. You felt more grief over Gabe."

Luke opened his mouth to argue but paused. He didn't even feel bad about that right now. He should be a blubbering mess like he had been in the office with Aeron. He'd been one for months. And he should be begging Aeron for her forgiveness, pleading with her to give him a chance to apologize, not rationalizing how to explain it to her. He closed his mouth, averting his gaze.

"What is wrong with me?" Luke whispered, pushing the mug away. "I feel. . . numb. Nothing. Is this like, denial?"

"No." Mason ran a hand through his hair. "Damn it. I was hoping with Maureen there. . ." he blew out a long breath. "You're experiencing the after-effects of Sin recovery. The drug invaded your brain. Your psyche was traumatized when memories were yanked from the recess of your mind while your grief and shame were used to torment you. So, your brain did what it's designed to do: protect your survival. It's restricted access to your emotions."

"No," Luke shook his head. That couldn't be it. "You can't just stop feeling things. I'm just. . . it's a lot. I just need a minute."

"The protocol for building Sin tolerance is slow doses and then months of recovery rebuilding the connections in your brain. You were dosed with a lethal level. Most people wouldn't survive that."

"So, I should feel lucky?" Luke asked. He could almost feel the swirl of indignation beneath the surface—but it slipped away.

"You should feel angry. Angry that they did this to you. Angry that your best friend is dead. Angry that we're not even close to being safe yet."

Luke sat back and crossed his arms. Anger seemed like a waste of time. Only one thing seemed important. Aeron. "Can I please go see her?"

"I've been through this process, Luke. A few times. It can be an asset to have the ability to mute the guilt. But it makes you someone you're not. You become an asshole and lose everyone close to you."

"You're not an asshole," Luke said. "You're one of the nicest guys I know."

"That's because I've integrated my emotions back in. I made the choice to. And it's not easy. We build a tolerance to Sin for two reasons: one, to get all secrets and weaknesses out on the board, and two, to learn to shut down the conscience. Don't get me wrong; it turns you into a hell of an assassin. But you become a terrible human being. Look at Maureen."

Luke didn't want that. He thought of Aeron and tried to pull a feeling from himself, love or hate. But nothing stirred in him. He could only feel the faint memory of them. "How do you fix this?" Luke asked.

"I can't," Mason confessed. "This is beyond my skill set."

"Then who can? I don't want to live like this."

"You're not going to like the answer. The only person I know who can help you is Maureen."

"She'll kill me," Luke said.

"You might die anyway. We're in uncharted waters with you. You received the serum, but that is only a small part of recovery." Mason ran a hand through his hair. "She might help us if I give her what she wants."

"What's that?

"Her kids."

"One of them is dead," Luke said, unsure where Mason was taking this.

Mason nodded, a sad smile crossing his face. "Don't worry about that. Do you have the locations of Katherine's safe houses?"

Luke nodded. He did, but so did Maureen. "Yeah. But I already gave them to Maureen."

Anger darkened Mason's face, and he stood. Luke leaned back, the sudden height difference putting him on guard. "We're not telling Aeron about her mother yet—understand?" Luke nodded. "Good. I'll be right back. I need to make a phone call."

28

KAT

$\mathcal{K}$at traced small circles around the crude smiley face tattoo on Griffin's chest, her arm propped up on him to keep some swelling down. Her fingers were still numb, and if anyone touched her tricep, she would probably disembowel them. Griffin had found some pain blockers in the medicine cabinet, but all the good drugs were in the lab at Headquarters.

"When did you get this one?" she asked. She recognized the design, two stab wounds for eyes and a clean slice creating the look of a smile. It was a signature he left on most kills.

"Stab, stab, smiley face?" He asked, his chest bubbling with laughter. "The year after I left you. Once I realized you were avoiding me, I wanted to be reminded of you every day."

A smile crept onto her face. When they worked together, he would sign the bodies so her Granddad knew which ones belonged to him. He would even say that—'stab, stab, smiley face'—as he carved into the dead bodies and then grin up at her. She lowered her fingertips and traced the Reaper tattoo on his side, the Legacy Inc Rook with a miniature king's crown above it.

Her eyelids became heavy, and she dropped them closed. It had been the perfect night of violence and passion, followed by a confession of the last three days, from Luke's phone call to the final breaths of her mother. If there was any shot of her actually taking over Legacy Inc, she needed Griffin on the same page. And it felt good to confide in him again.

"So you really took out two-thirds of Legacy Inc last night?" Griffin asked, sounding impressed.

"Almost. I sent Carl to Europe to handle the international missions, but none of them should be returning. And I still need to handle the Reapers."

"I can handle the Reapers," Griffin said. "I've been wanting to clean house for a while."

"Not Star. She needs a promotion," Kat said.

"She should be eliminated for disobeying an order," Griffin countered.

"What order?" She opened her eyes, raising an eyebrow at him.

"Not to fuck up your protection detail," Griffin said, his eyes flicking to Kat's arms.

"She broke *my* orders to stay put in order to protect me. Are you jealous she showed up and saved my day?" Kat smirked.

"I'll always be jealous," he said with a matching smirk and kissed her hair. "So that leaves Division Three and the Reapers."

"And the Alliance," Kat said, unease settling over her.

"What are you talking about? The Alliance has been dead for over a decade."

She looked up at him. "Not according to my mother. The Alliance was there last night—all those bodies with the sword tattoo." He held her gaze. "And according to Decius, they were passing themselves off as Legacy Inc assets in Costa Rica."

Griffin's brow furrowed. "We don't have an outpost in Costa Rica."

"That's what I said. So, the Alliance. Don't forget about the International divisions and the worldwide mercenaries coming to collect on our heads."

"No problem at all."

"Yeah, no problem," she said with a laugh.

"Where does Mason fit into all of this?"

"I wish I knew. He's been the undercover righthand to my Granddad for nearly two decades. He's connected to the Alliance—I know it. I just don't know how."

"I can't believe I didn't know anything about them." She felt the shake of his head. "You know, for a while, I was sure Senior believed I was all in."

"You were all in. I fucking hated you."

"Obviously not," Griffin said.

Kat glanced up, unsure which part of her statement he was responding to. Perhaps both. "My first concern is making sure Headquarters is still standing. Then I need to find Perry and Ivan. We should get going."

Her phone vibrated on the nightstand, and she jumped up. Griffin reached behind her and grabbed it. "It's Mason," he said.

She grabbed it and put it on speaker. "About fucking time."

"What happened to Rufus?" Mason asked. No hello or making sure she was good. Just straight to vengeance. She could appreciate that. "I found Rosemary's body—nice work, by the way—and too many others to even justify what we just did. But I didn't find him."

"Last I saw, our mystery woman was chasing him out of the bullpen," she said.

"Amara?" Mason asked, his voice so low she could barely hear it. "Damn. Have you heard from Perry or Ivan? They haven't checked in."

"No. I'm about to head back to D.C."

He fell silent for a few moments; she could hear steady breathing on the line. "Be careful. Your safe houses have been compromised. All the ones Luke was privy to."

Her insides flipped. She swung her legs off the bed and leaned forward. Perry and Ivan's first checkpoint had been her safe house. Griffin sat up beside her, a hand running up and down her spine.

"I'll be in the city in ninety and let you know what I find. Where's everyone else?" Silence followed the question. "Mason?"

"Luke and Aeron are at her safe house."

It suddenly became hard for her to swallow. "Where's Decius?"

Mason's silence answered for him.

"Shit." Moisture gathered behind her eyes, and she sniffed, keeping the tears at bay. There wasn't a good reason for her to feel this upset, but there had been a moment in the Playhouse she could see them working together for a long time. "What happened?"

"All I got was that Luke accidentally shot him."

"Accidentally. . ." For fuck's sake. Luke couldn't catch a break. "How is he?"

"He may not be able to open the vault for a few days to be sure the Sin is out of his system, but he's alive for now."

Kat exchanged a look with Griffin. The haunted face of a Sin survivor darkened his features, and he looked away. "Is he okay?" Kat asked.

"Honestly, I don't know. Your mother gave him a lethal dose."

"How did he survive?" Kat asked.

"That brings us to our bigger problem. Amara is not who you think she is."

Kat didn't think she was anything. There was no information on the woman except the connection to Costa Rica. "She works for the Alliance," Kat supplied.

"No," Mason said. "She runs the Alliance, and she is going to be the only person who might be able to save Luke."

Kat laughed. Of course. "What other bad news do you have for me?"

"I'll save that for you in person. Call me when you have something on Ivan and Perry." He hung up.

That was the most candid Mason had ever been with her, and it didn't feel good. Like he may be setting her up. "That was unexpected."

"He must really like you," Griffin offered. "He never even talks to me unless ordered to. What does he want with Rufus?"

Kat shrugged. It wasn't her place to tell Mason's story. And as much as it pained her to admit it—she didn't fully trust Griffin yet.

She dialed Perry in a last-ditch effort to reach him, and it went to voicemail. She picked out a pair of jeans and a hoodie from her clean laundry pile next to the dresser and headed to the bathroom. The most likely scenarios ran through her head, but she liked the one where Perry caught wind of the safe house leak and was hiding until it was safe. Then she could rip them a new one for being fucking cowards. She grabbed her toothbrush, catching sight of herself in the mirror. Bruises and cuts painted her face, and her hair was pulled up into a bun. She smiled. Fuck her mother. Fuck her Granddad. She'd won.

"You're already dressed?" Griffin pouted from the doorway, still naked.

She raised an eyebrow at him. "We should be halfway to DC by now. You're making me late."

"Why? He's dead. Just let the whole thing burn." He came up behind her and wrapped his arms around her waist, fingers slipping beneath her shirt, and she had to fight the moan wanting to come out. He nuzzled her neck, and she turned and pushed him off playfully.

"There's an extra toothbrush in the bottom drawer. And I'm not leaving. Legacy Inc belongs to me now. Besides, you heard Mason. Do you think Amara will let me live after I attacked the Playhouse and killed just as many of her people as my own?"

"Okay. But what about Luke?" He opened the drawer, picked out a pink toothbrush, and grabbed the toothpaste from in front of her. He raised an eyebrow as he talked while brushing. "Technically, he's reigning Senior."

She worked her hair into a braid. "He doesn't want it. As soon as I can hook up with Mason and grab Luke back, he'll pass it over. What I'm more worried about is Amara and what her plan is."

He rinsed his mouth and put his toothbrush right next to hers; it looked good there. Then he grabbed her hips and pulled her in for a kiss. It wasn't feverish or needy like the kisses last night. This one was soft and possessive. She cupped his face, meeting his intention. His fingers unbuttoned her jeans and slipped inside the waistband, reaching around to cup her ass. He pulled back, moving to her neck. Her hands grasped his wrists, pausing his movements.

"Later," Kat said, pulling his hands from her body to re-button her pants. "Let's find you some clothes."

He smirked. "You're the boss." He put his hands in the air and backed up. Kat arched an eyebrow, her gaze lingering on his body until he was out of sight.

The helicopter landed on the helipad a block from Headquarters. Kat tossed the headset to the seat and jumped to the ground. She and Griffin raced the worn path to the backyard of the Rowhouses. Instead of entering on the ground floor, Kat scaled the back of the building. They ran along the rooftop to the eastern entrance, the one closest to her office and restricted to her family and Griffin.

Griffin opened the hatch with his biometrics and slid down the ladder first. Kat scanned the rooftops for anything out of the ordinary. Everything seemed fine. She stepped down the ladder, closing the hatch above her. She put her feet on mini slides just outside the metal handle and slid down the three stories, Griffin catching her by the waist at the bottom.

"I've missed that view," he said. Her cheeks heated, and she pushed past him to the door.

"Ready?" she asked.

"Sure. Rag and tag?"

Kat smirked. "It's my favorite game." She pulled the door open, Griffin's gun raised over her shoulder. Against the wall opposite the entrance leaned a petite brunette Reaper.

April pushed off the wall. "Back already? Perry said you'd be in New York until tomorrow. When the chopper landed, I was expecting Senior."

If Perry had made it here, why hadn't he checked in? "Senior is all over the place at the moment. I wouldn't expect him anytime soon. Perry was here?"

"Still is. He and Carl are in the office," April said.

Fuck. Kat narrowed her gaze, and April stepped back. Carl was a dead man. "Any other visitors?"

"Not that I'm aware of," April said.

If Carl had returned, she could guarantee it wasn't alone. "Gather the division and wait for my word," Kat said.

April nodded and backed down the hall.

Kat followed more slowly. She was going to skin Carl alive. No. Pluck his eyeballs out and make him eat them. Both. She would skin him alive and then make him eat his eyeballs. "Why didn't you just kill him?" Griffin asked, annoyed.

"He was the only one I had leverage on," Kat admitted. "And I wanted a contact in my debt in Europe."

Griffin raised his eyebrows and gestured at himself.

"Yeah. I made a lot of questionable decisions the last few days." She grimaced and hurried toward the office, Griffin running to catch up.

They stopped before turning down the long corridor to the Senior Assassin's office. She peeked around the corner. The door to the office was closed, and an unfamiliar guard leaned next to it, a semi-auto rifle in hand.

She took a few slow breaths. "Ready?" she asked Griffin.

"Always," he said.

She turned the corner, a sneer plastered on her face as she approached the door, Griffin falling back behind her. "Who the hell are you?" she demanded.

He pointed his rifle at her. "Freeze, by order of the Senior Assassin."

"You're fucking looking at her, you dipshit."

"I said stop where you are!" He pointed the gun more aggressively.

Kat lined herself up with his center, keeping her pace steady. She stopped ten feet from him and saw sweat on his brow. "Hey, dipshit. Duck."

He cocked his head, and she stepped to the wall, looking back. Griffin flipped him off and then flipped his head forward. His braid flicked over his head, launching his hair dart. It landed in the guard's neck. His gun fell, hands going to his throat. Deep red poured over the guard's fingers, and he dropped to his knees. Kat approached, kicking him over. "I said duck."

The scanner whirred to life at her palm print, the small prick of her hand unlocking the door. Griffin pushed it open, gun raised.

"What the. . ."

"Hey, Carl," Griffin said with a friendly tone. Griffin kept the door propped, and Kat entered. Her blood boiled. Carl sat on her desk, eyes widening in surprise. She shook her head. A snake is a snake in the garden or in a cage.

She glanced at Perry, unmoving on the floor, and then to a man with scars identical to her Granddad's, kneeling in front of the vault, his tablet on her desk chair. He had a black eye, a busted lip, and sweat pouring down his face. This must be Ivan. His looks negated the letdown of his name, at least.

"Katherine," Carl said. His hand hovered over his gun, eyes flicking between her and Griffin.

"What are you doing in my office?"

"I thought we were just claiming titles now—you know now that the real Senior Assassin is dead."

"Why would you assume that?" Kat asked, but the prickle of betrayal inched up her neck.

"Your mother told me."

"I'm going to kill her," Kat spat.

"You already did," Griffin said. He shut the door, but not letting it fully close, and stepped up next to her.

"Oh, that's right." Kat snickered. "Your turn."

Griffin fired. Carl dove at Ivan, and another man sprung up from behind the desk and fired at Kat. Griffin shoved her sideways. Pain ripped through her arm at the contact, tears springing to her eyes. She pushed her back against the wall, sinking to the ground and breathing through the fire in her tricep. Carl grabbed Ivan by the hair and pulled him to his feet, slamming his gun under his jaw.

"Griff," Kat said. She tossed a throwing knife in the air. He spun, back kicking the blade and sending it sailing forward. The unknown man parried it, but missed the two blades sliding from Griffin's fingers. They landed in his chest, his gun firing into the ceiling as he dropped. Griffin turned to Carl.

"Let him go, Carl. You're outmatched."

Carl grinned. "I don't think so. The European Division has some amazing tech. The silent alarm went off the second you killed Toby—the man in the hall. My team is already descending on the building."

"Your team?" Kat scoffed and rose to her feet. "You've been gone two days."

"I knew you were lying about Senior the second you mentioned moving up in the company. I've been working with the European Division undercover for the past four years. I've already moved up." Carl let go of Ivan's hair and pulled up his own shirt. A pointed crown sat above the Rook.

"What the fuck is that?" Griffin asked.

Carl sneered. "You did catch me off guard with my son. I thought I hid him well enough. But to make a move eliminating portions of my division—you wouldn't be bold enough unless he was dead. A quick call to your mother, and well, here we are."

"Only blood relatives can open anything inside that vault," Kat said. Even if you got it open. . ." Perry. She looked over at him, the slight movement of his chest indicating he was breathing. Carl needed him alive.

"And now I have two of you, just in case." He removed the gun from Ivan's chin and pointed it toward them. "Keep working," he said to Ivan.

Ivan's eyes slid to Kat, his terrified gaze begging her to do something. An alarm sounded from somewhere within the building. They'd been breached. "How many?"

"Enough to eliminate everyone in this building. That's what you were after, right? A full rehaul. It's a brilliant plan."

"I know," Kat said. "Too bad you have no idea what you're up against."

"You won't make it out of here alive," Griffin said and dove at Carl, tackling him to the ground and disarming him.

Kat moved to Perry's side, rolling him over. He had a cut across his temple, and blood stained the side of his face. "C'mon," she said and slapped him. He roused, and relief spread through her.

"Carl—"

"Yeah," Kat said. "Get up." He sat up, and Kat moved to Ivan. "We have to go."

"I can't," Ivan said. "The code will go rogue if I just rip it out."

"What does that mean?" Kat asked and glanced at Carl and Griffin. Griffin was taking his time, reminding Carl where his place was in the hierarchy.

"You do know what rogue means, right?" Ivan asked.

Kat curbed the urge to punch him. Perry joined them, steady on his feet. "Yes, she knows what it means, but if you like living, shut up and do what she says," Perry said.

Ivan nodded. He punched in a few more lines of code and then disconnected the cable from the vault scanner. Kat's stomach flipped as she waited to see what would happen. His screen went black for a moment, then a new series of codes cascaded down the screen.

"No, no, no, no," he said, fingers flying across the keyboard. The door to the office slammed open, and Kat looked back. Star stood in the doorway, eyes moving from Griffin and Carl to them.

"What is it?" Kat asked.

Star held up her phone, and Kat looked at Ivan, his face paling.

"I'm sorry," he said. "The entire hit list just went live."

29

AERON

The door creaked open, but Aeron kept her eyes closed under the covers. She'd had three visitors so far. Rita had come in to check on her and left plates of food. Mason had tended to her side and injuries, but she couldn't tell you what he talked about. And Tommy popped in to let her know Luke was awake. She didn't say a word to any of them. It was like Shannon all over again. The boxes she'd built to keep herself sane had cracked open. But this was worse. So much worse. She was stuck in a bubble, drowning in her repressed memories—the painful ones and the joyful ones.

The footsteps neared, and the mattress sunk under the weight of someone sitting down. "Aeron," Mason said. "I can't give you any more time."

She pulled the covers off her face and squinted against the incoming sunlight. Mason's slight frown pulled her into a sitting position. "What's going on?" she asked, her voice hoarse and her mouth dry. She cleared her throat.

"Ivan sent a distress signal to the home computer. Go shower. It's time to roll."

Aeron's parched mouth suddenly felt full of sand, Ivan's face floating into her mind. There was no way she was losing anyone else. She tossed the blankets on the floor and stood up, the world spinning around her. Mason grabbed her arm and steadied her. Her fingers wrapped around his forearm, and she used him to ground herself in the moment. It took several deep breaths to build a box large enough to surround her pain. Once contained, it became smaller and smaller with each breath until her chest did not ache with each inhale.

"Ready?" he asked.

She opened her eyes and met his intense gaze. There was no humor in his face, no compassion in his eyes. He was heartbroken and ready for war. "Is there a plan?" She released his arm and grabbed a glass of water off the desk. She gulped it down, her body craving the nourishment. With a clearer mind, she scanned her surroundings. Plates still filled with food and cups of tea and water sat untouched around the room. The open med kit spilled out onto the desk. All evidence of her grief. She needed to clean it up—erase it before she returned.

"I've got it," he said, reading her mind and grabbing the closest plates. "Go shower."

But she didn't want to shower. "How is Luke?" she asked.

Mason paused, hand hovering over a plate of toast. "Luke is. . ." he sighed and turned to look at her. "Why do you care?"

Because there was hardly a memory of Decius that came during her grief that didn't have Luke attached to it—she hated Luke and had more than one solid thought wishing he was dead. Why should Decius be gone while Luke gets to walk this earth? Luke didn't deserve to be here. In the same moment, she pitied him. He'd been blinded by grief and tricked into believing a lie—and if she hadn't seen Decius die in front of her, who knows what she would believe or how far she would go?

"Because I love him," she said. "And fucking hate him at the same time. Because Decius loved him—he died making sure we gave Luke the benefit of the doubt."

Mason picked up the plate and stacked it on top of the others in his hand. "What happened in the Playhouse? Luke hasn't said much."

She sighed. He was checking her, making sure the pain was tucked away for a later day. It needed to be done. "He was in a bad state. I left him in a room and told him to wait so I could clear the hall. Decius showed up. We crossed paths with some people he worked with in Costa Rica—some women named Izz and Jude, who actually saved our lives. Luke must have fought through the Sin for a few moments and came into the hall. There was a threat directly behind me, and Luke aimed for them. Decius didn't see Luke as Luke. He only saw an unidentified target with those fucking contacts. When Luke pulled the trigger, Decius dove in front of me. For all intents, it was an accident. Yet, if Luke just stayed where I fucking I put him, Decius would be alive." She kept her voice even, her emotions in check, crammed inside the box.

Mason nodded, satisfied. "Go clean up."

Aeron grabbed a towel from the hallway and shut the bathroom door behind her. It wasn't until she was under the shower that she realized Mason never answered her question about Luke.

The room was spotless, the bed remade, and Decius' clothes folded on top of it when she returned from the shower. "I'll meet you downstairs," Mason said and excused himself before she could even thank him. The clean room gave her some relief. She would get through this.

Aeron wrapped her hair in a t-shirt to keep the water from dripping down her back, then pulled on a pair of sweatpants and Decius' hoodie. The smell of him engulfed her, and she took a deep breath, securing his scent in her mind. When she arrived, the kitchen was full of activity, and it reminded her of her first days at

Ernie's. Food was being cooked, plans were being made, and people who didn't belong together making life happen.

The room quieted when she reached the bottom step, eyes turning to her. She didn't want to look at Luke, sitting and eating a sandwich where Decius had been only days ago. And Mason avoided looking at her altogether, grabbing food from the fridge and passing it to Rita. She looked past them all to Tommy, sitting in front of Ivan's computer.

"You better not have used all the hot water," he said.

"I did," Aeron said jokingly. "And I used your favorite towel." He flipped her off, and it felt perfect. She laughed and dropped into the seat beside him, avoiding Luke's questioning gaze. "What's happening?"

"I'm not sure. I don't really understand all of this, but there was a message flashing—an S.O.S. that they had been caught," Tommy said. The screen looked exactly the same as the other night, with the security cameras up and the hit list in the corner.

"I've already called Kat," Mason said, taking the seat across from her. "She's headed to DC and will update us. Not much we can do until she calls, which should be any minute."

"Hungry?" Tommy held out a bag of chips to her. He tipped them so she could see the front: cracked pepper. Her stomach gave a desperate rumble. She could eat.

"You should eat something more sustainable," Luke said. Aeron looked toward him out of reflex and stared. There was something off about how he was sitting—straight-backed and hands folded on the table in front of him.

"What?" Her defenses flared.

"You haven't eaten in days. You need something healthier than chips. Here." He stood, and her gaze followed him as he opened the fridge and pulled out a bowl of cut cucumbers, holding it out to her. "Take it."

"What the hell is wrong with you?" She cocked her head and glared.

Confusion crossed Luke's face. "You need food."

She stood, too, not touching the bowl. "You don't get to tell me what I need." Anger buzzed in her system.

"Aeron—" Mason tried to intervene, but she cut him off, her focus on Luke.

"I needed you to stay put," Aeron said. "I needed to not worry about you for five minutes."

"If I stayed put, you'd probably be dead," Luke said, his voice even.

"Then you should have let me die!" she yelled. "Just like you should have all those months ago."

"Don't say that." Luke put the bowl down and shook his head. He reached for her. Aeron threw a punch, her fist connecting with his face, and he stumbled back. She swung again, and Luke caught her arm and pulled her close, wrapping his other one around her waist. Her breath caught in her chest, her body sending mixed signals to lean into him for comfort and to push away in disgust. "I could never live in a world without you," he said, eyes boring into her.

"Then you should have taken the bullet instead of pulling the trigger." The anger and hurt in her voice for each life he'd taken spewed out. He released her and took a step back, eyes still trained on her.

"Maybe," he said, not rising to the bait. He was too calm, too collected, and it unnerved her. He should be feeling more pain than she did. He should be suffering. "But it's too late to change it now." He turned and retreated to the living area he'd recovered in.

Her chest heaved, trying to keep herself under control. A hand touched her shoulder, and she spun, grabbing onto it, her other fist cocked to strike. It was Tommy. She released him and took a few steps back. "Sorry," she said. She shook her head and sat back down.

"That went better than expected," Mason said, leaning forward and grabbing the bowl of cucumbers. "Did you want one?" He raised an eyebrow and tipped the bowl toward her.

Her stomach growled, and she nodded, taking a few and pairing them with the chips. Luke's reaction had been cold. She'd meant to hurt him with her words, but they barely even made a dent.

"What's wrong with him?" Aeron asked.

Mason took a bite of cucumber before answering. "What do you mean?"

"That's not Luke," Aeron said. "Not the Luke I know."

Mason gave her a measured look and shook his head. "Not yet. Let's wait until everyone gets here. I'll explain it then."

The computer screen flashed beside her. Five pings echoed from the speakers. Tommy moved the cursor to the flashing window in the corner. Not a security breach, but an update to the hit list. The final five names were uncovered. Eileen Gale, Betty Wayward, Perry Wayward, Katherine Wayward, and Luke Wayward.

Luke reappeared in the doorway. "Was that the list?"

Aeron nodded, turning the screen toward him. The color in his cheeks paled. Mason moved behind Tommy to get a look. "Ah, fuck," Mason said. "That's going to be a problem."

30

KAT

"**F**uck." Kat didn't move her gaze from Ivan. "The whole list?"

"Eileen Gale, and then Betty, Perry, Katherine, and Luke Wayward," Ivan recited, putting the cords into his pocket, and tucking the tablet under his arm.

"How much am I worth?" Kat asked, curiosity getting the better of her.

"Really?" Perry asked as he moved to pull Griffin off of Carl.

"Seven million," Star answered. "Perry, you're worth six. More importantly, there is a ten-man team moving this way as we speak, and at least three other smaller teams attempting to clear the buildings."

Griffin shook off Perry's help and hauled Carl to his feet. Bruises had already formed on Carl's face, and blood trailed from a cut across his temple.

"Call them off," Kat said to Carl.

He bared his bloody teeth. "I'd rather die."

"Good, that makes my life easier." She turned to Star. "You take Perry and our new friend back to the helicopter. Griffin and I will clear the building."

Star shook her head. "No. Kat—your head is worth seven million dollars. You made it public knowledge you were in charge. They will be heading here to find you."

A buzzing started in Kat's stomach. Seven million was a lot of money. Add Perry's in, and they were sitting at a thirteen-million-dollar bounty. She'd garnered some trust within Legacy Inc, but cash like that is hard to pass up. "What about the Reapers and Division Three?"

Star glanced at Griffin, and he cleared his throat. "In order to keep you safe from Senior, I made it abundantly clear to my Reapers that I wanted nothing to do with you."

"There are a few of us who will defend you to the death, but—"

"But thirteen million," Kat reiterated and ran a hand over her face. "Got it." The door behind Star dinged with gunfire. Kat pinched the bridge of her nose. "Okay. We need to make it out of this office and halfway down the hall. The door to the left leads to the secret passages. Blood-only biometrics. We'll have a better chance running behind the walls."

"We just have to get there," Perry said. He opened the desk drawer and pulled his gun out.

Star signaled them to line up next to the wall by the door, Griffin in line first with Carl. If anyone was going to be shot, it would be him. Kat stood behind Griffin, and Perry, who was in charge of Ivan, was behind her. A tactical exit.

"Ready?" Star asked. Griffin nodded. Star pulled the door wide open and pressed herself against it. Bullets flew into the office, metal on metal rebounding through the room as they bounced off the vault. When the shooting paused, Griffin shoved Carl into the doorway first before stepping behind him. No shots went off. Star peered around the edge of the door and shook her head.

"They must be camped out around the corner," Griffin whispered. "Let's move." Star and Griffin took the lead, and Kat grabbed Carl's arm. They stepped over Toby, the air thick with anticipation, with the entrance to the passage only feet away. Before they reached the retinal scanner, it exploded into pieces. Griffin fired a shot down the hall, and Star dove on top of Kat while Carl made a break for it. Kat's tricep connected with the ground, and vomit accompanied the pain. Kat pushed Star off of her and retched. Her entire body shook.

"Get off me!" Kat snarled. She pushed Star away again and sprinted after Carl, Griffin yelling at her to stop. Carl was not getting away from her. Griffin cursed behind her, his blades flying past her toward the few heads peering out from the hall, attempting to shoot.

Kat tackled Carl to the ground. Griffin, Star, and Perry ran past them. Carl turned and kicked at her face. She backpedaled, and he returned to his feet. She didn't wait for an invitation. She charged forward, her elbow making a solid connection with his nose, the crunch giving that satisfaction only breaking bones could. He stumbled back, and she struck again, sliding her arm across his face until her hand covered his nose and mouth, and her other hand secured the back of his neck.

The blood pooled behind her fingers. She grasped his hair and pulled his head back, sticking a leg behind him and tripping him to the floor. Her hand slipped from his face, and she dropped a heavy knee to his chest, re-securing the hold over his mouth and nose, forcing the blood back into his sinuses and down his throat. Bullets cracked the wall beside them, but she watched with a smile as he struggled to gasp for air, clawing at her hands.

"You should have agreed to work with me." His eyes widened, and once Kat was sure the blood pooled into his mouth, she let up, allowing him to gasp and pull the blood into his lungs; she repeated the process, slowly depriving him of oxygen and flooding his lungs with blood. When his cough became difficult and his breath raspier, she rose, wiping her stained hands on his shirt and leaving him to drown in his own blood.

Griffin and Star were already around the corner. Perry signaled for Ivan to leave the office, and Kat joined them. "I don't want to die here," Ivan said, terror etched beneath his scarred face.

"Then just follow our lead," Kat said.

She peered down the hall. Star and Griffin posted further down the other end, now holding semi-auto rifles from the dead bodies. Griffin signaled the all-clear, and they moved down the hall. Perry and Kat stopped only to pick up their own weapons. They needed to get behind the steel-lined walls.

"Maybe they retreated further into the building," Star said.

Kat sighed. Aeron really fucked her timeline for a smooth takeover of Legacy Inc. She didn't have the assets in place or the leverage to make many moves. "Two hallways until the next entrance."

Griffin peered around the corner and snapped his head back as a bullet raced past him. He shoved Kat back the way they came. "Fuck. Reapers headed this way." He fired a few shots down the hall and peeked again. "They're holding."

Kat closed her eyes and leaned her head back against the wall. She should have dissolved the strip club and left—taken Dom, Gunnar, and all those kids back to the Caribbean. A thumb brushed her cheek, and she opened her eyes, Griffin inches from her. He leaned in for a kiss, cupping her face and pressing his body into her. She laced her fingers in his hair, pulling him closer. She could taste the goodbye on his lips as he pulled away, and her heart thumped against her ribs. He was going to do something stupid, but she wasn't losing him again.

"Take it," Kat said.

Griffin cocked his head. "Take what?"

"Legacy Inc. The Reapers will follow you. And there's no evidence Senior is dead. And there never will be."

"Senior is dead?" Star said, shock in her words proving Kat's point.

"Yes. Can you hold them off?" Kat asked. Star nodded and fired down the hallway.

"Perry, give him the phone." Kat looked at Perry expectantly.

He hesitated, eyeing Griffin. "That's a lot of power, Kat."

"And if we don't make it out of here, it doesn't matter. I'll catch you up when we're safe, but he's our biggest ally."

Perry held her gaze for a moment and then conceded, passing the phone to Griffin. "It mimics his email and phone number for outgoing messages, but you cannot receive any in return."

Kat's stomach flipped when Griffin grasped the phone. She grabbed his hand. "Don't you fuck me over," she said. "I'll be back as soon as I can."

Griffin licked his lips. "The only thing I want to fuck you over is the desk in front of that vault."

Her core tightened at the thought. "I'll make sure that happens."

"How does you fucking her on a desk help anything?" Ivan asked, breaking the moment. Kat glared at him, and he cowered back against the wall.

"We need to be seen on their side," Griffin said.

Kat held up her rifle. "And we need to be seen trying to kill them."

"Great," Ivan said, his voice a few octaves higher.

Perry grasped him by the shoulder. "Your only job is to follow my lead and not get shot."

"Let's go," Griffin said, turning away from them. He and Star cleared the hall of the two Reapers and then hustled to the next corridor, peering down it. Griffin looked over his shoulder at her and signaled three more Reapers. She nodded at him and swallowed hard. An intrusive thought entered Kat's mind—that he had only slept with her to get more information about her Granddad. But he could have killed her at any moment; there was no need for the charade at this point.

He turned to face her and fired. The wall above her head exploded, and she kept her eyes on him. He and Star backed into the hall, and Kat raised her gun, firing toward them.

"About damn time!" Griffin yelled down the hall. "I've got them cornered by the office. Where is everyone else?"

"It's a shit show, Reaper," one of them said. "We were defending HQ against an outside attack, and then we got the alert. What is Senior thinking?"

"They tried to kill him," Griffin said.

"Damn."

Kat fired again, and Star peeked her head out, firing back. "Can I get some assistance?" she asked. Three Reapers rounded the corner, Kat picked off two, and Griffin shot the other from behind. He motioned Kat forward, and she signaled Perry and Ivan to follow.

"One more hall," Perry said as they reached Star and Griffin.

Before they could round the corner, a six-man team of Reapers appeared. Kat stopped in her tracks and shoved Griffin forward, kicking his back. He turned, and she landed a solid punch to his face. Perry did the same to Star. They engaged themselves, so it would be impossible for them to shoot Kat or Perry without also killing Griffin or Star.

"Grab that man!" Griffin ordered. Kat looked over at the team, all frozen, unsure of what they should be doing. "They were trying to break into the office!" Griffin yelled. "Secure Mr. Wayward's asset and get him down that hall!"

The words jump-started the Reapers. Two females moved forward, grabbing Ivan. He tried to struggle, and Kat shook her head. "Just go!" she yelled at him. The other three descended upon Star and Perry, the last stood staring at her. Griffin swept Kat's feet, and she landed on her back with a thud. He pressed a blade to her neck. Her chest heaved, her entire body shaking with pain.

"What are you waiting for?" one of the Reapers asked.

Griffin shifted his gaze from her. "If we return them alive, we make way more money," he said. "I bet seven million apiece."

"I'd rather not make that bet."

Before the Reaper could even raise his gun, Griffin released Kat.

She rolled to her side, grabbing the Reaper's ankles, and dropping him to the ground. His gun fired as he fell, and she looked over her shoulder at Perry and Star. One of the Reapers spun, the bullet landing in his back. When she looked back down, Griffin had already sliced the Reaper's neck. The remaining two Legacy Inc assets turned to her.

"Fuck," Griffin swore under his breath. He glanced at her, and she nodded. He backhanded her, but she wasn't quite ready and fell sideways, landing hard on her sliced-up arm. She closed her eyes and dropped her head back, blackness threatening to take over as the pain filled all of her senses. "Kat!" Perry yelled.

She tried to turn her head, but it wouldn't cooperate. Two shots went off, and footsteps sounded around the corner. It felt like ripping glue from her eyelids, but she forced them open, and rolled to her knees, trying to take in the chaos in the hall.

Star lay in a pool of blood on the ground. Griffin was engaged with the two hostiles, and Perry scrambled to her side as the two female Reapers returned. He administered a headshot to the first one and then rolled in front of her as the other fired, the bullet flying past Kat's ear. He aimed again, hitting her in the leg, and she dropped.

"Get out of here!" Griffin yelled.

Perry pulled Kat to her feet, and they ran. Ivan's motionless body met them in the hall by the door. If he died, they'd failed. "Ivan!" she called out.

Ivan's head popped up, swiveling to find her. He grinned when he spotted them and clambered to his feet. "I figured if they thought I was already dead, they'd leave me alone."

Kat laughed in relief. "Not bad for a techie. Let's get out of here."

Perry leaned in front of the retinal scanner, the door unlocking for him. He shoved Ivan in and grabbed Kat's arm to push her next, his hand closing on the raw skin beneath her hoodie. A scream left her, and she stumbled, clutching the door frame for support, eyes falling closed.

"What's wrong?" He released her arm, his hand covered in blood. She must have ripped the bandage; her hoodie sleeve was soaked.

"A farewell present from my mother," she said. "It's fine. Let's go."

"What did she do?" he demanded; his mouth downturned.

"She filleted my tricep. I'm fine." Perry looked across the hall to the medical lab entrance. "No." She shook her head and grabbed him. "We can get supplies anywhere."

"I'm not risking you passing out again before we get off the property. It will take less than a minute. Ivan, don't move." He pulled Kat across the hall before she could protest, Ivan staring at them as the door clicked shut. With a quick palm scan, the medical lab door slid open, and the lights turned on when they entered.

The room was colder than the hall, and Kat pressed against the closest metal table, trying to lower her body temperature. Her head said they needed to leave now, but her body was grateful for the pause. This was the biggest benefit of Legacy Inc—access to cutting-edge technology and medical science. Complete pain blockers and super-meds for faster recovery only scratched the surface of what they had access to, and those were game changers.

Perry headed straight for a supply cabinet, grabbing cleaning solution, Lidopen—the pain-blocking gel—and new clear bandages. "Let me see," he said.

Kat removed her arm from the hoodie, and he sucked in a breath. "Okay, maybe longer than a minute."

"Just throw the gel on and re-cover it. We don't have time."

"We're making time. Ivan is safe, and we can't be tracked. Brace yourself," Perry said. He pulled the bandage, and it came away easily, blood and puss having busted through it.

Kat's knees buckled, her vision blurring when he rinsed the area, her arm shaking. "Fucking hell, Perry!"

"Almost done. Suck it up." He smiled at her glare and held up the gel. "See?"

Kat grit her teeth, trying to hold her arm steady. The cold gel coated her wound, and an immediate relief from the pain took effect, her blood pressure lowering considerably. "Thanks."

"Did she suffer?" Perry asked, applying the bandage. "When you tortured and killed her."

The knowledge he knew her so well brought a genuine smile to her face—she wouldn't be here unless her mother was dead. She pulled her hoodie back on. "For the time I was allowed? Yes."

"Good. Let's get out of here."

The door slid open. She covered the left, and he covered the right. The coast was clear, and she sprinted, opening the passageway and immediately turning to cover him. The coast was still clear. Perry ran, and a shot echoed through the hall. His body spun off course, and he crashed to the floor.

Kat's insides turned to liquid. No. Absolutely fucking not. This was not happening tonight. Kat searched for the shooter but saw nothing. Another shot rang out, and Perry's body jerked with the impact. As a bullet grazed her shoulder, Kat threw herself back into the open doorway for cover. She spotted the shooter to Perry's right, lying prone just out of sight. Motherfucker. She fired several shots, none landing, but they retreated.

"Ivan, help me!" Kat yelled. She kept the shooter's position in sight. Ivan grabbed Perry by the shoulders and pulled him into the hidden hallway, the steel door closing behind them. He lowered Perry to the ground and backed away, visibly shaking. He leaned against the wall and slid down; eyes wide.

Kat dropped to her knees at Perry's side. He blinked a few times, but his jaw remained clenched. "You're going to be fine," she said and lifted his shirt to find the wounds, but he'd been struck in the back, and there were no exits out the front.

Perry clasped her hand, shaking his head. "No." He raised his other, holding out a small medical bag he'd grabbed. "Take it." Blood stained his teeth, and as he tried to suppress a cough, it sprayed across his chest.

Tears burned her eyes, and she blinked furiously to let them fall. They had made it this far. She wasn't going without him. She tossed the small bag to Ivan and dropped to her butt, pulling him between her legs. Maybe it was just a shoulder or a flank shot. She rolled him to his side, his head resting against her thigh. Hot blood soaked into her jeans, and he struggled to catch his breath. A sob escaped her. Both bullets had pierced his lungs.

"No. No, Perry." Another sob left her, and she wiped her face. "This isn't how it's supposed to happen. You're supposed to lead with me." She cradled his head, his hands grabbing onto her arm. They'd been thick as thieves since day one—he'd been her best friend. "You know you're my best friend, right?" she asked. "You're not allowed to leave me."

"You don't. . . have. . . friends," he managed to get out.

"Shh. We're going to get you out of here." She looked at Ivan, his gaze locked on Perry's bloody back. Perry's body shook on her lap as he struggled to breathe. A thud against the door startled her, and she jumped, eyes flying up. Someone slammed against it several more times, and the high-pitched sound of bullets ricocheting off the metal followed. They wouldn't be able to get in, but they couldn't stay here much longer, or their exit would be blocked.

Perry gasped, getting some air, words fighting to get out. Kat leaned closer. "Give them. . . hell." Words jammed in her throat. She didn't want to do this without him. She didn't want to leave him here, but she had no choice if they were going to get out alive. "Make it. . . quick," he said, looking up to meet her eyes.

His face blurred, and she nodded. She wiped her nose on her sleeve and pulled herself out from underneath him, laying his head gently on the floor. "I love you," Kat said. She pressed a kiss to his forehead and stood up. She grabbed the pistol from his hip, squeezing the grip to keep from shaking.

"What are you doing!" Ivan scrambled to his feet and yanked her shoulder before she could aim. She ripped her arm back and aimed at Perry's head, throat swollen with words he would never hear.

She should have been more vocal about how important he was to her—how much she appreciated him. Needed him. She held his gaze and waited for permission. He gave a small nod. "Cover your ears," she said, leaning her ear to her shoulder and covering the other. She pulled the trigger.

The shot echoed in the steel-lined walls, and Perry's body went still, the red halo surrounding his head. She closed her eyes, taking several deep breaths. They only had to get two hallways over to reach a rooftop entrance.

She didn't look back at Ivan. She could imagine the disgust on his face. She would see it herself the next time she looked in the mirror. She tucked Perry's gun into her belt and started down the hall. "Let's go," she said over her shoulder.

She led them down the twisting and turning hallways, needing to double back twice because she had missed the turns. Her head swam with Perry's final moments, the things she should have done differently. She should have forced him into the passageway. Ivan remained silent on their trek until they finally came to a ladder. She grasped the rails and paused.

"Are you okay?" he asked.

"Shut up," Kat said, leaning her head against the cool metal rung. The shooter had come from the same direction as the office. The only way a shooter could have made it past Griffin was—no. Either Griffin was dead, or he betrayed her. Her heart seized at the thought. He better be dead.

"Katherine?" Ivan said. He put a hand on her shoulder. She turned, wrapping a hand around his throat and slamming him against the wall. He squeaked in surprise, clawing at her hand.

"I just killed one of my last family members. And I think I may have been betrayed, again, by my oldest friend. So, I am not okay. Honestly, I can't even think of a good reason at the moment to bring you out of here alive. You failed to cash in on the only thing of value you had to offer me."

He shook his head against the wall, eyes bulging and face

turning red. "I can fix it," he said. He held up the tablet, and she released her grip. "I know how to get in, now."

"Now is too late." She released him and turned back to the ladder. The only possible leverage he offered her now was a bargaining chip with Mason and Aeron for Luke. How could she tell Luke what she had to do? She clenched her teeth and shook her head.

Give them hell.

She'd sacrificed too much to give up now. She needed to see this through, or all of it was pointless. And if Griffin thought he could betray her again and not suffer a fate worse than her mother, he had another thing coming.

31

KAT

K at pulled onto the gravel driveway. She could make out the red barn house in the darkness, with huge garage doors on the right of it.

"This is it?" she glanced at Ivan. He'd remained quiet except to give her directions to his safe house after confirming with Mason it was still secure.

He nodded. "Pull around back."

She rounded the building and saw four vehicles parked along the back wall. The rear door was open, a silhouette waiting in the lighted entrance, their leg bouncing. Kat parked and cut the engine. The sudden quiet consumed her ears. The figure bounded for the car, and Ivan threw his door open. Aeron wrapped herself around him, Ivan nearly melting in her arms. The sight hurt, and Kat turned away, opening her door, and exiting. Her tricep burned, the feeling completely gone from her fingers. She tucked her left arm into her hoodie pocket for support.

She felt Aeron's gaze on her and looked back. Aeron looked to the back seat and back to her. Kat swallowed hard, her face contorting to keep back any more tears, and shook her head. Perry wasn't with them. Aeron's face dropped, and Kat remembered Aeron had lost someone too. "I'm sorry about your brother," Kat offered. There really were too many dead for her to quit now.

"I'm sorry about yours," she said, the words nearly crippling Kat's composure. "I know how close you and Perry were." Kat nodded and followed Ivan and her into the house.

They entered a kitchen with a round wooden table, mismatched chairs, and mugs of steaming liquid sitting on top. There were three doorways off of the room—one to the left, which probably led to a garage, one straight ahead that looked to open into another room, and one to the right that led upstairs. Mason rose to his feet, eyes scanning over Ivan before enveloping him in a hug. These people and their freaking hugs. She looked at Luke, seated at the table with a laptop. He seemed healthier than she expected, with only superficial cuts and bruises on his face. But he didn't look up when they entered. Maybe they already knew Perry was dead.

"Where's the crew?" Ivan asked.

"Ernie is in the garage. Tommy and Rita went upstairs when you all pulled up. There's food in the fridge when you're hungry," Mason said.

Food was the last thing Kat needed. She gazed down at her hand, stained with blood, and caught sight of her blood-drenched jeans, imagining her face looked the same. She moved to the sink. The pump for the hand soap turned red as she pressed, the smell of vanilla overwhelming her. She rested her left forearm on the edge of the sink. The water burned, and she kept scrubbing until her hands were mostly clean. The water ran red again as she cleaned her face.

"Where's Perry?" Luke asked across the kitchen. Her back stiffened.

"He didn't make it," Ivan answered, his voice cracking with emotion.

She waited for a response, for Luke to rage, scream, cry out. But nothing. She turned to look at him. He met her gaze with disinterest and shrugged, returning to the computer. A small thread that was holding her composure snapped. She turned off the water, grabbed a towel to dry her face and hands, the green fabric turning red, and tossed it to the counter. She slid her left arm back into her front pocket and cornered Luke.

"That's it? That's all he gets from you?" Kat demanded.

Mason stepped in front of her. "Wait. There's something you need to know."

"What I know is Perry is dead, and this fucker literally just shrugged his shoulders and went back to playing solitaire on the computer."

"I'm searching for leads on Maureen," Luke said, the words earning him a glare from Mason and piquing Kat's interest.

"Who's Maureen?" Kat asked.

"Don't say another word," Mason warned Luke.

"On the contrary," Kat said. She pulled Perry's gun from her hip and pointed it at Aeron. "You better start talking."

Aeron froze, her hand reaching out for her mug, but Luke simply looked from Kat to Aeron, and back. "You kill her, and I'll never help you get into that vault." His words were calm and even. Not an ounce of emotion behind his eyes to indicate he was worried about her at all. It reminded Kat of her mother. She lowered the weapon. This wasn't Luke.

"What happened to you in the Playhouse?" she asked.

"That's what I'm trying to tell you," Mason said. "Here." He passed a yellow mug to her. "There's creamer in the fridge. Let's all get a drink and have a seat."

Kat retrieved the creamer and took a seat at the table. She poured until the dark liquid turned light brown and took a sip. It was the perfect balance and reminded her of Perry. He always made her coffee. She closed her eyes and took a deep breath. There would be time to grieve when she won back Legacy Inc.

"What happened at Headquarters?" Mason asked.

"No. What happened to Luke?" she countered.

"He was given a lethal dose of Sin and tortured by your mother."

Kat's eyes widened, and she looked back to inspect him. He looked fine. Oddly formal and stiff but alive and kicking. "How the hell is he alive?" Mason pressed his lips together, and she could see the war waging behind his eyes over what to say. She looked to Luke instead. "How are you alive?"

His eyes flicked to Aeron before answering. "Maureen Seward saved me."

"Damn it, Luke!" Mason yelled, slamming his fist on the table.

"What?" he asked. "Aeron has the right to know. And if you think we can just waltz back into Headquarters with the Alliance and whoever sabotaged your Headquarters mission after us, you're insane."

Mason pinched the bridge of his nose, and Kat looked at Aeron. Her mouth was open in shock. Kat imagined that would be her face if her dead mother suddenly wasn't so dead. "What did you say?" Aeron whispered.

"Your mother is alive and well. She's been running the Alliance for the past thirteen years," Luke said.

Aeron gazed at Mason, disbelief on her face. "Is this another side effect of Sin? Hallucinations, confusion, and complete lack of any emotion known to man?"

Mason released a long sigh and laced his fingers behind his head. "Lack of emotions, yes. His ability to connect emotionally to anything or anyone has been severed. Sin uses memories, guilt, and grief to torture you. The recovery serum shuts down those connections to save your mind. Normally when we build a tolerance to Sin, there is a reintegration process we take months to work through. But because of the circumstances, the reintegration portion of the Sin recovery wasn't performed on Luke."

"He's going to be an emotionless asshole forever?" Ivan asked. Kat quirked her lips. He had a knack for saying the dumbest thing at the right moment.

"I'm sitting right here, jackass," Luke said.

"I don't know. We might be able to save him," Mason said. "But we will need Maureen." The room fell so silent at the confirmation that Kat could hear the clock tick on the wall.

"So, she is alive," Aeron whispered. "My mother is alive?"

32

AERON

"My mother is alive?" Aeron repeated, louder this time. She was going to throw up. Everything her father did—everything Luke did was because her mother was killed. She pressed her fist to her mouth, but it didn't help. She stood, and Katherine was already at the door, holding it open. Aeron stepped out into the blissfully cold night air and vomited next to a garbage bag.

Everything she'd ever been told was a lie. Every motivation for the last six months was based on a lie. But she'd heard her mother die; listened to those tapes with Decius. Oh, Decius. Her heart pounded in her throat, and she swallowed it down. He died without knowing—maybe it was a good thing.

She wiped her mouth and walked past Katherine, stopping inside the threshold in case she needed to run back out. More so, though, because she didn't really want the answer to her next question. She didn't want to be close to Mason if his answer was anything but 'no'.

"Did my father know?"

Mason nodded. "We saved her the night of the car crash."

The full weight of the betrayal crashed into her, and she stumbled back. Ivan was at her side and guided her to a chair. Everything they'd done, all the people she'd killed, the lying to Decius. "Fuck all of you," she said and leaned into Ivan, but she immediately pulled away. He'd worked with her father and Mason for years. "Did you know?" she asked.

He shook his head. "No. I swear." Aeron scooted away anyway. She didn't know what to believe. Who to believe.

"Looks like betrayal is in the air," Katherine said. Aeron looked over. She was leaning against the kitchen sink, drinking coffee, and staring daggers at Mason. "I think it's time Mason shares everything he knows." Aeron couldn't agree more. "Why don't we start with who you really work for?" Katherine said.

Mason shook his head. "Why don't we start with what happened since we left the strip club and lost Decius and Perry."

"He works for the Alliance," Luke supplied.

"Oh, my fucking god," Mason said, standing up. "Luke, shut the *fuck* up. You have no idea what you're talking about."

Kat smirked. "I might actually like this Luke better. Please, Luke. Continue."

"You can't trust his memory of events," Mason countered, resignation in his voice. "He's been conversing with the dead."

"And I don't trust you, Mason," Katherine replied. Her focus shifted to Luke.

Luke hesitated. "He might be right on that."

"Oh, don't try and find your tact now," Katherine said. She moved closer and placed her mug on the table. "Please, enlighten us."

Aeron's head pounded, and she pushed a palm to her forehead. It was information overload, and she couldn't sort it out in her head. Before Luke could answer, Aeron asked, "Why is she suddenly back in town? She's been gone all this time. What made her show her face?"

"The hit list and the vault," Mason said.

"Is she trying to collect on our heads?" Aeron whispered. Wouldn't that be the final nail in her coffin?

"The contrary. Her only mission has been trying to protect you since she left."

"She's done a shit job of it," Luke said. "Decius is dead."

"You're the one who shot him," Aeron snapped. Luke closed his mouth and sat back.

"Okay," Katherine said. "Perhaps starting at the beginning would be beneficial to get all of us on the same page." She took her seat again. Something about her posture, the direct eye contact with each of them, even the tone of her voice calmed Aeron's racing pulse, and she realized—she respected her. "I'll start. I made a bad judgment call, possibly two." She sighed, directing her attention to Mason. "I made a deal with Carl."

"Motherfucker," Mason said under his breath.

"I'm assuming, then, you knew he was deeper than just a Liaison?"

"There is so much you have no idea about, Katherine," Mason said. "You were never meant—"

"If you say to be in this deep, I will fucking ball-kick you," Aeron interjected. "We are not children or damsels in distress. I feel like you and my father, and even Luke's parents, have been playing us like pawns on a chess board, never giving us enough information to make a good decision but enough for us to hang ourselves with when you look away. The only one I would trust at this point is Mrs. Gale."

"Oh, I wouldn't," Luke said. "She's the Shannon to your mom."

"She saved you," Mason said incredulously. "She went against Maureen's orders to save you. Stop talking. You are helping no one."

"My mother was going to kill him?" Aeron said, her voice cracking, the words 'my mother' feeling foreign leaving her mouth.

"Enough," Katherine said. "Back on track. I made a deal with Carl, and he returned with enough assets from Europe to cripple the remainder of Legacy Inc—Reapers and all. He assumed—correctly—that Senior is dead. That's how Perry and Ivan were caught."

"I can get you into the vault now," Ivan whispered. "I need about twenty-four hours, and I can have an entire program written so you can just plug in. We can get it to what's-his-name you left in charge and be free and clear of this by tomorrow night."

Aeron liked the sound of that. "Let's do that. I just want to be done with all of this."

Mason cocked his head. "Who did you leave in charge of Legacy Inc, Kat?"

"That brings me to bad judgment call number two." She took a few steadying breaths before continuing. "Griffin."

"Why is that a bad judgment call?" Mason asked.

"The shots that dropped Perry came from the direction he was holding. So either he is dead, or he shot Perry, and we're fucked."

Mason scoffed. "There is no way in hell he would have shot Perry. You know he's not infallible, right? I get it—you're hurting. But that man loves you. They may have just slipped past him. And if he is alive, that is probably the smartest decision you have ever made."

"How would you know?" Aeron asked because Katherine looked like she might launch herself at Mason at any second.

"Because I offered him a shot at power not too long ago, and he refused. Said his fate was tied to yours, Kat."

She shook her head. "I'm done taking chances. We need the list shut down. And I need to reclaim my fucking spot at Legacy Inc. Ivan—if you can get that code written I'll, consider us even."

"He doesn't owe you anything," Aeron said with an urge to protect Ivan. "I brought him to you as a favor, not the other way around."

"Perry couldn't—I had to—" Katherine took a deep breath.

"Perry didn't make it out, so I'll consider us even when Ivan gets me back into that vault."

Aeron opened her mouth to argue, but Ivan put a hand on her arm. "I'll do it." He stood up, hand tightening on Aeron for a second. "I'll get started now. I'm going to need that." He collected the computer and looked at Katherine. "Thank you for saving me. For. . ."

Whatever Kat had done, they couldn't even speak of it. Kat nodded, wiping at her cheeks, and Ivan headed upstairs.

The open space beside Aeron left her vulnerable. Luke gave no comfort, she couldn't bring herself to look at Mason, and Katherine's strong presence fluctuated from comforting to scary within seconds. She grabbed her now lukewarm tea and held it between her hands.

"You had to put him out," Mason whispered. Aeron looked up, but his eyes weren't on her.

Katherine bit her lip, gathering her composure. "He had sucking chest wounds. He never would have survived if we had made it out of the building. He didn't want to slow us down."

"Fuck. I'm sorry, Kat." Mason stood and began pacing. "We need to figure out who is in charge of Headquarters to get Ivan back in safely."

"I need to know about the Alliance," Katherine countered. "Before my mother so gleefully tortured me, she alluded to the fact she was working with them."

"Tortured?" Mason asked.

Kat nodded.

"Is that why you're favoring your left arm?" Mason asked.

"It's fine," Kat answered. "I need to know, was my mother working with them?"

"Yeah, Mason," a female voice called from the open kitchen door. "Was her mother working for the Alliance?"

Aeron spun in her chair. Kat pulled Perry's weapon back out and pointed it toward the woman standing in the entryway, her hands up in surrender. The entire side of her face was twisted into scars, and her hair was braided down her back; it was the woman who saved Aeron in the Playhouse.

"Amara," Katherine spat. "I've been looking for you."

Mason stepped in front of Kat's raised gun. "Kat, wait."

"No," Kat said. "You infiltrated Legacy Inc. Decius told me about Costa Rica. The only thing is, I can't find a trace of you anywhere."

"That's because her name is not Amara," Luke said. "Hello, again, Auntie Moe."

It took a few seconds for his words to sink in. This was her mother? Aeron's world tilted, and she fell toward the floor. She connected with a solid body that engulfed her in their arms.

"You okay?" Luke asked.

Aeron shoved him away and grasped the table instead.

"Touch her, and I'll finish what I started, Lucas," her Mother said from the doorway. Aeron looked over at her. The smile warped her face—like a living nightmare. "It's good to see you, Aeron. Where's Decius?" The room fell silent. Even Luke did not speak. Her mother's eyes searched every crevice of the kitchen as if he would appear out of thin air. She stepped fully inside. "Where is my son?"

Footsteps raced down the stairs. Her mother looked over, eyes lighting up, and Aeron looked over, too, although she knew it couldn't be Dee.

Ivan appeared. "We have a security—" he froze at the bottom step, panic twisting his own set of scars, "—breach."

"You must be Ivan." Her mother closed the door, making the room stuffy without the cool breeze. "Please, join us. I'm getting reacquainted with my family."

Ivan nodded and passed Luke to be at Aeron's side. She wanted nothing more than for him to go back upstairs. The room was too full—too dangerous. He latched onto her hand and squeezed it, and she held tight.

"Why are you here, Maureen?" Mason asked.

"I heard about the attack on Legacy Inc Headquarters. It would seem we have a vested interest in working together. You guys are on the list, and I need information from the vault. I am proposing a truce between the Alliance and the remaining misfits of the Legacy. Now, where is Decius?"

"He's dead." The words left Aeron with anger, and she clamped down on the box trying to spring open in her chest. How dare this woman waltz in here like a savior.

"Excuse me?" The scars on her mother's face twisted in rage as she glared in her direction; Aeron glared back.

Katherine stepped between them. "You know, I'm really over mothers treating their daughters like shit," Katherine said. "He died in the Playhouse. If you hadn't snatched Luke, none of this would have happened. So why don't you take a good long look in the mirror at who is to blame for this one."

Aeron tightened her grip on Ivan's hand, and her mother turned to Mason; he leaned against the fridge, arms crossed, expression neutral.

"Did you do it?" Her mother asked him.

Mason's jaw ticked. "Do what?"

"You know what."

"Body swap him the way I regrettably body swapped you? No." He frowned. "I couldn't save him." The words broke as they left her Guardian. "Not this time."

"Shannon is dead. Decius is dead. Where's Perry? Did you fail on that front too?" her mother demanded. Aeron could tell the words were meant to dig at Mason, but he clenched his jaw, not responding. "You had one job," her mother ground out. "Keep them alive. Keep my fucking kids alive."

The words snapped something in Mason. His face darkened, and he pushed off the fridge, an arm flinging out to point toward Aeron. "Two out of three ain't fucking bad, Maureen. Don't you think? She should have been dead a long time ago. You should be grateful." Mason snapped his mouth shut, face falling as if he'd said something he wanted to take back. But the words were already out.

"Two out of three?" Luke said. Aeron looked over. His gaze was on them as some unseen piece of information clicked into place. "Holy fuck. The sister—the girl you traded for Maureen's life? That's Katherine?"

33

KAT

*A*ll eyes in the room turned to Kat, Luke's words sinking in. Her system couldn't take any more surprises today, and she looked past Maureen to Mason, her eyes begging him to tell her it was a lie.

"Andrew should have shot you when he had the chance," Maureen said to Mason, shaking her head.

"Be quiet," Kat said, her voice level, although her insides were nothing but. This couldn't be her mother. She'd just killed her mother—tortured the fuck out of her. Enjoyed every second of the vengeance she'd been planning, and it was a lie? "Mason?"

"Yes, Kat."

"Did I not just torture and kill my mother?"

Mason nodded. "You did. But Maureen is your biological mother."

Kat's entire world suddenly made perfect sense, and a weight lifted from her. She was not a Wayward. All those punishments and impossible expectations she could never understand. The disregard for her well-being that she chalked up to her being a girl had nothing to do with it. She was never meant to lead Legacy Inc. Was this why her mother—why Rosemary hated her so much? How she could watch Kat suffer again and again? Had she been just some prize Rosemary won and had the pleasure to torture and shape to become her enemy's worst nightmare? That had bitten Rosemary on the ass. And this would bite Maureen too.

"Great. So, I have two moms who didn't want me. It's no wonder I have trust issues." Kat pushed away the feeling of being unwanted—she didn't need any of them.

"Katherine," Maureen started.

"Shut up," Aeron said from behind Kat. "You don't get to speak."

"Aeron." Maureen stepped forward.

Kat raised the gun again, shaking her head. "You heard her. Shut up."

"You think you scare me?" Maureen asked, a crooked smile contorting her face.

"I think you should have stayed dead," Aeron said, coming up beside Kat, and it felt right to have her by her side. "And you're not here for us. I don't care what Mason said. We're a side quest that's gone wrong. If we all died in that Playhouse, you wouldn't weep for us. You would go after what you're really here for—whatever is in that vault."

"That's not true," Maureen said. "I have always had your safety as a priority."

"Maybe Aeron and Decius'," Kat said. "But certainly not mine. Get out."

"I'm not going anywhere," Maureen said.

"In case you missed it," Aeron said, "we each already killed our primary parent. And I was quite fond of mine." Aeron said, now standing beside Kat. "I don't think we'll have any reservations about killing you."

"I'm always down for some matricide," Kat added.

"I heard you're really good at it," Aeron added.

Kat laughed and looked over at Aeron. Her sister. Warmth filled her chest at the thought. Belonging. That was the feeling Decius had given her in the Playhouse. The warmth evaporated. Her brother. She'd had a brother.

"Maureen, I think it's best if you leave," Mason said.

"Kill me, don't kill me," Maureen said, unfazed by their casual conversation of her demise. "Bigger issue: Legacy Inc being leaderless. When was the last time you paid your assets, Katherine?"

"I haven't," Kat said, changing gears. Because as much as she hated the woman in front of her, she was right.

"And what about contact with StormTracer for the government contracts?"

Kat lowered the gun. "I've been a little preoccupied, mother, with a hit list and trying to retrieve Luke, the one person who could give me access to the finances."

Maureen raised an eyebrow at the jab but said nothing about it. "Then our first order of business is to—"

Glass shattered behind Kat, and she turned and dove on top of Aeron. Everyone dropped to the floor. The back door burst open and a woman with dark skin and a mohawk backed in, firing into the night before closing the door.

"What is it?" Maureen asked.

"Rufus, with a shit ton of people."

Kat looked at Ivan. "I thought you said you had this placed locked down."

"It is. But someone," he glared at Maureen, "hacked in and shut down the alarm system. I only knew she was here because I saw her on the screens."

"Way to go, Maureen," Mason said. "Couldn't just make a phone call, could you? How many people, Izz?"

The woman smiled appreciatively at him, eye fucking him from across the room. "At least twenty."

"How many did you bring?" he asked.

"Just me and boss lady," Izz said. "But what, there's seven of us? Where's Decius? That boy could knock some heads around."

"He didn't make it," Kat said, and she tried to ignore the pang of sadness in her gut. "How did they find us?"

"Doesn't matter," Luke said, and another shot entered the room. "We are short on weapons and even shorter on skill at the moment."

Two items clattered through the window, bouncing off the table and to the floor. Smoke bombs. "Clear out!" Kat yelled, her lungs already burning as the room filled with smoke. Kat had no idea where to go. The back door banged open, the cool air blowing the smoke around. Before she could get to her feet, the room was filled with people. There was yelling and flesh hitting flesh. Kat couldn't see who was friend or foe. Someone grabbed her by the arm, and she yanked it away, swinging, and connecting with a body. No one was dumb enough to fire blind. As the smoke began to dissipate, a single figure dominated the door frame, his eyes landing on her.

Everything inside her panicked. Rufus lunged, grabbed a fist full of her hair, and pulled. She tripped over an unseen body, her hands holding onto his for some semblance of control. But he was too strong, and she screamed for help as he dragged her out into the night.

34

AERON

*K*at's scream pulled Aeron's eyes to the door. Rufus had her by the hair. Someone grabbed Aeron from behind. She tossed her head back, connecting with their face, and then elbowed them in the gut. They released her, and she ran toward Kat. Another man appeared at the entrance, and she didn't slow down. She kicked him in the chest and he stumbled back as Aeron raced past him.

Rufus had only made it to the rear of the cars. Aeron launched herself on top of the closest vehicle. She ran over the roof and jumped toward Rufus, a flying knee smashing him in the face. She didn't stop to strike again. She grabbed Katherine by the arm and hauled her around the side of the building, bodies hugging the wall. She peered back toward Rufus. Mason had engaged him, a fury in her Guardian's face Aeron had never seen.

"Are you okay?" Aeron asked, looking back at Kat. Besides her hair being a mess, she looked fine.

"That's the second time you saved me from him," Katherine said.

"Hopefully, the last. C'mon, I've got someone in the garage. We can get back in through there." The front of the building was deserted. Aeron paused outside the garage entrance, hand on the door handle. When her father had come to retrieve her for the funeral, could he have ever imagined this? Her gut flipped. Had he known about Katherine?

Glass shattered inside the garage, and Aeron pushed the thoughts aside, throwing the door open. Kat raised her gun, and Aeron pulled a dagger from her forearm sheath. The windows of the Camaro she and Tommy had been working on were broken, with Luke engaged in hand-to-hand combat with two men beside it. Ernie was backed into a corner, fending off a man with a tire iron, his shotgun on the floor. Aeron threw her knife, which embedded itself into the man's arm; he turned and charged, and Ernie grabbed him from behind, rendering him unconscious with a few blows.

"The big tattooed guy is one of mine," Aeron said to Kat. "Don't kill him."

"Got it. I'll help Luke."

Aeron rounded the Camaro and met Ernie, his face red with exertion and she checked for any life-threatening injuries but saw none. "I'm sorry about this," Aeron said, looking around. The door to the house opened, and three more of Rufus' cronies entered, firing shots as if they didn't care who they hit. They probably didn't. There were nearly 22-million-dollars' worth of dead bodies in this room. Fuck.

The bullets sprayed across the room. Ernie threw Aeron to the ground behind the blue car, Luke vaulted over the top to land next to her, and Katherine rolled under it, bumping into Aeron's back. Aeron moved out of the way, and Katherine crawled up between her and Luke, pressing herself against the car door and shaking her head. "I have three shots left," Kat said, holding up her gun.

"I don't even have a weapon," Luke added.

Aeron pulled up her sleeve. She had two blades. "Ernie?" She looked at him.

"Just a few shells left for the shotgun."

"Damnit," Luke said.

"For the ten minutes you were my sister," Kat said softly beside her, "you didn't annoy me. I'd call it a win."

Aeron's lip quirked. "We're not dying, Katherine. The blue toolbox to the right, bottom drawer, has handguns and ammo. I'll go for the yellow toolbox over to the left; it has knives in the top." She leaned forward, looking at the drop cloth on the floor holding car pieces. "And Luke, we have some heavy projectiles at the front of the car; cover us?"

"I'll cover you, too," Ernie said. Aeron looked up at him. "Go get 'em." He popped up, shooting over the roof. They moved. Aeron dive-rolled from behind Ernie, Luke heading the same direction, the drop cloth sliding behind the car as she passed it. The wall above her rained drywall as she reached the toolbox, spinning it around on the wheels and kneeling behind it. The gunfire ceased for a moment, the sound of metal crashing onto the floor.

"Spread out!" Someone ordered from near the door.

Aeron reached into the top of the box and sucked a breath in as her fingertips slid against the blades. Once she'd grabbed hold of them, she leaned forward. The room now had six of Rufus' guys. Gripping the first blade, she threw it—then another, and another, and another. They barely stuck into the fabric of her targets. For the last two she aimed for the neck. She found purchase in one, and the woman dropped to the ground. Her companion turned. Anger filled her face, and she charged toward Aeron. Fuck. She threw the last blade, the woman parried it with her rifle, then pulled the trigger. Aeron closed her eyes in anticipation of the hit.

"No!" Ernie yelled.

Aeron snapped her eyes open at the sound of bullets piercing flesh right in front of her. Ernie dropped at Aeron's knees, his body knocking her backward. She cupped his face. "Ernie?" She turned his face to her, and his lifeless eyes stared back. But she couldn't stop to grieve.

Aeron vaulted over his body and shoved the woman's rifle up, rounds hitting the ceiling. She grabbed onto the woman's shirt, yanking her in, and head-butted her several times in the face until she dropped unconscious. Aeron unclipped the Sig from the woman's hip and checked the magazine—still loaded—and then administered a kill shot.

She looked to Katherine, bashing a head in with a car alternator, and to Luke, under a man trying to beat his head in with a wrench. Aeron turned to help him, and a shot zipped past her, knocking the threat aside. She looked over her shoulder. Maureen stood in the entryway to the kitchen. "Aeron! Katherine! Let's go!" Hate coursed through Aeron's body. She would rather die here than go anywhere with that woman.

"Fuck off," Katherine said from across the garage. She dropped the bloodied alternator and stood up. "We're not going anywhere with you."

Aeron turned back to Ernie, moving through what felt like quicksand to get to him. She dropped to her knees, her vision blurring. Luke joined her, crouching on his other side.

"He was important to you," he said.

"You have no idea. He was a dad to me."

"You had a father," Maureen said. "And he was better than that man ever could be."

Aeron clenched her fist, her other hand tightening on the Sig. She should kill the woman and be done with it. But first, Ernie. She reached forward and closed his eyes. A slap sounded from behind them. She turned. Katherine glared at their mother, who held her hand against her cheek, eyes blazing.

"Don't disrespect the man who just sacrificed his life for hers," Katherine nearly growled. "You'll never understand that kind of love."

Maureen advanced toward Katherine, and Aeron rose to her feet. If Maureen wanted a fight, she had one. Luke grabbed her shoulder, though, and walked past her, stopping in front of Maureen.

"We aren't out of the woods yet. Can we in-fight later?" he asked.

"In-fighting suggests we're on the same team," Aeron said.

"In this case, we are," he countered. "There are still a handful of people in the vicinity trying to collect the 22-million-dollar bounty sitting right here."

Izz appeared behind Maureen. "We've got a small window. We need to go."

"Girls, please come with me," Maureen pleaded. "We can sort this out later."

"That's your problem, Maureen. You think of us as helpless girls. Your girls died the day you left them. We're badass women. We don't need you," Aeron said, letting the venom in her words spew out. Maureen's features darkened, and Aeron recognized the danger in them.

"I'm with her," Kat said, standing beside Aeron.

The creak of the front door caught Aeron's attention, and she turned to look. A single shot resounded through the garage, and Aeron's body jerked, her feet stumbling back to hold her balance. Pain seared into her shoulder, and she looked down, already knowing what she'd see. She'd been shot.

35

KAT

The bullet flew past Kat's face, the sickening sound of a projectile hitting flesh meeting her ears. She returned fire into the darkness of the open entrance. "Luke, go check!" she called and turned around. Aeron's weapon tumbled from her hand, and Kat's gaze followed it. Her stomach turned at the steady stream of blood that dripped from Aeron's fingertips onto the gun. She pulled her gaze up, and Aeron reached forward, Kat catching her before her knees kissed the ground.

"Whoa," Kat said, "I've got you." She wrapped her arms beneath Aeron's armpits and hugged her close, stumbling back and dropping to the floor. More commotion sounded behind her, and she hoped Luke would keep them occupied. Aeron slid to her side, head falling back against Kat's shoulder, her breath labored.

"Fuck, that hurt." Aeron grimaced, trying to sit up straighter. She clawed at the neck of her hoodie, trying to pull down the collar.

"I'm sure it's just a flesh wound," Kat supplied. "Hold on." She looked around for something to cut off the fabric to see the damage. Kat spotted a throwing knife on the ground and leaned for it. Aeron cried out, and Kat stopped moving, the knife just out of reach. Her finger inched along the floor, her arm stretching a little bit more. A hand closed over the blade and grabbed it. Kat snapped her gaze up, ready to defend Aeron to the death, and Mason looked down at her, his face a mask.

"Thank goodness you're here," Kat said.

Mason's face remained stone, and he dropped beside them. "Hey, Aer." He kept his voice light and full of hope, and Kat clung to it. She was going to be fine. "I'm going to check that out, okay?"

"Don't patronize me," Aeron said and looked up at Kat. "If I don't make it out—"

"Nope." Kat shook her head, a knot forming in her chest. "We're not doing that."

"We need to lay you flat," Mason said. Aeron looked at him and nodded, clenching her jaw as Kat shifted out from underneath her. Aeron's complexion paled immediately, and a horrifying thought invaded Kat's mind. What if the bullet ricocheted inside? She squeezed Aeron's hand to help keep her eyes open and focused.

"Kat?" Aeron's voice was hardly a whisper.

"I'm here," she answered as Mason cut open Aeron's hoodie. A scream left Aeron as he slid the garment down her arm. Sweat formed on her brow, and Kat wiped it off. The bullet had just pierced the shoulder.

"Pressure," Mason said, and Kat circled to the other side, applying pressure to the wound, hands shaking. Aeron grunted again and looked up at Kat, tears in her eyes.

"Decius would have been stoked," Aeron said. "To find out you were family."

Tears filled Kat's eyes, too. This was her family. She had a chance to have a real family, a better family. "He saved me in the Playhouse. Twice. He was a total hero. You'll have to tell me all about him sometime."

"Swap," Mason said from beside her. "Three, two, one." Kat moved her hands, and Mason dug his finger into the hole, looking to the source of the bleeding, then started feeding the Quikclot into the wound. Aeron screamed again, Kat grimacing along with her. The dressing burned, smelled terrible, and was far inferior to what they used at headquarters. From behind, Kat heard Maureen scream out, "No!" but she didn't turn because Aeron's eyes had dropped shut.

"Aeron?" Kat yelled, the air leaving her lungs. She tapped her face hard, but her complexion had gone pasty. Aeron's eyes fluttered open. "Hey, you're going to be okay," Kat said. "You're the one who said no one is dying."

"I know. . ." Aeron said. "It's just a. . ." she trailed off. "It's a. . ."

Kat looked at Mason. His hands worked quickly, but his chin trembled, and Kat's heart cracked in two. Was she about to lose her sister? But she'd just learned about her; she just got to know her. No. The universe would not be that cruel. Surely, she'd lost enough already.

"I'm not—I'm—not making it," Aeron said, blood staining her teeth, a sob leaving her. Mason's face crumbled, but he kept working, and Kat looked down again. "I can—I can feel it." She brought her hand to her chest and tapped it.

A cry broke out of Kat, and she cupped Aeron's cheek. "Please," Kat begged. "Don't leave me. I just found you. I need you."

Aeron leaned into Kat's palm, moving her hand to hold it there. "Even when you wanted to kill me—I thought you were pretty badass," Aeron said with a laugh, followed by a cry of pain. Mason secured the wound with a bandage but refused to look up.

"I've always wanted a little sister," Kat confessed. "I mean, I didn't know that's what I wanted until you came to my club. You are everything I need in my life. Just hang on a little longer for me."

Aeron nodded. "I can do that." She reached for Mason's hand. He took it.

"Don't tell anyone," Mason said. "But you're my favorite."

She smiled with a soft laugh. "I love you, Mase. Keep Darth safe. And help Luke." Mason's chin trembled harder, and he nodded. Kat looked away, giving them their moment. Luke, Maureen, and Izz were fighting a new wave of threats, and a fresh surge of adrenaline pumped through her. They needed to get Aeron out of here, stat.

"I thought Izz said there was a window," Kat said.

"A very, very small one to get away from Rufus' men. But Rufus leaked the location to the hit list server. Everyone is coming here."

"You didn't kill him?"

"I knew you guys needed help."

Kat's jaw dropped open. "What about your vengeance?" Shock coated her words; after years of waiting, she couldn't imagine not getting her revenge. But Aeron moaned beneath her, and she swallowed hard. If she could do it over, Kat may not have been so quick to go to war. The cost of her vengeance may have been too high, and they were still paying it.

Mason shook his head, meeting her eyes. "Nothing is worth losing you guys." He looked down at Aeron. "It's always been you guys." His brow furrowed. "Aeron?"

Kat looked too. Aeron's eyes had fallen shut, her head heavy in Kat's hand. Mason slapped Aeron's face a few times, but there was no response. No, no, no, no, no. Kat's lungs forgot how to work, her heart beating hard enough to crack her ribs. Aeron was going to be fine.

Mason's hand slid to Aeron's neck, checking her pulse. He wiped his hand on his pants and checked again.

"What is it?" she asked, hoping the fallen look on Mason's face didn't mean what she thought it meant.

Mason's composure completely crumbled, a sob racking through his body. "She's—She's—"

Kat refused to believe it. She checked for a pulse herself, Aeron's head lolling to the side as her fingers left a bloody smear on Aeron's neck, then her wrist, and then her neck again. "No."

Mason dropped his head to Aeron's chest, a broken sob leaving him, the sound pulling Kat's buried sobs out from her. Who cared if she died here? She had no one to go back to. No reason to keep fighting. No family to protect her. Aeron was gone.

"Kat!" Luke's scream broke through her fog—they were far from safe yet. She looked over. The room had been cleared. Maureen wrapped her arm around Luke's throat, pulling him backward, with her gun slammed so deep into his neck there would be a bruise the shape of the muzzle there.

Mason responded before Kat did. He hopped across Aeron's still form, sitting low against her body, one knee bent in front of him with his arm resting on it. He pointed Aeron's fallen Sig lazily toward them with a look of pure hatred on his face.

"Let him go," Mason said.

"Is she. . ." Maureen trailed off.

"Want to come see for yourself?" Mason asked, ice in his words. "That's three I am burying since you showed up, and you accused me of playing the long game. Does Eileen know you had Rosemary on the payroll the night Shannon died?"

Maureen removed the gun from Luke's throat and fired at Mason. Kat flinched away, but Mason didn't move a muscle. Luke screamed when she dug the gun back in, the metal melting his skin.

"Stop!" Kat yelled, rising to her feet, and stepping forward. "Why are you doing this?"

Maureen's twisted face sneered at her. "I'm not leaving empty-handed." She looked at the entrance to the house.

Izz held the door open. "Let's go."

Maureen dragged Luke with her. His gaze fell on Aeron's body behind them, and Kat could see the trigger of something happening in his eyes. "Aeron? Aeron! No! Let me go!"

Kat swallowed back her urge to lunge forward, afraid Maureen would shoot him out of spite. Luke wasn't lost yet. "Mason," Kat said under her breath, "we have to help him."

"We will," Mason replied. "She won't kill him until they breach the vault. There's time."

Kat held Luke's pleading eyes until they were out of sight, sending a silent promise that they would save him. The room fell silent, allowing Kat to hear how loud the ringing was in her ears.

"Damn it!" she yelled. She grabbed the closest item, a wrench, and hurled it across the room. It slammed against the wall and clattered to the floor. The pent-up anger coursed through her. This wasn't fair. She continued to destroy whatever her hands could get a hold of—a mug, a throwing knife, a brake caliper. She threw and screamed until her arms refused to lift anymore, her fingers numb and tingling. She dropped to the ground, leaning forward, head pressed into the cold cement, and took a slow deep breath.

"Mason?"

Kat tilted her head toward the kitchen, keeping the cool floor against her forehead, slowing her heart rate. Ivan had his eyes on a tablet, scrolling.

"I got the security back up and running. Maureen cleared out, but there's another group of mercenaries heading this way. Tommy and Rita are loading the car now." He looked up, surveying the damage with interest. "We've got eight minutes to—" His eyes landed on Aeron. Kat bounded to her feet, trying to put herself between them, but his look of interest dissolved into horror. "No." He shook his head, tripping over his feet to reach Aeron. Kat tried to head him off, but he shoved her away.

"Ivan, no. You don't want to—"

"Aeron!" Ivan threw himself onto her lifeless body. Mason grabbed him by the shoulders and hauled him back. But Ivan clung to her, and Aeron's body lifted off the floor.

"Ivan, stop!" Kat said, catching Aeron's head before it could hit the ground. He released her, and the full weight of Aeron's body dropped back down. Kat gently placed her head on the floor, and it lolled to the side when she let go. Kat stared at the distraught man clinging to Mason, tears unashamedly pouring down his face.

"I loved her," Ivan sobbed. "I never told her that." Mason released him, and he knelt back down by her.

"Ivan, I'm so sorry," Mason whispered. "You said we had a short window." Ivan nodded, hands on his thighs, eyes fixed blankly on

Aeron. "We don't have time. This is the life. This is the cost. Pack it away—we gotta go."

Ivan nodded again but remained stuck in that position. Kat moved beside him, his broken breathing tugging on her chest, and she shook her head, refocusing on the most important task—escaping. She gently rubbed his back.

"She loved you, too," Kat said. "I don't know if it's the way you wanted, but she protected you tooth and nail from me." Her words caused another round of sobs, and she looked to Mason for help. She had no idea how to console this man.

Mason picked up the fallen tablet. "Two minutes," he said.

"She didn't die for you to get caught here," Kat said. He nodded and wiped his face on his arm. He leaned forward and placed a gentle kiss on Aeron's forehead. Kat choked back her own sob and pulled him to his feet. When he looked at her, there was a steel wall behind his eyes.

"We are getting into that vault before Maureen," he said.

Good. He was focused and had a purpose. "We are," Kat agreed.

Mason handed back the tablet and looked at Kat. "I assume you have a safe house where the kids are stored?"

"In Arlington," she said.

"Go. I'll reach out to Ivan when I get this taken care of."

Kat took one last look at Aeron before Mason covered her face with the drop cloth and scooped her body off the ground. Kat grabbed Ivan by the arm, leading him to the car they'd arrived in.

A man and woman stood by one of the vehicles. Kat raised her gun, and Ivan put her hand on top of it, pushing it down. "That's Tommy and Rita, Ernie's family. Aeron's family."

They looked past her to Mason, the color draining from Tommy's face, and Rita grabbing onto him for support. Kat didn't want to look back and see what they saw. She wanted to keep the vision of Aeron in her mind. A beautiful and feisty woman with a contagious smile and a light that turned heads. A ruthless assassin who gave Kat a run for her money and made grown men cry. A friend and a sister that Kat wished she'd been given the time to get to know.

She got in the car without saying a word to them, Ivan doing the same. It started without an issue, and she backed up, headlights shining light on Mason closing the back car door and Tommy sliding into the front seat. Mason waved to her, and she nodded back.

"What's the plan?" Ivan asked as they pulled onto the road.

"Aeron told me before the Playhouse that I should take the fucking crown," Kat said, speeding off toward DC. "We're going to get my crown."

36

LUKE

Izz slammed Luke into the back of the van, hopping in beside him and closing the doors. His head pounded in agony, flashes of grief and anxiety seizing his mind and then disappearing, only to be replaced with an inexplicable rage, which vanished before his thoughts could form. He was going insane.

His wrists ached where they'd bound them, and he pushed himself up. There was no need to restrain him. His reason for living was gone. Aeron was gone. He leaned against the wall of the utility van, his head bouncing as the van drove down the road. His body shivered, the familiar cold spot burrowing into his spine, and he smiled. They were back.

"What are you smirking at?" Izz asked.

Luke closed his eyes and didn't answer. They would all come to watch him suffer if he waited long enough.

"Hey!" Izz kicked his leg. "Answer me."

He squeezed his eyes shut tighter, the kick sending a wave of pain through his back, fear gripping him. He knew fear. He understood fear. And then a sob caught him off guard. Aeron was gone.

"Oh shit," Izz said.

The van took a hard turn. Luke landed on his shoulder, muscles spasming. They came to a stop, and Maureen's scarred face sneered at him from the driver's seat. "Pathetic." She climbed into the back, checking his pulse and forehead. "No fever. That's a good sign. But his heart is racing."

"What's wrong with him?"

"Where'd you get your serum?" Maureen asked, grabbing Luke's chin, and making him look up. "Where?"

"Dr. Shea," he said. A movement to the front of the van caught his attention, and he slammed his eyes shut again. He didn't want to see him, Decius, covered in blood. Dead.

"How many vials? Did you miss a dose?"

"I don't know. I woke up. That's all I know."

She dropped his chin. "We're making a quick stop and changing vehicles."

"Yes, ma'am," Izz said. The van started forward again, and Luke rolled back into Izz. She put a hand on him, and as much as he didn't want to, his body leaned into her warmth. "C'mere." She shifted to sit beside him and put his head in her lap, running light fingers through his hair. On his next breath, his sobs started. His best friends were gone. Fuck.

His heart ached like it would explode out of his chest, the ice-cold stares of the dead drilling into his back. He covered his head, pulling his knees to his chest. He'd killed his best friend. Everything he did to protect them, and he was the one to pull the goddamn trigger. And Aeron—anger surged through him, and a scream replaced his cries. Rosemary and Maureen had stolen his last chances with her. He was a fucking asshole to her before she died.

Izz rubbed his back, and he quieted, his breath coming in shuddered gasps. "I'd put you out," she whispered, "but we need you alive and with a clean system."

Luke didn't care. He'd exhausted his sudden overflow of emotions, and they were gone as quickly as they came. The ice in his body disappeared, and his mind told him to sit up and clean up.

He wiped his face on his sleeve and sat up, his breathing regulating out.

"Water?" he asked, voice raspy.

Izz cocked an eyebrow at him. She opened a plastic water bottle and held it out. Luke drank it in two long gulps, feeling better. "What was that?" she asked.

He didn't answer right away because he didn't know and could still feel a residual pull in his chest, the sadness that just tried to drown him. He looked up and jerked back hard, slamming his head into the side of the van. Aeron sat crossed-legged in front of him, her beautiful smile tugging at the corner of her lips, her face spattered with blood. "Boo."

"Fuck!" He tried to back away, but there was nowhere to go.

Izz jumped up, looking around. "What is it?"

It took several deep breaths, but his heart calmed, and Aeron flickered slightly. He reached forward for her face, pausing for a moment before making contact. His hands went right through her, and then she vanished. He locked his fingers together to hide the shaking and tucked them between his legs.

No one spoke, but Maureen sped up.

The van finally came to a stop. Luke pulled his eyes open, realizing he must have fallen asleep. Perhaps seeing Aeron had been a horrible nightmare. Being under Sin and hallucinating was one thing. Being sober and still having the effects, he wished he'd been shot too.

Maureen opened the rear doors. She and Izz escorted him out of the van and right into the back of an ambulance. They sat him down on the stretcher, and Izz attached his tied hands to the railing.

"Just a precaution," she said. "But if you're into it, I'm not judging." She winked at him and hopped out the back. He leaned forward to see who Maureen was talking to.

"I gave him a single dose when he was here with instructions to give him five more doses every two hours, the next one within ninety minutes." It was Dr. Shea.

"Did you even ask how much Sin was administered?" Maureen demanded.

"I was preoccupied with a dying man on my table, ma'am. I did not ask. I assumed it was a normal interrogation dose."

Maureen's voice dropped low. "Who was on your table?"

Dr. Shea hesitated. The anonymity of his practice kept him well-employed by the Underworld and Legacy alike. Luke held his breath, leaning forward to hear more. He heard Maureen's gun cock instead.

"Decius Seward, with a gunshot wound."

Panic seeped into Luke's system. He couldn't remember if he told Dr. Shea that he'd shot him or not. If Maureen found out he killed Dee, he had a feeling his last brush with Sin would be a cakewalk.

"What happened to him?" Maureen's voice was even.

There was another hesitation, and Luke swallowed hard, heart hammering and making it difficult to hear. He leaned forward further, wrists pulling against the restraint.

Dr. Shea coughed and let out a short yell. "I, uh, I—"

"He could probably answer better without the gun pressed into his jugular," Izz said softly.

"You can answer me now, or I will shatter each finger until you do, and you will never work again. Tell me, what happened when Decius Seward was brought in here."

"Luke Wayward brought him, said Katherine had sent them. He had massive internal damage consistent with shots to the chest with a vest on and a single bullet wound entering through the armpit. There was too much damage to save him. I tried."

"And did Luke say who shot him?"

Dr. Shea stuttered over his words.

"Spit it out," Izz encouraged. Luke pressed his eyes together as a scream broke the night air. "You didn't really need that little finger, did you? How about this one?"

"Wait! Wait! He shot him." Luke's insides turned to liquid. He yanked up on the rail and it rattled but didn't budge. He scanned the ambulance for anything he could reach, but the words left Dr. Shea before he could find anything. "Luke shot him."

Luke moved his gaze to the open doors, and Izz's face peered in, a pair of bloody pliers hanging lazily in her hand. "Are you sure?" she asked, eyes on Luke but waving the pliers in the air.

"Yes. Please, I don't want any more trouble."

Izz's eyes narrowed, and her lip curled. Luke's entire body began to tremble, and he shook his head at her. She tossed the metal tool to the floor and looked back at Dr. Shea, head nodding.

"Thank you for your time," Maureen said. Luke waited for the gunshot. Instead, she appeared beside Izz, pulled herself into the back of the vehicle with a purple container in her hands, and sat beside the stretcher. Izz pushed the doors closed and got into the driver's seat.

Luke kept his eyes averted from Maureen, terror rocking his core. They drove in silence, Luke swaying back and forth slightly, afraid to move a muscle as if being frozen would keep her wrath to a minimum. What was she going to do to him? She couldn't drug him or kill him. All she needed from him was a handprint and a heartbeat.

They hit a bump. A spike of the electrical current ran up his spine to his shoulder blades, and he bit through his lip, holding in his scream, the blood trailing down his chin. He still did not move. Maybe the Sin wasn't out of his system yet. If he could keep his cool, maybe he would lock them out of the vault when his biometrics read the Sin.

Her fingers grabbed his jaw, turned his face to her, and wiped the blood from his chin. "They've started again." He didn't answer. She slapped him, bringing back the vivid memory of Aeron hitting him in the Playhouse. He could almost feel the string that connected them pulling in his mind. If he closed his eyes and tugged—she slapped him again, his eyes snapping open.

Maureen shook her head and opened the box. Inside were yellow serums nestled in black foam and what looked like prepackaged alcohol wipes. She pulled on a pair of gloves and opened one of the packages. She took the small white pad and wiped it along his forehead. It was cold against his hot skin, and he fought off a shiver. She held the pad between two fingers and waited. It remained white, and she laughed.

"I can't decide if I want to torture you for killing my son or study how the Sin affects you. Maybe I'll do both." She pulled the gloves off, the white pad folded inside, and tossed the gloves.

"It was an accident," Luke said, his voice wavering.

She raised an eyebrow and cocked her head. "Do you think that matters to me? Two of my children are dead. Everyone responsible will pay, one way or another."

Luke nodded, his mind clearing at the moment. The fear subsided, and the ambulance snapped into focus with a single rational thought: his fate was sealed the day he said yes to his Granddad. He could try and play out how things may have gone differently. But they hadn't, and every decision had led him here. There was really no other way for this to end.

He cleared his throat. "What was in that box?" he asked, voice steady.

"A quick and dirty Sin detection kit. Dr. Shea was kind enough to lend me his."

"I'm sure his kindness had nothing to do with the imminent threat of bodily harm," Luke responded and then snapped his mouth shut. This was what Mason had warned him about.

"Huh." She looked him up and down. Could she see a physical change when his mind snapped to attention? "The Sin is out of your system. We open the vault tonight."

Luke pushed his luck. She was answering questions, and he

needed answers. "Okay. What about the pain and visions I just had? Is it simply residual side effects that will wear off?"

"You should be dead," Maureen said, leaning forward. "Or, at the very least, an emotionless machine as you seem to be at the moment. There is something faulty up here." She tapped his head a few times. "I've experimented with many variations of reintegration after Sin, depending on what I need someone for. But you—you weren't reintegrated. In fact, I was one hundred percent sure you would die even if we got you the serum, because Rosemary accidentally double-dosed you. My personal blends of Sin are much more potent than Legacy Inc's."

"Would you be able to keep me like this?" Luke asked. The idea of feeling nothing ever again seemed pretty enticing at the moment, and he would rather die than end up stuck in limbo between this and the all-consuming wave of emotion he'd just had.

She reached for his face, and he stilled as her finger traced his jaw. "I want to know how you're flipping that switch. Or. . . how it's flipping itself." She quirked an eyebrow. "Perhaps I'll get my hands on Aeron's body and see how your brain likes that." Luke's mind flooded with anger, and he jerked back, suddenly unable to breathe at the thought.

She smiled in victory. "Thought so."

"I'll open the vault," Luke said, pushing away visions of Aeron's body being strung up by her mother to torture him. He grasped for the calm he'd had just moments ago, but it was gone. "I will walk you straight to that office and open the vault. But please, let me go after that." He tried to keep the calm facade, but Aeron flickered into existence beside Maureen, and he backed away.

Her lip quirked in a half smile, and the effect twisted her entire face. "I'll consider it. You should get some rest. We have a few hours before we arrive."

"I'm stopping for gas," Izz said from the front.

"Good. Then you heard the man; let's go to D.C." Maureen patted him on the shoulder, her body moving forward through

Aeron's, and it disappeared. A burner phone stuck out of Maureen's back pocket. Izz made a hard left, and when Maureen's body swung close, Luke let the restraints slice deep into his wrists and secured the phone without notice. He dropped to the side, head resting on his hands to hide it until she was seated.

Izz parked the ambulance. "I'll fill up. Can you get caffeine?"

He could feel Maureen's gaze on him, and he remained perfectly still. "Sure. Shoot him if he tries to escape."

Luke waited until both doors closed and opened the phone. He dialed the Legacy line, hoping Mason still answered.

"Go."

Luke released a sigh of relief. "Mase, we're headed to the vault. We're a few hours out." The line was silent on the other end. "Please, I only have a minute. It's not a trap," Luke said, realizing how it sounded, and the urge to cry snapped into his chest. The yo-yo effect of the after-Sin effect gave him a migraine, and he let out a sob. "She knows I shot Dee. She's going to torture me for the rest of my life." Another cry rocked his body again.

Mason sucked in a breath on the other end. "Fucking hell, Luke. How?"

"Dr. Shea told her."

"No, how are you. . . feeling?"

"That's what she wants to know. Please, just get there and kill me before she gets in."

"Luke, I promised someone I wouldn't do that."

The driver-side door opened. "Please," Luke begged and ended the call. He erased any trace of it and dropped the phone to the ground. He closed his eyes as the passenger door opened, biting into his swollen lip to stem off the sobs, praying Mason would get to him in time.

37

KAT

"Are you okay?" Ivan asked.

Kat glanced over. They'd been driving for hours in silence, Ivan working on his tablet and Kat holding the steering wheel in a vice grip. Her knuckles ached, but her heart hurt so much more. The work of shutting down the emotions wasn't as easy this time. Perhaps it had been the hope that Aeron offered her —a new start, a new family. Hope never brought anything but pain with it.

They were thirty minutes from the safe house. "Just be quiet," Kat said.

"I'm not okay," Ivan continued, and Kat swallowed hard. "I would have said that to her, and she would have rolled her eyes, but she still would have listened." Kat didn't respond, and he kept going. "Did you know she gave me this scar? The first night we met." Kat glanced over, and he ran a hand over the scars on his face, the ones identical to her Granddad's.

Kat shook her head. "I helped Luke pick out the damned thing that did it."

Ivan laughed. "It had been a complete accident when training, and she felt awful about it. I was mad, but I knew that day—I would go to the ends of the earth for her."

"I get the feeling a lot of people would," she said, hands relaxing on the wheel, her shoulders settling. "I know I would have. Will you tell me more about her someday?"

"Yeah," he said softly. "I would love to."

Her left arm dropped, now her fingers were no longer latched to the wheel, and a shot of pain raced through the tricep. She winced. Fuck. The pain blocker must be wearing off. They fell into silence again, the air around them relaxed, and she opened and closed her hands a few times, her left one not cooperating. That would be a problem for later.

They pulled into the driveway of a two-story house. The property was isolated, and a perimeter was set up to let Dom know when someone was approaching. She turned off the engine but didn't get out of the car. "Perry's mom is in there," she whispered. "How the hell am I going to tell her he's dead?"

"You could lead with your mother is dead? I heard they didn't like each other very much," Ivan offered.

Kat laughed. He wasn't wrong. She took a deep breath. She could do this. "Let's get it done." They exited the car, Kat leading Ivan around the back of the safe house and unlocking the metal door with her retinal scan. It swung open. She slid her dirty shoes off before stepping inside, Ivan doing the same, and closed the door behind them.

She peered into the next room—a lounge area they used as their security room, armory, and bar. Dom waved at her, and she nodded to him. Across from him, monitors were mounted across the wall, each currently cycling through the many security cameras on the property, and behind him was the bar, which concealed an entrance to a mini armory tucked behind the liquor shelves.

Dom raised a glass to her, and she nodded back. She stripped down, removing the stiff bloody clothes and tossing them in the trash. She hadn't realized how filthy they were and shook the thought of Perry and Aeron away for the moment.

"What the fuck happened to your arm?" Ivan asked; his hand reached out but didn't touch her.

"My mother."

"Which one?" he asked, and Kat laughed.

"I was going to say the shitty one, but that's both. Rosemary."

"Fucking hell," Dom said, moving to the mudroom. "Do you want me to get Betty down here to look at that?"

Kat sobered up and glanced over to the bathroom door. She wanted nothing more than to wash herself off. "No. Not yet."

"Okay. Who's this?" Dom quirked an eyebrow at Ivan. "Bringing home strays?"

"This is Ivan, the techie I've been searching for." Dom's face lit up. "Ivan, this is Dominic."

Ivan extended his hand. "Nice to meet you."

"Dom, we've got a program we need completed ASAP. Get him set up." She entered the bathroom and turned the shower on ice cold. She glanced in the mirror, turning to see her tricep. It was red, swollen, and bloody as hell. Her fingers ran across the clear bandage where a burning sensation had started. She would have to clean it soon.

The cold water shocked her system, sending her mind into problem-solving overdrive. Anything that couldn't be fixed or changed was immediately dismissed or shoved so deep down it wasn't a thought anymore. She dried off and wrapped a towel around her. When she re-entered the lounge, Ivan and Dom had computers and tablets running across the bar top. They didn't acknowledge her when she rounded the bar, grabbing a glass and pouring herself some rum over ice. She swirled it around, not understanding half of what they said to each other.

"Ivan," she said, looking up from her glass. Luke's screams for Aeron kept creeping into her mind, and no matter how much she shoved them down—they stayed. She needed to get him back, and not just because of the vault. "You said you needed twenty-four hours. Can you get it done sooner?"

"I believe so," he said.

She couldn't even muster a smart-ass remark for him. "I need to go talk to Betty. Did you tell her about the hit list?" she asked Dom.

He shook his head. "Ivan updated me about Perry. Kat—"

"No. It's buried. It's staying there. Once the program is done, I need one more favor."

Dom's eyes narrowed. "You don't ask for favors."

"If I don't make it back here, you sell Rockstars and take these kids and Betty to the islands. Or give Betty Perry's cut. Whichever she wants."

"You can't be serious."

"I'm dead serious." She held his gaze until he nodded. "Good. Get working. I'm going to break my aunt's heart."

Kat carried her drink with her. The basement stairs led to the kitchen. There was a laundry room off the back and an open floor plan for the living and dining rooms. Not a single toy lay on the floor, and the kitchen was spotless, the complete opposite of the last safe house. Her footsteps to the second floor were muffled on the carpeted stairs. The lights under the doors were off, and she veered for the last guest room. Someone had made her bed, and her clothes were out of the go-bag and hung in the closet. She gulped down her drink, the cool liquid burning. With a slight tug, she pulled a green tank top off a hanger and then dug around in the dresser drawers finding underwear and black sweatpants. She looked back at the queen bed for a moment, the soft comforter calling her name. But if she sat, she wouldn't get back up.

She retreated back down the hall, heading for the master bedroom. They'd given it to Betty. There was a slight flicker of light beneath the door, and Kat knocked. It took a few moments, and Betty pulled the door open a crack, her eyes looking down as if expecting a child. When her eyes lifted from Kat's kneecaps, they widened.

"You're back," she said, surprise in her voice.

"May I come in?" Kat asked. Betty opened the door, and Kat walked past her. The sleeping area on the right side of the room held a king-sized bed, the covers untouched even at this late hour. "Can't sleep?"

Betty closed the door and motioned for Kat to take a seat near the lit fireplace. Kat eyed the bookcases on either side of it. "Eliza has been having nightmares," Betty said, folding her legs beneath her in the chair. "I've been reading up on ways to help her sleep better." She held up a book on childhood trauma and sleep.

Kat gave a small smile and lowered herself into the comfortable blue chair across from her. "Perry's dead," Kat said, the words falling out before she could filter them. Betty's face froze in shock, the light of the fire dancing across it in shadows, and she lowered the book to the table in between them. "I'm sorry," Kat adjusted. She was terrible at this. "We lost Perry during a raid at Head-quarters."

Betty pressed her lips together, tears welling in her eyes, her head nodding slowly as if she knew this day was coming. She probably did. "What about Luke? Did you find him, at least?"

For the first time, it occurred to Kat that she had a wealth of information right in front of her. An exiled team member of the key group of the Alliance—an unwanted illegitimate Wayward. "We did. But I have some questions, and I need honest answers if I'm going to be able to help him."

Betty adjusted in her seat, wiping the wetness from her face. "I can do that."

Kat let out a sigh of relief. "You may want a drink first." Betty leaned forward, opened the bottom of the round coffee table, and retrieved a glass and a bottle of whiskey. She closed the hidden door, poured a healthy amount, and held the bottle out to Kat.

"No, thank you. I need to be ready to go."

"Of course."

Kat waited for her to settle, debating where to start, and

deciding the most important information needed to be discussed. "First of all, your name has been released on the hit list. All of our names, including Mrs. Gale. As long as you stay in the safe house, you should be fine until I get it shut down."

"How do you plan to do that?"

"Dom and a friend are working on a program now, and as soon as it's ready, I go back in. If I don't make it, Dom has instructions to get you set up."

"Katherine," Betty shook her head. "Ask your questions."

Kat leaned forward to gauge her aunt's reaction. "Did you know Rosemary wasn't my mother?"

Betty choked on the sip of whiskey she'd taken and coughed. "What?"

Apparently not. "Rosemary was not my biological mother."

"Well, that explains a lot," she said. "You're too good for them anyways. And they fucking hate you. But no, I didn't know."

"Hated," Kat clarified. "Rosemary is dead."

Betty's lips quirked into a smile, pulling one out of Kat too. "That's a fortunate turn of events. If she's not your mother, then. . ."

"Maureen Seward," Kat supplied.

The glass nearly tumbled from Betty's hand, and she put it on the table instead, clasping her hands together. Not the response Kat was expecting. "You're fucking kidding me."

"Don't I wish I was. Here's the kicker: she's alive and running the Alliance." Even in the dancing shadows of the fireplace, Kat couldn't miss the flash of terror cross Betty's face. "You're scared of her."

Betty looked away, heaving a sigh. "You don't cross Maureen and live to tell about it. Unless she's dead."

"Oh shit," Kat said. "What did you do?"

She rubbed the back of her neck, eyes on the floor. Kat gave her time to answer. Whatever it was, she'd thought she had been free and clear for years.

"It seemed trivial at the time," Betty said. "A misunderstanding between two teammates about the direction of the Alliance. I thought we were taking down Elijah. He'd threatened us and our children. Maureen had other plans. She wanted to build a new empire and destroy the Legacies. I wasn't opposed. I just didn't see the point. Why not just remove the man in power and restructure? It would create fewer enemies and we already had the resources in place, along with access to the government contracts. Maureen discovered my distaste for her vision while I was under Sin and saw it as a threat. There was no convincing her that I wasn't against it all."

She took a deep breath and looked away, shame filling her face before continuing. "I'd always been the outsider in the group. They were a team long before Paul and I got together. I knew I would lose if it was Maureen's word against mine. And I wasn't ready to lose. I wanted to see Perry grow up. So, I gave up their location to Elijah."

Kat gasped and then put her hand over her mouth.

"I should have taken my chance with the Alliance. Elijah saw my weakness and pounced. Paul was dead shortly after that, and so, we thought, was Maureen. And Perry's life was stolen—chained to that monster."

Kat blinked a few times. What a horrible fucking family she had —on both sides. She shook her head. "Holy hell."

"There is nothing holy about it," Betty said. "When Maureen died, I thought at least I was in the clear from her rage." Betty picked back up her drink and took several big sips. "But that means you have siblings. Aeron and Decius."

Kat's chest ached for a moment, so she grabbed the whiskey bottle off the table and took a big swig, putting her head back and letting it burn all the way down. She imagined it drowning out the image of Aeron in her arms, the hollow feeling when she realized Decius was her brother.

"Oh, no," Betty whispered. "Both of them?"

Kat nodded and contemplated taking another gulp, but put it

down instead, wiping the back of her hand across her mouth. Betty shot to her feet, and Kat jumped, looking over her shoulder.

"My god, what happened?" Betty's eyes weren't behind Kat—they were on her arm.

"Oh. My other question. Can you help me with this?"

It took an hour for Betty to clean her arm. For the first fifteen minutes, Kat bit into a washcloth so she didn't wake the kids with her screaming. After she had cleaned it up, Betty's ability to fluently swear in multiple languages and make it sound coherent impressed Kat and kept her mind off the nauseousness attempting to overtake her.

About halfway through, Betty called Gunnar to bring in some food, insisting Kat needed to eat. He gagged when he entered the Master bathroom carrying a tray of sandwiches and fresh veggies for her.

"It's not that bad," Kat said from the empty bathtub, her arm propped over her head.

"It looks like someone took a tiny vegetable peeler to your arm and couldn't decide how much flesh they actually wanted to take off," he countered. He shivered and pushed his fist against his mouth as he left.

"How is the feeling to your fingers?" Betty asked, gently smoothing the Lidopen gel on her tricep, and the pain instantly dissipated.

"She must have damaged a nerve or two," Kat said. "I can move them, but it's numb."

"Nothing we can't look at later," Betty assured. "Why don't you get some sleep?"

Kat pushed herself up from the tub, her hips screaming in protest from being still so long. "Because I don't deserve sleep. Not until I've accomplished what every person who died in the last forty-eight hours fought for—me in that office shutting down the hit list and fixing the fucked Legacy our families left behind."

A knock came from the main room. "It's open!" Betty called out.

Dom appeared with a phone in hand. "The program will be ready in thirty minutes."

"That fast?" Kat asked.

"Don't sound so surprised." He shook his head. "Mason's on the line." He held out the phone. Kat nearly snatched it from his hand.

"Go," she said and walked out of the bathroom, pacing the master suite.

"Maureen is making her move."

Kat's entire nervous system went into overdrive, her body buzzing with anticipation and fear. This was it. "What about the Sin?"

"She knows Sin better than anyone alive. I was guessing how long so we didn't get locked out. She probably already tested his system."

"Fuck."

"They said the program is good to go?" Mason confirmed.

"Thirty minutes. Have you reached Griffin?" She wanted to trust that Mason was right about him—but how could she trust anything? Everything in her life had been a lie.

"Still radio silence, so we're going in blind," he said. "I'm going to meet you there, but we need to discuss something before you leave. Are you alone?"

38

KAT

Kat looked up at Headquarters, the row house facade her favorite part of the building. Less than twenty-four hours ago, it had been hers, and she wanted it. Now? It wasn't hers, but she needed it. She did a full perimeter sweep. The building was quiet, and the security doors were all still locked—at least on the ground. Mason would be coming from the roof.

She reached inside her security vest, pressing against her chest, double-checking that Ivan's programs were still tucked in her bra. The side entrance to Headquarters would lead her to the basement, where none of the assets could access. If Griffin had betrayed her, he would have guards lined up waiting for her. She didn't scan her hand. Instead, she reached into her bra, pulled out the smaller thumb drive, and inserted it into the side of the scanner. Ivan's secondary program would allow her to enter without detection in case they'd beat her there, and Luke had restarted the security system.

The lock released. Kat grabbed the thumb drive and pushed the door open, raising her gun. The stairwell was clear. She padded down to the basement floor, cautiously approaching the hallway. Leaning forward, gun at the ready, she checked both ways and then let out a long breath. Still clear. A weight lifted from her shoulders, and she picked up her pace.

The thumb drive opened the next door, the basement entrance to the passageways. The steel walls were closer together down here, the stairwell built beside the main staircase. She moved as quickly as possible without losing her breath through the labyrinth, cramming down any thought that didn't get her closer to the office, such as she wished Perry was by her side right now.

It was as if the thought brought her to his resting place faster. She paused at the end of the hall, catching sight of his body. She could have gone another, longer route—but time was not on her side. She slowed to a walk. If she blocked out the blood and the hole in the center of his forehead, he could be napping. Or playing a prank. Careful not to disturb him, Kat stepped around him. She pulled her eyes away and reached for the exit. She would be back to bury him properly.

She turned the handle without an issue, but the urge to look back at him begged her to listen. She raised her weapon and pushed the door open, ready to shoot. This hallway was empty, too, except for the bodies they'd dropped just yesterday. The first scents of death already lingered in the air, and Kat scrunched her nose in disgust. If she survived, her first order of business would be to burn this place to the ground and start somewhere fresh.

The phone in her back pocket vibrated, and she quickened her pace. She didn't need to check it. Mason made it to the rooftop. She pressed against the first corner and froze, the flash of Star on the ground returning to her. Beyond this corner, Griffin could be dead. Kat shoved down the dread crawling up her spine. Her knee bounced as she prepped herself. The phone vibrated in her pocket again. She needed to get to her office and stop Maureen.

She let out a long breath of air and rounded the bend, ready to fire. The bodies had been moved, cleared off to the sides. Kat scanned them, relieved not to see Star nor Griffin amongst them.

She kept moving, slowing only to admire Carl's body still where she'd left it, and then paused—there was an addition to it.

His shirt had been folded to expose a slice slashed post-mortem on his stomach. Kat squatted down, lifted the shirt's edge, and shook her head, the dread inside her evaporating. Carved into his stomach was a message from Griffin. Although it'd been years since she'd seen his signature in the flesh, she could hear him saying it as he engraved it. 'Stab, stab, smiley face.' It had always been cocky and juvenile. And right now, it reminded her that she enjoyed this life and her job more than anything. That he loved her and protected her. And that no one, especially her mother, was taking that away.

She dropped the shirt and closed the distance to the office. Carl's guard, Toby, still lay on the floor. She picked his arm up, rested it against the door, and then put Ivan's program in again. She adjusted her grip on her gun and tucked herself out of view, waiting for the whir of the lock to disengage. As soon as the lock clicked, she pushed the door, and Toby's arm fell forward to prop it open. No one fired, but the sound of people still reached her.

"I wasn't sure if you would make an appearance," Maureen called. "Come on in and join us. Drop your weapon on the desk."

Fuck. Kat tightened her grip and pushed the door open enough to enter, stepping over Toby. The sight of Griffin met her first. Izz straddled his lap, her hand fisted in his hair pulling his head back and pressing one of his hair darts against his neck. She had fresh slices across her cheeks and a deep cut along her jaw, blood dripping.

"Looks like you missed her throat," Kat said to Griffin, glaring at the older woman. He smiled but didn't dare move his head. Kat turned toward the now open vault and looked straight into the barrel of Maureen's Sig, with Luke standing behind her. His posture was hunched, and his hands shook as he sorted through the paperwork.

"Hey, Luke," Kat said. He nodded in her direction but didn't respond. She caught sight of his red eyes and a bloody, swollen lip that looked like he tried to bite through it. "Even as an emotionless asshole, he wanted nothing to do with you. What'd you do to him?"

"We didn't do anything yet," Izz said, and Kat glared at her. "Drop the weapon, or I'm going to have the immense pleasure of penetrating this god-like specimen with his own stabby tools."

Kat raised an eyebrow at her and looked back at Maureen. Griffin would be dead before Maureen hit the ground. "Congratulations," Kat said. "You win." She'd held up her hands and gingerly placed the gun on the desk. She scanned the rest of her office. They were alone.

Maureen sighed, pulled out another stack of folders, and passed them to Luke. He flipped through each one, searching for something. "This was never about winning," Maureen said. "This was about power." She pulled a folded piece of paper from her back pocket. "And I have it. Why are you here?" she asked and slid the paper back into her pocket.

Kat licked her lips and stuck her hands in her pockets. "Maybe I'm looking for answers. It's been a hell of a few days. I missed out on years of planned vengeance—twice—although I did get to spend a few hours torturing my mother. It was cut short by about a week, though." Maureen quirked her lips, and Kat continued. "I took charge of the deadliest institution on the East Coast only to wind up on an international hit list, which stole my crown from me. However, I am worth seven million dollars, so that's a bonus. I was betrayed and ended up killing my best friend, although I know Luke can relate to that one."

Kat saw the twitch of anger cross his face before he could school it. Good. He wasn't gone yet. "Then I learned I wasn't who I always thought I was. The mother I took such pleasure in killing wasn't even my mother. I admit I was disappointed to learn that. Imagine my surprise to learn my biological mother is a traitorous bitch, who traded my life for her freedom. I guess Rosemary took a page out of your book when she raised me."

Maureen's eyes narrowed. Kat had hit a nerve. Perfect. "But there's an upside, right?" Her phone vibrated in her pocket, and she took a step forward. "I got myself some new siblings, but wouldn't you know it—my brother is dead, and my sister dies in my arms. Tell me, did you enjoy the few weeks in Costa Rica with Decius?"

Maureen sneered at her, "Watch it, child."

"Sorry, Mother, did I hit a nerve?"

"Katherine," Izz warned from beside her.

Kat turned and faced her. "Rag and tag?" Kat asked.

"What?" Izz asked.

"Knock, knock, bitch," Kat said and kicked her hard in the chest. Griffin bridged his hips, knocking her off balance. Maureen's gun fired, and the wall behind Griffin exploded. "Don't let Maureen leave," Kat said and kicked Izz again, this time in the side of the face, and she fell to the ground. The door to the office sprung open. Mason stepped inside with a battered, bruised, but very much alive Aeron at his side, guns ready.

"No!" Luke yelled. Kat slammed her foot against Izz's throat and turned. Maureen jammed her gun into Luke's back, holding him in front of her for cover. His face had completely crumbled, all control lost, tears streaming down his cheeks, his breath hitching. Mason had said he was seeing ghosts. Did Luke think she was haunting him?

Maureen's eyes stared over his shoulder, disbelief in them. "How?" she asked, her voice wavering. "I saw her."

Mason chuckled. "Like mother, like daughter," he said. "No offense, Aeron."

"None taken. Returning from the dead is probably the only thing I want to get from her."

"Cover this?" Kat asked softly to Griffin. He nodded, moving close enough to place a kiss on her forehead before they traded spots. Kat grabbed her gun off the desk and joined Aeron by the door. "Glad you didn't die," she said, eyeing Aeron's left arm in a sling. She really shouldn't be here.

"Same," Aeron said.

"You're outmatched," Mason said.

Maureen glared at them. "You can't kill me."

"That's okay. I have years of vengeance that needs to be paid," Kat supplied. "I would rather do that anyway."

"How about you let Luke go, and we'll let you walk," Mason offered. Kat sent a glare at him. She did not want to let this woman walk. She wanted to rip her to shreds.

"You're not going to kill me," Maureen repeated. She took a step forward, pushing Luke with the gun. "You're going to let us leave, and I'm taking Luke."

"Please. Mason, please don't let her!" Luke cried.

"I've got you," Mason assured. "Maureen. I have three people in this room wanting you dead. Take my offer."

She shook her head, stepping out of the vault. Kat raised her gun, aiming past Luke's head at Maureen. "Let me do it," Kat said to Mason.

"You can't," Maureen said and took another step.

She was right. Kat's Granddad had been blinded by his greed and paranoia. It had made for a messy fallout from his death. The Alliance, according to Mason, would make the last few days look like a summer vacation, and they couldn't afford to take any more hits. Kat couldn't afford to lose any more people.

"Let her up, Reaper," Maureen said, taking a few more steps, Luke's body trembling in front of her.

Griffin looked at Kat, and she nodded. He removed the boot from Izz's throat. She massaged it out and stood up, her tongue shooting across her lip. "If I was going to die, that was definitely a top-five choice for me." She blew him a kiss and moved to the door, Mason, Aeron, and Kat shifting in unison to keep them in their sights.

Luke avoided looking at them and focused is eyes on the floor. Something was wrong with him. Kat saw the decision in his posture before he moved, and she pushed Aeron back as Luke lunged toward them. She and Luke collided. His body was on fire, his eyes wild in his head. "I'm sorry!" he yelled toward Aeron, desperation dripping from his words. Mason charged at Maureen, and Kat focused completely on calming Luke down.

"Hey! Relax." Words did not penetrate his mind. She wanted to help him—wanted to save him. He'd sold his soul to help her. She punched him across the face instead, but it didn't jar him. He kept trying to get past her to Aeron. Kat grabbed him by the hair, bringing his head down to meet her knee. If she couldn't calm him, at least she could knock him out. That didn't work either. He stumbled back and shook his head. He dropped to his knees and grabbed his head. Kat stepped toward him. "Luke?"

Above him, Izz dropped low. Griffin yelled and stumbled back against the wall, a dagger protruding from his leg. Izz threw an elbow, knocking him out, and then spun around, her eyes scanning, landing on Kat and then, behind her, Aeron.

Absolutely fucking not. Kat fired, and Izz dove at Luke. "Damn it," Kat swore. But Izz already had a grip on him and yanked him to his feet, the gun jammed under his chin. She walked them backward toward the door.

"Enough!" Izz called out. "Let her go, Mase, or he's dead."

Mason and Maureen broke apart, both looking like they'd gone ten rounds in a cage, chests heaving and Maureen wiping the blood from her lip. "You're not taking him anywhere," Mason said.

Maureen bent forward and picked her Sig off the ground. "Yes, we are. Now, Katherine, you're going to have to rebuild this place from the ground up after the chaos you orchestrated in the Playhouse. Let me help you."

"No," Kat said and glanced over her shoulder at Aeron. She'd propped herself against the wall, her gun trained on Maureen. She was pale and sweat drenched her face. "We can figure it out on our own."

Maureen smiled. "I'm sure you will. You're just like me at that age: headstrong and full of revenge. If you change your mind, let me know. Let's go, Izz." Maureen rounded the desk and pulled the office door open.

Kat clenched her teeth. Everything in her screamed to shoot this woman. She was nothing like her. She would never sell her family for her freedom. "Wait," Kat said. Maureen looked back, hope in her eyes, and Kat smirked. "Aeron, check her back pocket." Maureen's look melted into a glare.

Aeron walked past, signaling with her gun for Maureen to put her hands up and turn around. Her fingers reached into Maureen's back pocket and pulled out a single piece of folded paper. She held it up. "This?"

"Yeah."

Aeron passed it to Kat. All this death and destruction for a piece of wrinkled paper? It was from a standard notepad and had stains of what she could only assume were coffee and maybe blood. She opened it. A single name was scrawled across it. Her heart quickened. How the hell did Maureen know where to find this?

"What is it?" Mason asked.

"It's everything," Maureen said, meeting Kat's eyes. "I look forward to doing business with you."

Kat swallowed, the words feeling more like a threat. She placed the paper in her own pocket. "You're not taking Luke," Kat reiterated.

"He killed your brother. Where do you think you got your taste for vengeance, darling? I'm not leaving here without him. Izz and I can do this all day, and we already established you're not killing us."

"Mason," Luke pleaded. "Please don—" Izz pistol-whipped the side of Luke's face. He dropped to his knees. Aeron cried out, and Kat threw an arm out to stop her from going forward, fisting a hand in her shirt—but Aeron's gun was raised.

Luke's tear-stained face turned to them, his eyes pleading for someone to save him. "Aeron, please," Luke begged.

"No!" Maureen yelled.

Luke's head snapped backward. Blood splattered across Izz as his body landed on her and then dropped to the floor, a single gunshot to the forehead. Kat jumped, eyes darting to Aeron. Her gun trembled, tears freely falling down her face. Did Aeron just. . . Kat uncurled her fingers from the shirt and moved her hand to Aeron's gun, pushing it toward the ground. The heat confirmed Aeron had fired the shot. Kat's heart constricted. How much more death could they survive? How much more loss?

"How dare you!" Maureen said, stepping toward Aeron.

Kat stepped in front of Aeron, a protectiveness coursing through her she couldn't explain. Mason moved in front of them, his eyes wide with disbelief but locked on Maureen. "Now you can leave," he said, ice in his words. Maureen glared daggers at them but stepped over Luke's body and left, Izz on her heels. Mason followed them to the door.

Aeron moved past Kat and dropped to her knees beside Luke. Her gun clattered to the floor, and she ran her shaking hands over Luke's hair. "I can't—I can't. I'm so sorry, Luke." A sob rocked through Aeron, and Kat pulled her eyes away from the grief, looking to Mason.

"How do you know they'll leave?" Kat asked him.

"Because Maureen is a self-preservationist and a business-woman. And seeing Aeron alive did exactly what I wanted—gave her hope of a future with her daughters."

"That will never happen," Kat said, eyes returning to Aeron. She'd dropped her head to Luke's chest, small sobs leaving her. Kat swallowed her own emotions. No matter what Aeron claimed or how angry she'd been, it took an act of love to pull that trigger and save Luke from himself and whatever hell their mother had in store.

"Sometimes it's okay to feed the delusions." Mason took a knee beside Aeron, a hand running over her back. Kat stole a glance at Griffin. His pants were soaked in blood from the knife, but his chest moved up and down. He could wait a moment; her sister needed her.

"Are you okay?" Kat asked, joining them next to Luke. He looked peaceful, and it was the first time Kat had ever seen his brow not furrowed, and his jaw unclenched. Guilt dug into her chest. It wasn't all their fault, but each of them had a hand in pushing Luke here.

"No," Mason said. "But this is better than the alternative."

Kat leaned forward and met Aeron's eyes. Aeron swallowed hard and shook her head. "I promised I would save him," Aeron said and let out another sob. "I just wanted to save him." Mason scooped her into a hug as she broke down, and Kat stood, leaving Mason to console her.

She swallowed her own sob. Consoling the sad wasn't something Kat was good at, and she didn't want to crack open her own dam of emotions here. Instead, she moved to Griffin and shook him awake.

His eyes opened, and he smiled at her. "Am I in heaven?"

She laughed with a small shake of her head. "No, we can't get in there. C'mon." She hoisted him off the ground, helping him back into the chair. "That looks nasty." She pointed to his leg.

"It will add character to my swagger," he said, his eyes flitting over to Luke and then back to her, concern etched on his face. "Fuck. Are you okay?"

"I will be," she answered.

"I know you will be, but right now—are you okay?"

"No," she admitted, blinking away the tears. "Far from it." He laced his fingers through hers, and she leaned into him. "What happened to everyone in the building after I left?"

"Perry had StormLink on the phone you gave me. Star and I were able to eliminate the entire building with a quick game of hide-and-scope with a few alterations to the program. Is he with Ivan?"

Kat's gut clenched, and she closed her eyes. "He didn't make it out of Headquarters, Griff. For a second—" she wasn't going to start off by lying to him. "I thought you killed him," she admitted, shame heating her face.

"What? Perry?" Griffin tried to get up. "I would never—"

"I know that now." Kat shook her head and put a hand on his shoulder, pushing him back down. "But a shot came from over here."

"Must have been Delilah," Griffin supplied, "the woman he shot in the leg. I heard her firing, but when I got to her, the hall was clear." He pulled her close, wrapping her in a hug. Her body calmed instantly, like she needed the confirmation that Griffin was the good guy. He'd always been the good guy. How had she ever believed he wasn't? "I'm sorry," he whispered and rested his head against her.

"Me too." She pulled away and wiped at her face.

"So, uh." Griffin cleared his throat. "Your mother, huh?"

Fuck. She couldn't process anything else right now. They had bodies to bury, a vault to clean out, and open contracts and missions that needed to be handled before someone realized Legacy Inc had fallen. Maureen was low on her priority list at the moment. "Yeah. I'll tell you all about it later." She turned to Mason. "So, what do we do now?"

He got to his feet, pulling Aeron with him. She swayed again and leaned into him. "We get Aeron into recovery. I think you've earned a few days off." She smiled, but it didn't reach her eyes. She would need a lifetime off after what they'd just been through—after what she'd just done. "What was on the paper?"

Kat had already forgotten about it. She pulled it out and unfolded it, turning it around for them to see.

StormTracer : Kara Lourde

She may have eliminated almost the entirety of Legacy Inc, but if they played their cards right, she had all she needed to rebuild bigger and better. A Legacy 2.0.

"Holy shit." Mason took a step closer, eyes scanning the paper again and his face lit up with joy.

"What is it?" Aeron asked. Griffin leaned forward too.

"Not what, who," Griffin said, eyebrows flying up. "That's StormTracer? I never would have guessed."

"I'm lost," Aeron said, and it reminded Kat how different they were, even if they were sisters. Aeron grew up under the protection of the Legacy, where they had curated training and missions and no concern about where anything came from. Kat had grown up knowing the only point of life was to make connections—the more powerful the better—and then to exploit them or end up dead. This connection was the motherload.

"StormTracer is the exclusive contact within the government which assigns all black ops and off-the-book missions," Mason clarified. "When we originally launched the StormLink program, they reached out to us. I don't know how Maureen knew that information was in the vault, but the identity has been a tight-kept secret for over a decade. It's where Senior's political power and unlimited funds have come from."

"With this information. . ." Kat looked at Griffin, hope daring to fill her fractured heart. Until this point, there had never been a long-term plan. Get vengeance or die trying; shut down the hit list or run. With the most powerful Underworld and government connection, her world seemed full of opportunity because she could run a business and get vengeance simultaneously. "We could build a whole new empire—a better one."

"And if Maureen gets to this woman before us?" Aeron asked, hesitation and fear in her voice.

"Let her," Kat said, smiling at Aeron's use of us. They were in this together. They'd suffered too much loss at the hands of their mother not to be. "It's not going to matter. We have something she doesn't—access to StormLink. It gives us an automatic in. But just in case. . ." She turned to Mason, his lips stretching in a smile as if he already knew what she was going to ask. "Mason, will you help us take down our mother?"

He tipped his head. "It would be my pleasure."

THANK YOU

I hope you enjoyed The Assassin's Sin!

They have secured the vault. They have bodies to bury. But is the hit list down? Will Maureen give Kat the space to breathe? Or are Kat and Aeron's troubles just getting started? Find out in The Assassin's Storm.

If you would like access to exclusive content and updates on the next books in the series, join my newsletter. If you enjoyed this book please consider leaving a review to help other people fall in love with this world too!

ACKNOWLEDGMENTS

To all of you who made it through The Assassin's Sin trenches with me—all the love and thanks!

My husband & kids, for your unending support & patience with my crazy writing schedule & rants made The Assassin's Legacy Series possible. Thank you.

Ms. Donna Cromeans, thank you for your invaluable feedback & ability to help me dig deeper into the characters & always asking, 'But what if. . .' truly leveled up this manuscript.

To my beta readers: Kristina, Colby, Malia, April, Emily, Shannon C., Kadee, & Beans. Sorry for the emotional torment, but thank you for your unending love for the characters! And Shannon W. for your genuine excitement & support on the entrepreneur journey.

Kristina, your enthusiasm for my fictional world inspires me to keep writing, & your joy, support, & constant reminder that I am actually a good writer fills my soul. Thank you for being my person.

Colby, I am so glad we have crossed paths. Your unwavering support & excitement inspires me daily, & the weekly meetups have kept me focused & motivated. Thank you, from the bottom of my cold dead heart. #2grateswitwerdz

Martial Arts & More—my second family. Thank you for your continued support of my writing & training, for the inspiration & opportunities to choreograph fight scenes, & for a safe place to be me.

To the 20booksto50k community—the real MVPs for any Indie

Author. Thank you for the knowledge & support to take on this journey full force. And for the new goal: to be invited to the castle one day.

ABOUT THE AUTHOR

After a childhood filled with James Bond marathons with her father, Libby brings to life a world of assassins and badass heroines.

When not writing, Libby spends her time enjoying the art of jiu-jitsu or napping. She loves English Breakfast tea, campfires, and loud music.

www.ingramcontent.com/pod-product-compliance
Lightning Source LLC
Chambersburg PA
CBHW032155190726
48290CB00005BC/1572